About the Author

Clara O'Connor grew up in the west of Ireland where inspiration was on her doorstep; her village was full of legend, a place of druids and banshees and black dogs at crossroads. Clara worked in publishing for many years before her travels set her in the footsteps of Arthurian myth, to Mayans, Maasai, Dervishes and the gods of the Ancients. The world she never expected to explore was the one found in the pages of her debut novel, *Secrets of the Starcrossed*, which is the first book in the The Once and Future Queen trilogy.

Clara now works in LA in TV. At weekends, if not scribbling away on her next book, she can be found browsing the markets, hiking in the Hollywood Hills or curled up by the fireside with a red wine deep in an epic YA or fantasy novel.

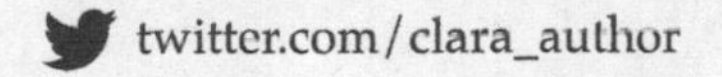

Books by Clara O'Connor

The Once and Future Queen Series

Secrets of the Starcrossed

Curse of the Celts

Legend of the Lakes

SECRETS OF THE STARCROSSED

The Once and Future Queen

CLARA O'CONNOR

One More Chapter
a division of HarperCollins*Publishers* Ltd
1 London Bridge Street
London SE1 9GF
www.harpercollins.co.uk

This paperback edition 2020

First published in Great Britain in ebook format
by HarperCollins*Publishers* 2020

A catalogue record of this book
is available from the British Library

ISBN: 978-0-00-840766-7

Printed and bound in Great Britain by
CPI Group (UK) Ltd, Croydon CR0 4YY

I dedicate this first step to
My posse who said I should
My dear KL who helped me realise I could
My family who assumed I would.

Thank you
So much.

BRITANNIA
ALBA
CARLISLE
PENRITH
KESWICK
MERCIA
YORK
CONWY
ANGLESEY
DINAS BRÂN
GWYNEDD
CYMRU
POWYS
BELINUS LINE
ANGLIA
MAY LINE
DYFED
OXFORD
GWENT
LONDINIUM
AVEBURY
CANTIACORUM
KERNOW
GLASTONBURY
IMPERIAL
PROVINCE
OF
BRITANNIA
TINTAGEL
DUBRIS

Prologue

I scowled as I studied my reflection. Something was off... I couldn't quite place it, but I could see it was there. Or not there. And if I could tell, others would too. There would be consequences. I just wasn't sure what they would be yet.

I shut my eyes, seeing again the blood soaking into the sand. The red spattered across the golden grains, the flashes of neon from the screens high above reflected on the pale arena walls. The red soaking deeper into the gold. You would think it would disappear, but it doesn't. The dark stain just sits there as witness to the damage.

The humidity of my bathroom was at odds with my dry mouth and the wind whipping across the sands in my mind.

I should never have intervened. Until him, I had followed the Code unwaveringly every day of my life. And now our fates were aligned. If he was proved to be a Codebreaker, I too could be deemed guilty.

I lifted my promise ring to my lips, the warm, familiar weight grounding me, giving me focus. Clarity. The promise that kept me going, a family that would be truly my own. Somewhere I would belong.

If anyone ever learned of my impulsive actions, I wouldn't just stand out anymore, I would be thrown out. Of class. Of home. Of the city.

If I was lucky, most likely…

Promise broken.

My chest felt tight.

What had I done?

Part One

THE NEAREST COAST OF DARKNESS

Thither he plies
Undaunted, to meet there whatever Power
Or Spirit of the nethermost Abyss
Might in that noise reside, of whom to ask
Which way the nearest coast of darkness lies
Bordering on light; when straight behold the throne
Of Chaos, and his dark pavilion spread
Wide on the wasteful deep!

– *Paradise Lost*, John Milton

Chapter One

Londinium, Imperial Province of Britannia

In the reign of Caesar Magnus XVII

The morning shivered awake grey and wet, putting my hair in danger of severe frizzing ahead of the Mete this evening. I had an early class so caught the gleaming monorail straight to the forum, dashing past the merchants preparing their stalls for the day without a glance to spare for their sundry wares.

As I entered Basilica Varian, my eye was caught by the graffiti on the wall. How anyone had managed to deface the facade of a building inside the forum without either the sentinels or the cameras catching them, I could not begin to imagine. Maybe the graffiti was right, that there really was "chaos in the Code". There would have to be. I forced myself to look away – there was no point paying it any attention. The sentinels would have it removed in no time. No doubt they were already on their way.

"Good morning, Cassandra," my locker offered loudly, the door swinging open as I approached. I really did need to change the settings on my utilities more often. Even though it was nearly the end of the course, I just hadn't gotten around to it yet. I should really; it was such a bonus to even own a locker. One of the perks of having a prominent merchant as a father. Most of my classmates had to carry their belongings around while we attended classes in the basilica, but through his business connections at the forum Papa had somehow arranged it.

"Cassandra," Ginevra greeted me, swinging off her scooter. Luckily, this part of the forum was quiet in the mornings, but if anyone saw her gliding across the mosaics, there would be Hades to pay. Not that Ginevra ever seemed to care for such rules. I, on the other hand, preferred to stay well within their boundaries at all times. My parents insisted on it, stressing that as my future would be in the public eye, my past must be beyond reproach. My own personal code to live by.

"You have any mid-terms this morning?" Ginevra asked, throwing her exquisitely embroidered jacket into my locker.

"No, just a history lecture on the Reformation of the Province for me, I think."

Ginevra was examining her nails as I rummaged in my pocket for my mini slate. Hopefully, no tiny smudge was lurking. We had little enough time after class to run home and get ready for tonight. Having to redo nails would completely throw out all our careful planning.

"Schedule," I said, glancing at the data the slate offered up. "Yep, just a regular class. I'll see you for lunch after, yeah?"

But she had already gone, not waiting for an answer. One of my favourite morning tunes started to play in my ear as I swayed towards my class. I walked through the gallery, using the portico covering for as long as possible to stay out of the rain. Crossing the corner of the expansive courtyard, I took the side entrance into the central part of the basilica before turning up towards the civics centre where the citizenship classes were held.

My usual seat beside Ambrose was taken, leaving me to weave my way to an empty place. But my attention was caught by a device, a glint of impossible gold from the jacket pocket of a boy in a seat to my right. Distracted, I missed a step and stumbled forward.

I braced myself for impact, but a hand grabbed my arm and steadied me before I could fall in an inelegant heap in front of the entire class.

"Thank you," I said, looking up at the boy who had restored my balance. My breath caught as our eyes connected, his midnight gaze burning into mine. Magnetism seemed to sizzle in the air between us, the lines of his face becoming sharper, his presence building to a crescendo in my mind like a song… until his lids lowered, cutting me off, and his gentle hands released me.

What just happened?

"Cassandra Shelton," a voice snapped from across the room. "If you would?"

Shaken from my stupor, I took my place, my cheeks hot.

I looked again at the boy in the seat next to mine, that hint of illegal tech in his pocket no longer visible.

Devyn, that was his name. I had to dredge the word up from some shadowy recess of memory, but even holding the thought in my mind felt wearisome and wrong. It was so strange – in that moment of contact I had felt solid unyielding muscle. Yet that reality clashed with what my eyes were now telling me, that this slight boy would be knocked over by an overly aggressive wind. It was like his very appearance had shifted beneath my gaze, like a mask falling back into place.

I tried to focus on the lesson, but my concentration was shot. I felt hyperaware of the boy next to me in a way I never had before. Not with Devyn, who I must've shared classrooms with for almost a decade. Not with *anyone*. Which was odd, because what would be the point? I knew exactly where my story ended. What on earth was I doing getting distracted by old classmates and impossible devices? Ridiculous.

I shook off all thought of glimmering gold and midnight eyes, and even managed to take some notes, until our tutor encouraged us to move our desks back and make a circle with our seats.

These classes were a formality really, but every now and then you got a teacher who wanted to go the extra mile. One for whom the Code was not just a set of rules to live by but the very foundation on which the Empire existed. As a class of elites, the chance we would fail to achieve citizenship was incredibly remote. But we had to be seen to complete the same formalities as every other young adult in the city.

Devyn ended up in the seat next to me again, his chair uncomfortably close. I was so concerned with not touching him that I managed to stumble clumsily for the second time. His jacket was hanging off the back of his chair and whatever none-of-my-business thing was in the pocket scraped my leg as I rearranged my chair next to his.

I scowled, rubbing at the spot as I retook my seat, only inches between us now. Imperial tech was always superbly finished, uniform silver, smooth, and compact. Not gold like glazed amber, and certainly not *sharp*. It could only have come from beyond our walls. But where would he have sourced such a thing? And why? It wouldn't even be compatible with our hardware.

I shook my head, trying to focus. The Reformation was one of my weaker subjects, but the bar was low, given the selection of mostly dusty legislative classes we were required to attend, packed with mind-numbing civic obligations and duties.

"When Aurelius XV became consul, the Britannia Province wasn't much more than the city itself, and the citizens were deemed to be half-native," Professor Livius droned on. "Hard to imagine now, but in a world where the Olympian myths and the Christian god of earlier generations had faded, some had even adopted the religious practices of the Celtic kingdoms, and druids could be regularly found *inside* the walls."

I jotted down the years: 1521, new council begins era of reform; 1528, introduction of imperial Code of Conduct and expulsion of Britons from the city; 1540, end of the Tewdwr dynasty leading to the Two Hundred Years' War; until the eventual Treaty of 1772 and the establishment of agreed borders between the imperial Province and the rest of the peoples of Britannia.

Devyn Agrestis.

How long had we been in the same classes? I couldn't seem to recall. We didn't share the same social circles and certainly not the same virtual ones. I knew nearly everyone in this particular round of citizenship classes. I should, I went to school and college with most of them. Beyond them, there was an even wider circle of people all across Londinium whose views I knew on every topic from celebrity homes to upload damage whom I might not even recognise if I met them in real life.

I realised I actually knew little to nothing about Devyn. Even though we were in the same civics class and, thinking about it, I was sure we had attended the same secondary school as well.

My eye ran from his loose, dark curls down his straight nose, over his lips, past the column of his throat, to the rise and fall of his chest. He was sort of... well, nondescript, but my eyes kept wanting to trace his features. I froze as I saw his brows pulling together over those dark eyes. He had noticed.

I cringed, quickly redirecting my focus to Lucia Lonis, who had the floor.

"It goes without question that the introduction of the imperial Code of Conduct paved the way for the Glorious Reformation. Imagine the city if it was still overrun by natives, freely walking our streets, marrying into our families... It's bad enough that they're allowed in for the Treaty Renewal. At least that interaction is limited, but even that could and should be reduced. Why can't the Renewal be done outside the walls?" she implored the room, delicately shuddering, as if allowing Britons entry into the city for one week every four years was going to contaminate us in some way.

Lucia's dramatics only called attention to the rumours that had followed the Lonis family for the last few generations that before the introduction of the Code the family had been much less worried about relations with the local inhabitants. Particularly during periods when it had been economically advantageous to do so. By all accounts, at one point the Lonis family had been more native than not, some sections of the family choosing to make their fortunes outside the walls in the wider province where intermarrying with Britons reduced some of the more threatening aspects of life in the Shadowlands. These days, nobody could question the purity of the Lonis blood and their commitment to the imperial Code, if Lucia's performance was anything to go by: she was the very model of modern Roman elite; she could be a woman from the age of the ancients reborn. I had once yearned for the glossy black curtain that Lucia flicked behind her shoulder. My own hair was a rather gaudier colour.

Lucia's interminable monologue was cut short by sentinels silently entering the room, their dark red cloaks almost as black as their uniforms from the rain. They slid in through the door, expressionless, still… like a breeze, almost unnoticed but cooling the temperature imperceptibly.

Time felt sluggish to me, and I noticed them a fraction of a second before anyone else in the room responded. Lucia stopped speaking. Everyone went utterly still. Why were they here? Or rather, who were they here for?

Devyn, they were here for Devyn.

Seated beside him, I swore I could feel the heavy thump of his heart, rapid and loud before it returned to slow, steady composure. Much quicker to return to normal than anyone else's. But there remained a coiled tension that seemed to pulse off him.

That glint of gold in his pocket, I hadn't imagined it. It wasn't imperial technology. I was sure of it now.

And that's when I did it. I put my hand down in the space between our chairs and reached into his pocket, my fingers closing around the strange, unfamiliar shape they found there.

"Devyn Agrestis." The uniformed sentinel spoke softly into the unnaturally still room.

Devyn rose, his exit from the chair taking him a fraction further than necessary, so he stood between me and the sentinels, allowing me an extra moment to tuck the device into my pocket and lay my once again innocent hand back in my lap. My entire being was focused on appearing normal. Slow, heart, *slow*. I blinked dismissively at the sentinels' intrusion into my day. My features composed themselves into their usual agreeable – if a little haughty – expression, not dissimilar to everyone else in the room.

Despite the unlikely chance that anyone in the room had ever so much as littered, everyone wore a studied kind of indifference at the shocking appearance of sentinels in our classroom. I looked around at my classmates, many of whom, like me, had known Devyn for years. Yet we all sat there, unflinching.

The stern-faced lead sentinel motioned Devyn forward. My stomach folded in on itself. When he reached them, they surrounded him as they left the room together.

The class immediately resumed, water closing over the submerged stone of the interruption, barely so much as a ripple left on the surface. The only sign anything untoward had occurred was the empty cooling seat beside my own.

While I remained calm on the outside, my mind was churning, sifting through recollections of the lean shadow that was Devyn Agrestis, attempting to find a pattern, a truth that made sense.

Chaos in the Code. The graffiti I had seen this morning flashed through my mind.

There were some in the city who were not fans of the Code, people who preferred to push against the limitations of the walls rather than embrace the security they gave us.

Dissidents talked a big talk, but beyond a bit of graffiti they made little impact on city life. Occasionally a hacker was arrested, someone who, in the name of chaos, breached the digital firewalls which were every bit as vital to the protection of the city as the physical walls themselves.

If Devyn had been questioned with unauthorised tech on him, he could have been accused of sympathising with such people. I wasn't sure what he might need such a thing for but being mistaken for a dissident would have been bad, perhaps even fail him in our civics course. What was he playing at? He was an *elite*. He had access to all the tech he could need. Some people just had to poke at things better left alone, I thought, tidying a loose tendril of hair behind my ear.

Outrageously, what perturbed me most in the immediate aftermath, making my thoughts teem and jostle against each other, was that *feeling*. The scalding awareness that had exploded between us the second I touched him. What was it? Where had it come from? And more pressingly, would I experience it again?

Even though I had known Devyn for ever, I felt like I had never really seen him before today.

I hoped we never had an exam on the topics covered in the rest of the morning's classes, as unless it was on the shape and texture of the thing in my pocket and the myriad possible explanations for it and its owner then I was doomed.

At lunch, I grabbed a juice blend from the fruit seller in the forum, momentarily pulled from thoughts of Devyn at the sight of a pineapple. I adore them, but they hadn't been readily available in recent months, which usually meant that traffic from the tropics was being impeded. It would explain my father's lousy mood of late. Double bonus to see it in the market today – happy father and delicious tangy beverage. I sipped my juice, wondering if they had released Devyn yet. After all, they would have no reason to detain him now that I had the device.

I took a perch on the stairs of the arch nearest the silk seller's shop, an old favourite from when my father would bring me to the forum and I would wait quietly, mesmerised by the colours and feel of the exotic material. The spot on the second gallery also offered an excellent view of the vast marketplace below. The rain continued to pour down on the shoppers, merchants, gossips, and general loiterers milling about in the ancient venue, dodging around stalls and statues, sheltering under the grand columned entrances of the basilicas, keeping to the porticoed arcades as much as possible.

On the pedestal in the courtyard below me, a sharp-featured man was speaking against the lack of privacy in the city. It was a not uncommon complaint from those who took a stand on the forum's stage, where citizens could voice their opinion free of repercussions. Taxes, overpopulation, warmongering, and privacy were the topics most commonly debated at length here. Occasionally, some fool would even take the stand to rail against the imperial Code that shaped our society. Those were rare though.

Honour, loyalty, justice, city, empire – these simply weren't smart targets to take aim at, and anyone fool enough to attempt it ran the risk of the crowd in the forum dealing out their own form of justice even if the sentinels didn't.

Today's speaker wasn't even particularly witty or original. If you were going to stand up in the forum to tackle a topic like privacy and the obligation of every citizen to live with complete transparency under the council's watchful eye, then you really had to bring something new to the debate. This fool seemed to like the sound of his own voice more than anything else.

Ginevra joined me just as he was reaching his concluding arguments in a voice that suggested he, at least, was terribly impressed with himself. Raising one perfectly arched brow, Ginevra took a seat on the step beside me.

"I hear your Reformation class was a little more interesting than usual," she said.

I tilted my chin up to indicate she should fill me in on what she'd heard. Gossip-lover that she was, she didn't have to be invited twice, proceeding to regale me with the best of the questions and speculation zinging between our classmates. What could the sentinels want with him? Was it anything to do with tonight's Mete? If so, what could it be? Had he fallen victim to a street swindler? Had he witnessed something?

If only they knew. It never occurred to any of them, elites as they were, that one amongst them might have actually broken the Code. The Code outlined our duties as citizens, it was our moral centre, the foundation of our city and our lives within it. Why would we ever do anything to defy it?

I answered Ginevra's questions about what had happened, honestly, with a few minor omissions. No need to mention the physical awareness I suddenly had of a boy I had barely noticed before or the small matter of the strange device I had stolen from him. As Ginevra didn't know to ask those questions, it was unnecessary to lie, which I had never been particularly successful at. I hadn't needed to be.

Maybe a good liar was someone who practised more often. Perhaps the more you crossed the line, the better you were at it. I wasn't in the habit of thinking of myself as inhabiting a space anywhere near the line – until today, anyway – and I was certainly uncomfortable with my current proximity. I would be more than happy to back further away. The device in my pocket was small enough that if I really tried, I could almost forget it was there. If it were to drop out as I walked home by the river, then it would be as if the whole thing had never happened.

"I have Prof Livius next myself," Ginevra announced, popping up. "Do you think he'll know more or could I squeeze in a hair appointment if I leave now?"

"I think even if Prof Livius knows something he would never say anything. Especially if it's anything juicy."

"Right, as if Devyn Agrestis would have broken the Code."

"You never know." I shrugged with as much indifference as I thought she would buy.

"Maybe we'll see him on the sands," she said, wagging her eyebrows in a faux-ominous manner before dashing off, checking her hair out in a shop window as she made her way down the arcade.

A pang of unease washed through me. Having illegal tech could be a serious offence. Devyn undoubtedly took a risk in carrying such a thing into the heart of the city. But if the sentinels were questioning him, and he knew where it was, being caught with it in my pocket certainly wouldn't aid my plausible deniability if Devyn gave me up.

I hurried through the forum, wondering what on earth to do with it until I passed by the Great Basilica. It was more properly known as Basilica Garai, in honour of the Governor who had rebuilt after the early Londinium settlement had been burnt down by some Briton queen. The basilica was home to a library that was the pride of the city. The lines and lines of dusty tomes hidden inside spoke of age and erudition nearly as much as the ivy that crawled up the stone walls and the impeccably preserved mosaics on the floor. Overtaken by technology, the books had little utility now and rarely left the shelves, which was perfect for my purposes.

I moved past the students and academics making use of the workstations, heading towards the deeper, dustier rows. I ran my fingers lightly along the edges of the books until I found a title that practically whimpered as it was pulled off the shelf.

Social Conventions and Concerns of the Shadower Woman in the Age of Sentenus VII, vol. 2748.1.

Hopefully the anthropology students had moved on to more significant issues by now than whatever petty concerns those who lived outside the walls had protested about nearly two centuries ago. The book had broken away from the spine, leaving just enough space for me to slip the small golden device inside. I pushed it back onto the shelf and walked back through the shelves, looking around casually before making my way swiftly home to change.

It would be safe there. I breathed a sigh of relief, my thoughts now turning to the big night ahead.

If anyone had told me yesterday that I wouldn't even have started getting ready for my first Mete at this point in the day, I'd have thought them suffering from some kind of mind glitch. But here I was, only hours away from being there in person and from seeing Marcus in real life for the first time in years, and I hadn't even done my hair yet.

Chapter Two

I made my way down to the lobby, my hands still smoothing my carefully selected outfit. I had spent weeks searching for precisely the right skirt to go with the aqua silk blouse I had bought almost a year earlier because it matched my eyes. My long hair was tied up in the elaborate braids that showed off its multiple hues to best effect. My mother might prefer it if I kept my hair tidied away, but I had moved on from my childhood desire to blend in and preferred to see my red-tinted hair as my signature not my stigma.

I surveyed my appearance in the mirror one last time. Satisfied, I headed for the door, smiling back at our maid Anna as she handed me my wrap on the way out. This was a once-in-a-lifetime event for most citizens. While it was not likely to be the case for me, I meant to savour every heartbeat of my first one, every scent, every sound to be imprinted on my mind for ever.

Attending the weekly Mete was a privilege afforded to few, as there was only room in the ancient amphitheatre for the greatest citizens: the council, of course, and the chosen of the city, those who had been recognised as having served the state and who were honoured by being granted a seat for the duration of their lifetime. The most prestigious families had boxes, many of which had belonged to their houses since the founding of the city. Then there were a couple of hundred seats left that were allocated either by lottery or charitable auction – or in my case because I was in the current civics class. Or rather, because I was in the civics class in the forum; other civics classes in the city weren't afforded a similar privilege.

Too excited to wait around, I had decided to walk across the city rather than take the monorail. All the better to fully appreciate the day, or at least the evening. In light of earlier events, I felt, for the first time in my life, slightly worried about my own place in society. Up until this morning, I had been the most upstanding of citizens, could have walked with my head held high into the amphitheatre. Now I felt somehow tarnished, but I pushed the thought aside, determined not to let it ruin my evening.

The walk would take an hour or so, and I needed every minute of it to get rid of the jitters that had beset me since I arrived home. I didn't often walk, usually taking the trains or the elevated red buses that sped around the higher levels of the city. But sometimes I was overcome by a restlessness, a sense of being caged that sent me out into the streets, walking until I was too exhausted to feel it anymore.

Constrained by the walls that protected it, Londinium could not move freely outwards, and so the city had instead built upwards, ever higher and higher into the clouds. I followed the layers of the city into the sky. The grand avenues, interlaced by the medieval lanes and alleys, wound upwards through a city of concrete and steel, marble and glass, the lower levels dotted with the temples and buildings of the ancients.

The few areas where the sun shone all the way down to ground level were exclusively reserved for the first imperial jewels: the forum, the Governor's Palace, the amphitheatre, and the White Tower, protected over the ages by the council. The historic temples and some public parks were also conserved, but the scrapers still straddled them, casting them into shadow. Only a handful of ancient buildings were so prized that miles of unhindered sky was kept free above them. It was these precious few that held the most fascination for me.

Sometimes I felt overwhelmed by the chaos of the world I lived in, lives taking place at different layers of the city. There was the bustle of the ground, the merchants and traders, each street-level front door and window plying their wares in the various sections – Rope St, Candle St, Tailor St – by the forum. There was Services St, Design St, and the like past the financial district up by the silicon roundabout. Surgeons and plastics and dermatologists inhabited the Harley St area. The city was fed via the great Tower markets – meat at Smithfields tower, fish at Billingsgate. Fruit and vegetables had moved from Covent Garden further east towards the docks as the inner West End and Drury Lane tower became a hive of theatres and entertainment centres.

As I made my way through its labyrinthine grandeur, the thought of that strange stolen device was a loaded stone in my heart. What had I been thinking? Even to touch such a thing was a sin against society. Our city might be seen by the Caesar as a remote outpost, but here we considered it a shining beacon of civilisation, one that should be nurtured and protected. Even if it wasn't actively dangerous, illegal tech of any kind was a threat to the city I loved and the people in it. I vowed to throw it in the Tamesis as soon as I could – as I should already have done. That would be an end to it.

I had purposefully chosen to take a highwalk, the curling path taking me through the neons of Piccadilly. It skimmed across the top of the theatre district, many floors above the older theatres and opera houses at ground level and past the more avant-garde centres where the live-streamed dramas and comedies my friends and I watched were produced.

I kept my eye out for a glimpse of any actors, who could sometimes be seen exiting the stage doors. The die-hard fans always knew how long it took their favourites to end a scene, get out of costume, and hit the exit, so I slowed whenever I saw a group gathered beside a door.

But I couldn't afford to linger, even when I noticed a particularly large crowd outside the Windup Theatre which broadcast my latest favourite period drama, set in the reign of Governor Jerolin, who had ruled during the war years before the Treaty. As I approached the Bailey Tower my heart started to beat faster. I went up a couple of levels to ensure I came out at one of the higher balconies, all the better to savour every moment of my approach.

The bustle and excitement of the crowd swept me along to the southwestern balcony above the amphitheatre. I looked up to savour the darkening sky and, wriggling through to the front of the gallery, I let my gaze drop down the vast expanse of air, taking it all in: the northern and eastern balconies, the lights of the housing behind lowering as the balcony curtains were dropped, the oohs and ahhs of the crowd making their way onto the terraces as the neon display screens perched high on the surrounding buildings came on. It really was the most spectacular sight and I had timed my arrival perfectly. I smiled my delight into the cooling evening air as my gaze dropped level after level until I could see the oval of the arena itself. The hairs on my arms raised. I could barely believe I was going to be down there.

"Cassandra." I turned at the sound of my name, scanning the people milling about on the balcony behind me.

"Cassandra, over here."

Redirecting my search over to the balcony on my right, I spotted Ginevra and Ambrose waving excitedly. I grinned back at them, indicating I would meet them at the nearest lift. Taking one last glance at the arena below, I started to push through the second wave of the crowd entering the balcony. Unlike some who had apparently been holding their spot for hours, these people seemed happy to arrive with only half an hour to go and jockey and jostle each other for whatever view they could manage to get from further back on the public galleries high above the arena.

I was scanned for my right of admission and, at a nod from the sentinel, skipped over to where Ginevra and Ambrose waited. Ginevra was talking nonstop as we stepped into the glass cube that swept us down to ground level, the cubes synchronised so that the entry of the arena's audience was efficiently and gracefully controlled.

I could see that the stone walls and the original cobbles were dusted with sand as we got closer. I could scarcely believe how familiar and iconic everything was, yet also how strangely new it felt seeing it firsthand like this. I reached out and trailed my hand along the ancient honey-coloured stone walls of the entrance. What must those awaiting judgement feel now? I shivered at the thought.

What type of offences would be on show tonight? I hoped it was something good. Last Saturday's event had been something of a damp squib, definitely the least interesting

Mete from recent months. Those in my class whose surnames began M through Q had been disappointed, though they, of course, had still been all about their experience in class on Monday. The worst of the criminals judged last Saturday had been sentenced to the stocks, which those classmates had made sure to visit during the week, if only to lob a piece of bad fruit at them for not having committed something more worthy of what was likely to be the single visit of their lifetime to the amphitheatre. As we followed the signs to our allocated seating, Ambrose and Ginevra speculated animatedly on the type of Codebreaker we might see this evening.

Nearly every seat was taken when the high council entered, the twelve senators elegantly taking their seats; their immediate families were already seated further back on the balcony. I recognised the Lord Procurator who held the purse strings of the city, Senator Jerdin beside him with whom my father had occasional dealings, then Senator Dolon on the far left. I cast around for his son Marcus, gnawing my lip; I would have expected to see him in the family area behind the council. Was he not coming? It seemed unlikely – if I had a permanently available seat I would never miss one – but I couldn't see him. I felt a pang of disappointment. I had tried not to think about it too much, but I had secretly hoped to see him in real life this evening.

I scanned the tier of boxes occupied by the great houses once more. Ah, there he was. A burnished head sat amongst a glamorous group in the Courtenay box. Of course, he would have a box, inherited from his mother's family, along with his surname which was one of the oldest in the city, and correspondingly one of the largest boxes. Ginevra caught the direction of my gaze and coughed pointedly at catching me mooning over the city's most eligible son, before bursting into a fit of giggles at the resulting flush of colour on my cheeks. But I could hardly be blamed for looking, as Ginevra well knew.

"All right, settle down," I pleaded with my friend, trying to conceal my blushes from the rest of the group, whose attention was being drawn by her peals of laughter. My connection to Marcus Courtenay was not public knowledge and I frowned at my friend's lack of discretion.

The announcement of Governor Actaeon and Praetor Calchas thankfully drowned her out, and an expectant hush came over the crowd as the pair made their way solemnly to the front of the council's box in full ceremonial regalia.

The stern-faced governor strode to the front of the box and solemnly cast his gaze around the arena. I was torn between looking at the big screen above the highest tier of the amphitheatre to take in the high-definition close-up of the most important man in our province, and looking at the actual man standing not twenty feet to my right. I finally settled on watching the man in person as I could always re-watch the actual broadcast later. He looked smaller in real life, as he delivered the traditional welcome.

"Friends, Romans, citizens, we are gathered here once more in Londinium's great amphitheatre that has witnessed our dedication to the imperial Code for two thousand years. We are the first and last defence of the Empire. The walls keep us safe, but our Code keeps us strong. In the Code we are one."

And the entire arena responded together, "We are one in the Code."

The moral and ethical Code protected us all. It was the system we all relied on as much as the programming Code given to us by tonight's honoured citizen, the legend and genius that was Louis Vanders, who in his youth had brought new depths to the computing languages on which the technology underpinning our world ran.

I followed the direction of the Governor's nod to locate him. He was on the far side of the arena, a woman who must be his nurse or daughter helping him rise to accept the crowd's applause.

The crowd grew silent again as the great doors to the arena opened, and the governor took his seat.

Praetor Calchas, the highest judge in the land, and commander of the legions stationed in the province, and who was rather more approachable-looking than the governor, stepped forward.

"Bring forth the accused," he directed at the sentinels who flanked the shadowed entrance.

Tonight's accused, wearing standard black uniforms, shuffled into the arena. The traditional masks and hoods that covered their faces were in place, beneath which their hearing would also be blocked so they were unable to hear what happened to their fellow accused. This meant they existed in a state of stasis at the side of the arena until it was their turn to be brought forward and judged.

The silence was unnerving. I was used to hearing the swell of the signature music that accompanied the entrance of the accused into the arena. Then the stamping began, each member of the audience contributing to the pounding which reverberated through the building. I shivered in response. The accused must be able to feel it – the thud of the crowd, a vibrating baying for their blood. I marvelled at the revelation. Familiar as I was with the Metes, I had already glimpsed an authentic aspect of the event that I could barely have guessed at watching the broadcast.

What must the accused make of it? This unexpected

pounding that vibrated through the very foundations of the ancient building must be disconcerting at the very least.

I wasn't sure why I was spending so much time thinking about the accused and what they must be feeling. Usually, I was too busy making sure I had everything I needed for the Mete when I watched at home. I took my obligation to judge very seriously, often taking notes to make sure I followed the more complicated cases.

My mother's approach was much less considered. She usually judged the person on the way they took the sands to face judgement, often before the first clip had been shown. She had a pretty shoddy record in other aspects as well: it was mandatory to vote on at least 80% of judgments but my mother, at 84%, was well below the average. Usually, it was because she was out socialising and used the time of the broadcast to whip across the city in a fraction of the time. My father and I took it much more seriously, he at 98% – exemplary – and I at 91%. This was low considering I had never missed a broadcast since I turned eighteen, but I was squeamish about voting in capital offence cases. My father even allowed me to leave the room during the executions. He had taken me aside earlier in the week to warn me my vote would likely be under more scrutiny while I was in citizenship class. I needed to redress the balance so that my lack of voting in more serious cases wasn't so apparent. I hoped there wasn't anything horrible here tonight. I had no desire to witness blood on the sand.

The first of the accused was walked into the centre of the arena, guided by two sentinels. His hood and mask remained firmly in place – justice had to be blind so we wouldn't see their faces until after the vote had taken place. The mask also had a switch that was controlled remotely so they could hear the evidence against them when it was their moment on the sands.

The praetor's voice rang around the arena as he spoke the most iconic words in our city.

"You are accused of crimes against the Code. How do you plead?"

The crowd held its breath. The man in the hood fell to his knees; he chose to deny the accusations, to throw his case open to the judgement of his fellow citizens. The amphitheatre broke into delighted applause. The entertainment was underway.

Praetor Calchas waited until the applause died down before pointing up at the screen.

"The accused has been charged with breaking the Code by failing to pay taxes owed to the city."

The film rolled, compiled by the sentinels from the city's pervasive cameras. In it we watched as a tall ship sailed up the Tamesis. The name was blurred out – a precaution to ensure voting was as unbiased as possible – just as the face of the accused in the footage was blurred in bright red; any bystanders in the shots were also blurred out in grey to ensure no innocent party was targeted after the Mete by members of the public. After all, they weren't to know that they were associating with a Codebreaker. *Unless they did,* I admonished myself.

We watched as the ship's cargo was offloaded onto the docks, inspected, and duly signed off by the customs officer. Fast forward to night time, and the ship's captain – for that was who the accused seemed to be – returned and entered the warehouse where he cut into a number of the bales carrying cotton from the Americas and pulled out several small bags. As he exited the warehouse, the sentinels closed in. The camera panned in for a close-up on the bags as they were opened and nuggets of gold were produced from within.

The crowd roared and the captain pushed himself up to a standing position. The crowd roared even louder at his impudence. It was far too late to attempt to get out of a public vote. The severity of the sentence tended to be influenced by the results of the election, and the evidence here left little doubt.

Praetor Calchas raised his fist, thumb out to the side and the crowd fell silent for the sixty seconds accorded to the Public Vote. I reached into my pocket and clicked the button to indicate guilty. Around the city, I imagined the thousands of others who were doing the same as the clock counted down.

The dong signalled the end of the vote, the sentinels removed the man's hood and mask, and he watched as the praetor took the note handed to him and his thumb pointed down.

"Captain Delmer, you have been found guilty of smuggling and in light of a 99.87% conviction rate you are sentenced to our most severe punishment for evasion of taxes. You are to serve the city for ten years, during which time you will take no profits from your work, and at the end of this period your case will be reviewed."

The man sagged onto his knees once more. He would be utterly ruined, but the sentence was just; this was what happened to those who stole from the city.

The crowd applauded again but politely, their interest waning. There was no further fun to be had with this one then. Calchas raised his hand once more.

"In light of your freedom to exit the city, please note that should you attempt to flee your sentence, your family will be held accountable, and their blood shall stain the sand in your place. This is the sentence of the city upon you."

The sailor on the sand nodded, accepting his fate. He walked from the sand, but as we were waiting for the next accused to be brought forward, our attention was caught by activity happening off–screen.

The sentinels were dragging a new hooded figure onto the sands. I had no memory of anything similar ever happening before, either of an accused arriving after the opening ceremony or of them being dragged in unable to walk on their own. The man was thrown into the cage where the others waited, and was left by the sentinels sitting propped up by the wall of the arena. I looked to the big screens but the cameras hadn't shown this unusual event; only those in the actual arena would have witnessed the late entrant. The swirl of the praetor's robes caught my eye as he turned to glare at someone behind him – a praetorian guard hurrying forward to whisper in his ear. It appeared Praetor Calchas did not approve of this event either. Was the latecomer unexpected or was he just annoyed at the untidiness of his arrival?

The next accused was marched to the centre of the sand. Praetor Calchas's voice rang out once more.

"You are accused of crimes against the Code. How do you plead?"

This man, slighter than the last, also knelt. Another citizen wishing to put his fate in the hands of the people. The crowd roared their approval.

Calchas again pointed up at the screen.

"You have been accused of theft."

The screens lit up with the evidentiary reel. An apprentice – the accused – toiled away at a work table cutting and sewing cloth. The finished products were cheap and of average style. Disappointing.

My attention wandered, the attraction of checking out Marcus Courtenay – golden prince of the city – too difficult to resist. He sat in the middle of his box, the charismatic centre of his group of friends, the last scion of the old blood, descendant of the rose king of York. My heart fluttered. It was hard to believe that the stranger on the other side of the arena was my soulmate.

I caught myself. I knew better. That word, the concept of someone being the predestined other half of your soul, was outdated, like religion or one of those twentieth-century cars that ran on fossil fuel or something. I'd studied enough literature to know that in earlier times it had been a matter of luck: you met and married the nearest person to your village who was also looking for someone, usually based on status or looks or, hard though it was to believe, physical strength. I'd seen this whole series of bursts on it. The idea had intrigued me though. The bursts were on a sociological matrimonial study. Each looked at a different aspect of how matches were made in real time through the eras. Even early online experiences had been hit and miss with a laughably low ratio of successful matches, but steadily online rates had improved as real-time opportunities became fewer. New technological advances had also helped, mainly the take-off of pharma combined with wearable technology that added a chemical dimension to the psychometric to allow the sequencing that ultimately perfected the matching system.

At a gasp from the crowd, I quickly refocused on the giant screens as the apprentice took a bolt of extremely expensive-looking cloth and put it inside his coat. He was then shown walking out of his master's studio, with it still hidden inside his coat. It seemed a straightforward enough case, but the film kept rolling. We were shown the apprentice in a shabby room, crowded with people – his family, presumably. Once they were all asleep, he got up and, despite the long hours he had already worked, sat night after night, cutting and sewing the cloth by candlelight. The dress he produced was remarkable, an object of incredible beauty. The footage concluded, as it always did, with the sentinels arresting him. His mother was screaming, his brothers and sisters crying, as he was pulled unresisting from his home.

The vote began. There was no denying that the crime had been committed and by kneeling the apprentice had chosen to throw himself on the mercy of the city. In some cases, sentences were lightened if the city could see a mitigating motivation or another factor that inspired mercy. In this case, it looked as though the apprentice was hoping the end would justify the means. He shouldn't have stolen from his master, but the dress he had produced had been a credit to the rich cloth.

Wary of my father's warning, I hesitated over the judgement. The young man's talent had been suppressed and I inwardly applauded his courage in doing something he knew was wrong to attain something he felt was right. I twisted the platinum ring on my left hand, closing my eyes as I pressed guilty with my right. I could only hope the wider audience had voted innocent. The clock counted down and the young man flinched as the dong signalled the end of the vote.

The man's mask was removed, revealing a thin, pale face, his frail frame looking as if he would crumble at any moment. The praetor accepted the note and on reading it, his thumb pointed down.

"Apprentice Oban, the city has spoken and has found you guilty at a rate of 62.38%. It appears many citizens of the city wish to grant you some clemency. Having previewed the case, we had prepared for such a result. Master Simmonds, take the sands."

The camera panned to the apprentice's master in the box reserved for the witnesses that were on occasion called on to answer a question or report on an event not caught on camera. The fussy looking master tailor seemed startled as he took his place in the centre of the arena beside the apprentice who had stolen from him.

"Lord High Justice," he called up to the council's box, "I don't understand. I have done nothing. This man stole from me and I reported the crime. Why must I stand here in the place of judgement?"

Praetor Calchas did not appear pleased to be spoken to out of turn like this and stood in stony silence until the tailor stopped talking.

"It is for me to decide who stands in judgement on these sands, Master Tailor, not you. Am I understood?"

Despite it clearly being rhetorical, the man hastily nodded his agreement.

"We stand here today in judgement of a man guilty of theft. However, the city, in its wisdom, has indicated that it wishes to show leniency. We find that this man's crime was caused by a more insidious crime – that of stifling the talent of a citizen. Master Tailor Simmonds, we find that you are a fool and as such will be attired as befits that status."

The sentinels pulled Master Simmonds over to a small tent at the edge of the arena. The praetor turned his attention to the trembling young man who was watching in shock as his master was led away.

"Apprentice Oban, theft is not an offence to which we usually grant leniency. Yet it would be a shame to leave one of those talented hands upon the sands here today. Therefore, you will share your master's punishment."

At his nod, the young man was also led away by the sentinels towards the tent. Praetor Calchas turned and spoke to the governor until laughter broke out from the crowd as the pair reappeared. Master Simmonds, his dignity clearly much offended, was dressed as a clown, while his red-faced apprentice followed behind dressed in a larger version of the dress that had been his undoing. The praetor's face lit up in amusement as they retook their position to the jeers and catcalls of the crowd.

"You have been dressed as befits your crimes, sirs."

The oddly attired duo stood awaiting their sentence.

"For the crime of stupidity, Master Simmonds, you must bear this costume for a month as you go about your daily business in the hope that you remember not to waste opportunities that are gifted to you. Apprentice Oban, you too shall don this outfit for a month while you serve your master honestly. After this time, you will attend the College of Design to be more appropriately trained as befits your talent. You will thereafter be established with your own shop. The fees for your education and shop will be taken from your profits, after which you will donate 30% of your earnings for your lifetime to a fund to educate other deserving citizens who would not otherwise be given such an opportunity."

He paused, allowing the audience a moment to appreciate his mercy.

"This is the sentence of the city upon you both."

Both men nodded their acceptance, the apprentice clearly still shocked by the turn of events. He must have entered the arena today expecting to lose a hand, the customary punishment given to those found guilty of petty theft. Instead, he would be walking away to a future so much brighter than the one he'd had before committing his crime. I felt a flash of relief at his sentence too, grateful that my attempt to improve the weighting of my own voting record hadn't harmed him in any way. He was rained with flowers as he left the arena wearing the dress that had so changed his fate. I spotted the fashion-forward Ginevra tucking his name away in anticipation of his shop opening. It shouldn't take too long for him to discharge his debt and set up shop.

I refocused on the remaining cases. Most were minor and were sentenced to the stocks or other public humiliations. The last but one was a shocking adultery case. Crime in the city was low, but crimes against family and loyalty – the core of the Code – were beyond rare, especially given our matching system. The woman stood, head bowed, as she took her place at the centre of the arena, which meant the footage captured must be impossible to deny. Her lover had fled into the stews, but it was only a matter of time before he too was brought before the city. The woman's mask was removed to reveal a tear-stained face. She was summarily sentenced to exile from the city, stripped bare before us all and redressed in sackcloth, her hair shorn, then marched out of the arena. She would be walked to the eastern gate at the end of the Mete and thrown out to meet whatever fate awaited her as a destitute beggar in the Shadowlands. The route to the eastern gate would take her across the city and undoubtedly would be full of people turning out to shower her with further humiliation.

The woman was barely off the sand before the crowd in the arena turned their attention with interest to the latecomer who had been dragged in. He stood now, having found his feet at some point during proceedings, alone in the cage.

He shrugged off the hands of the sentinels as they

attempted to march him to the centre of the sands. Despite the mask blinding him, he strode in the direction he had been facing until at their command, he came to a stop. His hearing must have already been restored, his spine straightening further at the sound of the crowd jeering him for his attitude.

"You are accused of crimes against the Code. How do you plead?"

It was a surprise to no one when the man refused to bend the knee. The mob erupted, clamouring to see the evidence, condemning him already for the insolence he had shown to the sentinels. The praetor raised his hand to command silence. When the deafening noise subsided, he spoke directly to the audience.

"You are accused of hacking."

I lifted a trembling hand to my lips. Hacking struck at the very heart of our security. The walls were the physical symbol of our defences against the island's natives, but it was our technology that was the real deterrent to the armies that occupied the lands around us, keeping them from attacking. Hacking was, therefore, a capital offence. My dream evening had turned into my worst nightmare. I dug my nails into my hands to prevent my face from revealing my horror. I could abstain from the vote, and no one around me would know, but I couldn't avoid watching the blood spill on the sand. I was in the actual live audience; I couldn't risk the camera panning to me and be caught not showing the proper form for an execution of someone found guilty of such a heinous crime against the state.

The crowd was in a frenzy at the prospect, but I watched as the praetor spoke in an aside with Governor Actaeon, and a couple of other senators. When he returned to his position at the front of the balcony, the amphitheatre fell silent in panting anticipation.

"Sir, you have been found guilty of hacking and damaging the security of the Code – the Code of tonight's most honoured guest."

I could barely hear him over the sound of my pounding heart.

"As you have damaged the city, the city in its turn demands you be damaged in punishment. You are sentenced to public flogging."

The crowd buzzed as everyone turned to their neighbour to check if they had heard correctly. This man was to get off so lightly…? What was going on? The praetor stood impassively as the crowd began to hiss in disgust and anger at being denied a capital vote as the hooded man was strung up and his back bared.

Any earlier delight at how close my seat was to the front evaporated. I felt only churning dismay as I watched the flecks of blood hit the sand. From where I sat I was looking at his front so thankfully I couldn't see the lash gouge into his flesh, but I could see the impact of each hit, his body arching in agony at each blow. His chest was already coloured in fresh bruises. Had he fought the sentinels? Was that why he hadn't made his entrance with the others? I strained to control my own body's flinch each time the whip came down, twisting and turning the ring that felt so heavy on my finger. The crowd stopped jeering as it delightedly took up the count. While an execution didn't come along all that often, floggings were pretty rare as well. Devyn's face flashed into my mind. He had been taken this morning… but no, my imagination was running away with me. No way was this man an elite. What motive would one of my class possibly have to do something so criminal?

I struggled to keep the contents of my stomach on the inside as the count reached the high teens. Blood ran down the man's body onto the ground beneath him, trails of it dripping off the whip as it was raised each time. I glued my eyes on a point on the distant wall behind him. I really was going to throw up if I continued to watch. At least it would appear as if I was looking in the right direction. I kept my face impassive even as Ginevra leaned in to calm my fingers worrying aggressively at my promise ring. My eyes met those of Marcus Courtenay, who finally looked my way, but I was too numb to acknowledge him, each blow causing my gaze to lose more and more focus.

Twenty.

Finally, it was over.

The man fell to the ground as he was untied. Sentinels picked him up directed by a praetorian guard, the laurel emblem on his chest silver rather than the standard red of the sentinels. Why would a praetorian be overseeing the clearing up of a punished Codebreaker? It was lowly work for the esteemed guard of the council. Praetor Calchas thanked the citizenry for their duty, and we all stood as the senators and various dignitaries made their exit.

The crowd was mostly discussing the hacker's light sentence as we made our way out of the arena. I overheard two senior men discussing the possibility that the hacker would be put to some other use by the city. My friends were less concerned at the hacker's fate and more disappointed at not being shown the adulterer's footage, but I could barely force myself to listen to them as my stomach was still in danger of revolting. A last glance at the arena before we exited showed the last accused, still masked, being dragged across the sand. He wasn't moving and his head was hanging on his chest; I hoped he wasn't conscious.

As we walked out, my thoughts turned to the crime I had witnessed – participated in – this morning. I needed to rid myself of all ties to it. While being in possession of black-market tech was a long way from hacking, I was still perilously close to a major transgression. With this fresh reminder of how the city frowned on any violation of the Code, I was stunned at my earlier actions.

What had I been thinking?

Chapter Three

"Where is it?"

"No 'hi, hello, thanks for saving my skin'?" I asked, even as some part of me unclenched at finding myself cornered by Devyn Agrestis, dark eyes glaring down at me in an intense way that seemed at odds with my memories of his usually diffident character.

"Cassandra." My name was half command, half frustrated exhale. "Just give it to me, and we can pretend like this never happened."

My jaw dropped. Obviously, pretending yesterday's blip never happened was the best way forward and certainly what I had resolved to do after my meltdown last night. But a little appreciation of the risk I had taken wouldn't hurt either.

"Never happened? You… are you kidding me? First off, you smuggle some kind of nonregulation device into the forum of all places, then you get picked up by the sentinels, and"—my hand lifted until I was jabbing him in his surprisingly firm chest—"then you disappear for the rest of the day. I've been going out of my mind. There was a part of me that even thought maybe you were that hacker, last night, the one…"

My finger changed from being a taut instrument of accusation as a thought occurred to me, softening as its fellows uncurled to join it. Was it possible? I traced the outline of his chest with gentle fingertips, shaping, learning as they travelled the length of his torso around to his back where I pressed hard watching for a flinch. No reaction. I sagged in relief even as my fingers continued their path down his unmarred muscular back. He wasn't the accused flogged last night. My breath hitched as I once again felt that odd tingle in the current that flowed between us.

I shook my head to clear it.

The sound of Ginevra calling my name made us turn – and taking this in, Devyn stepped back towards me slightly.

"Cassandra"—his tone softened to a hesitant plea—"I was hoping you might take a walk with me later, after class, perhaps?"

Before I had time to tell him in no uncertain terms what kind of walk he could take, he was gone, consumed by the tide of people who were making their way to the licensing offices.

I picked up my tablet as the last class of the day ended. What should I do, meet him? My stomach felt hollow at the thought. What did I know about Devyn, really, much less his damn illegal tech? What on earth was he doing with it and, more importantly, what did it do? The sentinels had dragged him out of class, but what had he told them? He couldn't have said anything incriminating. They surely wouldn't have let him out if he had. Nor would I be sitting here wondering whether or not taking a walk with a boy was going to land me in more trouble than I had ever believed possible.

I was not a rule breaker; I ticked every requirement of the Code. I was obedient, a good daughter, a moderate but diligent student. Abiding by the Code wasn't even something I usually had to give any thought to; it was second nature. What on earth was I thinking? I wasn't going to get involved, I should never have taken the device out of his pocket in the first place. It was none of my business. Devyn and his technology, wherever it was from, had nothing to do with me. All I needed to do was give him back whatever it was and I would be done with the whole business. In a few days, I could forget this had ever happened.

Resolved, I stood up and made my way down the hall towards the library in the Great Basilica.

Until a hand slid into mine and tugged.

And that quickly I was undone.

Up the hall and to the right lay sanity and sense: collect the tech, meet Ginevra, walk home via the river, toss it in… It would be that simple.

But somehow, I found myself traipsing after the slight figure in front of me, his movements lithe as I followed in his wake. He no longer held my hand and yet my path was unwavering, as if he had clamped a manacle around my wrist, the other end attached to his. I couldn't have turned around and walked away if I tried.

Somehow, Code breaking felt more right and more natural than the Code compliance I was usually so good at.

I trailed behind Devyn as he wound his way through the porticoed arcade and out of the main entrance of the forum, moving west through the streets. The neon lures of the shops on the bridge were projected out before us – the latest running shoes briefly adorning his feet, a version of myself twirling in the most adorable little skirt as we passed one of my favourite clothes shops, the blue eyes of my avatar flashing as my body spun, long bright hair streaming. I brushed it away, irritably.

He led us through the financial districts, winding along the tangled walkways that curled around the grand formal architecture at this level, across the square that roofed the ancient Temple of Diana towards one of the great parks that sat at mid-level.

We turned right, continuing to walk along the open galleries until we hit the edge of the Pleasure Gardens, half a mile above river level, a wide expanse of manicured hedges, exotic trees, and lush flowers, paths curling in and around to their best advantage.

Devyn's pace slowed, his dark head turning to acknowledge me for the first time since he touched my hand in the hallway, indicating that I should catch up to him. I paused. Was this a good idea? Would it be better to leave now?

Devyn's head turned a little more. His eye caught mine, and his eyebrow raised ever so slightly. He knew I was nervous and yet he was daring me to do what I did not want to do. I took a step forward, and another, until I was alongside him.

He smirked, fiddling with his wristband.

"We are free to talk here." Despite his words, his voice was still low.

"So… are you going to tell me what's going on? What were you doing with that tech? What is it? What did you say to the sentinels? Wh—" I stopped and stared at him mutinously. "Tell me."

"It's sort of a long story, Cass." His dark eyes fixed on me and I forgot to object to his irksome shortening of my name. "Why don't we sit down?"

We sat on an old bench beside a fountain, the wood grey with age and warped at the joins. Few people came to this part of the gardens and, more pertinently, there didn't seem to be a single camera in sight. It was rare for a place to be so unobserved, but I was grateful for it. The last thing I needed was the city's surveillance catching me associating with someone recently questioned by the sentinels.

"I wasn't expecting… that yesterday morning," he began.

I snorted. "I don't suppose you were. What were you doing bringing unauthorised tech into class?" I lowered my voice. "Into the forum?"

His lips lifted in the corner like I had said something amusing but only he was in on the joke. It was the first time I had seen the expression on his face but I was already starting to find it incredibly annoying.

"No," he corrected, "I meant I wasn't expecting you. Why did you help me? You didn't have to get involved."

Why *had* I helped him?

"I-I don't know," I stammered, thrown. "It wasn't planned. But I couldn't let them arrest you with the device on you, so it seemed… for the best."

"Ah, so you thought it through then?"

I really hadn't. My heart thumped at the recollection of that moment. I just hadn't wanted him to get caught; it had been a reflex more than a decision. And I had ended up an accomplice to a major Code violation as a result.

Devyn reached across and patted down my pockets before he looked up and, taking in my expression of outrage, regarded me oddly. His hand lifted as if compelled and tucked a stray lock of hair behind my ear. My breath hitched as, again, the nondescript boy I knew seemed to morph into someone I felt I was conjuring: lean, intense, strong; the cheekbones sharper, shoulders broader.

I blinked. A trick of the light? But no, I hadn't forgotten that feeling when he caught me in class, or what I saw when I touched him in the forum. Something very odd was going on.

I jumped up; I was out of here. I stepped jerkily back out of reach, the breath in my lungs suddenly lacking in oxygen. I couldn't get enough air.

Once again, Devyn was there, in front of me, his soft brown eyes locked with mine, an arm looping around the small of my back pulling me close as he laid his hand on my chest, the weight steadying me, connecting me to the ground, to him. I stood still, dragging in deep steady breaths in time with his.

"Okay?"

I nodded and he stepped away, backing out of my space as unobtrusively as he could. Something unreadable flickered in his eyes, an action that nagged at me like a cut on the inside of my lip, unnoticed until eating food containing salt when the pain would burst into life leaving you wondering how on earth you had forgotten it was there. Now, as the pain zinged through me, I noticed how much care he took not to touch me, doing so as little as possible. Yet he had already touched me more often in the last two days than anyone else had all week. As he backed away, I stepped towards him without conscious thought, drawn to him like metal filings to a magnet.

His knees hit the bench and he allowed his tall length to fold in on itself. I continued forward, letting my fingers run mesmerised through his dark hair and down his strong jawline.

"Who are you, Devyn Agrestis?"

"Same guy I've always been." He pulled back, putting

himself out of reach of my searching fingers. My eyes struggled to focus and I blinked down at the skinny, unremarkable boy looking calmly up at me from the bench.

"No, no, you aren't," I insisted. "I know what – okay, I don't know what just happened – but I know that something did."

He looked back at me impassively with polite confusion.

"I'm not crazy," I insisted, at his raised eyebrow. "You're doing someth—"

"Cass," he cut across me, seeming to lose patience. "Look, I really appreciate what you did for me yesterday. Honestly, you saved my ass, but if I could just get the ah… thing back, you can go back to your life and I'll go back to mine."

Was he kidding?

"No. Absolutely not. You," I said, poking him in the chest, that deceptively solid chest, "you are going to tell me what is going on here."

He returned my gaze with that same inanely mild expression that suggested I was imagining things.

"I told you, thanks for helping out yesterday. I was holding on to it for a friend, but I really will need to get it back. To return it to him."

I looked at him mutinously. He was actually going to keep up this act, this fraud, this fake—

Well, too late. The genie was out of the bottle, the cookie jar was open, the milk was well and truly spilt. But if he wouldn't level with me, what was I actually accusing him of? *Hey buddy, you're actually a lot hotter than you let on.* Or no, maybe the thing I should ask is why, after knowing him for years as a background figure, I suddenly felt like I couldn't breathe around him? Or rather, that it was only when he was near that the air had any oxygen in it at all, oxygen that pulsed through my body, making me feel more alive than I had ever been.

He met my look with patent expectation that I would be happy to put this behind me. Let him slither back into the shadows. A contrary impulse made me smile and I let my lashes fall before stepping away from the bench.

"The tech… no problem. I was so nervous with the sentinels on the prowl that I hid it. There's a party at my place on Friday night. Everybody's coming. Why don't you come over? I'll give it to you then."

I watched smugly as a not-so-innocuous flash of annoyance crossed his face, momentarily marring his mild-mannered facade.

"Oh, a party," he drew out the word as if he was actually contemplating it. "Thanks, but it's not really my thing. I can meet you by your locker tomorrow at the forum."

I took another step away from him.

"I don't care if it's not really your thing. Being dragged off by the sentinels and thrown into the arena is most definitely not my thing. So you can suck it up and come over to my place with twenty or so close classmates where it's pretty dark, where there's loud music, and where nobody will be watching us too closely." I paused to take a breath. "See you on Friday, yeah?"

It looked like Devyn was having a moment of difficulty holding on to his diffident manner. He took a moment before answering.

"Sure, Cass," he eventually got out between gritted teeth. "Friday it is."

I swung away to head out of the park.

"And stop calling me Cass."

He answered with a not-so-meek chuckle, a dirtily amused sound that I felt in the pit of my stomach.

What was going on with me? Why hadn't I got rid of the unauthorised tech already – much less held on to it as bait? I walked between the clearly codified lines; I followed the rules of our society as well as anyone who didn't want to end up on the sands of the arena. A tremor ran through me at the thought of ever having to—

No, I pushed the idea away. It was unthinkable. Yet the memory of touching him clung to my fingertips, almost a physical thing.

I might not know what Devyn was up to but I couldn't seem to stop myself. Despite all the reasons to walk away, I couldn't. I simply had to know more about him. I was used to getting what I wanted. And what I did know was how to work a party.

One way or another, I was going to figure out Devyn Agrestis's secrets.

Chapter Four

Everything was as it always was – at least to anyone watching, nothing would appear different. But it *was* different, I thought, taking a sip of my drink, only half listening to Ambrose's latest plan for retail innovation.

"I know it's been done before, but I think my take on the kinetic approach would be sensational. A revolutionary way of merchandising…"

Ambrose's voice faded into the general hum and beat of the music as I became increasingly focused on Devyn sloping around the edges of the party.

There was a real art to the way he seemed to be barely there. Most of my friends wanted to be noticed, talking animatedly about something clever or topical, laughing brightly in a way that drew attention to their pearly teeth or witty comments, dancing in their perfectly on-trend clothing that flattered their best features. Long legs, tiny waist, broad shoulders, lustrous hair – girls and boys alike primped and preened. Not a great deal of touching went on – no one wanted to risk that – but the general attitude was that it didn't hurt to look and be looked at.

But not Devyn. He didn't lurk exactly, as that would draw attention. He was part of the party: he talked to people, but no one in particular; he laughed softly with others, but was never the one to incite the hilarity. He didn't really dance but moved with the music, as if he had moments where he failed to take notice of himself, and the rhythm happened to catch him in its current.

I was all too aware that I had been watching him all evening. I only got to throw a party once a season or so. I loved to party – or rather, I loved to dance – and my father was happier letting me throw one than he was about me going to other people's. He almost never granted me permission to go to a club in the West End, and clubs at the outer walls were utterly out of bounds. And here I was spending so much time tracking Devyn bloody Agrestis that I was utterly wasting this one.

He'd been here for two hours, and so far he'd made no attempt to talk to me at all. He acted like he came to our parties all the time. Maybe he did. In fact, suddenly I was sure he did. Like the brush of a tune that you suddenly realise you've heard countless times and even seem to know a few lines of. He'd been here. Last time for sure, and maybe the one before that. Delving into half-remembered parties, the endless glimpses of Devyn rolled before my mind's eye.

He always came to my parties. Scanning through memories of social events over the last few years it seemed like he was always there. I shook my head, trying to clear the picture; I could sense him there, in corners, on the outside of groups, I just couldn't focus on his face… It was like a strange optical illusion that was almost impossible to penetrate. Once you knew it was there and you focused hard, you could see it for a moment before it faded away again.

"Cassandra, Ca-ssan-dra," Ambrose was waving his hand in front of my face.

I turned to him, smiling vaguely.

"Uh, yes, sorry, what was that?" I struggled to recall what Ambrose had been talking about – something about augmented reality.

"Where did you go?"

"Nowhere, I was just worrying about the catering. I think we have plenty of everything though." I hesitated before continuing. Somehow I didn't like drawing attention to Devyn but I had to test my theory. "Ambrose, what do you think of Devyn Agrestis?"

Ambrose looked at me blankly for a moment.

"Devyn Agrestis," he drew the name out slowly. "Devyn Agrestis… right, yeah, I know him. He's in our class. Nice guy, sort of tall, no, average height, black, maybe brown hair. Yeah, yeah, nice guy."

Wow, Ambrose would be quite the witness for the state. Talk about failing to paint a picture with words.

Unable to help myself, I felt my eyes go to Devyn once more, now standing in a group talking by the drinks table.

"Does he come out with us much?" Maybe Ambrose could pinpoint him to specific parties for me.

"Uh, yeah, he's usually around."

"But when specifically?" I pushed.

Ambrose looked baffled. "Like, all the time. He was at… I'm sure I was talking to him the other week at Alianna's thing. We spoke about…" Ambrose trailed off. "Yeah, we had a good talk, caught up about things."

Ambrose, one of the top-scoring boys in our college class,

had the pedant's preference for specificity on all occasions. While he was clearly sure that Devyn was someone we socialised with, that he was unable to supply the litany of times or dates such a question would usually have generated was notable. Vague generalities were the best he could come up with. How curious.

I added it to the growing mental file labelled Devyn Agrestis. Right alongside my realisation that him not looking my way all night was far too deliberate for real indifference. People at parties scanned the room, as interested in the opportunities they were missing as the one they were in the middle of.

Devyn, however, was making an art of flitting his eyes across the room like everyone else, while studiously ignoring whatever part of the room I happened to be in. So, while it looked like he hadn't yet spotted me, I was willing to place a substantial wager on the likelihood that he could describe in minute detail exactly what I was wearing from my heeled sandals to my intricately painted nails. Not to mention every interaction I'd had all evening. Fine. Then let him get an eyeful of this.

I strode across the room to where Felix Thomas and his cronies were standing. Felix had always liked me. I usually wouldn't play up to that – my father had strong views on any kind of flirtation. He was pretty orthodox in that respect; even though some kids my age experimented lightly, my father saw it as disrespectful to one's true match. I had never felt like crossing that boundary before but I was willing to bet Devyn wouldn't be happy either. Not for the same reasons as my father, though.

Brushing my hair behind my shoulder to better display my neck in the off-the-shoulder top I was wearing, I sidled up to

Felix and greeted him by lightly laying my hand on his bicep, and letting it trail gently just a few millimetres – nothing too strong.

Felix turned, his eyes lighting when he realised who it was that had so blatantly invaded his space.

"Cassandra." He smiled his pearly cute-boy smile. "Great party."

"Thanks, I was hoping…" and before I could even finish one sentence, Devyn was at my shoulder. Well, that had been even quicker than expected.

"Cassandra, can I have a quick word?" he cut across me. Without waiting for my answer, he had cupped my elbow and was leading me down the hallway to the quieter reception room.

"What are you doing?" I asked, oh so softly.

"What you wanted me to do," he returned.

I shook my head, giving him my best confused look. "I don't know what you mean."

"No?" One eyebrow lifted. "I think you know exactly what I mean. Papa's little princess doesn't normally play with the boys."

He'd noticed I didn't really flirt with guys. How much more did he know about me? It was my turn to find out something about him.

"Are you sure about that?" Pulling my jangling nerves together, I reached out, repeating the move I had just practised on Felix. Devyn steeled himself as my hand came into contact with his bicep, tightening under my touch, the whipcord strength undeniable.

There was a truth touch provided that sight alone contradicted. I was increasingly sure of it: his body, the body I was so startling aware of, did not belong. There was something about him I couldn't quite figure out. How was he doing this? Some kind of new augmenting tech? He looked directly down at me, amused but alert.

"So confident, little girl. What are you going to do now?"

I pulled back my wandering thoughts. I wasn't going to back down, that was for sure. I moved squarely in front of him, lifting my chin in defiance. I lowered my lashes, letting my fingers drift up to his shoulder, swaying closer to him, taking my other hand and repeating the manoeuvre until both hands were on his shoulders, settling there. Our bodies now so close there was barely enough room for the breeze gently lifting the curtains to make its way between us. I tilted one hip and then the other.

I hummed the tune that was blaring through the walls from the living room where the party continued, unaware of the lines being crossed only a room away. His body was unmoving, refusing to take up the rhythm with mine but the awareness crackled between us. Devyn might be holding still, but he was far from indifferent; his entire body fairly screamed in its tension.

I risked a tentative glance upwards. Not a good move. Devyn's eyes glittered darkly, the appearance of mildness thoroughly dropped once more.

"Cassandra," he grated, "you play at games you don't understand. You've been a good girl all your life. Why change now?"

He warned me off, but he didn't move back and his hands didn't push me away. I met the darkly glittering eyes of this boy I barely knew and certainly didn't understand. The soft, slight version sharpened to reveal the truth of him. Why would anyone use cutting-edge tech to appear more ordinary?

A part of me wanted to back away. I felt intimidated,

threatened by this version of him. The tremble of a doe on seeing a suspected predator step out of the shadows ran through me. I embraced it, the electricity of my blood swirling through me, making me feel utterly alive. As if up until this moment I'd been sleepwalking, his touch pulling me out of a drugged sleep. Dry-mouthed, I wet my lips with a flick of my tongue, spotting his eyes track the tiny movement.

"Maybe I've never had anybody tempt me before. Why take a nibble of something you're not hungry for?" The huskily spoken words accurately summed up my previous indifference to the flirting that would so horrify my father. It was more than I had planned to share though.

"And you're hungry for me." Devyn's voice was low and deep as the darkness of the room seemed to enclose us in a bubble. A world of two.

Was that a statement or a question? I wasn't sure, and what did it matter? I moved closer until our bodies were fitting lightly together. Every atom that existed between us seemed charged. Was this what I had been missing out on by staying true to a boy I had met only once on my twelfth birthday? I glanced at my promise ring in an attempt to conjure up the most important reason not to move closer to the pulsing magnetic body so close to my own. Why would I not touch, embrace, feel…? The growl in his chest reverberated through my veins. I wanted to—

"Cassandra." Unnoticed, the door had opened and my mother was standing in the open doorway, her scolding glare melting the warmth that encircled me. I swayed as the coldness of my mother's gaze seemed to physically stab me.

Devyn moved as if to stand in front of me but then his head went down and he sloped – and by sloped, I mean he practically *oozed* around the tall, elegant brunette in the doorway – from the scene of the crime. Nice.

"What was going on in here?" my mother's question lashed across the room.

"Nothing, he's just a classmate," I offered, deliberately not naming Devyn. "He wanted a word about a girl he's friends with. Her birthday is coming up and he was wondering if it would be appropriate to get her a gift."

And just like that, I told the first outright lie of my life. I had spent most of my childhood drifting happily along in between the twin lines of expectation and appropriate conduct. In the last week, I had taken some significant excursions. I felt like I was going to be sick, my stomach churning with nerves. There was no way my mother was going to believe me. But given the slightly risqué behaviour I was describing versus the absolutely scandalous behaviour she had not quite witnessed, Camilla could only judge based on my past self rather than the new version of me that was emerging and had yet to be formally introduced.

She nodded, adding curtly that I was neglecting the rest of my guests, before sharply closing the door behind her. I staggered over to the open window and took a deep breath of air. I was trembling – from my mother walking in on us and from the heart-stopping almost-something with Devyn.

I realised that I had lied not to protect myself from my mother's condemnation, my father's disappointment, or even the possibility that my future partner would feel in some way betrayed, but for Devyn's protection. I had broken a code of honesty I had lived by my entire life so that he would not be noticed – because my parents would have ensured he got noticed. By the authorities, by the college board, by my classmates' parents, even potential employers, as we were now only a couple of months from graduation. Flirting with non-partners wasn't off-limits officially, but if my mother had walked in only seconds later, things might have progressed beyond a light touch on the arm. Not that it was actually against the code to get physical with someone other than your intended before marriage, but it was incredibly rare once matched. After all, why waste calories on some passing fancy when the most delectable custom-made dessert was waiting for you?

I looked out over the city, the dark void of the river visible between the illuminated tower blocks, and I allowed my heightened emotions to float out on the tide.

Devyn Agrestis was not good for me. I liked my life. I was looking forward to graduation, and most especially upgrading from promise ring to promise kept.

That was what was important.

The last seven days were the anomaly, as was the odd boy who had stepped from the shadowy wings of my life into centre stage. I needed to regain control and push the mystery of Devyn and his device out of my life for good, before it did any permanent damage.

Chapter Five

When I walked into the breakfast room the next morning, the atmosphere had the coiled tension of a trap waiting to spring. My darling mother had wasted no time. I shouldn't have been surprised. With my father, I often forgot that I was adopted. With my mother, I never forgot. But as I hadn't officially done anything wrong, I took my seat with a chirpy "good morning" to the room.

I glanced at Anna, the maid standing so quietly in the corner she was practically merging with the wall. Anna shook her head slightly. From her this was a big red flag crying out *go back, go back*. The maid rarely stuck her neck out. Camilla Shelton missed nothing so for her to dare this much meant I was in *big* trouble. Graham Shelton looked up grimly at my entrance, placing his cup gently back on the table.

"Cassandra." He paused, his eyes serious. "I hear you took some time out from the party last night."

"Pa—" He cut off my interruption with a wave of his hand.

"No, dearest. I was shocked to hear that you were in a room

with a boy on your own. This is not how you have been raised."

My head went back. On the scale of… oh, spilling some tea on the tablecloth to, let's say, having illegal tech hidden away in the forum, talking to a boy seemed reasonably innocent. My parents rarely had to chastise me and now I was to be taken to task for behaviour that would barely raise an eyebrow in any of my friends' homes.

"Papa," I sputtered, unsure how to find the right level of indignation and casualness. "Nothing happened. Nothing." I glared at my mother. "I don't know what you were told, but I was gone for five minutes." *Flashback of trailing my fingers along Devyn's bicep.* "We were talking, that's it." *The sway of my hips towards his, the warmth as the energy bounced in the tiny space left between our two bodies.* "I don't know what the fuss is about."

What *was* the fuss about? Why had I behaved like that? I stared down at my untouched breakfast, resolving once more to give Devyn back his tech and get on with my life. It was the right thing to do. I lived a charmed life, and unlike many of my friends was very aware of that fact. It was likely to do with being adopted, knowing that, but for the grace of my parents, my life could have been different. Who knew what life I might have led had my real parents been alive, but sometimes I found myself looking at and wondering about people who lived lives so different from my own. Slipping through the city on the train, I watch busy people hustling about the city. People unable to afford the monorail to take them to menial unrewarding jobs that I was barely aware existed. Or worse, the mudlarks who flooded the shores of the river at low tide, desperately looking for something that would get themselves and their families through another day.

I knew I should stay away from Devyn. Whatever he was

involved with… well, it could even be dangerous. *Chaos in the Code.* There were those who wanted to interrupt the order that governed our world, I knew. But for what purpose? Order and the Code were what kept our city safe. Did people want our lives to be like those who lived beyond the walls? Uncivilised? Primitive? I couldn't imagine why.

I snapped my attention to my mother to find myself subject to her trademark coolly assessing look.

"Cassandra, you may tell your father what you wish, but you were standing very close to that young man. I don't need to remind you that as our daughter, we expect you to be the best you can be. Your father is a prominent merchant in the city, and given the status of your promised partner, we cannot afford to have you behaving improperly with some nobody."

"I wasn't," I protested again. "Since when is it improper to just stand close to someone?"

My mother held my gaze before turning away to my father with a sniff. My father turned back to me, and his gaze softened as he smiled affectionately.

"Darling, I'm sure nothing was going on."

I'd never before given him a reason to think anything different. I shifted guiltily in my seat.

"Sometimes it's about appearances, and you are only a year away from handfasting. The year between graduation and handfasting is there for you to enjoy yourself and try different things before you settle down. I know some of your friends may even experiment a little, but I'd hate to see you do something you'll regret later when you are with your true partner."

He put his hand over my mother's, ever the peacemaker in the family, soothing her with his touch as he delivered an admonishment that would be far too light in her eyes.

I smiled gratefully, aware that timing was on my side here. Thank goodness for ships coming in: I had been right, the pineapple in the market was a sign that whatever had been disrupting the flow of goods into the city was now over and trade was good again. And so, therefore, was my father's mood. "Of course, Papa, I'll be more careful in future."

In that moment I truly meant it. I had no idea how I had managed to stray so far from my normal life. What was it about Devyn Agrestis? Whenever he was close, I felt like I was magnetised. I was playing with fire and was in grave danger of third-degree burns, the type that give lasting scars. If they didn't actually kill you. I was in possession of unauthorised tech that I was withholding from a potential criminal because I was flirting with him. Flirting with someone who wasn't my intended partner.

I knew what happened to people who infringed on the Code. The entire city got a weekly reminder, yet here I was dancing all over it and lying to my parents to boot. I needed to give Devyn Agrestis back his damn tech as soon as possible – and hopefully return to blissful unawareness of his existence immediately after.

Back at the forum on Monday, I realised my intentions were never going to stay the course. My eyes, of their own volition, were scanning the faces going by, seeking back and forth until they found their target.

He was loitering, almost invisibly, just down the passage from my locker. Even though I was looking for him, my eyes had slid past and had to track back when my brain insisted something wasn't quite right. He never seemed to take up too much space, blending into the background, staggeringly unremarkable.

His eyes flicked to me but didn't linger. Taking his cue, I continued to my locker and, after grabbing what I needed, started to move down the hallway. My breath quickened as I walked past the spot where Devyn leaned against the wall.

As I made my way to class, he didn't catch up with me, but I knew he was behind me, his presence – even seven or eight feet behind – a tangible thing. I paused outside the door to check my tablet. Was I even going to the right class?

He passed me with no acknowledgement but a feather-light touch on my hand… that I might easily have missed had it not blazed up through me. I lifted my hand to find a small slip of paper in my palm.

PARK 5pm

I blinked at the words, and they were gone. Looking up, I realised so was he. Our misadventure at the party meant I had failed to do the promised handover. So now I had to cross the city with the damn device burning a hole in my pocket for a second time. It had been bad enough bringing it to the party, my recent visit to the arena and the flinching body of that hacker adding weight to every step I took. Carrying it back to the forum and hiding it again after also receiving admonishment from my parents had almost broken me. Each step had felt like it was one closer to a dreaded fate in the arena.

My renewed promise to myself that I was backing out of whatever it was I had embroiled myself in had raised my fear levels to the extent that I didn't think I could ever touch the thing again without having heart palpitations. I leaned back against the wall outside my class for a moment, my mind swirling. Could I risk going back to the library so soon? Would this attract attention? Unease fizzed through me. Gathering myself, I crushed the paper as I dismissed all thoughts of Devyn. *Focus*. Just get through the day. Figure it out later.

"Did you bring it?" Devyn's cool voice from behind the bench we had shared the previous week startled me, even though I had been waiting for it.

"No," I returned, more sharply than I had intended, startled at his sudden appearance. "You think I walk around with it in my pocket all the time, on the off chance the opportunity to give it to you finally arrives? Are you crazy? "

A glint lit his dark eyes.

"I don't know. You've had plenty of chances. I'm starting to think Papa's little princess doesn't want to give it back."

"Don't call me that," I snapped. "What does that even mean? Of course I want rid of it."

"Do you?" he smiled. "You could have given it back to me straight away. Your life would have gone on with only that tiny mark to blemish your perfect record in your perfect life. But you didn't. You held on to it. You're interested in what lies behind the curtains."

I looked away. Was that it? Was it something more than Devyn himself that intrigued me? Was I interested in understanding the device as well as the boy, why he had it, and what he intended to do with it? Why he was risking his life for it? I was. Or at least I was *also* curious about that, I admitted to myself. I had originally held on to the irregular tech because in some way it was the concrete evidence I needed that Devyn Agrestis was more than he appeared to be. As long as I had it I could be sure Devyn wouldn't disappear again. He would have to show his true colours. The insignificant boy who lived in the shadows of my life would be forced to step into the light every time we discussed the device. The more it happened, the harder it would be for him to hide from me. I reminded myself that I was handing the gold tech back. I just needed to make sure that he was permanently in the open first.

"Maybe," I admitted. "What is it? What's it for?"

Devyn laughed. "You don't really want to know. Once that genie is out, you won't ever be able to put him back in the bottle."

I frowned. He might be right.

"I do want to know."

He looked at me speculatively. "I don't think so. I've been watching you a long time, Cassandra Shelton. You're a pretty girl with a pretty life, which you dance through matching your steps to whatever tune the piper is playing. You go to school, you do well – but not too well. Your life is neatly mapped out: you're comfortable, and your match is from one of the oldest families in the city. Why would you rock the boat now?"

His dark, intelligent eyes mocked me, his lips twisted in a curl that dared me to deny the insignificance of my compliant existence. My fists curled at my sides. He was right, I couldn't deny his words. He had me pegged; from his spot in the shadows he had seen everything. But that didn't stop it from stinging.

"You've been watching me?" I repeated testily. "Why? How

bloody creepy, who are you to judge me about anything? Why don't you go away and live your own life?"

His eyes had narrowed at my accusations, but he laughed, a harsh grating sound, before he responded.

"That's my plan. Or at least it was until a shallow little rich girl decided she wanted to play at things she doesn't understand." His face darkened, slivers of raw emotion leaking through his usually implacable facade. "Live my own life? Nothing would please me more. It's past time. But I need the device you stole to do that. I've wasted *years* on you, hoping you were someone else. But you're not. She's gone. You're nothing more than the pretty, superficial girl you appear to be. Nothing more."

He looked desolate as he trailed off, beyond grief, beyond pain. Unable to help myself, I stepped towards him, reaching up and placing my hand gently on his face. His body curved around mine as if we were two halves finally made whole and his heartbeat, thundering with the pain that thudded through him, slowed in response to my own gentle beat. It was the most utterly connected moment I had ever felt in my life.

"Damn it." He pushed back from me, glaring at me in angry consternation at how much he had revealed, before the blank expression slammed back into place.

"Who? Who did you think I was?" Thrown back to reality, I scrambled to gain a foothold in what he had told me before it too was pulled from under me once more.

His eyes were cold as he contemplated his response.

"That's not really any of your business now, is it? *Princess*."

Fine. I tried another tack.

"Where will you go? Why do you need the tech to get there?"

"Again, nothing for you to concern yourself with." Even

with our short acquaintance – on my side at least – I had come to recognise the particularly implacable look that settled over his saturnine features.

"Fine. Keep your secrets." I was almost shaking. For someone who supposedly danced unthinking through life, I was wrongfooted now and felt dangerously off balance.

For which I thoroughly blamed the mercurial aggravating cretin in front of me.

The dark shadow of a sentinel on foot was veering across the path towards us, unlikely to be anything to do with us, but conveniently timed for me because I was done with this conversation. I whirled away.

"But two can play at that game," I threw back over my shoulder. I'd show him. I wasn't just an insipid girl living her safe little life. I could be more, do more.

I could.

Chapter Six

There was no sign of Devyn at the forum the next day or the one after that. He had tried three times to get the tech from me now. Had he given up?

Maybe he was already gone. I didn't care. Or rather, I was an addict insisting to myself I didn't need a fix but I did. Badly. It was like nagging tooth pain – Devyn in the background of my life was a presence of which I had been ignorant until the cavity of his absence became a fact which was impossible to ignore. I turned our last conversation over and over in my mind. What did it mean? Who had he thought I might be?

He had waited years for what? Some sign, some evidence… why? Round and round it went in my brain. He had been watching me for years – this fact alone should have thrown me way more than it did. What was special about me? But then… apparently nothing. He had concluded I was nothing more than the spoiled daughter of an elite merchant. But he had hoped I was someone else; his disappointment that I wasn't had been a tangible thing.

That connection, his pain… I had never felt that before. It had wholly blindsided me. He was looking for someone. I had never really known who I was that's all it was. I had been promised that soon I would have all the connection I would ever need in my partner, not some freak moment with someone I barely knew.

On Saturday, I pulled myself together to go shopping with Ginevra to buy my graduation dress. My mother had made clear that I needed something spectacular, a stipulation that would previously have lit up my world with its underlying licence to consider money no object in satisfying this single criterion.

I had hoped that having Ginevra along would help me focus on my task, but I found her light-hearted chatter impossible to hold on to, so made do with offering up what so far had clearly managed to be the appropriate noises as she had yet to complain at my inattention.

"Maybe if you left your hair down, this one would do?" Ginevra mused as we watched my avatar twirl in front of us in the latest unsatisfactory outfit. Barely had she spoken and the elaborate updo dissolved and my long multi-hued tresses flowed down across my shoulders covering the awkward way the straps lay on my pale bare shoulders.

I stilled. My hair colour was unusual – the gold, red, and caramel strands shouted my adopted status to anyone paying attention. It wasn't a secret, but it wasn't public knowledge either. In fact, my mother went to some lengths to ensure it was not questioned, even going so far as to dye her own hair a lighter brown to discourage any potential raised eyebrows. I had never given it much thought before, but was this something I shared with the girl Devyn sought?

Who was she and why was he looking for her? I eyed the

avatar speculatively. Was she everything I wasn't? Was she worthy of the years he had spent looking for her?

Not a foolish girl who would never be anything more than an ornament on the arm of a more important male. Not just a pretty bauble to be displayed to best effect before being put back in its box.

"Ginevra, what was the name of that apprentice at the Mete?" I asked.

"What apprentice?" Ginevra was confused at my apparently random question. "We don't know any apprentices."

She stopped, her eyes lighting in sudden understanding. "You wouldn't."

"I would," I returned, shaking off the despondency towards which my thoughts had been dragging me. Getting the disgraced apprentice to make my dress would be a stroke of genius. It would indeed be spectacular, as directed, while also annoying my mother because of its less than salubrious origin. It didn't hurt that it also soothed my conscience, which had niggled at me ever since I had voted him guilty for my own selfish reasons.

We quickly looked up the address of Apprentice Oban, finding it amongst the reams of attention he had received in the feeds following the Mete. His home was buried in the stews, making Ginevra a little less supportive of my plan.

We wound our way out of the shopping district and through the West End. Our destination lay eastwards beyond the plazas and concrete and glass buildings of the financial district. It was a part of the city I didn't really spend a great deal of time in. The weekend atmosphere was eerie, all those buildings filled with thousands and thousands of empty rooms now that everyone had gone home for a day of rest.

Ginevra and I grew quiet as we continued past streets that were becoming less and less familiar. We were scanned and waved through the old wall at Aldgate. My father would not approve of my being in the outer eastern part of the city. We were quite a distance from the outer walls, but still… I was a little nervous about my plan by this stage but refused to turn around. I was not just a pretty girl in a pretty life. Not two streets from the gate, Ginevra baulked and turned back, unhappy that I couldn't be talked out of my course of action.

As I wound my way through the warren of narrower, older streets, I looked around, fascinated. It was so different to the western neighbourhood where I lived with its wide spaces between the buildings and unhurried green walkways. The homes here pressed tightly together, a legacy from the era when the Empire had been at its weakest. Londinium had struggled to cope with the numbers cowering inside the walls back when the border had stretched all the way to the gates of the city itself. Before we had the engineering skills to go higher, the poor had squeezed into every space offered between the original inner-city wall and the newer reinforced ones. Nothing but those great outer walls, built deep and high, separated us from the hordes of Britons who waited outside ready to burn us to the ground.

The stews held people of every shape and size, all exotic to my eyes. Grubby little hands grabbed at my skirts as we whisked by.

"Please, donna, spare a copper."

I snatched my skirts closer, looking nervously around. Even if I had physical currency to give them, begging was strictly forbidden. These children were risking the stocks by approaching me.

I shook my head at the children and they melted away into

the warren of streets. I paused every now and then to discreetly peek at my device to check I was still going the right way.

Eventually, a beep outside a peeling doorway indicated I had arrived. I knocked and, finally, an elderly man opened the door. Taking in the quality of my clothes, he winked at me and pointed to a door at the top of the stairs. Apparently I wasn't the first elite to deign to cross this threshold since Apprentice Oban's skills had come to light, too impatient to wait until he opened a shop in the inner districts.

I hesitated outside the door. This was a crazy idea. My mother would kill me and Devyn wouldn't even know, much less care, that I had got a tailor from the stews to make my dress. *Make my dress*. Ha, even my small act of defiance and social conscience was related to the role he had identified as mine: pretty little rich girl.

My shoulders slumped. I felt as if I had lost a battle I didn't even know had been engaged. I had stepped outside the safe borders of my world momentarily and, having skirted the edge for a while, I was now ready to scuttle back to the safety of my pampered life.

Only Devyn remained as a lure on the border, nagging at me to take another step, even though he had advised me to stay in my sheltered world. The other world, the one he inhabited, was no place for me. He had no place for me. I felt hollow at the thought. He was an insufferable enigma; the mask he put on made my fingers curl into claws in my desire to rip it off and reveal someone else. The man I had glimpsed. Dark curls, sharply defined features, intensity and determination blazing out of him. How did he hide that side of himself, and why? Would I ever know?

He had said he would be moving on, and so must I. Only,

what direction to take? My mind went in circles as I stood there in the dimly lit, dirty hallway. Home to my parents and friends, pretty dresses, and inane parties? Or should I push at the boundaries of my world to know something more? Something that tingled at the fringes of my sensibilities.

"Hello." The door had opened and I looked down to discover a dishevelled girl surveying me through dark, tangled hair. A shimmer of something ran through me, a shiver of something… like a hand held out over a threshold, drawing me in. I couldn't resist taking another tiny step. Just a little more, maybe.

"Hello," I responded, smiling slightly so she would know I meant no harm.

She eyed me warily, her survey comprehensive. No chance of this one being cowed by anything, I realised. Her gaze was bold and aware beyond her years, her head tilting to the side as if something about me had struck her as different. On closer examination, she was older than she looked, the tired slump of her shoulders making her appear young while a cough wracked her small frame.

"You looking for Oban?" she asked once the fit had subsided.

I nodded. She led me into the small, sparsely furnished apartment, vaguely recognisable from its moment of fame at the arena.

There was an older lady sewing in the light of the window who barely glanced up from her activity. A few more children huddled in another corner of the room.

The slight young man from the Mete was bent over some material, standing when his sister called out to him, alerting him to my presence.

"Donna," he addressed me formally as the street urchins had done.

"I was hoping you might make me a dress," I announced haltingly.

He smiled shyly, nodding, his survey of me less bold than his sister's but no less comprehensive for all that.

"I have no funds for the material, but if you buy it, I can do the rest," he offered.

"Deal," I said quickly. Standing here in this room with his family I felt deeply uncomfortable, my guilt at voting against him at the Mete gnawing at me, an unsettling anxiety crawling over my skin at the squalor of the room. I glanced over at the woman in the corner who sat sullenly watching – their mother, I supposed. As I submitted to Oban's measuring in the second room, the girl who had greeted me at the door left after confirmation that Oban would be able to manage both attending to me and the care of the two small ones on the floor, but not before her grey eyes settled on me once more. It wasn't a warning exactly but there was something about her that told me that should I do anything in her absence to hurt her family it would not be the last I saw of her. She was a slip of a thing yet I believed that silent promise.

"Have you had much business since the Mete?" I queried lightly as Oban continued to take my measurements, jotting down quick notes in a little book on the table.

He inclined his head in what I took for a soft yes. I made a few more attempts to start a conversation with him but they elicited little more in the way of response. Not a talker then.

A hacking cough in the other room indicated that his sister had returned, though I had not heard the door closing.

"Is she okay?" I asked softly to the kneeling Oban as he measured the inside of my leg.

He looked up, his eyes flashing with concern, before he again gave a small nod. I frowned at the conflicting signals.

"Has she been ill for long?" I tried again.

Another nod.

"Marina's not contagious," he said finally after another pause, clearly taking my question as worry for my *own* health.

I *tsked* in frustration. He looked up at me, startled.

"I wasn't asking for myself," I admonished. "I can bring medicine."

His face lost the inexpressive look that those in service so often used to hide all feelings and, more importantly, opinions from their customers.

He looked concerned again and then shook his head. "No cure."

"What do you mean, no cure?" I asked, baffled. Our society had little illness – most having been defeated by science and technology generations ago – and what remained was quickly remedied.

He shook his head and refused to answer any more questions, hustling me out of the house with a slip of paper containing the instructions regarding what material he wanted me to buy.

I made my way back to Aldgate deeply distracted by Oban's behaviour. Why would he not want his sister to get help? It was ridiculous. Was it the cost?

The thought of the dark-haired girl's illness niggled at me. When I returned two days later with the cloth, I made sure I had some medicine anyway, purchased from one of the few pharmacies in the city.

Oban was pleased with the cloth, as was I – the rich material glimmered as it caught the light that came through the grimy window, my signature colour turquoise shot through with indigo. He practically hummed with excitement as he felt it, showing me a couple of sketches he had done already that made my own eyes gleam in anticipation. We grinned at each other, appreciating the mutual pleasure caused by his vision.

His sister was bustling about in the main living area and when she popped her head in to ask Oban a question, I pulled the bottle out of my bag.

Marina stilled, the colour draining from her already pale face. There was an odd feeling in the room, almost a physical charge that raised the hair on my body. I rubbed at my arms to dispel the fanciful notion. I pulled my eyes from the girl to her brother to find he looked equally as upset.

"What did you do?" Oban whispered from bloodless lips.

"I–I…" I stammered, confused by the atmosphere that had descended so suddenly on the room, their reaction to the bottle of cough medicine as though I had taken out a bottle of poison. "I thought it might help."

Oban looked behind him at the top corner of the room where the ubiquitous state camera resided. They were supposed to be in every home but became increasingly rare in the higher echelons of society. He followed the trajectory of the camera and realised that the bottle was currently blocked by his own frame. He shot me a quelling look as he covered the bottle with the cloth and turned again to his notebook without looking at his sister who remained frozen in the doorway.

"Perhaps, donna, you would like something a little higher around the neckline in the fashion of the orient?" he asked, indicating his book. Rather than an adjustment to the sketch he had been happily showing me moments before, there was a hastily scribbled message.

PLEASE. NO HELP. NO ILLNESS. THEY TAKE HER.

I was deeply confused but, responding to the desperate

pleading contorting the two faces turned to me, I nodded. What was going on?

Troubled, I took my leave with smiling promises to return a week later for a fitting, my skin still tingling from the strange atmosphere that hadn't quite dissipated from their home.

They were hiding Marina's illness, but why? Because they would take her… but who were *they*?

The pharmacist had been slightly off when I bought the medicine, I now recalled, asking me who it was for and why I needed it. I had been vaguely annoyed at her questioning, having been already irritated at Devyn's elusiveness. I had assumed he would be back, cap in hand, to get his sodding tech but I had assumed wrong. I caught glimpses of him now and then but always at a distance, slipping away like a snake in the grass when I attempted to cross paths with him. It was infuriating.

"Aarghh." I released my frustration audibly, earning a startled look from the man in front of me in the queue to get back through Aldgate. I smiled guilelessly up at him. A Shadower from the look of his dirt-stained clothes, come to the city to sell whatever it was he grew in the lands beyond the outer wall. He looked prosperous, as he would have to be to have a permit to pass through the inner walls. Taking in my fine dress, he dropped his eyes and quickly turned away.

My mind churned over the conversation I had shared with the pharmacist. I had been haughtily brief in my answers but she had been noticeably insistent. Why had she wanted to know what I was purchasing medicine for? It hadn't been just the idle curiosity of one bored for lack of customers. She had been actively trying to discover where the medicine was bound.

I had, out of sheer ignorance, been vague about the

symptoms, for I had seen little more than the cough, but the keen-eyed pharmacist had asked some questions that had been unnervingly accurate. Flushed cheeks, slightly jerky movements? I had agreed under her soft interrogation, my memory of Marina remarkably clear for someone I had only met for a few moments.

As I walked up to the platform to take a transport across the city, I also recalled my father asking after my health that evening at dinner. He too had been oddly persistent, checking I was taking my vertigo meds, but I had laughed it off, teasing him for his excessive care of me. Had he known about the cough bottle? Had he thought it was for me? I couldn't imagine why as I was clearly quite well.

I felt unsettled as I took my seat to head west and home. Had my action been watched and observed? Was that why my father was asking about my health for no apparent reason? Why had Oban and Marina been hiding her illness? Who was it they were so scared of?

I stared out of the window, my mind racing. Usually the journey across the city was one of my greatest pleasures, whizzing through the teeming galleried warren of Londinium, millions of citizens busily going about their day, toiling at the lower levels, ascending into homes in the great scrapers. So many lives full of unknown joys and unknown dramas. Now all I could think of was one single citizen whose life I might have unwittingly made harder.

I had been trying to help. Had I blindly done the opposite? I cursed my ignorance, reproach washing through me. Had my blithe dance through life meant that I had hurt someone else? Devyn was right, I was a fool. *Stupid, stupid,* I berated myself.

Devyn.

Perhaps I could repair the damage I had done. Cover the

tracks I had left to their door. If anyone could help it would be him. I still had his device, but I couldn't afford to wait until he broke and approached me. I would have to swallow my pride and ask him for help.

At the forum over the next few days, I kept my eyes peeled but went from distant sightings to none at all. Didn't he plan to complete civics? Without a pass, it was not possible to graduate and become a full citizen. Or to travel around the Empire, as I assumed was his plan.

I was due back at Oban's for a fitting the day after. I really needed to catch Devyn before that. To understand what I had done and how to fix it.

Oban and Marina had been terrified. Whatever line I had inadvertently crossed, it was bad. The thought of something happening to the dark-haired urchin was more than I could bear. Devyn had to be around somewhere but how to flush him out? Would the ploy I had used with Felix work a second time, I wondered? It would be infinitely more damaging to be seen flirting with a boy in the forum than it had been in the privacy of my own home at a party. My reputation would definitely suffer this time. Besides which there was no guarantee that Devyn was watching anymore – he had said as much himself – now that I definitely wasn't the girl he was looking for. I felt strangely bereft at the thought. I shook my head.

In my first class, I asked Ambrose and Ginevra if they had seen him that morning. Ambrose thought he had but the closer I questioned him, the less sure he became. Maybe it hadn't been Devyn, maybe it had been someone else.

The more people I asked, the stronger this pattern

appeared. Some people couldn't recall seeing him in weeks, others had spoken to him that morning, but the topic escaped them, and then they became less sure they had seen him at all. How did he do that? Under any kind of focus, Devyn became even more mysterious as he deflected such scrutiny.

As I circled the forum at lunch hunting my elusive prey, I spotted that there were some mangos and bananas to be had. Pleased, I broke off my search to acquire a drink.

I thanked the vendor as he handed me the fresh smoothie, tapping my wrist in payment and bringing the straw to my lips with a sigh of pleasure. I loved the tang and exoticness of these fruits that travelled so far to wind up in the Londinium markets; they were expensive but oh so worth it.

"What do you want?"

I jumped at the dark low growl behind me. I turned straight into the solid chest of Devyn Agrestis. I looked up at him as he glowered down from his superior height.

"I need to talk to you," I said softly back, my lips barely moving, not even removing the straw in the hopes it would obscure my words to anyone who might be watching.

Devyn reached behind me and picked up a mango, turning it in his long fingers, a slight thinning of the lips the only indication he had heard me.

"You have something for me?" he asked lightly with a meaningful emphasis on *something*.

"No." I shook my head, before realising he meant the device. My body relaxed slightly; I had something to trade with. He would have to help me. "That is, I mean, yes. Sure, if you help me."

Still not looking at me, he raised a brow in query.

"I've done something stupid," I confessed under my breath.

"That is, I think I have. I bought some cough medicine for someone."

I broke off as the graceful fingers dropped the mango on the floor, and the vendor exclaimed loudly in wrath at the sight of his delicious and costly wares being so poorly treated.

Devyn apologised profusely before backing away, completely ignoring me. Stunned, I turned back to the vendor who had started to complain loudly about clumsy young men. I shrugged – nothing to do with me – and the vendor turned to his waiting customers, a trapped audience more sympathetic to his plight. Turning, I scowled in annoyance.

Damn it, he was gone.

I hadn't taken two steps before I felt a light touch on my fingers.

"We can't talk here," he said. "Come with me."

"Where to?" I protested, until he took my hand and, as easily as that, I found myself going with him. Because I wanted his help or because I liked the sensation of his skin touching mine, I did not know.

Any and all attempts to talk as we hurried across the city were silenced immediately by a harsh glare. I trailed behind, no idea where we were going, our direction too directly east to be headed to our usual park, and fumed silently.

I said nothing as we passed through the Bishopsgate – the northeast part of the city had more Christian churches than the Olympian temples nearer the river. I had never been in the area before and grew increasingly nervous as we walked further and further away from the inner wall, the area feeling distinctly seedier than the district Oban lived in. This was the deepest darkest stews, less the busy bustle of those who were poor but struggling to keep themselves above water, more the sinister sluggishness of those who were likelier to pull you down with them than look for a hand up. There were fewer people on the streets which made it seem even odder that nobody approached us to beg, even though with our fine clothes we stood out. A lot. Devyn held my hand firmly as we swept along, his step confident and powerful, his features stronger and more defined. And yet people here barely looked our way.

Finally, Devyn stopped and, pulling a piece of metal from his pocket, he inserted it into a hole in the door and we slipped inside and up the creaky beaten-down stairs until he stopped once more and repeated the exercise.

As we walked through the second door, he released my hand and my sense of security melted away, leaving me bereft and deep inside an area where I would never have agreed to go in the full presence of my wits. I was nervous enough about Oban's home, only two streets away from the old wall; the outer wall was way beyond my comfort zone.

"Caesar wept." I looked wildly around the room. "Where in Hades are we? I can't believe you. My father will kill me if he finds out I'm here."

I really was in trouble. My parents were reasonably lenient but the northeastern section of the outer wall was most certainly out of bounds. How had he managed to do that? I had just walked across the city, directly into the worst reaches of the stews, because some boy had held my hand.

"Your father would be a little upset at a lot of your recent activities, princess," Devyn said with a smirk. And then in a testing tone, he added, "Was it me who led you here? Or was it you?"

"What… what does that mean?" I lingered near the door as he strode into the small, dimly lit room.

"Tea? Water?" he offered.

I shook my head. "No, I don't want a cup of your cursed tea."

"Please sit down, Cass," he said, waving at the shabby couch in what I supposed was a kitchen area. It looked like it would most definitely leave a stain on my skirt.

"Uh, no thanks. I'm fine standing."

Devyn took a step towards me, lifting my hand and drawing me into the room, manoeuvring me until I stood in front of the grubby seat, at which point he pushed lightly on my shoulder and I found myself yet again in a place I hadn't agreed to be. I looked up at him, smug and so different from the mild Devyn everyone else still saw. He was intelligent and strong, far from the effete elite he affected to be most of the time. I saw through it. I saw him.

A fury I was utterly unfamiliar with overtook me. I was practically shaking with rage as I stood and crossed the room to him.

"Enough." My voice was sufficiently raised that there was every chance they could hear me back at the forum. "What are you doing to me? Why am I here? Who in Hades are you, Devyn? This is… this isn't just about that device, you… you're doing things that aren't possible. Don't you dare tell me that I'm imagining it. I know what I've seen. You are a lie, a complete and utter fraud. I don't know how you do it or why but that piece of tech is the least of it."

I had his tall, lean body backed against the wall but quick as a flash he grabbed me, reversing our positions, so I was the one with my back to the wall, him looming over me.

"Quiet," he hissed. "Lower your voice."

I glared mutinously up at him, my mouth opening to begin round two.

"No, Cass. Stop."

He was now uncomfortably close, my attempts to push away from the wall into the confining space between us bringing our bodies into intimate contact, a fact I was fairly sure he hadn't missed.

The tension dropped from me as he gently brushed aside the hair that had tumbled across my face and tucked it behind my ear.

"Can you keep your voice down?" he asked gently.

I nodded, and he stepped away with a heavy exhale, running his fingers through his thick hair. A flash of uncertainty briefly crossed his face.

"You can't shout like that. You'll draw attention to the flat and after I've explained, you'll understand why that is something we can do without. I'm guessing you've already done more than enough."

He gestured for me to sit again, refraining from manoeuvring me, somehow knowing that repeating his little trick was unlikely to end in the outcome he desired this second time.

"Talk," he ordered, taking a seat at a shabby table opposite me.

I glanced nervously up at the corners of the room, my awareness of the pervasiveness of the city's observation more acute now that I had something to hide.

"You can talk freely here," he advised. "Without raising your voice would be preferable, though."

I hesitated. Was involving him wise? Or was it the next step in my journey to finding myself in the arena again, only this time on the sands awaiting judgement? I felt suddenly that my life had shifted so far off the rails that my course to those pale ancient sands was the only certainty left. My breath felt shallow. I shook my head as Devyn tensed to stand, to come over to me. No, his touch would not help me think.

"How do I know I can trust you?"

He barked with laughter at my challenge.

"You wish me to prove my credentials as a dissident? Or are you asking if I'm a full-on Codebreaker?" he asked, a twitch of a smile tugging at his lips.

I nodded.

"What is it you'd like me to tell you?"

"How about starting with the device," I suggested. The tech I understood, the tech was real. Whatever else Devyn was, I was less sure I was ready to face.

"Right, the device." He was clearly happy to begin there too. "I shouldn't have brought it into class that day, but the basilicas have terminals that are accessible by students. I was debating what to do next. I needed some information to check what options I have now. I was careless. I'd grown complacent and I took a risk I shouldn't have. I don't know how they found out I had it but I'm glad they weren't the only ones who did."

At this last, he met my eyes in acknowledgement of my intervention.

"What do you mean options?"

His eyes met mine, assessing.

"The device allows me to introduce some chaos to the Code, creating a blind spot long enough for someone to get through the city's firewalls. A key, of sorts. The tech simulates an attack like the ones dissidents use to hack in. While the imperial defences are busy investigating the string of chaos, it allows me to slip through some of the less secure sections."

He was a hacker. What he was describing was a capital offence.

"Why would you need to do that?"

"It can be used to access information about citizens on their databases, or"—his eyes met mine, a provocative light glimmering in his otherwise expressionless face—"to create a gap in the Empire's security long enough to get someone out of the city."

"Get someone out?" I repeated. "Of the city?"

My mind whirled with the implications. He wasn't just some trouble-making boy in possession of black-market technology. Or even a hacker accessing classified files in his search for this lost girl. He was helping people get out of the city without the Empire's authorisation.

Devyn wasn't mysterious, he was *dangerous*. I'd be lucky to end up on the sands of the arena. At least there I could say I hadn't known what I was getting myself into.

I retreated to the corner of the couch, frantically assessing my escape options. Had he locked the door when we came in?

"Calm down, Cass," Devyn urged gently, reaching a placating hand towards me.

I scrabbled further back. "Don't touch me."

He stepped away, his hands spread wide, dark eyes meeting mine.

"Stop freaking out. You're not in any danger, I promise." He paused, correcting himself. "At least, not from me."

"From who then?"

He gnawed at his lip. "The council, the sentinels, the praetor."

I huffed a shaky breath. "Yeah, I am now. Because of you, you and your chaos key and whatever it is you're up to. If I'm in trouble, it's all your fault."

"You wanted to know." He shrugged. "Now why don't you tell me what it is that you've done?"

I shook my head. I needed a minute to think. "Who are you smuggling out of the city?" I demanded. "What have *they* done?"

"Done? And what did you mean, who am I? Ah, you think I'm helping Codebreakers escape the Empire." He shook his head ruefully. "That was more Linus's thing. That's not what I need the hardware back for."

A darkness passed behind his eyes. A vulnerable flicker.

"The person I sought is not here. It's time to leave to continue my search. That's hard to explain to sentinels."

He was leaving the city then. Leaving Londinium. Richmond, just west of the city, was the furthest I had ever been from home. He was pretty determined to find this person, whoever they were.

"Who is she?" I chanced. He had given years of his life already and now was planning to search the far corners of the Empire. My curiosity gnawed at me.

"Nobody you need concern yourself with. Now, tell me what is it you've done."

I shook my head. I wouldn't be put off so easily.

"No," I stated obstinately. "Not unless you tell me why you've been watching me all these years. I don't feel safe. You've made me feel unsafe."

Liar, my inner voice mocked. Even as he made my world tilt on its axis, his presence in it felt like the one thing I did believe I could hold on to. Those dark eyes considered me impassively, searching for the truth in what I was saying. Fearing that what I was saying held truth. I might not be the girl he was looking for, but it made him uncomfortable to think that I considered him some kind of a stalker. I could practically feel the distaste vibrating off him. I had him.

"Are you sure you want the truth?" he asked again,

echoing his previous warning. Once truths were known, there would be no putting them back in a bottle.

I wasn't sure but nodded anyway.

He studied me for a moment, before lifting a shoulder as he conceded to my pressure.

"You fit certain criteria, Cassandra. Very rare criteria. To be truthful, the kind of criteria that put you in danger. No," he corrected himself, "you've always been in danger, I'm just letting you know."

I raised my brow. "What's that supposed to mean? I am not and have never been in any kind of trouble. My father is an important merchant with friends on the council, for the gods' sake."

"Yes," he said cryptically.

I didn't think I'd ever met anyone I found more frustrating. Ever.

"What?" I pushed, not sure what he was implying. "You clearly have something you want to tell me. Out with it."

"Your father is not your real father."

"That's the big reveal? I've always known I was adopted."

"And that you're not city born?" Devyn fired back.

The wind tore out of my sails. The world actually spun, or maybe it was the room. I sat forward to let the blood flow back into my head, shrugging off Devyn's hand as it came down on my shoulder.

Not city born. Not city born. Not…

I was what? A Shadower? I sat up squaring my shoulders.

"There is no way I'm not a citizen." Citizens of the Empire were privileged. They lived inside the walls, lived by the Code. Shadowers were almost native. They lived in the Province, were tolerated by those inside the walls to farm the lands this side of the Celtic border, but they weren't citizens. They were in between. Belonging to neither.

"My father is an important merchant," I stated, in a last futile attempt to find safe ground. "This doesn't make any sense. My birth parents died in an accident. In the city. I've seen the news feeds. There is no way I'm not a citizen... look at me." I indicated my perfect hair, impeccable style, and state-of-the-art accessories.

Devyn gave me a somewhat exasperated look, followed by a top-to-toe inspection.

"Any stone can be polished and made to look like something it's not."

"Like a diamond," I shot back, "a dull, cloudy lump of carbon infinitely improved upon when cut, shone, and polished."

"Indeed," he said drily, "but just because someone has put a shine on it, a stone it remains nonetheless."

"I don't care about diamonds," I said, annoyed to have been so easily countered. "Why do you say I'm not a citizen? How do you know that?"

"I know lots of things," he replied equably.

Could he not just give me a straight answer?

Did I want a straight answer?

Devyn was clearly involved in crimes more serious than I could have imagined. Meanwhile, my life was just fine. I didn't need to get myself mixed up with whatever misguided nonsense this was. I could just hand back the device, do whatever was needed to conceal my mistake with the medicine and Marina, and get on with my life. I could graduate, find a nice place to live, marry the man I was matched to, have babies as the Code decreed. A family that was truly my own. This, whatever it was, was likely to mess with that.

I took in my surroundings again.

"Where are we?" Anything rather than continue the conversation in the direction it had taken. A next step that led to a road I hadn't ever seen coming. "Do you live here?"

"Hardly," Devyn scoffed. "How would I be able to go to a nice western college if this was my home address?"

"I don't know. You're a hacker, and there's something else, something more."

I paused, my mind working overtime. How was he doing this? He had been taken from class. How had he managed to convince the sentinels of his innocence when he was so clearly guilty of many, many crimes against the city? What was he up to?

"I don't know who you are, not really, and now you're telling me I'm not even a citizen." I stopped, unable to go on, this was too much. I wasn't political. I had no idea what motivated someone to hack the city's firewalls, much less what dissidents railed against. As for his statement that I was not a full citizen, I couldn't begin to put together the ramifications of what that meant. My mind reeled at the idea.

I ran a hand over my hair, my auburn hair, bright as autumn leaves, seeing the flicker of distaste in my mother's eyes when she looked at it. But it wasn't proof enough.

And what was the destroyer-of-the-world-as-I-knew-it doing now, having just delivered a truth of which I would happily have lived my life in ignorance? He was leaning back in his armchair, as relaxed as you please, that irritating penetrating gaze watching me absorb his bombshell.

"Why would you poke holes in the Code that protects the city? Why would anyone want to sneak out? How do you change your appearance, make people barely see you? Seriously, if the sentinels realise you can…"

I waved my hand in the air. I wasn't sure how he managed to be so unremarkable but I was reasonably sure it wasn't something most upstanding citizens were capable of. It must be some kind of chemical that worked on pheromones or new augmenting tech.

"Can you please, please stop messing around and give one of my questions a straight answer? Any one of them will do," I pleaded.

"This room belongs to my friend Linus."

I screeched.

"No, no." He laughed softly. "Let me finish. Linus needed to leave the city. He was sick. I helped him get out discreetly. Once he's better he wants to come back. I'm just keeping the lights on in his absence, so the authorities don't realise he's gone."

"Why didn't he just get healed here, with proper medicine?" I latched on immediately. Did this Linus have the same illness as Marina?

Devyn's lips thinned.

"Because medicine and shiny hospitals aren't as easily accessed when you live at the bottom of the pile. Also, some illnesses do better by not having the attention of the authorities on them."

"What kind of illness?" I pursued. What was it about the illness Marina had that so scared her and her brother of attracting the eyes of the authorities?

Devyn eyed me speculatively. "Are you unwell, Cass?"

The light in his eyes was almost eager as he leaned towards me.

"No, I'm fine."

He looked strangely disappointed at this and leaned back

again. "But somebody is ill. Cough, fever, fatigue, shakes, getting worse all the time?"

"Yes, well, just the cough that I'm sure of, perhaps a touch of fever, and her movements seem a little jerky. I bought some medicine but they refused to take it. I don't understand why."

Devyn glanced sharply at me. "Where did you get the medicine – a pharmacy, a doctor? Did you give them the name of the sick friend? Who exactly is sick? Where are they now?"

His questions came thick and fast, hardly drawing breath between them. I stumbled over the answers.

"I got the medicine in the West End. I didn't tell them who it was for." I paused, recollecting my father's questions the day after. Had he known I'd bought it? Suddenly I was sure he had. "My father knew. He was asking me the next day if I felt well. He was really persistent."

"I'll bet he was." Devyn was unsurprised.

"But it wasn't for me or one of my friends. It was for the sister of someone I know. Someone this side of the old walls," I continued.

A dark eyebrow raised at that. "Who do you know in the stews, princess?"

I really hated it when he called me that. What was worse was I could almost predict his smug smile when I told him who I knew.

"Apprentice Oban."

His look was blank; he didn't recognise the name. How was that possible?

"The tailor," I clarified, "from the Mete. The one with the dress."

Still nothing.

"You did watch and vote Friday before last, didn't you?" It was unthinkable that he wouldn't have. Devyn took care not to draw attention to himself and not voting was a significant thing to forget to do.

Devyn's face showed a slight hint of bewilderment before he shrugged it off.

"A tailor, you say? This is who is sick?"

"No, it's his sister. She looks like she's been sick for a while. But when I brought them the medicine, they were horrified." I looked over at him then. "Why wouldn't they want the medicine? Why were they afraid of anyone knowing she is sick?"

"I'd guess her problem isn't what she's done but what she is," Devyn said, back to his cryptic self.

I exhaled my frustration. "What does that mean?"

"It means you should stay away from her. There is nothing you can do to help her."

"I don't understand." I stood, walking over to him, the better to see his face in the growing dark of the evening. His face was its usual mask, but those dark eyes occasionally offered a glimpse into the true Devyn. This close, I was aware once again of how deceptive his appearance was. He gave the impression of a long, slight body, an aura of a quiet, diffident soul. Up close, this was a sham. His body was wide at the shoulder, long and lean as he sat in the chair with his back to the wall. The force of his personality crackled in the near dark, as if now that I couldn't see him so well, my eyes could no longer deceive me as to the reality of him.

I felt compelled to break down his façade completely. I reached out a hand to touch him, my fingers drawn to the strong column of his throat where it met his collarbone. He stood abruptly, causing me to stumble backward. He caught me before I fell, releasing me and hastily putting more space between us before going to stand in what light still came in through the window. The small of my back was electrified by his fleeting touch.

"She's most likely a latent," he said, distracting me from my purpose. "Those who are getting ill have some of the old blood in their veins. It doesn't have to be a lot but it makes them susceptible to this infection."

"But why would that make Marina afraid to get help?" Old blood… did he mean Briton? It wasn't unknown for citizens to have some Briton ancestry, a legacy from the era before the Code was introduced. Even more so here in the stews, where Shadowers mingled more freely with the population, accidents happened.

He took a breath, seeming to consider his words carefully before continuing.

"Because a few of them also have… abilities. Or rather the potential to. Latents, particularly those manifesting any abilities, have been known to disappear after they seek medical attention."

Even now he was being cagey with information. But I understood what he wasn't saying.

"Magic? In the city?"

He inclined his head, a silent confirmation.

I drew a steadying breath. Abilities. Old blood. People who could wield magic, here behind the walls. This was the reason it was against the Code to intermarry with Britons. Why Shadowers couldn't become full citizens. This taint in the blood. Magic was absolutely forbidden within the walls. It was the only way to keep our city safe.

If what Devyn said was true and I wasn't city born then… no, he'd lied, it wasn't possible… mixed blood. I had been adopted by a prominent elite family, I couldn't be tainted with Wilder blood. Without thinking, I used the slightly derogatory reference to the native peoples of this land. Nobody referred to the indigenous as barbarian anymore, but they weren't exactly civilised either.

"You think that's why they're hiding her illness. Because she has…" I couldn't bring myself to say it.

"It sounds likely."

"What happens to them? The ones who disappear?" I asked focusing on the impact rather than the cause. It didn't bear thinking about, if she really did have what he suggested. The sooner she was beyond the reach of the authorities, the better.

He shrugged. "I don't know, maybe they die like everyone else."

"You don't know for sure? Haven't you searched online? You must have some idea."

"No, I've tried to find out, of course, but there's no reference to them anywhere."

"Your friend, he decided not to stay to find out?"

"No, Linus decided to disappear himself for a little while, lie low, try to find out what he could beyond the walls," he said slowly. "He'll be back."

I slowly and shudderingly released the breath I was holding. This was real.

I had drawn attention to Marina; it was my fault.

I wouldn't stand by and do nothing. "Can you get her out?"

"What?" His features were in almost complete darkness. He was no more than a silhouette in the evening dusk.

"You helped get your friend out. Is there someone outside the walls who is helping him? Someone Marina could go to?"

He looked at me measuringly.

"Perhaps," he said softly. "But I will need my tech back."

"Deal," I said with alacrity.

He laughed. "It's not quite as simple as that. I'll need help. Are you sure you want to be more involved than you are already, princess?"

I was going to punch him the next time he called me that. I saw again the fear in Marina's eyes, the worry in Oban's.

"What happens if she doesn't get help?" I asked.

"She'll die."

"She can't go to the hospital because the sentinels will take her?" I guessed.

"They don't take everyone, but if she's as afraid as you say then she may suspect she is likely to be one of the unfortunate ones."

"I'll help."

"Good girl." He smiled a broad open grin I hadn't seen before. "Give me her details and I'll go and talk to her and see if she and her brother want our help. Then I'll see what I can do."

"What *we* can do," I corrected. I had got involved and I would see this through.

Again his dark eyes measured me.

"We'll see. I'll let you know if they agree to accept my… our help. Which means we'll need to talk freely again, about things we don't want anyone to hear. We're okay here – the house is a clean zone. It's been made safe."

"People can't hear us?"

"Not exactly, otherwise you screaming your head off wouldn't have been a problem," he explained. "It's more that what you say can't be picked up. Hang on a sec."

He got up, crossing to what passed for a kitchen, and pulled out a drawer. Setting it gently on the floor, he reached back in to the hole and pulled out a small package before returning.

"Stand up for a minute, Cass. You need to wear this at all times." He stepped behind me and placed a rose-gold chain with a plain disk hanging off it around my neck, his fingers brushing against the sensitive skin at the nape as I held my hair up out of his way. I could feel him standing there, his breath warm on my exposed neck, his touch lingering perhaps a moment longer than was necessary once he had fixed the clasp.

He returned into my line of sight and leaned against the wall.

"It's important you remember to use it when we are together. We can't let them notice any big change in your behaviour. Take the pendant between your forefinger and thumb before you say anything controversial, particularly if you're going to use keywords that they monitor for dissidents."

"Are you telling me that what we say is being monitored, that somebody is listening to us all the time?" I knew the council could watch citizens and that there were cameras everywhere, but I thought the surveillance of the level seen in the Mete's evidentiary real was only for those who broke the Code.

"This can't be news to you. The system tracks what you say to make your life as a citizen and, more importantly, as a *consumer* better, more efficient. When you walk into a shop, keywords are picked up, so that when you're looking for that perfect pair of boots with the *cute little strap*"—he mimicked a teenage girl's voice—"the shop assistant approaches you with a pair of boots in one of your favourite brands in your size. You know this, Cassandra."

"Sure," I replied. "They use that technology to optimise our time when shopping. Personalisation is much more efficient."

Devyn snorted. "Don't be so naïve. You think it stops there? You are monitored all the time. When you're online with your friends, at classes, walking through the shops with Ginevra, they are always listening. They don't record everything but every time you mention a brand name, ping, I want, ping, I need, ping, I must get, ping. We aren't free citizens, we're monitored consumers. Wake up." His eyes were alive with contempt.

"What's so wrong with that? I like that I don't have to waste time shopping. My clothes arrive with the right accessories and my outfits are adorable," I preened, unable to help myself.

"What's wrong with that?" Devyn took a step towards me. His intensity compelled me to listen to him. "Nothing, as long as you continue to be a good little girl, keep up with the latest styles, listen to the latest packaged pop star, watch the trending bursts. What do you think happens when you don't comply? When you're caught saying something against the Code? When you're caught breaking the Code?"

I saw again the blood speckled across the sand.

"All it takes is for them to catch you saying one thing that's outside the lines of what the Code allows for them to focus in on you and start monitoring you and every little thing you do."

I put my hand to the delicate chain, worrying the pendant up and down it. This was my only protection against the city's surveillance. An alarming thought occurred to me.

"What about the last times we met? We spoke about the tech. What if they've already heard us?" I asked.

"They haven't heard anything," he said, turning his wrist to show me that his wristband contained a similar disc embedded in the leather.

"Why are we here then? We could have talked at the park." He had relied on the protection offered by the disc before so what was different this time?

"I wanted to see how badly you wanted this favour."

Just when I thought he wasn't that bad, he had traipsed us all the way to the outer walls to test me. Right. Well, I had passed, I guessed.

I had come to him to figure out how to cover up my mistake so I could smooth over a wrinkle in my usually seamless life. Not only was it now well and truly rumpled, but if I was to believe what Devyn was telling me, it wasn't even my life. Not really. My life belonged to an elite citizen, not a –

I shuddered. One problem at a time.

"Okay, tell me what to do."

Chapter Seven

Devyn told me little about what he needed to do to get Marina out of the city. My main task turned out to be helping him track the patrols on the river. He was fine on his own while walking the riverbank but preferred to be in company when we hung around for hour after hour in the coffee shop, insisting that we were less conspicuous as a pair dawdling over what was an expensive pastime.

Even without the hardware I had hidden away, he was able to do incredibly advanced things. I had stood guard at the basilica a couple of times when he had accessed a terminal to check on any activity around Marina or Oban. Despite the absence of the chaos device, he was able to creep around at the higher levels of what should have been impenetrable systems. The speed with which he'd been able to get in and out had been jaw-dropping.

Coffee was imported from the Americas, with whom we did little trade, and from beyond the furthest reaches of the Empire to the south, so I was pretty sure we spent our time in that shop watching the patrols around the wharves less because of the advantageousness of the view it offered and more because Devyn adored the drink. His eyelids slid closed every time he took his first sip, a moment I watched for, his bliss at the taste one of the few signs he ever gave of enjoying anything.

It was on one such evening that he noticed me take my daily pill and snatched the bottle out of my hand.

"What is this?"

"Uh, mine." I went to grab it back but he pulled his hand out of reach.

He frowned, sniffing the bottle.

"No, really, what is it?" he insisted.

"They're just for my dizzy spells."

"What dizzy spells?"

"I don't have them now obviously," I said witheringly. "That's why I take these."

He glared at me in frustration which made my lips twitch. Not so much fun being on the other side, huh.

Devyn leaned forward, his hand reaching for the disc on his wristband.

"I… please… describe them."

I smiled. "Since you asked so nicely, I used to suffer from vertigo and fatigue when I was younger."

His brows drew together as he fiddled with his wristband after surreptitiously checking if we were within hearing distance of any other customers.

"I've never felt anything from you. Even a late bloomer would have shown some sign by now. I thought maybe you might just be a latent, which would serve their purpose if not mine. But perhaps you are a bit more than that," he said, inspecting the little bottle again.

I huffed. "Is there any chance you're going to explain that little chat with yourself?"

Devyn looked up, his eyes intent.

"You've never asked me anything further about not being a citizen," he commented, his voice low, taking no chance that he could be overheard by the customers sitting at the nearer tables. "Have you decided whether or not you believe me?"

"I'm not sure." To be honest, I'd done my best not to think of it at all… not entirely successfully. Something like that was hard to unhear. "I don't know how you can be so certain."

"I've spent a great deal of time investigating your birth and adoption. Even for someone of my skills seeing through the lie was… a challenge. Someone went to a great deal of effort to conceal your origins. I thought for a time you might even be a full-blood Briton."

That wasn't possible. A Briton?

No, it didn't make any sense. They weren't even allowed inside the city. The only time full-blooded Britons were permitted entry was during the Treaty Renewal when a heavily guarded contingent of Britons were escorted inside the walls to the Governor's Palace and then escorted out by sundown of the seventh day. Outside of that week, which only occurred every four years, they were *never* permitted inside the walls. No exceptions.

"Why would you think that?" I put a hand to my hair.

"Your history is fully documented, all nice and neat. Who your parents were, their parents, their siblings, school records, work history for generations. But if you know what you're looking for, the Code reeks of newness." He frowned. "I've crosschecked thousands of records. Even in the stews all births are accounted for. However the Sheltons got you, it wasn't from within the walls."

"Are you sure?" He gave me an affronted glare. I had seen enough of his programming skills to know that his information would be solid.

I couldn't breathe. My birth, my background, were fake. I had been born outside the city walls.

He tilted his head in acknowledgement that my impending panic attack was warranted. And we were having this conversation out in the open. I gripped my pendant like my life depended on it. Which it might. Not to mention his. He had risked his life to hack into those records. The nightmare of that man's blood flecking across the sand flashed before my eyes.

"You... did that... it must have taken..." My mind boggled at the amount of time he must have spent behind the firewalls scouring the records to be so confident. "Why, in the name of Caesar, would you do something so reckless?"

His lips twisted at my invocation of the ultimate authority.

"I told you I was looking for someone. The more I investigated you..." He shrugged. "It seemed worth the risk. I needed to be sure. But I've been watching you for years. Even those who don't manifest until late show some signs by adulthood. I was so sure, but then you turned eighteen and still nothing. I couldn't give up though, so I gave it another year, and another."

He was almost speaking to himself.

"In the end, I wasn't sure if I was here because it might be true or because I just couldn't give up hope. You've never shown even the smallest sign, whatever your origin; your blood doesn't appear to be even a latent carrier. But perhaps..."

He weighed the pill bottle in his hand contemplatively.

"Perhaps what?" I asked. Honestly, who could deal with

this level of cryptic nonsense on a daily basis? Once this was done, I would be happy to see the back of Devyn. Totally.

"Perhaps what?" I repeated when no answer was forthcoming.

Devyn smirked, pocketing the pills.

"What on earth do you think you're doing?"

"I need to check something."

"That involves stealing my pills? Have them." It was my turn to smirk. "I have plenty more at home."

That wiped the smile from his face. Devyn took my hand, his face serious, his expression intent.

"Please, Cass, I need you to stop taking them. I think you may have been suppressed." He rubbed his face with his hand. "I was so sure that you were at least a Shadower latent, but maybe you *are* more. I can't be sure unless you stop taking them."

More? What did that mean? Was he suggesting I didn't just have Briton blood but I might have actual magic?

I shuddered. The Empire loathed magic. For good reason. In the early days of the Empire the balance of power in Britannia had lain with us against the unorganised warring tribes of natives. Under Governor Hadrian, Roman rule had gone almost as far north as Alba. The territories south of Hadrian's wall had never stopped resisting though, their ranks swelling over time from regions long subdued, Saxons, Danes, Normans, Basques, all fleeing the reach of the Empire.

The turning point came when the Lady of the Lake appeared and joined forces with the kings of Mercia and Anglia, and the druids. The Rose Kings had united with the Celtic tribes and by the time the Tewdwr dynasty rose to power, the Britons had the Empire pinned in Londinium and a handful of other walled cities in the southeast. But the

Reformation empowered the citizens behind the wall and they had stunned the Britons with a surprise attack.

With the Tewdwrs gone, the Briton alliance had fallen apart. Yet their magic had held off our superior forces in a series of fierce battles that had raged across the Chiltern hills for the next two hundred years.

The magic of the Britons and the disruption of the ley line on the border managed to keep us confined in the southeast. At the same time, the pure magic of the ley lines beneath the sea prevented the Empire from deploying mass forces and attacking from the north, a geographical impediment the neighbouring island also utilised.

Eventually, technological advances had levelled the playing field; both sides were tired of war and finally agreed to terms. The 1772 Treaty established the territory ruled by the Empire and kept the Britons firmly on their side of the border, running along the May ley line, which sliced through the land, aligning with sunrise on the 8th of May.

Now we stood at a détente that kept us confined in the province of the southeast, or the Shadowlands as they were commonly called, sitting as they did in the shadow of our great walled cities. While Shadowers farmed the countryside in between those strongholds, their lives were hard since modern technology often failed outside the walls, the cars and trains that transported citizens around the city being replaced by more traditional modes of transport.

The power the Britons wielded was what kept Roman citizens confined behind the walls. That and the magical energy lines that ran below ground that made advanced technology unstable, limiting the means by which both the sea and the land could be crossed. It was easy to repel an attack that moved slowly across the heavily wooded countryside when it could only move as quickly as its slowest mule and cart as opposed to the hovercraft that skimmed across the river and high in the upper streets here in the city.

The thought filled me with unease and a growing sense of certainty. *That* was what he had watched me for all this time... for years, in my classes in college, and now in citizenship prep at the forum. He believed the ability to touch that power might be in my blood.

"Will you think differently of me if nothing happens?" I wasn't sure why, but this was important.

Devyn looked at me in surprise and I glimpsed a flash of something so intense I couldn't even begin to identify it.

"No, of course not. You'll always be the same perfect princess to me."

"If there *is* something the pills are hiding, could that mean I might be who you're looking for?"

A more decipherable look passed over Devyn's face, a reluctant bruising sliver of hope quickly damped down before he looked at me blankly.

"We'll have to cross that bridge when we come to it." Discussion closed. But I was becoming increasingly curious about this mystery girl he so badly wanted to find.

Despite his refusal to tell me more, I did what he asked and stopped taking any more of the pills. It was the least I could do given the risk he was taking to help me.

My parents started paying more attention than usual to how I spent my time. My mother wasn't so easily persuaded that what she'd seen the night of the party was as innocent as I made out. My behaviour since then probably also fell into a less recognisable pattern. I spent more time out of the house and was always careful to have a cover to explain my absences. I used them rarely but I was also less forthcoming about what I was doing and who I was with than I used to be as a result of Devyn's advice: never offer too much information. It only adds to the lies you have to keep track of.

I had spent most of this hidden time with Devyn. He had met Oban and Marina – the toughest twelve-year-old I had ever known – and saw that her brother watched her all the time for signs the illness was getting worse.

I paid more attention now to the rare reports that showed up about the strange illness that was increasingly striking people down. The illness was rare in my circles but more cases had been surfacing elsewhere. On the couple of occasions I had managed to slip across town to bring Oban and Marina extra food supplies (against Devyn's express command) I noticed more people in the stews with glazed eyes and jerky movements, which I now recognized as early symptoms. There were still only occasional sightings, but the way people moved in the street to give them a wide berth made them relatively easy to spot.

I spent hours at a time with Devyn watching the patrols go by the coffee house nearest the warehouses on Shad Thames. I plagued Devyn with questions about life outside the walls. I had never been beyond Londinium – had he? How did he know people to send Linus and now Marina to? On certain topics he was utterly intractable and it was infuriating. He had warned me against searching online. Now was not the time to start showing an interest in the world beyond the walls.

But that time of watching and waiting was over now. Devyn was moving the date up… to tonight. I sucked in a breath. I'd already had my nails done this week, a beautiful cerise shade with a light diamante finish, so what else did I have to do with my evening?

I touched the disk hanging off the chain around my neck, rubbing my thumb against the faint engraving inside. Noticing, Devyn raised his eyes to mine, frowning questioningly. I shook my head. I didn't have anything to say, it was just becoming something of a nervous habit when I felt… well, nervous.

Still holding the pendant in my fingers, thus ensuring no one was listening in, I gathered my scattered thoughts.

"Everything is in place?" I asked. For all that Devyn had involved me in his scheme, he had been sketchy on the details. I wasn't sure if this was because he didn't trust me with them, or because the plan was still coming together.

His eyes searched mine briefly before nodding as if satisfied with what he saw there.

"Yes, everything is ready." His long fingers tracked back and forth across his wristband. "We've got to do it this evening. I've been monitoring the sentinels' database. They know Marina is sick. She's going to be picked up so I've hidden her at Linus's place until we can get her out. The new timeframe limits our options. I'm afraid you're going to be more involved than I had hoped. We need to move fast."

I waited, but apparently that was all I was getting for now.

"Do you need the…" I hesitated, despite Devyn's promise that the pendant would conceal any use of words the authorities were listening for. Now that I knew they were listening, I was reluctant to take the risk. "…Notes I took for you the other week in Reformation class?"

Devyn raised a brow.

"Yes, Cass, the notes you took for me will come in most handy. Are they at your home?"

"No, the forum. If I take the monorail I can be there and back in an hour." I scowled. "If you'd told me you needed them this evening I could have brought the notes with me."

"I didn't know myself until an hour or so ago," Devyn explained quietly. "Do you need me to come with you?"

I shook my head and stood up from the table, grabbing my bag from where it lay slung over the back of the chair.

"I'm fairly certain I can make it to and from the forum without an escort. I'll meet you there?" I checked. By now I was reasonably confident of finding my way to Linus's on my own.

Somebody was following me. I hadn't seen anyone, but I was pretty sure of it. The monorail platform had been quiet when I got there. Not terribly surprising as it wasn't the cheapest mode of transport. I had recently become aware that it wasn't a cost that fit comfortably into the budgets of those who lived between the walls. It bypassed the guarded gates of the inner eastern wall, making crossing town a relatively simple affair without the admittedly remote possibility of being pulled aside to have my papers checked. When I changed lines and was boarding the second train, something made me stop and turn as I was about to get on the train. Nothing out of the ordinary, I told myself, trying to dismiss my feelings of paranoia.

As I took my seat on the near-empty train, I held my bag closer to my body. *I'm imagining it,* I repeated to myself as the transport whizzed through a tunnel. I felt a little dazed this evening, struggling to contain my thoughts, which felt loose inside my head. I needed to focus, and not on what I was about to do. My stomach fizzed with nerves as it was.

I looked past my reflection out to the city beyond as the monorail wove its way through the urban maze. I busied my mind by identifying the styles of the many layers of the city outside the window: the austerity of the lower layers spoke to the strict rule of Governor Garai; the arches of the great conquering Governor Varian; the swirling towers were favoured during the period of Governor Jerolin when really the more practical procurator had controlled the city in everything but architecture; the whimsical fancies and decorations from the short-lived Emperor Dorian; the military austerity and transparency of the post-reformation era during the wars which had left an indelible mark on entire levels in the upper part of the city. Since the Reformation, the solidity and privacy afforded by stone had given way almost entirely to glass. The open galleries crisscrossing the city at that level allowed passersby to see into homes, eschewing privacy in an architectural statement that each citizen was content to be on display, perfectly at ease living transparently within the Code.

Me, not so much anymore.

But could fear and paranoia account for the vague sensation of being watched that I couldn't seem to shake? The feeling almost overwhelmed me as I pulled the book from the shelf at the forum and retrieved the device from its spine.

I nearly jumped out of my skin at the sound of the train door closing. Marina was counting on me. I had promised Devyn I could do this alone.

What was wrong with me? I put my head in my hands.

I was travelling across the city carrying illegal tech in my pocket which I was going to deliver into the hands of someone I knew would use it to hack through the firewalls. Once I delivered it to him, I was going to help him get a sick girl out of the city before the sentinels came for her.

I had lost my mind. Of course I felt like I was being watched. I was going to end up standing in front of the praetor as the entire city sat in judgement of the undeniable evidence of me knowingly helping him commit crime after crime.

I believed in the Code. I had always lived by it. Being a good citizen was as natural to me as breathing and I expected to graduate with flying colours. Yet, over the last weeks, I had aided and abetted crimes that introduced chaos into the Code.

More troubling was that I was doing it all for a boy… a boy I thought about all the time.

I didn't understand the way I acted with Devyn. I couldn't help myself. I touched him all the time. My fingers brushed his as he handed me a coffee. I touched his arm when I asked him a question or when he made me laugh with his unexpected teasing humour. I didn't like others in my space, yet I had traced his chest, head, face, arms within days of meeting him. Was I really risking everything I had for Marina's sake as I had been telling myself, or for his?

For a boy who provoked me. Disturbed my comfortable life.

Told me I was not a citizen.

Dared to ask more of me.

I couldn't stop myself. He kept showing me the boundaries to my cage, the lines of my world, and I kept crossing them. This was not the way of the Code. This was not the way of a girl already promised elsewhere. Once Marina was safe, I would have to return to my own life. Away from Devyn.

Before it was too late.

If it wasn't already.

Chapter Eight

Having applied the finishing touches, I sat back to admire my handiwork.

"Take a look."

Marina's face lit up as she caught her reflection in the dirty mirror at Linus's place, her usually wan face a picture of health and wealth, which was more important than ever in order to move openly throughout the city. I looked back over my shoulder at her fretting brother.

"Look, Oban." She touched her face in wonder as she turned back once more to the mirror.

"You look beautiful, Mari." Oban took a step forward, his hand coming to rest on his sister's shoulder as he turned her back to face him. His hand rose to touch her face as if to prove to himself that the vision before him was real, a temptation I quickly quashed, slapping his hand away.

"Don't you dare undo all my hard work," I scolded, my tartness covering up the welling emotion at the tender scene. Even though I was risking so much to help Marina, somehow seeing her dressed like a mini version of myself made her seem more real, her dark hair wrapped like a crown atop her head, her silver eyes bright. She looked beautiful, elegant… elite.

As individual as she was, in all her adorable, fierce, prickly self I realised I had mostly still seen Marina as a street urchin, someone to aid but not really someone who was the same as me. I flicked a look up at Devyn, who was always so adept at reading my true feelings. I hoped he couldn't see into my soul at this moment but he too was absorbed in the scene before us.

Yes, I was helping Marina, and tonight I would be risking a great deal to do so, but really, up until this moment, the little girl had remained *other*. A diversion from the straight path through shops and the pretty, petty things with which I filled my day. Something I could point to and say, there, see, I did something unselfish and risky and proved that I am a better person than I might at first appear to be. Demonstrating my compassion to my lesser man. Or to Devyn, perhaps.

I unhooked a piece of hair from my elaborate updo and pulled it to my lips to hide the tremble that was emerging there.

What had I been thinking? I wasn't dallying here; this was no food run into the stews. I would throw myself under a hackney bus to save Marina. In fact, if tonight didn't come off, I would have failed to protect her and I knew I would never get over it.

Squaring my shoulders, I tucked the lock of hair back into place, impeccable once more.

Devyn nodded, his expression grave. There was sorrow at the back of those dark eyes, empathy perhaps, for the girl about to go into exile, leaving behind all she knew. She was only twelve, too young to leave home, but at least she wouldn't be alone. Oban was reluctantly leaving the other two children in his mother's care. He couldn't risk staying once

Marina disappeared. One transgression might be forgiven but two would be fatal. Marina obviously couldn't stay though I still wasn't entirely sure what happened to the sick who got picked up by the sentinels. Devyn said he didn't know but I guessed he was hiding the answer from me. For my own protection or for his?

"Right, we need to make a move." He crouched down to Marina, his hand smoothing back the intricate elite style I had given her, careful not to touch the makeup that disguised her illness. "Are you ready?"

Marina stood, her chin lifted, and she gave him a solemn single nod.

His dark eyes flicked up at me.

Mirroring Marina's conviction, I too gave a single nod and swallowed my fear.

"Good."

A single word of encouragement. A nice speech wouldn't have gone astray, something more than one bloody word. Anything to delay walking out of this room and irrevocably putting everything on the line. My life as I knew it, Marina's actual life, both of the men's lives. If Oban made it out through the outer gate before nightfall, he was free and clear. It was up to Devyn and me to deliver his sister safely to him on the other side. Walking through the gate was not an option as Shadower children were never issued papers granting them access to the city; there was simply no need. Adults came into the city to trade or work but their children remained firmly outside the walls. And no citizen ever left the safety of the walls for the Shadowlands. It was unthinkable

Oban patted his top pocket for what must have been the hundredth time since I had arrived earlier that evening. The papers resting there were one side of the key to his escape from the city, documents that proclaimed him a Shadower, permission granted to enter and exit the city during daylight hours.

The other half of that key lay in the heart of Devyn's device and his ability to inject some chaos into the Code and plant a corresponding file that verified the papers. I had seen someone fail that verification a few years earlier. I wasn't sure what happened to Shadowers found within the walls without the right documents as they were not tried publicly like citizens. But the woman the sentinels had caught that day had not gone quietly. Her screaming had haunted my dreams for weeks after, despite my father's assurances that it was a legal matter which far from warranted such fuss.

I had never quite been able to gloss over the fear that sat at the core of those screams.

I went over and patted Oban's papers for myself, my hand resting on his briefly.

I met his grey eyes, so like his sister's.

"Good luck." I smiled as encouragingly as I could with the replay of that woman's arrest rattling around in my head.

Oban smiled his shy grin.

"Don't you worry about me, love, you got enough to do yourself. You get my Mari through this night and there is nothing I will refuse you from now till the day I draw my last breath."

He looked directly at me, for once not showing the bowed-head deference those in this part of the city usually showed the elite, his eyes locked with mine as he made a vow I knew to be more than just mere words. It was unlikely I would hold him to it, for once out he could never return to the city. I would never see either of them again.

He extended his arm in farewell in what I vaguely

recognised as the Briton version of a handshake, ready for his life beyond the walls. I awkwardly responded in kind. He gripped me on my forearm and I felt a pulse along the touching veins of our inner wrists.

"Don't take any chances you don't need to," Devyn ordered us all.

I nodded. There was a small chance my voice wasn't quite as steady as I would like it to be. I saw no immediate need to communicate that to the rest of the room.

"Get through the East End as quickly as you can; you'll stick out more the further you get into Stepney." He nodded towards Marina but looked at me. "You need to look like you know where you're going. Let her guide you."

I nodded again.

"Don't take any transports; you'll be tracked. Better if nobody is able to follow your activity this evening"—he paused—"just in case…"

We got caught. No need to finish that particular sentence.

"Cass, are you listening to me?"

"Yes, yes, I'm listening, straight through, no transports. No dawdling when we get to the river, up the quays, through the XVII wharf, meet your friend, get to the end of the tunnel, and wait for you." I gave him my most confident withering stare.

"Right then." He nodded.

No matter how many times we went over it, Devyn clearly didn't think I had the compos mentis to retain the plan. He'd gone over it and over it. We were ready.

It wasn't really the plan he had a problem with. It was me. Devyn had made it very clear that he didn't like my being so involved. If Marina hadn't deteriorated so rapidly in the last few days and come to the attention of the authorities, he would be following the original plan, a better plan that didn't involve me. The checks through the eastern reaches of the river had tighter security due to the presence of non-citizens on the boats. To minimise the risk we were going to board beyond the old wall in a blind spot so there was no record of our passing. As a merchant's daughter, if we were stopped I could provide a reason for us to be in the Docklands, and as an elite, it was unlikely I would be questioned anyway. As far as anyone was concerned, we were two sisters going to meet our father at his place of work.

I gathered up my coat and handed Marina's to Oban so he could help her into it, my old jacket slightly dated but refreshed thanks to Oban's skill with needle and thread. Devyn had ruled out any purchasing of clothes for Marina. It would be recorded and I would have a hard time explaining why I had bought a top-to-toe outfit for a twelve-year-old. Instead, I'd clambered into the storeroom when my parents were out at a social function last week and rooted through the boxes stored there until I found suitable clothes, shoes, and accessories to create the impression that Marina was every bit as elite as me. As long as she didn't open her mouth, we'd be fine.

Oban had his arms wrapped around his sister like a man afraid he would never see her again, which was a reasonable fear.

Marina gave him a kiss on the cheek and untangled her arms from around his neck.

"It's fine, Oban, we'll be fine. Cassandra will look after me. I'll see you in a little while." She gave him a wide smile which her brother returned.

"Right you are, scrap." He looked over at me. "You take care of her, donna."

"I will."

"Oh, wait." Oban indicated a large box that I hadn't noticed in the otherwise bare rooms, sitting on the floor under the table. "I finished it. I hope it fits right."

The dress that I had ordered from him weeks earlier, and which I had forgotten in all the subsequent drama. I nodded my thanks distractedly. With that, I hooked Marina's arm in mine and stole one last look at Devyn, who still looked extremely displeased with the whole situation. Well, tough. I was the only person for the job and if he couldn't accept it that was his problem. Sweeping round him, we exited the small room and headed down the rickety stairs into the late afternoon.

We wound our way along arm in arm, Marina occasionally tugging me discreetly in one direction or another, through the warren of the East End. A wistful glance from my guide alerted me to the presence of a music hall, the tinkling music and laughter wafting out the door into our path as we hurried by. The further we went, the greater the presence of activities and merchandise that I considered quaint, if not outright antiquated – from the sound of the live music to the glimpses of people in the open doors of their homes huddled in front of braziers cooking meals. If I wasn't so scared I'd be fascinated. We hurried through streets where smiths wielded hammers that sent sparks flying as they went about their craft. The smells were overwhelming, if not downright toxic, as we swept through a street clearly inhabited by candlemakers whose wares were a far cry from the elegant, fragrant spires that occasionally graced my parents' dining room table, a decorative accompaniment to the powered lighting. I had no idea what went into the making of the candles offered to the masses who couldn't afford electricity and, shuddering at the acrid smell, I hoped I would never find out.

As we finally came out of the dense buildings into a small

park, I breathed deeply, pulling the somewhat cleaner air into lungs starved of oxygen after our trip through the sour aromas of the deep East End.

A man loomed out of the shadow of a tree as we moved to cross the park. He leered over at us, taking in our finery, his eyes calculating risk versus reward.

Marina hissed at him. He peered more closely, taking in her braids and tailored clothes, the silk wrapped around her throat that contrasted with her don't-mess-with-me gimlet eyes and bared teeth as she dared him to come at us.

Deciding we weren't worth the trouble, he grunted and turned away.

"Thanks." I smiled down at my petite warrior except, with the departure of danger, my warrior didn't look so fierce anymore as she crumpled to the ground.

"Marina, Marina," I sank to my knees beside her, my hand reaching for her forehead and finding not only that it was warm but that she was in a full sweat. This was not the time to have a relapse. We had none of the rough, illicit medicine with us that Devyn had managed to procure. We had decided not to risk carrying something that would identify her as ill.

I swore. What in Hades was I going to do? I looked around. The street was quiet apart from the departing shape of our unfriendly recent chancer.

"Marina, sweetie," I urged. "Are you with me?"

"Sorry…" Her small voice came even though she hadn't yet managed to open her eyes. "I'm sorry. The way is longer than I remembered and I'm tired. I just need to lie down for a minute."

"You've got to get up. C'mon, up you come." I put my arms under her shoulders and hoicked her up, feeling like the worst kind of bully. "We've got to keep going. Oban is waiting, remember."

At the reminder of her brother, Marina opened her eyes and determinedly put one foot in front of the other.

"This way."

I was completely outside of my comfort zone; I had zero knowledge of this part of the city. I wasn't even sure how close to the river we were. The original plan would have taken her to the old inner walls on the river. Plan B not so much.

"How much further?"

Marina paused in her slow steps.

"Dunno. Maybe a mile."

A mile. She was never going to make it another mile in this condition.

A hackney passed us, nearly silent as it swept by in a gleam of silver. I weighed my options. I could flag one down – I knew hackneys went back and forth between the city and the outer wall carrying citizens for both work and pleasure reasons. While I couldn't claim I was out here for business, if challenged I could perhaps claim I was here for pleasure. Some of my friends occasionally visited the clubs by the wall. It wasn't approved of but it wasn't entirely unheard of either.

I didn't really see how I had any other option and as another carriage rolled towards us, I put my arm up to wave him down.

Marina became fully alert as the hackney pulled up beside us. Her eyes were wide as every muscle in her body went taut.

"Cassandra," she said. "We aren't supposed…"

I shushed her as the driver opened the door and ushered Marina gently but firmly into the seat. Sitting back in the familiar comfort of the backseat, relief at the quick solution to

"All good?" I asked softly.

The small dark head nodded.

"Impressive accent there, Donna Marina."

She gave the ghost of an impish grin.

"Where to now?" I asked, taking Marina's hand once more. I looked around. We were back in a busier part of town, neon lights of all colours welcoming punters into bars and clubs of all shapes and sizes. Lifting my gaze, I could see the wall looming behind. If my awareness of this part of town was correct, we were in Mile End, a long way from the river.

Why on earth had Marina brought us here? Despite us completely breaking rule number two, we were no better off than we had been – rule number one being, *don't do anything stupid*. Too late.

Maybe I had broken rules one and two.

Looking back down at the guide who had brought us so badly out of our way, I discovered a cocky grin waiting expectantly.

"We can get a boat on the canal. They'll take payment other than credits," Marina offered before continuing with clear relish, "but if you're ever asked, the worst you've done is sneak to a party in the district with your mates."

I grinned back at her despite myself. No one could ever accuse Marina of lacking street smarts. Upping my own game, I pulled out some of the small coins Devyn had given me that were used as currency by those who traded in something more tangible than credits. Two well-dressed young girls might just about walk the streets attracting a minimum of notice. Casual onlookers would suppose we were taking a short trip between some merchants and our waiting cab. The same two girls on a working barge were likely to be a lot more noticeable. Given the area we were in, it was a matter of moments before we came across a shop selling hooded cloaks to wrap ourselves in. This part of town could be relied upon to help cover up any indiscretion a citizen might wish to commit – it was merely good business.

We retraced our steps and just beyond the bridge took the steps that led down to the canal and made our way to a lock. True to Marina's suggestion, it wasn't long before we convinced one of the bargemen to earn a couple of extra coins by taking us downstream.

Streetlights were starting to go on as we jumped off the barge at the last lock before the canal joined the river. Back in more familiar territory – I had loved to visit the docks with my father when I was a child, not to mention repeated trips to watch the patrols more recently with Devyn – we quickly made our way to XVII wharf and with slightly less ease found the door to the warehouse to which Devyn had directed us.

My quick tap on the door was answered almost immediately by a woman who hugged the shadows, ensuring we couldn't get a good look at her face before she beckoned us in.

Once inside, she turned without further exchange and began to lead us through the poorly lit passageway and out into the central storerooms, which were full to the brim with goods. The huge stacked crates had always intrigued me as a child. From the outside they were so plain and uniform but inside lay treasures from across the globe: silk from China, spices from India, carpets from Persia, paper from Egypt, coffee from Columbia. Delicacies from exotic places I had only ever seen in digital form. Places I was unlikely ever to be able to venture to given how dangerous sea travel was. A classmate in college had grown up in the Caribbean, enthralling everyone with tales of sugar plantations, endless blue skies, and balmy turquoise waters that one could swim in since the islands tended to be held in their entirety by either citizens or Wilders in that part of the world with walled towns to retreat to in times of unrest.

Marina's stumble brought me back to the present; she was tiring again.

"Not much further," I whispered encouragingly, earning a glare from our silent hostess.

I wrapped my arm around Marina to provide more support as we hurried through the gloomy warehouse. After weaving through interminable lanes created by the stacked crates, the woman came to a stop and, pushing a single container aside, revealed a trapdoor in the floor.

With some effort, she raised it and, handing us a light, ushered us down the dank steps, pointing into the dark.

"River." With that one word, she started to lower the trapdoor, sealing us into the tunnel. She paused briefly before the door hit the stones with a bang.

"Good luck."

We made our way to the bottom of the stairs, or at least where the stairs met water.

I raised the light in a weak attempt to see where we were going. Nothing but light reflected on the black water so there was no way of telling how deep it was or, more to the point, what was in it. I shuddered. I didn't want to begin to imagine.

I stepped gingerly down and then again, and again. Tapping about, I realised we were at the bottom of the steps. Thankfully it appeared the lightly moving water was only shin deep.

"Marina, it's okay, no more stairs. Are you feeling all right, sweetie?" I spoke quietly. There was no fear of being overheard down here, but it felt wrong to talk at a normal pitch.

Marina's response was mumbled which not a good sign. I decided against asking her to repeat herself, figuring she probably had enough on her plate just staying upright on the slimy surface of the tunnel floor. We sloshed through the tunnel which took us under the warehouses and out to the bank of the river.

Finally, we turned a corner to be greeted by an orange evening light dancing over the river. Devyn had said he would be here by the time the sun hit the horizon but looking out at the river it was difficult to tell whether the sun had fully set yet or not. It had certainly left a spectacular sky on its way down though. I moved us further back so we wouldn't be visible to any passing boats, the river still bustling with empty barges and other vessels heading back down to the docks after delivering their last loads of the evening to the warehouses.

As the minutes slipped by, Marina was clearly losing the strength to stand, and, believing Devyn would be here soon enough, I decided that sitting in the water was the lesser of two evils, rather than standing until Marina collapsed.

Marina huddled against me in the darkness of the tunnel. Shivering with fever, she was starting to lose consciousness. Where was Devyn? If he didn't come soon, we were in serious trouble. The low tide was turning. When it entered the tunnel in which we were hiding, we would be below the surface of the water. There was no way I would be able to carry Marina far on my own, but if I didn't make a decision soon we would be swimming, and that was going to attract attention. A lot of attention.

I peered out into the waning light, rubbing Marina's arm in a vain effort to warm and comfort her. Or maybe it just reminded me that I wasn't alone.

The cold was starting to seep into my bones. Warm for

spring though it was, we had been here over an hour. I rested my head back against the slimy walls, tired from crouching forward in the curved dankness.

Listening carefully over the sound of our shivering, I thought I detected a change in the sound of the water lapping against the edge of the embankment.

"Cass." The call came softly and it lifted my heart in joyous relief.

"Marina." I shook the little girl to rouse her. "He's here, Devyn's here."

She barely responded.

'No, no, no." We were so close to getting Marina the help she needed. I couldn't lose her now.

"Devyn," I called, my voice low but urgent.

No response.

What was I supposed to do?

The water had started seeping back into the tunnel and I couldn't leave Marina unsupported. She would sink unresisting into the murky water if I did.

I couldn't do that.

I wouldn't.

Chapter Nine

The fiery colours of the setting sun glinted off the icy water, lighting our path to the river while behind us the dark was closing in. The distance between us and the tunnel entrance wasn't huge – surely I could carry Marina that far? I pushed off the wall and stood with the girl in front of me then, bending down, I put one arm around her neck and another under her knees. I had her, I could do this. I adjusted my grip slightly and took a tentative step forward. One down, twenty or so to go.

Making progress through the sloshing water was not easy. Each step was tentative as I couldn't see what I was stepping on and couldn't afford to lose my balance with the unmoving Marina in my arms.

Was she still breathing? I paused to check, listening in the twilight for a sign that the body in my arms still supported life.

"Come on, Marina," I urged. "Please be okay. Your brother is waiting. He's got help for you."

My arms were tiring. Why hadn't Devyn called again? Had I imagined that first call? Maybe he wasn't there at all and I was going to arrive at the top of the tunnel to nothing more than the swirling eddy of the incoming tide. I had to get us both out of here one way or another, and if Devyn wasn't waiting, I would figure out my next move then.

Hopefully, it wouldn't end with me in whatever dungeon they threw traitorous fools into. My mother would be mortified by the scandal. Though what crime had I committed? Trying to help a minor leave the city undetected… I shook my head. Yeah, I'd be able to explain that away, no problem. I mocked my optimism. I wouldn't even be able to explain why Marina needed to get out of the city. That we had met when I rebelliously went to Oban to design a dress, sure, so far the story made sense. Her illness, why it needed to be hidden from the authorities… well, I couldn't answer these questions even if I wanted to, I realised belatedly. I had surface knowledge, but nothing solid.

Maybe that was the answer. I could claim ignorance, that I didn't know the child, I'd merely seen her fall into the river and had jumped in to save her. That might work.

Each step continued to bring us closer to the end of the tunnel while my mind worried over solutions to problems I could barely believe I had.

I peered out into the gloom. Darkness had fallen and the lightest sliver of new moon was all that illuminated the river.

"Devyn," I called again. My arms were incredibly tired and I slumped against the wall. I couldn't hold Marina much longer.

The river flowed past, heavy and dark on its interminable journey out of Londinium. A seagull flew upstream, its wings spread wide, its belly mere inches from the water and I could feel the joy of its glide, its sheer effortlessness. I tilted to the right as if angling to catch the current of the wind better and the gull's wing dipped to catch that same current. My breath caught…

"Shhh. Cass, keep your voice down." The words were practically whispered into my ear. Startled, I lost my grip and Marina started to slide out of my hands.

"Easy," Devyn hissed as he reached up out of the small boat that he had manoeuvred, unseen, beneath us.

The tide knocked the boat against the wall as he took my precious cargo out of my arms and laid Marina gently in the boat before turning to offer me a hand down.

My less-than-elegant arrival into the boat set it rocking as I practically fell into Devyn's arms.

"Whoa." Before I could get comfortable or even right my balance he had pushed me off and into a seat at the prow of the boat.

"Is she all right?" He nodded at Marina's prone form at my feet, his brow furrowed, his hand reaching down and registering the fever that had taken hold since he saw her just a few hours ago.

"I'm not sure," I admitted. "I couldn't wake her up."

I moved to sit on the floor of the boat, but Devyn's hand restrained me. He shook his head.

"Cass, the only reason you're here is so that I visibly have a paying customer in the boat, not to nurse the child."

"What's the point of any of it if she doesn't make it?"

His eyes glittered. "I'm taking more risk than I should having you in this boat at all. If you can't do your part then you can get out now. Marina won't be saved because you're brushing her hair back from her face." He pointed to the seat I had abandoned. "What hope she has requires you to look like an elite princess visiting her father at his warehouse so I don't get stopped for having a hackney this far out of town. Now sit."

He pulled a tarpaulin over Marina after making sure she was as comfortable as he could possibly make her, given the raging fever and wet clothes and the fact we were trying to elude the sentinels and escape the city for who knew what destination out there beyond the walls.

Settling himself into the boatman's spot at the base of the boat, Devyn triggered the engine and brought us around until we were headed downstream in the non-commercial channel.

Sitting upright in the passenger seat, I turned my head enough to allow my low words to drift back to Devyn.

"Oban? He made it out?"

"Yes. They barely glanced at his papers."

"Then what took you so long?"

A humph. I turned to take in his expression, unsurprised at the look of exasperation I found there.

"I had a fare."

"What?" I wasn't sure I understood. "What do you mean you had a fare?"

"When I was picking up the boat, a group of sentinels hailed me down," he explained. "What reason could I give to refuse the job? It would have been suspicious, and the last thing I needed was them taking down the name of the boat and tracking the licence. Like I say, I had a fare."

It was my turn to humph. I couldn't argue with that.

"Now, please, face forward and no more talking."

I lifted my chin and did as requested. This first section of our trip was the most dangerous in a lot of ways. The Limehouse Reach was always busy, this section of the river having the most docks and warehouses. The tall ships swayed all along the shore as dockhands worked through the night unloading them, the warehouses of the hungry city emptying as quickly as they were filled with the imports on which the city survived. Londinium might be a leader in technology, a very wealthy city despite its location at the edge of the Empire, but it was also one of its most isolated. While the city had control of most of the southeast since the Treaty, this was hardly enough to feed the millions huddled behind the safety of the city walls.

As we swept along the river, I watched the bustle with interest. In truth my father rarely permitted me to come this far east and certainly not without him. The rougher edges of the city towards the outer wall were not something to which he wanted me exposed. The old inner city was deemed sufficient exposure to a world I didn't really need to become familiar with, while, obviously, the East End proper was pretty much out of bounds. I had friends whose fathers worked in the financial district or technology towers just to the north that I had visited, and I had made frequent visits to the forum at the heart of the old city even before I attended classes there.

But most of my life was spent in the villas and open leafy levels of the western suburbs and bankside, our summer sojourns out in the country in Richmond as far from the outer walls as I had ever travelled. Not that anyone really considered Richmond all that far outside the walls. There were no arteries in or out of the city on that side. The lands out there were heavily patrolled and were strictly for citizens of Londinium only.

My attention was snagged back to my current location by the deep creak of timbers in the nearest ship. Deep voices speaking a foreign tongue and a glimpse of brightly coloured robes suggested it was likely traders from mineral-rich central Africa. When I was a child I used to beg my father to take me on the river to see the traders from other parts of the Empire and beyond. They were not permitted ashore so sightings of the Cherokee or Shawnee with their long black hair, Aztecs and Incas from further south in the Americas, wealthy Africans, and white-robed Arabs could only be had on the river.

The tangled web of rigging and sails on the great boats tethered ten-deep on the docks was thick tonight, leaving only a small narrow channel to enter and exit. I wistfully took in the tall ships as we passed. What places might they have come from? What adventures? How many had been attacked by Caribbean buccaneers in their fast sloops or Northmen in the colder waters of northern Europe? I sighed. As the cossetted daughter of Graham Shelton I was unlikely to ever find out. *Adopted* daughter, I corrected myself, a differentiation I had been acknowledging more of late.

As we swung beneath the Isle of Dogs, Devyn hoisted the small sail of the taxi.

I turned in surprise.

"What are you doing?"

"Power might go in the engine before we exit the Greenwich Reach. It happens sometimes. Best to be prepared. We can't afford to be dead in the water," he explained.

I frowned. "But we aren't even at the outer walls. Power should be steady here."

"Not always, princess. There's an energy line running underneath this section of the river and occasionally the power fluctuates out here. They don't even bother to set up the monitoring here because the cameras just get fried."

At that, the engine sputtered and died. Given the relative peace on the water, I felt I could afford to turn and watch as

Devyn deftly raised the sail, his muscles flexing as he pulled a rope here, deftly let one out there.

For the first time ever I could be certain we were out of range of any listening devices as well as cameras. I braced myself to ask the question that had been burning inside me for weeks.

"Devyn, are you a spy?"

He stilled.

"No."

"But you're not… your family, they're not citizens, are they?"

"No."

He was a Shadower then, here without papers, passing as a citizen. "You said before that you're here alone, but I remember you from school. Exactly how long have you been here?"

Devyn looked at me as if weighing his answer.

"Ten years."

"You've been living here alone since you were twelve?" I gasped.

"Not quite, I was sixteen when I arrived in Londinium."

I shook my head. "I don't understand. That doesn't add up." My maths was average, but it wasn't that bad. Ten years ago we had just been entering secondary school.

"I'm a little older than I appear," he explained wryly. "I am actually twenty-six years old."

"Why join a class four years younger than you?"

"I needed to be in that class," he replied ambiguously.

"Why?"

"For you."

I gritted my teeth. Getting anything more than I already knew from Devyn was an exercise in restraint that would test the most patient of souls.

"Because you thought I might be this girl, the one with magic in her blood?" At this point, I had turned all the way round to face him so he could see how openly crazy he was making me.

"There was a chance..." He paused, no doubt assessing how much would be just enough to shut me up. "I had to start somewhere. Why not with the little girl who had just been matched to the York prince?"

"The York prince?" My brows crinkled. "Oh, you mean Marcus."

On my twelfth birthday I had been promised to Marcus Courtenay, scion of one of the pre-eminent Houses in the city. His line had sat on the high council for centuries.

Marcus's family had been an instrumental part of the Treaty: the Britons had married one of their princesses to Marcus's great-great-whatever, making him a prince of the House of York.

"How did you know?" Matches were not exactly public knowledge.

"The Anglians take an interest."

Spies. Even if he was claiming not to be one, the Britons had spies in the city. I barely knew what happened in Rome, or even Dubris on the coast for that matter, but somehow the Britons knew about Marcus's match.

"Why?"

"Why what?" He gestured for me to duck as he tacked, and the boom swung to the other side of the boat.

"Why did my match make you think I might be her?"

Devyn contemplated me in the dark.

"You don't find it unusual that a little adopted nobody was matched to the Courtenay heir?"

It had been a massive coup for my mother to discover that

the girl she had adopted was matched to House Courtenay. At times I felt that from the day they had matched me to Marcus, Camilla had seen me less as a daughter to raise and more as a future first lady of the city to shape and polish.

I felt as if he'd slapped me across the face. I'd spent my whole life trying to ensure I belonged, that I fit into the Shelton family, to my group of friends, to the city, to my match.

"I am not a nobody. How dare you."

"Really?" he fired back. "Twenty years ago, your father was a moderately successful merchant, then he acquires a daughter and suddenly he has more council business than any other merchant in the city. You don't find that a tiny bit odd?"

"Coincidence," I snapped.

Devyn smiled his infuriating half smirk and raised his brow. Double whammy.

"Sure," he said patronisingly, "Then when you turn twelve, the youngest possible age at which a citizen can become matched, you are betrothed to the single most eligible boy in the entire city."

"So?"

"I found that interesting." He lay back against the tiller.

I felt like bashing him over the head.

"Interesting enough that you gave up your own life to sit in the back of classrooms watching me live my life," I threw at him.

"I didn't have anything better to do," he drawled. "So many pieces fit. But it seemed less likely the more years that passed. I haven't been able to find another lead as strong, otherwise I'd have been long gone."

He'd been here for years… since he was little more than a child himself.

"Do you manage to get out to visit your family often?"

His mouth twisted. I suddenly had a really bad feeling.

"Devyn, where does your family live?"

"Uh, northwest of here." Both brows dipped as he gave his answer.

"Northwest," I repeated. That bad feeling solidified into a stone wall inside me. There was nothing to the northwest. No Shadowers lived in the borderlands that side of the city; it was a wasteland.

Dark eyes awaited my realisation.

"You're not a Shadower… you're a full-blood Briton," I said in a strangled voice. "How?"

"Not entirely, but my father was one. My mother was a citizen and they got married and one night they… *Ow*!" He acknowledged my direct hit to his shin.

"How come your mother married a Briton?"

"She was from another part of the Empire, the other side of the Mediterranean. She fled her country, ended up on a ship that was bound for Eireann, and, fortunately for me, it stopped to do some trading on our western coast."

"Don't you miss her?"

"I never really knew her. She died when I was very young." He looked down and checked on the sleeping Marina. "She died of the Mallacht."

"The what?" The word sounded like it was in one of the Celtic languages.

"The illness."

"But that was twenty years ago. The illness hasn't been around that long."

"Not here, but in other parts of the Empire they call it the Maledictio."

The Curse.

We spoke the common tongue like most parts of the

western world, but as an elite I had learned old Latin.

"But there's nothing in the feeds about that."

Devyn looked at me, his face impassive. "You know what they want you to know."

My mind absorbed this. Was he right? Were the authorities hiding the truth? Had there been instances of it that far back? They controlled everything. His mother had fled for the same reasons Marina now ran; no wonder he had been so quick to help. Despite the danger, he had risked his life to come here. If the authorities caught him…

"Devyn Agrestis." My jaw dropped. His name, Agrestis, meant rural, *wild*. "Is this all a joke to you?"

"I was sixteen when I chose it." His lip tugged up at the corner.

"And Devyn?"

"My real name."

"Right." My mind was reeling. "If you're discovered… how could she be worth risking your life?"

How had he lived for so long in the city, undetected, as a minor?

He stayed silent.

I stared at him in frustration until he finally shrugged.

"It didn't seem a big decision for me. If there was a chance I could find her, I had to try."

"You came here alone. You were only sixteen. How did your family allow it?" What must it have been like for him to leave everyone and everything he knew to live in a place where he was alone and in constant fear of being discovered.

He shrugged. "Didn't have much family to speak of. My father and I haven't spoken in a very long time. What other family I have left was better off without me. I volunteered to do this."

"Volunteered…" I whispered the word. He was here illegally, a Briton on the wrong side of a boundary that had been created centuries ago. The two societies shared this island, living separately in clearly marked regions of it. Crossing the border was frowned on. Since the Treaty, fatally so. My heart was beating a wild tattoo in my chest. Why was he admitting this to me now?

Devyn's eyes snapped from my face to somewhere behind me.

"Face forward."

A guard boat had begun to glide by us, its sails bigger than ours, catching the wind and surging perilously close to our much smaller vessel.

A light shone along the length of our boat.

I raised an arm to shield my eyes even as I gave them my haughtiest expression. I was in a boat with a Briton and a sick child fleeing the authorities. Despite the chilly night air, I was perspiring madly. Evidently satisfied, the larger boat skimmed ahead of us in the direction of a barge coming upriver on the other side.

I let my muscles unclench, my heart pounding.

Devyn's hand captured and squeezed mine briefly. "Good girl, nearly there."

I slowly relaxed, the adrenalin leaving my body somewhat shaky.

"That, princess, is why it was necessary to have you along. Being out here on my own with a young girl would have been suspicious. Ferrying a snooty elite princess downriver, not worth the hassle of stopping." He smiled smugly.

I frowned. Now that I was finally getting answers out of him, I was not going to be distracted, not by cruising sentinels and not by faint praise.

"You volunteered to come here to check me out?" I prompted him to return to his story. "If you were caught... it's an instant death sentence. Why would they let you come? It doesn't make any sense. It would be a major political disaster if you were caught here."

I turned to look at him but all I could make out was his silhouette in the dark.

"When I said I volunteered, I didn't say that anybody else deemed it a good idea," he replied.

"Then what changed their minds? Was it really so important to find out more about who was matched to Marcus?" I shook my head. "It makes no sense. The Britons have never cared before who Marcus's line married... or have they?"

"In Anglia, they have become more interested as the Plantagenet line has thinned out. Technically, your future husband is the heir to the York crown. But I'm not from there so I don't care so much about that." He adjusted the blanket around Marina, tucking her in against the cold on the open water. "I told you I was looking for someone."

This conversation was beyond frustrating – like all conversations with Devyn – forcing me to circle back again and again as his answers hid as much as they revealed. I had been educated in a system built on straight lines and this conversation was making me dizzy as I chased after the answers to the questions that had been burning inside me. But if I had to keep circling back endlessly, I would; I had to know. Who could possibly be so important to a sixteen-year-old that he would give up his world and risk his life to find her?

"And you thought it might be me? Because I was matched to Marcus? So they sent you to check it out?"

"Not exactly."

"What do you mean, not exactly?"

"There is no reason to believe..." He hesitated. "That is, everyone believes she died years ago. I thought... there was a solid chance that you might be her. You're the same age and the colouring is right. Nobody else would even consider it because they're sure she's dead. I've never felt it to be true." Another significant pause. "And over the last few years, I have even more reason to believe she's alive."

"Why?"

No answer. Whatever strange impulse had loosened his usually circumspect tongue seemed to be wearing off.

No, he couldn't stop now. I couldn't bear it. I turned around to face him again. We were past the tall ships, and here in the less populated part of the river, in the dark, we would see any boat approaching long before they were close enough to see that the passenger and driver were unusually deep in conversation.

"But you don't think I'm her anymore?" I tried another avenue. I wasn't sure I wanted to be this girl Devyn had risked all to find, but I was pretty sure relief wasn't going to be my next emotion if he confirmed that I was nothing more to him than a girl he had reported back on as being nothing special.

Devyn checked the sail, tightening the ropes before answering me.

"I know you're at least a Shadower, possibly a latent. But no more than that. I thought maybe the pills were some kind of blocker but it's been weeks since you stopped taking them. She was from a powerful bloodline and I have reason to believe her magic would have manifested by now. I need to accept that she's not here. I should have left years ago. She's still out there. I just have to keep looking."

He stared grimly across the dark water. I couldn't help

myself. I reached out and laid a hand on his cheek until he looked back at me.

"I'm sorry."

"It's not your fault." He ran a hand through his hair, slightly long for a citizen but still short, a habit I realised now he had probably learned as a child when his hair must have been long in the style of the Britons. "It was the foolish dream of a child. I wanted to restore my family's honour, to save the girl. As it is, if I make it out of the city I'll be lucky if my lord doesn't take my head for what I've done."

I stopped to consider the life he'd left behind. I really wanted to know who it was he'd been looking for but I was loath to push my luck – he'd already revealed more in the last ten minutes than I would have believed possible. I realised the discovery that he was Briton should have horrified me more but instead I was intrigued, curious. As we sailed along I toned it down, keeping my questions simple, asking about daily life and the land of his birth. When it came to the vast spaces, trees, and natural life, he couldn't resist describing the lush hills and valleys of his childhood.

Mountain ranges and endless skies and eagles, things I could only imagine.

Freedom, and the beauty of endless landscape rather than confining concrete. Visiting the parkland out at Richmond Hill always made me feel less weighed down. The city was still visible but the open space, the green, the wandering deer all combined to draw dark energy out of me. What must the places Devyn described be like? The deep forests of Anglia, the high mountains of Cymru, the distant beauty of the Lakelands of Mercia?

"You said you serve a lord?" I recalled. The Briton territories stretched from Alba in the far north through Cymru to the west and as far as Kernow to the southwest; the Mercians held the north and the Anglians the midlands from York down to the borderlands. All of them were feudal societies. Cymru and Kernow had multiple princes while Alba, Mercia, and Anglia were all Kingdoms. Devyn's previous life had begun in one of their ancient castles.

"Yes," he responded tersely.

"In the north or the west?" I asked.

"North." We were back to pulling teeth it seemed, his fealty clearly a no-go area, but I persevered. "Alba?"

"Close. They are also Celts, at least."

"I can't tell," I said as I surveyed his features. Should I be able to guess? "I've never really met a Briton."

"Of course you haven't." He smiled. "Apart from me."

"So, you're not from Alba? Uh, who else is mostly Celt... Kernowans?"

He ran his hand through his cropped hair again.

"I serve a lord in Mercia."

"Aha, I know that one," I said, recalling my second level geography. "It's in the northeast. You're from the Lakelands?"

"My lord is," he agreed. "I am from Gwynedd."

I wracked my brain. Mercia ran from the Cumbrian Lakelands down to Lancashire and all the way across to the Umbrian east coast

"It's in North Cymru," he said taking pity on me.

"Then why are you serving a house in Mercia?"

His face went stony. "My family owes a debt."

A debt that he had walked out on when he came to Londinium, which would explain why he felt he would be in trouble when he returned. I wondered again who was so important that he would give up so much. A sister, perhaps?

"What kind of debt?"

"Quiet now, we're approaching the barrier." He shrugged deeper into his hood, indicating that I should now don mine. What convenient timing. Though to be fair, even as I asked the question, I hadn't really expected an answer. Debts and family honour did not really fall under topics of casual conversation.

We slid through the water. It was choppier here than it had been, our little boat bobbing up and down in the rougher water by the open barrier. Devyn pulled alongside a column of the tidal barrier and hooked us on with a rope. He pulled us closer then stepped out onto the concrete. He took from his pocket the all too familiar sliver of illegal tech and inserted it into the console he had opened above the waterline.

"You haven't sorted this out already?" I asked aghast.

"I told you, power is sketchy out here. There is a ley line running through here and also elements of this system are local so it's got to be done here," he said abstractedly. I watched him work, bright lines of code flickering on his monitor. After a few minutes, he disconnected and the barrier lifted as he stepped back into the bobbing boat.

We sailed through uneventfully. Devyn took us close to the northern bank where the small light of a lantern sat. We tacked towards a small pier and two men materialised out of the darkness, a whinny in the dark behind them indicating waiting horses.

"Stay here," Devyn told me as he lifted the limp bundle that was Marina. I placed a small kiss of farewell on her damp forehead.

"Be well, sweetheart," I whispered, my heart heavy at saying goodbye and at how ill she appeared. Would I ever see her again? Would she make it? In a short space of time, she had become someone I felt bonded to and the thought that this might be the last I saw of her felt deeply wrong. I tucked her cloak about her. I would see her again. The Wilders would help her. They must.

Devyn carried Marina down to the waiting men, who came to meet him leading their horses and they exchanged words. From my place in the boat it looked like an argument was taking place. The taller of the men caught hold of Devyn's arm. I did a quick count: there was an extra horse. Surely Devyn wouldn't leave me here. Was that why he had told me the truth of his background? Not because we were outside all possible surveillance but because he was leaving? Now? Tonight?

He couldn't abandon me here. I couldn't sail this thing. I sat up to get out of the boat and make sure he wouldn't leave me when he pulled away from the man who held him and jogged quickly back down the pier, untying our boat before we drifted back out onto the Tamesis.

Minus one girl. Her fate was in the hands of the Wilders now.

The pain of sending her away with strangers was almost a physical thing, as if I could feel the distance between us stretching.

"What was that about?" I asked as the wind and tide sent us speedily back towards the city.

"Nothing."

"I thought you were going to leave me there."

His lips thinned and he gave no answer. Just like that, regular service had resumed.

Whatever had taken place during the handoff made Devyn retreat and his mood was sour for the journey back.

My own mood was irrepressible. The release of pressure fizzed through me and by the time we got back to Linus's place I was positively giddy. Even my taciturn companion was starting to unclench at my constant stream of nonsense as we made our way through the winding streets. Once so grim and threatening, even they seemed lighter and more pleasant tonight.

"We did it."

Once inside the relative safety of Devyn's friend's dingy flat, a fresh rush of jubilation and adrenaline ran through me. Without thinking I threw my arms around Devyn who finally gave in to my joy. Catching me, he lifted me into the air above him; I smiled widely and inhaled deeply, taking the moment in.

Taking *him* in, and just that quickly the moment changed. Became aware. Tingled.

Devyn lowered me slowly and stepped away and, much like a moth to a flame, I followed.

I raised my hand tentatively, not sure that I was doing this even as my hand found the back of his neck and pulled his head down towards my own.

Our lips touched, held, tangled. I might never have kissed anyone before, but I knew this wasn't a standard off-the-shelf kind of kiss. What had been part curiosity, part experiment on my side was quickly becoming something more than I could handle.

Devyn's hands were moving now, roaming, tracing and retracing my body. Pulling me closer until we fit like two pieces of the same whole.

I yanked myself free, shocked and heaving to breathe.

He couldn't touch me like that. I was horrified. What was he doing? What had I let him do? What if he did it again? Would I be able to stop him? Would I want to stop him? My skin still pulsed to the track of his fingers. My heartbeat was deafening in my ears.

"I'm matched," I protested. The word throbbed through

me. Matched. 100% destined for another, for someone I was meant to be with, our DNA aligned to give me the perfect mate, and here I was risking that. With a Briton. A Briton who was leaving. Who had kissed me. "Officially and utterly matched and promised. You… you can't touch me like that."

He leaned closer again, not touching me this time, but his eyelash fluttered against my cheek. His breath shuddered in and out of his chest, but he didn't touch me. We were just close, the warmth of his body an almost tangible thing along the length of my body.

"I know," he said.

He pushed back, putting distance between us.

"You should go." His voice was chipped with ice.

And the room actually felt colder.

My life was all planned out; I had a perfect man all lined up for me. All I had to do was stay the course. I barely even had to do that, just not mess up. I had done what I had set out to do. I had helped Oban and his sister leave the city. Who knew what would happen to them now, but Marina was such an independent thing and it felt right, like her path was meant to be outside the walls. The city would only stifle her; her life would not be a long one if she stayed here. She was better off outside.

My life, on the other hand, meandered through the city, taking in all the sights anybody could ask for. Stepping off that path was not a good idea.

Marina was safe. Devyn had his tech back. He was moving on in his search for some missing Shadower girl who was not me. I hadn't been arrested and I wanted it to stay that way. Didn't I? Hadn't that been the whole point?

I took a step forward, placing a hand on Devyn's shoulder. A shudder ran through him. I took another step, impulse or instinct or whatever it was taking over, and wrapped my arms around his rigid form as he stood looking out of the window.

I could feel the warmth seep from my body into his, yet his form remained unyielding.

"I hope you find her."

He stiffened and pulled out of my arms. "Why, because you think she's my match? The most I can hope is that she lives, more than that is not even—"

He stopped, scrubbing his hands across his face and hair.

"Go, Cass," he repeated. "Just leave. Go back to your life."

"Will you leave now?" I asked. Much as I couldn't imagine never seeing him again, he needed to leave soon. I couldn't believe he'd remained undiscovered this long.

"It'll be easier if I have my citizenship papers if I want to keep looking within the Empire. So I'm here until graduation at least."

There was a flicker, a hesitation. There was something he wasn't telling me, but I nodded, relieved to know he wouldn't be leaving just yet.

"Will you go back to visit your family before you move on?" I should leave… why wasn't I putting myself on the other side of that door?

"It's not really on my way."

How could he be so dismissive of the people who cared for him? He'd left at sixteen so surely going to see them before he headed deeper into the Empire would be worth it. It had been years.

"Surely you could take a little detour?" I persisted.

"Enough, Cassandra. My life and my family are none of your business." His eyes blazed with anger before he shut them and when they opened again, they were the dull, forgettable mud-brown behind which he hid his real self.

As I watched, the mask dropped into place. The intense coiled man disappeared behind the mild-mannered illusion. *Illusion*. The word rang like a bell inside my head. He was a Celt – this wasn't some kind of augmenting tech.

"You're not just a Celt. You… you… you're using…"

Magic. That was it. That was how he seemed so different. He was using magic. The illegal tech was nothing – that he had helped someone slip out of the city was one of the naughty antics of a misguided youth in comparison. Helping Marina leave no doubt broke the Code. I'd known if we were caught we would wind up on the sands but I didn't think it was a capital crime. I wasn't sure, as this wasn't a crime I'd ever witnessed; nobody voluntarily left the safety of the walls. I'd thought about it a lot, but between my father's influence and my lack of awareness, if it was an actual crime, I was hoping the punishment wouldn't be too severe.

But Devyn. He was so much worse than that. He was a Briton… with magic, whom I had been seen with. Whom my mother knew I had covered for. I didn't know what they did to Britons when they caught them and I didn't know what they did to the people who associated with them either.

Because this never happened. Or at least it hadn't, not in centuries. If he was caught and revealed to be a Briton, it would likely mean his death. But the death of a Briton with magic would mean war. There was a reason the walls and our advanced technology existed. It kept the Britons and their magic out.

"The tech, the chaos in the Code. That's what it is. You've found a way to inject your hocus pocus into the technology that protects the city. Are you planning to attack? Why? There's been peace for centuries. What are you doing? Why don't you just stay on your side of the wall?"

"Hocus pocus?" A hint of amusement tugged at his lips.

"Seriously?" I asked back. "I could be on the sands just for having this conversation. And you're mocking my choice of words."

"The tech is what got Oban and Marina out," he said in a calm tone. "And only tech."

"But you *are* using magic," I insisted. "Don't lie to me."

He drew in a deep considering breath and the illusion dropped. He immediately felt more present, more alive, more charismatic and more physically impressive. Now I was sure of the difference it was shocking to me that I had ever doubted what I had glimpsed.

"Seems we're a little past that now," he said. "Yes, it's a skill I have."

"How?"

"I have abilities that allow me to blend in, to manipulate the perceptions of others. They appeared when I was sixteen."

"Sixteen?" The age he had been when he arrived in Londinium.

"It's part of the reason I was so convinced she was here," he said, confirming my guess that the events were related. "These are skills that would allow me to protect her. I'm more adept than anyone of my line in generations. It's also how I met Linus. He saw through the illusion I maintained to avoid drawing attention to myself. He sought me out, helped me, and when he got ill I was able to return the favour."

He was using magic.

As did the owner of this flat. And it seemed Marina would too. If she survived.

My heart pounded in my veins.

"You said before we couldn't be overheard here, right? How are you doing that?"

He stood and pulled back the threadbare rug on the floor to reveal a mark etched into the floorboard underneath: a triangle of three leaf-shaped loops, entwined by a circle.

"It's a Celtic knot, a triquetra. It symbolises the Celtic Trinity and the circle woven through it makes it a protection charm," he explained holding out his wristband and twisting the disc held in it to display the same symbol hidden on the underside. My fingers found the etchings scratched into the rose gold disc that hung around my own neck. I let loose one of the more interesting new phrases I had picked up in my recent tours of the docks.

"So graphic, Cass." His dark eyes gleamed his amusement.

I struggled to smother an even more choice phrase.

"If you were caught, they would burn you alive." I might not know what they did to captured Britons but I knew the punishment that used to be dealt to users of magic.

He shrugged. "Possibly." His eyes lost focus as he contemplated his situation. "It wouldn't really matter."

"It wouldn't really matter," I echoed. My blood was pounding against my skull. "It matters to me."

I stepped back.

"I can't do this. I can't be here." My mind had gone into complete meltdown.

I took another step. Back on to my path.

"Stay away from me."

I reached for the door. My hand trembled, waiting for him to call my name, but it didn't come. I took hold of the doorknob.

I turned it.

And left.

Part Two

ALL WE NEED OF HELL

My life closed twice before its close—
It yet remains to see
If Immortality unveil
A third event to me

So huge, so hopeless to conceive
As these that twice befell.
Parting is all we know of heaven,
And all we need of hell.

– *Parting,* Emily Dickinson

Chapter Ten

Over the next weeks, I threw myself into my courses at the forum as college results were released and graduation fast approached. I refused to look for Devyn. He was there though, back in the shadows, occasionally passing me in the halls or on the stairs. He never looked at me, but sometimes I could feel his gaze move across me, never stopping.

I didn't care. I refused to care.

I had no way of explaining the kiss or the moment we had shared that day, but I felt hollow when I thought about it. I reached more frequently for the pendant I still wore around my neck, the only substantial proof I had that anything had ever happened. I knew with its Celtic symbol it was also evidence to others, but I couldn't quite bring myself to take it off and throw it into the river. Instead, I completely blocked out any further thoughts about Britons, magic, or the last few weeks. It was over. After graduation he would leave on his search and that would be it. I could forget any of this ever happened.

By the time graduation came, I almost felt like my old self – at least, I was pretty sure I would appear like the old me to anyone who cared to look. I dressed for my graduation dinner carefully. My new dress had a fabulous bias cut which flattered my slim figure, and the long cuffs were to die for. It wasn't a patch on Oban's beautiful creation, but I couldn't bring myself to wear that now. The dress that symbolised my moment of defiance had arrived at our door a few days after – and it had lived in its box under my bed ever since.

Its significance had changed from a moment of stupid, childish rebellion against my mother into something more. Something I couldn't articulate, jumbled as it was with my new fear of the authorities and my worries for Oban and Marina. Not to mention the seething morass of unidentifiable emotion that Devyn incited.

I sighed as I twirled my hair up, the brightest strands catching the light wonderfully as I leaned forward to put in my earrings. They had been a gift from my father on my twenty-first birthday; he would expect to see them.

Sure enough, he smiled fondly at me as I entered the room, his smile growing wider as he spotted the earrings swinging jauntily.

"Darling." He hugged me to him. "Well done, we're so proud of you."

"Thanks, Papa." I smiled back up at him. This alone made putting my defiance behind me worthwhile. If he ever found out how badly I had betrayed the Code he would be heartbroken.

My mother entered the room from behind me, her fingers sweeping lightly across the collar of my dress, slightly smoothing the ends, before she turned around to wave in the man loitering in the hallway.

what could have been a significant problem washed through me.

Until I realised the driver was looking at me expectantly. I needed to give him a destination. I couldn't give him the address of the wharf that we were headed for. If this journey were tracked I would be leading the authorities straight to Devyn and anyone else who had helped us.

Marina looked at me and thankfully, comprehending my dilemma, offered a solution.

"Rhodeswell Bridge, if you would, sir," she clipped out in pristine plummy tones.

I gulped to swallow the surprised giggle that bubbled up despite our dire circumstances.

What seemed like mere moments later, the cab arrived at our destination. Pretending for all the world like I knew exactly what I was doing, I smiled coyly at the driver, ducking my head to look up at him shyly through my lashes. At least I hoped it was coy; I felt like an idiot.

"Is there any chance I could pay extra to be dropped in the city?"

The man looked at me blankly. "As you wish, donna. Where would you be off to?"

I smiled again, a butter-wouldn't-melt smile. "How about Spitalfields?"

"Certainly, premium rates for that trip," he returned, not the first time he'd had a citizen ask him to record a trip that did not end under the walls.

"Of course," I replied as coolly as I could muster. I tapped my chip against the scanner, somewhat horrified at the charge the blackguard had put on the screen.

Out on the street again, I checked Marina to see how she was faring.

Marcus Courtenay.

My smile froze. What was he doing here?

"We thought it would be nice if Marcus could join in the celebrations."

My mother flashed her teeth at the room. The perfect smile. But her eyes didn't meet mine. My slight trespass all those weeks ago had not been forgotten and my behaviour since had done nothing to smooth over the turbulence caused by Camilla witnessing Devyn and me standing a little too closely together. If only she knew.

"Hello, Marcus." I looked at him and then quickly dropped my lashes, concealing any emotion that didn't belong in my eyes.

"Cassandra." He greeted me in the modulated, well-educated tones one would expect from Senator Dolon's son.

I knew he was handsome; this was a well-established fact in the city's high society gossip feeds. Marcus was occasionally photographed attending the theatre or the opening of a glitzy restaurant with his close circle of friends. His athletic form was impeccably suited and booted, his chestnut-brown hair holding the most delectable wave that occasionally looked like it would break free of the perfection of its cut. But it never did. His clear green eyes were warm when in conversation with his friends and disdainful when looking directly at the camera.

Now his eyes were politely warm as he gave the most courteous semi bow.

I inhaled deeply – this man was well outside my experience. I knew I looked the part, my delicate appearance a fitting foil to his burnished golden-boy looks, but I felt like an imposter as we exited my parents' apartment and stepped into the waiting town car – a luxury even for my parents.

My parents' chit chat with Marcus took us across town as

we smoothly moved through the streets, neatly passing the trams and the hackneys which were our more usual form of transport.

My father took my mother's hand to help her out of the car as Marcus came around to extend the same immaculate manners to me. My wrap slipped and he lightly lifted it around my shoulders again; as I looked up to thank him, the flashes started. The paparazzi. Now that I had graduated, like any child with parents considered high society I was officially fair game. My parents were just about in that bracket and my match with Marcus would guarantee it once it became known.

I grimaced and heard my mother tsk, reminding me that I had a duty if not to myself then to the parents who had raised me. I smiled my most dazzling smile directly at her.

Marcus's bright eyes lost a little of their warmth as he took in our exchange. Great. Not off to the best start there then. I turned, tucking my arm into my father's as he entered the restaurant.

"Not a fan of the paps?" Marcus leaned down to murmur as my parents stopped to talk to yet another couple as we made our way through the buzzing lobby. I wasn't the only graduate of the Basilica Varian class being treated to a celebratory meal at the city's most exclusive restaurant tonight.

"Just not used to it," I responded softly, grateful he had chosen to interpret my behaviour as dismissive of the photographers rather than disrespectful of my mother.

He sighed ruefully.

"It's not so bad, and unless you give them regular fodder, they won't bother with you unless you happen to be in their direct path."

"Like dining at the Ritz on graduation night with the one

and only Marcus Courtenay?" I delivered breathlessly in my best impression of a gossip reporter.

"Yeah, like that." His eyes were warm again as he put his hand in the small of my back to propel me forward in my parents' wake.

My body flinched. It was a small flicker really, a reaction to his touch, a memory of another man directing me. One whose merest touch could persuade me to follow him anywhere. His sheer existence gave me polarity, reducing me to a satellite happy to orbit wherever he happened to be.

We made our way through the hall towards the dining room, our footsteps sinking into the deep pile of the Persian carpet. The murmured conversations and tinkling laughter of the elegant crowd bounced off the exquisite décor which was nothing to the decadence of the dining room with its lush artwork, gilded wall carvings, immaculately laid tables, and entirely handcrafted china and silverware. My spine tingled as my head turned to take in the room and I realised the music was actually live. One corner held three musicians, their fingers moving lightly across ivory and string sending a waft of melody across the room. My fingers lifted as if to touch it. I snapped back at the realisation. How odd.

We followed as the maître d' led us across the room and we were formally seated at our pristine table. I looked down at the menu blankly. I could still feel the music, its tangle swirling around the room as a beautiful lilting tune danced like a giddy child around our heads, first a merry toddler before emerging like a graceful dancer with her arm stretched out, one note reaching for the next. I had to concentrate fiercely to read the list in my hand My attention was finally caught by the fact there were three different types of fish on the menu, at least two of them unfamiliar to me. Salt-water fish... my mouth watered in anticipation.

My father politely questioned Marcus about his experiences in the hospital he was working in with various accident victims and the like. I tuned back in at his mention of the mysterious illness among the poor.

"We've tried everything," Marcus was saying. "We aren't really equipped to deal with a virus of this type. Most of the work to eradicate or contain viruses like the common cold was done centuries ago. We've figured out how the research was done but it's not been the province of medicine to do this kind of work in generations."

Father nodded gravely. "There's talk that this is plague," he said, "that Governor Actaeon and the council are trying to keep it quiet."

Marcus smiled. "No, plague it most certainly isn't. The Great Plague was caused by external factors, fleas on the rats that came in off the boats. It then passed from patient to patient; once someone was infected, it was virtually impossible to contain it, particularly in the outer wall area which is so congested and next door to the Docklands."

He rubbed his jaw in a gesture that spoke of frustration and fatigue.

"Similar symptoms have popped up here and there for years in different parts of the Empire but this wave is worrying. It's never been seen in these numbers here before," he said. "We've ruled out external factors and there just isn't a clear pattern in those who start to exhibit symptoms. The cells start to die and each one sets off the next and the next until they finally come in to the hospital, too far gone for us to do any more than make them comfortable."

I had, by this time, read as much about the illness that was popping up throughout the city as I could manage discreetly. There had been sporadic reported cases over the last few years but the number of instances had grown dramatically over the last couple of months, while at the same time the official press had toned down their reports. It had gone from being big news with accompanying pictures of grieving families, since the stricken nearly always died, to being rarely, if ever, reported. Still, the chances were if somebody in the inner walls died under the age of ninety it was the illness that had done it.

I searched my mind for something to ask, Mother's eyes boring a hole in the side of my head as she mentally urged me to take an interest in Marcus's depressing work. Little did she realise I was very interested, mostly in the patients who disappeared, but how to find out more without raising suspicions…

"Do you ever catch it in time?" I asked. My question was inane as he had just said it was a death sentence. Even I knew that much.

He looked over at me and smiled politely.

He bowed his head before finally responding in a voice so low it was nearly impossible to hear him over the background din.

"I'm not really supposed to say," he said before adding, "but we've had some successes recently. It's early, so we aren't quite sure what it is we've found, but it's hopeful."

"Oh." I was honestly a little shocked; this was most certainly not public news.

My parents' display of delight was immediate though it was hard to tell with my mother if she was pleased a cure had been found or that she was one of the first to know.

"Have there been many cases?" my father asked.

Marcus shook his head. "Only a handful so far, and those

patients were caught in the very early stages, but any progress is great."

"I should say so," my father affirmed, as pleased and proud as if Marcus himself had come up with the cure.

"Which hospital has recorded the successes?" Mother asked – she had friends on the boards of some of the few hospitals in the city. Knowing my mother, she would now hold it against those who had failed to bring her the news first hand.

"Uh, Barts," Marcus answered, starting to look like he wished he could take back the revelation he had shared more freely than he should.

St Bart's was the hospital where he worked, the name a relic from the phase of Christianity the Empire had gone through in earlier centuries. I might not have been in the same room as him in over ten years, but I had kept up with what was going on in his life. He was, after all, my match, the mate I had been promised, the husband I would have for the rest of my life. "Have you seen some of these cases?"

I knew he didn't want to talk about it any more but it was impossible to pass up the opportunity to get more information. Perhaps it could help Marina if we could get a message to her.

He nodded.

"Did you work on any of them?"

Another nod. No further explanation offered. He was clearly trying to back out of the conversation. After spending so many weeks with Devyn, it was a technique with which I had grown all too familiar.

"Did you treat them with something in particular?" I followed up.

Marcus shook his head lightly, straightening his shoulders and sitting back in the chair. "I'm afraid not. We tried several things, but success in one case wasn't always repeated in the next. It's hard to identify what's actually working. We've repeated treatments which seem to have no effect, only for the patient to take a turn for the better just as we were giving up."

He reached for his glass and took a long drink.

"So you have no idea how to cure it?" My voice clearly conveyed my disappointment, which earned me a glare from my mother and a rueful flash of pearly teeth from my date.

"I'm afraid not. Most of the successes are moved to a different hospital for further study," he replied civilly before smiling in obvious relief at the arrival of our next course.

As I ate the expensive meal, I wondered whether those successes were also latents with hidden magic and if that was why they were moved. I wondered what had cured them, and whether Marina was healed now, wherever she was, or whether she would have been better off staying here where at least some were recovering. Though it didn't sound like those who recovered got to go home precisely, so maybe she was better off where she was. Free.

My parents moved quickly to the door of our building when we got home, hurriedly calling goodnight as they went through the doorway before Marcus had finished helping me out of the car.

My breath hitched. How embarrassing. My cheeks felt warm as I took a quick glance at Marcus to see if he'd also seen through the not-so-subtle removal of their chaperoning presence.

Marcus's fingers held onto mine as he pulled me towards the shadier part of the sidewalk. Yeah, he'd noticed.

"It was nice to meet you again, Cassandra." He really did

have the loveliest velvet tones; his bedside manner must practically heal his patients through speech alone.

I gnawed on the side of my lip.

"I'm better company now than I was at twelve?" I asked, laughing up at him, at the recollection of our match celebration on my twelfth birthday. I'd barely looked at him all night, thoroughly intimidated by his seventeen-year-old sophistication.

"Slightly." His lips quirked in a half smile as he lowered his head and softly pressed his perfect lips to mine.

I gasped as he lifted his head again.

When Devyn looked at me, my connection to reality wavered; when he touched me, I knew I would follow him into the pits of Hades without ever questioning why; when he kissed me, the universe trembled and blinked out of existence.

When Marcus, my match, my fated soulmate, kissed me for the first time, I felt…

Nothing.

Chapter Eleven

I was adrift. Marcus was my reward for walking the line laid out in front of me. My fingers worried at my promise ring. Our intended partnership was part of the Code that made up my existence. This didn't make sense.

After a restless night, I slipped out early. Devyn would have the answers. At least, he bloody better have. I didn't have the address to the apartment that was his official residence. I couldn't contact him online because he'd have a fit if I put something out there that connected us. I played with my mobile device, idly flicking through my feeds, scanning photos of my friends' graduation parties hoping for a glimpse of someone barely there in the background, dark head averted from the camera. But there was no sign of him. There were plenty of comments about me and the papped pictures with Marcus before dinner though. We looked like the perfect couple. No one looking at these pictures would think we were anything but matched. The speculation was rife that this was the case and it easily made the—

Oh no. There was one of us outside my building. I was half

hidden in Marcus's arms as he bent down to kiss me; I looked like I was in heaven, eyes half closed. Little did anyone know it was in rejection of the man kissing me, in the faint hope that when I opened them, it would be to the face of—

Linus's place.

Devyn would have gone to Linus's place if he didn't want to see anyone. If I had seen him kissing someone else, I would have wanted, needed, to be alone. Besides which I didn't have any better idea.

I changed into the shabbiest, most nondescript clothes I could find before packing the cloak I had procured at the outer walls into my bag. I raced across town and despite my building anger at Devyn, I kept to the protocols he had taught me before Oban and Marina's escape.

As I passed through Bishopsgate, I put on the cloak, pulling up the deep hood to hide my face, a face that was now splashed all over the society feeds, which were as avidly consumed here between the walls as they were in any other part of the city.

I was out of breath as I finally crossed the threshold of the dilapidated building, making my way hurriedly up the rickety stairs before pounding on the doors.

No sound inside. Yet I could feel him; I knew he was there.

I banged again.

"Devyn, open the cursed door," I whispered urgently holding on to the pendant. The flat inside was protected to prevent listeners but I was less sure about the landing.

The door opened and I went in.

Devyn was moving towards the small kitchen area.

"Chamomile?" he offered, not turning around.

"No, no chamomile," I gritted out.

I waited in mutinous silence while he busied himself with

making his cup of the hot tea so prevalent in the stews, his movements unhurried. He wasn't as casual about my arrival as he let on though. He still hadn't managed to look at me.

Finally, he turned, his face unreadable, and indicated that I should sit as he took a seat at the small table.

I glared at him.

"What did you do?"

"Do?" he repeated, surprise colouring his voice. "I haven't *done* anything. You wanted me to stay away, I've stayed away." He raised his cup in a toast. "Happy graduation. I see you celebrated in style. Is Marcus Courtenay everything you thought he would be?"

If only I had said yes to that chamomile. A hot cup of scalding liquid would make for such a satisfying missile right now.

"No, no, he isn't. Someone *somewhere* has made a mistake. He's everything any girl could want but he's not for me… We're not actually a match at all. They've messed up. The matching system failed. I'm going to have to go to my parents and let them know just how wrong it is. They have to get me out of it. They *have* to."

Devyn cut across me. "You can't do that, Cass."

"What do you mean I can't do that? We are *not* a match." I halted. Devyn had that intense, determined look on his face again. "I don't understand. What difference does it make to you? You're leaving, aren't you? In search of this girl. What does it matter to you who I spend my life with?"

"This time it's not about you," he offered bitterly.

I was missing something here. If it wasn't about me then it had to be about Marcus, who Devyn had explicitly told me he didn't care about. "Why are you so interested in Marcus all of a sudden?"

"He has Briton blood from a high family. A bloodline that has power. The council know all about it which makes him impossible to get to. I've been trying to get more information on him for weeks. All his data is locked down. I need your help; you're my only way in."

"I'm your only way in? What are you talking about? I thought you were looking for some girl. What does Marcus have to do with you?"

Devyn's only answer was to run his hand through his hair and stare at me tight-lipped. It wasn't the inscrutable mask he usually showed me when he didn't want to answer something. I could see the internal battle waged in his dark eyes.

He turned away and looked out the window onto the bustling street below.

"You remember the men on the dock who took Marina?"

I nodded.

"I had sent word out of the city for help in getting Marina out. She's barely more than a child so she needed more help than Linus did. I believe she has abilities and I had to be sure she would make it well beyond the reach of the council. I had to seek help from people who could help her, people from my past."

He'd argued with those men on the dock. Was that what this was about?

Devyn exhaled. "I have new orders – or at least, I've been ordered to stay a bit longer. I was already inside the walls anyway, so they asked me to take a closer look at the illness. It isn't just here, it's travelled beyond the borderlands. They believe it's something the Empire is doing, but they don't know what. It seems to attack those who have magic in their bloodline whether there's any manifestation of it or not. There were cases like this years ago in other parts of the Empire, places where magic has now been almost entirely eradicated. They hunted down the sick – no more magic, no more illness." He shook his head. "Marcus Courtenay is the only known person of a magical bloodline in Londinium. He's not ill, but he works in a hospital that's had some success in treating it and you have access to him. We want to find out what he knows."

"You want me to spy on him?" I shook my head. "No, Marcus is my future partner, my match."

"You won't do this because you think he is your match? Didn't you just say you know he can't be?"

"He was chosen for me by the system," I insisted helplessly. This had been my truth for half my life. I didn't know what to do with what I felt – or didn't feel – for him.

"No, Cass, you were chosen for him by them. My guess is it's because of your blood; they want to pair you both. Marcus is fifth generation. His great-great-grandmother, the one who married into the Courtenay family as collateral in the 1772 Treaty, was a Plantagenet. Her line was incredibly powerful. The city's council never knew how powerful. You are just a foundling child to them, but genetically, if you are from outside Londinium, your blood is likely to be at least a carrier, if not a latent or something more. Princess Margaret was married to one of their own, and their child married a citizen, and so on. That line is running thin which is why they've now matched him to you. It's probably the only reason they didn't kill you when they found you, or let you rot in the slums of the outer walls."

I shook my head, not sure which piece of information I was having more trouble processing.

They knew I was a Shadower. Marcus was not my true match. Rather, we were being put together to give the next generation of House Courtenay a bloodline that was more likely to carry magic.

"They want to breed us, is that what you're telling me?" My voice was on the high side.

"Yes, we think so."

"For what purpose?" I asked.

"We're not sure. It's got to be connected to the illness. It can't be a coincidence – a sickness attacking latents at the same time as they make moves to strengthen the only major latent bloodline in the city. We need to figure out what they're up to. The council must have been planning this for years: your adoption by your parents, their subsequent rise in society, being matched to Marcus, whose father is actually a member of the council. They're all in on it. It's clearly important to them, but why? Beyond eradicating magic, the Empire has never shown that much interest in it before."

He was talking about geopolitical machinations, but all I really heard was that my promise of a happy, blessed future with someone who would be my real family was all a lie.

"No." I stumbled as I stood. "No, I've done everything, everything the Code asks and now I don't even get to have my true match?"

I felt like someone had punched me in the gut. The future I had been working towards was no more.

And now what? What was Devyn asking of me?

My eyes stung and watered as I stared at him, at those dark, dark eyes – almost black as the shutters came down trying to veil the confirmation of what I now knew to be true. The city might be using me but he was no better. He wanted to make me his creature, a puppet he pulled on a string.

It served him now that I stay close to Marcus. Because I danced where he led, I couldn't help myself. I would do anything he asked me to. Just to be able to spend more time with him. Just to be near him.

My stomach seemed to fold in on itself as emotion slammed into me. No. No.

I stared at him, anger tearing through me.

"You, you are my real match, right?"

He stood immobile, staring down at me, a slight tick in his jaw the only sign he had heard me.

"Right?" I repeated, my tone demanding an answer.

His eyes closed briefly as he shook his head tersely.

"Outside the walls, we don't believe in matching using the codified system," he demurred.

Liar. What I had felt when Marcus kissed me was platonic compared to the quicksilver that whipped through me at Devyn's touch. I was drawn to him. He made me feel… more.

He wasn't saying he felt nothing for me. I knew he felt something. Maybe they didn't believe in matches in the Wilds, but there was something between us. How dare he. How dare he tell me more half-truths while my entire future was crashing down about my ears. I launched myself at him blindly, my fists raining down on his chest, violence surging through me looking for an outlet, for relief that could only be achieved by denting that impermeable surface.

Devyn took a step back in surprise as he found himself under attack, his arms coming up to capture mine as he lost his footing and we were falling, back onto the low, plain bed that sat behind the table.

I landed squarely on top of him, my wrists caught in his hands, our bodies in total contact. His midnight eyes opened wide in awe as he looked up at me. Then a flicker took his gaze lower, to my lips. Then lower still to the cleavage that pushed up where my chest met his, and I felt him change, felt him shift lower down. His hips moved to assuage his newfound discomfort, seeking an angle at the joining of our two bodies that would give him more space… or perhaps less.

My breathing quickened, became shallow, the anger fading from my melting bones.

I lowered my head until our lips were a sliver away from each other, his tilted slightly to one side, and then we were locked, our tongues dancing as the flames licked along my bones.

I pulled my hands out of his, freeing them to roam through his thick tousled hair, across his back, tracing the line of his spine, needing to learn him as his hands too danced from my hair to my breasts, moving restlessly, possessively, as our mouths met and merged.

His large body pushed me down into the mattress, his hardness driven against the junction of my thighs, pressing in to close any air between us, despising the trappings of our clothes.

And then his big hands came up and cupped my face, pushing me away from him.

His head was already shaking in denial, a denial his lower body was eagerly and assuredly in conflict with. My skirt had ridden up around my hips as I dazedly struggled for breath beneath him.

Sanity slowly returned to his eyes as a broken sound left my swollen lips. Yet it still took him another moment to gather his reserves of determination, his eyes steeling as he peeled himself off me, fixing my skirt as he went.

He sat on the edge of the bed, his head in his hands. "Cass, I'm sorry. That shouldn't have happened. We…" He paused, his head lifting as he ran his hand through his hair before half turning to look at me, still spread out on the bed. "That can't happen again."

My heart caught in my throat. I was reeling, my body still readjusting to the lack of him. A lack, it seemed, I was destined to feel from here on out.

Gritting my teeth, I sat up, looking anywhere but at Devyn as I adjusted my clothing. Finally, I got up and went over to the window; I watched the flow of people on the street below, which gave me something to focus on. Anything not to look directly at the man who had just rejected me.

I felt as though I had just run a race, a race where everything had been up for grabs, adrenaline and hormones whirling and surging, now with the anguish of defeat sucking me down.

My mind felt strangely calm, detached, and logical, assessing the next moves in the chess game. His kind might not believe in matches and my tech-oriented civilisation might scoff at soulmates but he was mine. *I* knew it. *He* knew it. But it seemed that reality wasn't something he was willing to admit to… because it was at cross purposes with his new mission or because it went against his commitment to this girl he sought, I didn't know. Devyn held all the major pieces and I could walk away from the board with no further harm done but I didn't want to give up. Too little experience of not getting what I wanted left me unwilling to concede the life I'd thought I would have with Marcus as well as the feelings I had whenever I was near Devyn. To play the game as it stood would be to suffer a drawn-out inevitable defeat and that didn't appeal either.

Which left me with only one option: pick up my queen and leave his game.

"You want me to ignore what's between us to continue to

help you and betray the city I live in, is that it?" I asked, turning back to face him in the dirty, dark little room.

Devyn looked back at me, his expression intent.

"Yes."

I shook my head in disbelief.

"I don't think so. I helped you get Oban and Marina out of the city. That's it. That's all I signed up for. You tell me I'm a Shadower and expect me to believe you just because I'm adopted. You can't prove it and I wouldn't care anyway. I like my life, I like my home and my clothes and my friends. I love the city." I took a step towards him. "The only thing missing is a future partner because I certainly don't want the one that they, whoever 'they' are, selected for me. I don't know why they want to reintroduce more Briton blood into House Courtenay. And I don't want to know. I don't want anything to do with any of it." I glared down at him. "As for you and your friends… why would I help them? What is it they're trying to do? Take down my city? You think I'm going to help the Britons overthrow us and haul us all back to the dark ages? Just because you asked nicely? To Hades with you."

Devyn pushed himself up off the bed.

"Don't be so naïve, Cass," he scoffed. "People are dying. This isn't about what you believe or what you want. Or what I believe or what I want. I've been asked to put those things aside and help. Because I can. You talk like it has nothing to do with you, like the pampered life you lead is yours by right and that you have no obligation to those less well off, whether those people live inside or outside the walls. You'd rather think about whether or not your shoes show off the latest fashion."

I shook my head in denial. I was pretty, popular, smart enough. I was not someone who was going to change anything more significant than myself. I didn't want to. Sure, it would be nice if people weren't getting struck down by this illness, but that was the concern of the council. It was up to them to make the world better. As for outside the walls, I had only the vaguest idea of how Shadowers lived and knew almost nothing about how the Britons lived in some feudal state where people didn't even have… well, I didn't have the least idea of how they lived with no technology.

I'd never really been all that interested. Britons existed; their visit to Londinium at Treaty time was an opportunity to ogle the pageantry of their entry into the city and attend the social events that surrounded the week, my primary interest lying in the strange fashions of the visitors to our city. It was also an excellent excuse to have parties. And that was a pretty satisfactory arrangement as far as I was concerned.

It had little to do with me and I was happy for it to continue that way. If the Britons wanted to know more about Marcus and his work, that was their business. Not mine.

"You're right," I directed at him, my hands balling into fists at my sides, "and right now, these delectable little shoes are getting me out of here. Away from you. Away from whatever it is you and your kind want from me. You want Marcus, you can have him, but it turns out he's not mine to give. You… you are…"

Devyn's whole body stilled, his face completely blank, his eyes black.

"You are nothing to me either." I had to brace myself in order to get the words out. It was the worst lie I had ever told in my mounting pile of them. But damn it, I had to scrape whatever pride I had left off the floor on my way out.

"Goodbye, Devyn."

Chapter Twelve

It was a glorious day in Richmond. Coming out to the villa was something we did every summer to enjoy a break in the holiday town with family and friends away from the hustle and bustle of the city. Of course, this far out tech was more temperamental but I always relished the relative peace it offered.

Mother coped less well, but the sight of Papa sitting out on the balcony reading physical books in a lounging chair was a sight that always gave me pleasure.

There had been no sign of Devyn, which was good, but I felt out of place in the beautiful house in which I had spent so many summers. This summer I felt utterly drained and found myself drifting listlessly from one room to the next. Without the endless stream of music, blasts, newsfeeds, and updates that filled my time in town, I was left to my own unquiet thoughts… thoughts that circled endlessly around Devyn. Out boating on the river with my friends, I wondered what he was doing and how he was spending his days. Playing tennis on the immaculate lawn courts perfecting my serve, I guessed at whom he might be spending time with. Though it had nothing to do with me anymore.

I was increasingly suffering from strange episodes where I ceased to be entirely myself. As I sat by the river with my friends gossiping about the latest insane fashion Miranda Decian – our summer nemesis – was wearing, watching weekenders row by in the little rented boats, sitting in the dappled sunlight under the trees a light breeze would float by and suddenly I would be mesmerised by the glimmering play of lights on the water as the river reflected the sun. Mesmerised was too light a word for it – I was less me and more there. The sunlight glimmer, the tilting breeze, called me to play and I was helpless to resist. My soul would soar out of me and dance merrily, freely, with my new playmates, returning clumsily as my friends would eventually notice that I had spaced out when I failed to answer a direct question, but then they would laugh and call me back… at least, that's how it started. As the episodes grew more frequent, Ginevra took to sitting by my side to nudge me urgently when I failed to respond when addressed. Sometimes I had actually just tuned out, bored by the idle chatter that up until recently engaged me fully.

I wasn't sure how to explain what was happening to me. When I took flight, I could actually see and hear what was happening around the bend in the river. I had contemplated starting to take the pills again, but it was hard to resist the pleasure I felt when my soul soared. I also needed to know the truth for myself. I couldn't bring myself to suppress the evidence that not only was I almost certainly a latent, it was probable I was something more. It was a link to the truth, whatever that might be. I could live my life in the city and marry Marcus, but the temptation to find out just a little bit more about who I was and where I was from was impossible to ignore.

Since the episodes were starting to attract attention, I tried to keep as busy as possible, which seemed to help. As long as I was active and focussed, I seemed to be okay, but that was exhausting, which made me irritable and less than fun to be around… which in turn didn't help in the keeping busy stakes.

Ironically, I was also spending quite a bit of time with Marcus.

We strolled along the riverbank in the glorious sunshine at weekends when he took the boat downriver to visit me. The days were filled with blue skies and music and brightly dressed people flitting about. We walked and talked, gradually getting to know each other.

I still felt nothing more than vague warmth towards him but when I had hinted at the idea that we might not be properly matched my mother immediately latched on to the notion that the boy from my party might be responsible. To keep her from turning her attention to Devyn despite our lack of contact, I was forced to play along.

What reason could I give for throwing over the most eligible man in the province? Better to just go along with it, for now… at least while Devyn remained in the city.

My friends were delighted at these visits, more than happy to be seen hanging out with the senator's son and keen to finally ride the wave of glory by association, their reward for having been discreet about my match for years.

To be fair, he was any girl's dream, and in a world where you had your partner handed to you by the Code, I had little reason to be disappointed. Watching him as we poked around the ruins of the old Briton palace, I had to admit that he put any man I'd ever met to shame. He was tall and had the most perfectly broad shoulders that tapered down to lean hips which were attached to long legs with a smooth stride that proclaimed his easy confidence to the world. There was no room in which he showed anything other than his absolute belief that he belonged… which was actually sort of starting to bother me until I realised that it was entirely faked.

As we spent more time together, I found that the master-of-all-he-surveyed, entitled senator's son was, if not a complete sham, then certainly more of an image he worked pretty hard to project than the real him.

It was a sham that, as far as I could tell, pretty much no one saw through, except perhaps his father. At the summer fair a few weeks earlier, we had bumped into the right honourable Matthias Dolon after we had been messing about on the river and taken a soaking when our boat tipped over. Our attempt to skirt the fair and get back to the villa as quickly as possible had been blown in the worst way possible.

We were giggling like children as we hurried along the street in our sopping clothes. I snorted at the sight of the river weed coming out of the back of Marcus's trousers where it had caught in his belt.

"Well, this is a sorry sight."

Looking up to find his father on the path in front of us, Marcus's laughing response to his unwanted tail died on his lips.

"You will be more suitably attired for the dinner party this evening, one hopes." His father raised a sardonic eyebrow at his bedraggled son, turning to flash his teeth at the elegantly attired group with him.

"Of course, Father," Marcus returned easily, or at least so it would have looked to anyone who hadn't spent as much time with him as I had. Although I wasn't sure if my newfound skill at seeing beneath the surface of things wasn't something I hadn't acquired under Devyn's tutelage.

His father laughed, every inch the doting parent as he gestured for the group to continue. "Out here in the countryside, I suppose the temptation to embrace nature is irresistible, eh, son?" Out of sight of his companions, the once-over he gave Marcus contained the edge of a sneer.

Marcus looked like he'd been slapped across the face. He bowed his head and his father passed on. I reached out to place a hand on his arm as he stood there while the group disappeared around the corner. As my hand touched him, he flinched away and continued stiffly and silently towards my house.

"Marcus," I called after him, not quite sure what had happened to leave him so changed.

He paused as we reached the drive to the villa before veering off and taking one of the trailing paths that wound through the villas back in the direction of the river. I followed, unsure if I was wanted but driven by the guilty awareness that if it were Devyn, I would want to know what was wrong and how to help. I owed Marcus no less.

Finally reaching the folly, he sat down, grimacing as he realised the river weed still remained attached to him. His expression was raw as he turned to find me hovering at the entrance, unsure of my welcome. Giving me a small smile, he ran his hands over his face before sweeping them decisively through his thick wavy hair.

Sitting up, he pushed his shoulders back, before looking at me again. I sat down gently beside him, reaching out to touch him comfortingly. This time he didn't shrug me away.

"I'm sorry," he said quietly.

"I don't understand. Sorry for what? What just happened?"

"I suppose you should know. It's only fair."

I suddenly had an idea about what was coming.

"I'm not entirely civilised," he began to explain. "I'm not sure if you're aware of the history of my family."

I was. Of course I was. His family was studied in my history classes, but if he wasn't already aware of his own coverage in our education system then this didn't seem the time to fill him in. Besides which, I wasn't sure where he was going with this.

"In the last set of wars between us and the Britons, part of the Treaty was that they married one of their princesses to my great-great-grandfather. She was the favoured daughter of the king of Anglia, and it was felt that the Treaty would be more secure if there were one of them in the city with us. It was essential if the Empire wanted to remain unmolested in the southeast, and for the last couple of hundred years, we've been able to farm sizeable tracts of some of the best land on the island… not to mention have access up the river to the sea for trade purposes."

I nodded, smiling wryly. "I am vaguely familiar with the terms of the 1772 Treaty. I did recently graduate, you recall."

In reward, I got a fleeting smile before he braced himself once more, his usually unguarded face suddenly anything but.

"I'm the last of Princess Margaret's line."

I bit my lip, unsure of what he was expecting me to say as it wasn't exactly a state secret.

"Wow, that's impressive," I finally responded. "Actual royalty in our midst."

He frowned. "Cassandra, you're missing the point."

"I am?" What deep dark secret would I have to keep now? I was starting to hate secrets.

He shot me a pained look before finally spitting out the words as if they were coated in acid.

"I'm one of them. I have Briton blood running through my veins."

I laughed in relief.

"Hardly *new* news." I waved a hand in the air to dispel the heavy atmosphere between us.

"Well, my father is all too keenly aware of it. He's not the greatest fan of my bloodline," Marcus said.

"That's a bit rich. After all, your father sits on the high council in the seat he married into, the seat that belonged to your mother's family, right? Which of course came down through the Courtenays, from Tobias Courtenay who married that Anglian Princess." I was outraged on his behalf. What *hypocrisy*. Says the girl who just pretended she didn't know every detail about his family.

He laughed, taking a small step back towards the Marcus I knew.

"That's true, but I think my father could live with it better if I at least looked more Courtenay or Dolon and less Wilder." He shrugged bitterly. "Apparently, if my face is anything to go by, my blood must be nearly completely Plantagenet."

"Ah." I suddenly saw why our encounter today had been so poorly timed.

A thought struck me.

"Your father married your mother and looks every inch the natural born senator. You sort of forget that, in fact, that seat was your *mother's*, the Courtenay seat. Shouldn't it be yours now?"

Marcus's laugh came more easily this time, the golden-boy aura almost entirely back in place around him.

"Yes. Which is possibly the only reason my father didn't

outright forbid me from becoming a doctor, rather a non-profession in his view."

"What do you mean, a non-profession?" I asked.

He threw his chin up and in his father's perfectly modulated tones continued, "*Medicine…* What is the point, Marcus? Proper citizens don't need your services and the rest can't afford it. What a waste of your time. But if you must, I suppose it's a way to fill your days until I retire and you take my seat on the council."

My jaw dropped. "No way. He's letting you work as a doctor, but only so he can continue to sit in the council seat that's rightfully yours? That's outrageous."

"Yep, and he was fairly happy about it, up until the outbreak. Now he's less happy. I'm fairly certain it's only out of fear that if I were to catch the illness and die, they might take the seat from him."

"Outrageous," I repeated, shaking my head.

"He's not entirely wrong though," Marcus added.

"Wrong about what?"

"Proper citizens have very little need for clinical medicine. Sure, for surgeries and so on, but diseases, viruses, and such are rare." Marcus flicked me a glance. "My mother died when I was young. She was ill for a long time – they couldn't help her – but a few years after she died, I was ill for a while too. I promised myself if I got better, when I grew up I was going to help people like me."

"People like you?"

"With Briton blood."

"You think you were ill because of your ancestry?"

"That's what I thought when I was a child since my mother had been ill too. Recent research seems to confirm it."

There it was: my opening to ask more about the illness. I

had told Devyn I wouldn't though. It felt like a betrayal to ask Marcus more about that research now.

"Their name and their blood."

"What?" I had been so caught up in my own internal debate that I'd missed what he said.

"That's my inheritance, and it will be our children's." He looked at me keenly to check I understood what he was telling me.

"Their name?" I asked.

"Yes, just as I was obliged to take my mother's name rather than my father's, I also must bear the Anglian name. My full name is Marcus Varian Edward Plantagenet Courtenay."

"That's a lot."

"Not only am I the last Courtenay, I am also the last Plantagenet," he said, returning to the subject of his Wilder lineage. He huffed out a laugh. "Did you know that the line of that house hasn't broken in almost one thousand years?"

"Really?"

"Mmm, they fled Normandy after the Empire crushed some rebellion there, came here and conquered Anglia… and apart from a spell in Mercia, they've held the kingdom ever since. All those Edwards, Margarets, and Richards for hundreds of years."

"Why were they in Mercia?" That was where Devyn's lord lived.

"Oh, we held Anglia for a century or so but the Plantagenets fled to their cousins in the north. They eventually came together under the rose banner – forming the Union of the Roses – and pushed back."

I frowned. "Mercia is ruled by the Plantagenets as well?"

"It was at that time. But the last of the House of Lancaster, as that branch was known, was killed in battle. His widow married a soldier called Owain Tewdwr from House Glyndwr. Their son married the Lady of the Lake, who was a distant Plantagenet cousin, I seem to recall, and started a *new* dynasty."

"The Tewdwrs." I had followed enough of that to identify possibly the most famous of all the Briton dynasties. Even *I* knew of House Tewdwr. "How do you know all this?"

Briton genealogy wasn't required knowledge, much to my recent frustration.

"When I was a child, I was ill. I had a lot of spare time. And the last of the York kings had just died, so it was in the feeds." He shrugged, glancing wryly down at himself. "Let's go and get out of these wet clothes."

The subject of Briton blood hadn't come up again but it played on my mind as we walked along the river a couple of weeks later and, on impulse, I led him up the track that went to the old Briton ruins.

"It's odd to think that this used to be territory held by the Britons only a few hundred years ago," I commented, looking around what I supposed would have been a small courtyard or an entrance hall – it was impossible to tell on this side of the buildings. Some were better preserved, the beautiful stonework redder near the crenellations, the foundation stones dark to the point of being black, from age perhaps, or maybe even the fire that had destroyed it hundreds of years earlier.

Marcus surveyed the ruins. He looked exhausted, I realised. He turned to me, the side of his mouth tilting up.

"Indeed, we'd have been stuck inside the city walls."

The period during which this castle had been inhabited had

been a low point in the ebb and flow of control of territory on the island. The Empire had been pushed back and limited to the walled cities: Londinium, Cantiacorum, Dubris, and a handful of other towns.

"We would have been killed on sight this far out of the city."

"I might have. Your ancestors probably danced in these halls." The lie came easily. For all that Devyn assured me I wasn't city-born, I had grown up believing myself civilised and that hadn't changed overnight because of some throwaway claim by a boy with a clear motive to lie to me… however much I was increasingly inclined to feel that it was the truth.

"Touché." Marcus acknowledged the hit. "I suppose they probably did."

I looked around, imagining that far-off time. On this very ground, the last great House of the Britons had lived and laughed and, by all accounts, generally made merry in between waging war with the Roman city on its doorstep. High King Arthur had been a clever leader despite suffering from poor health most of his life. The last of his line, the Tewdwrs, had united the tribes of Britannia and built their castle boldly on the very doorstep of the Empire's capitol. Arthur had expanded his reach through his marriage, a dynasty ended by the fire that had taken the high king and his Basque queen.

There had been rumours that his brother, Henry, and his niece had escaped the flames, but a dark war-torn era had ensued on the island, and the records were hazy regarding what had been going on outside the walls beyond the battles that had pushed the borders north again. That is, until the 1772

Treaty some two hundred or so years later had finally delivered respite from the constant warring.

"Do you ever wonder what your life might have been like if your family hadn't married into the city?" I asked, a thought that had recently been surfacing in my own mind. The expression I received clearly questioned my sanity before he even opened his mouth.

"Why on earth would I? I'm, what, a *fraction* Anglian? Besides which, if my great-great-whatever-grandmother had married into her own society, I, Marcus, wouldn't exist at all." He spread his arms wide to take in our surroundings. "This world is not mine; the one that takes place out here in the country isn't even one I particularly care for. I love the city, the towers reaching to the sky, the bustle of people toing and froing in the streets and along the river. The lights that keep our city bright, the technology that allows us to live lives that are fuller than they would be if we had to live in the primitive homes of the Britons." He smiled gently. "I'm pretty much only out here in Richmond because of you. I have no plans to ever leave Londinium."

My stomach dropped. I knew he didn't entirely love it out here – tech tended to be patchy this far from the city... something about the ley line that ran close to the surface. While I also loved Londinium, I felt restored after a summer out in the open air. I sighed inwardly. Would I have to give this up too once we were married? *If* we married.

As if sensing my reaction, which I felt I had hidden from him reasonably well, he held out a hand.

"But if my lady cares to dance while at court..." he offered, in the fashion of the stately Britons.

I smiled shyly, accepting his hand.

Evening was starting to fall, and there was the most

spectacular red and pink light in the sky. There in the court of the Tewdwrs he swirled me around, our laughter at our foolish behaviour echoing back off the ruined walls.

Until a wave of sorrow hit me like a wall.

I wanted to be in Devyn's arms. He wouldn't twirl me in a mocking parody of a courtly dance. I somehow knew that here on this ground he would hold me close, respectful of the dead who once lived in these halls. Fierce and proud, taken down before their time by sentinels who had crept in at night and lit up the sky in red and orange flames that would have been seen from the walls of Londinium itself.

I felt my bottom lip tremble… whether from the echoes of that night held within the ruined walls that left me unsteady on my feet or the lack of Devyn to support me as I crumpled to the ground, I couldn't be sure.

Marcus attempted to catch me as I fell, but I was at arm's length when my legs went from under me.

"*Cassandra*." He knelt beside me, his hands moving across my forehead and taking my pulse, automatically doing medical checks.

My eyes fluttered open, struggling to focus on his face.

"Hey." I felt terrible.

"Are you all right?"

"I'm fine."

I was not fine.

For a moment I had *been* there in the night, seen the flames licking out of the windows and up the walls of the building opposite, heard the sound of people screaming and running in their nightclothes from figures I recognised as sentinels on account of their night-black tunics and dark red cloaks. They were somewhat more martial than the version worn today, what with the breastplates, but recognisable forebears of the ones who had taken Devyn from class all those months ago.

The sights and sounds I had seen in that moment replayed in my mind. Most vivid were the sounds of horses, their screams almost human, their hooves battling against stall doors as the smoke and sparks invaded their space.

"This was a stable," I murmured.

There, in the last stall, a door burst open and two horses galloped out into the chaos.

The first bore a large man with a dark red beard atop a horse who mowed down a sentinel who stood in his path before being cut down by another. The second horse reared but the two riders held their seat, an adolescent boy fighting to stay in control, hesitating, before taking advantage of the distraction provided by the fallen man and riding for the gate.

Behind the rider was a small child.

She turned and looked directly at me, glittering green eyes in the most terribly angry face. A child with bright red hair. She had escaped.

Tears sprang into my eyes. But was it relief at the fate of a child who had lived and died hundreds of years ago or concern that I was finally losing my mind?

"What? How do you know?" Marcus asked. His hand softly stroked my hair back from my face.

I shook off the last vestiges of my latest and weirdest episode. How on earth could I explain my latest sign of lunacy?

"Know what?" I looked back at him as if I didn't follow his question.

"You said this was a stable," he offered softly.

"I did? I can't imagine why. Maybe because I felt like I'd been kicked by a horse."

Marcus chuckled softly.

"There aren't any horses here now. Are you feeling better? Can I help you up?"

"That would be good."

He started to stand, reaching beneath me to help support me as I went to sit up.

"Oh," he exclaimed, pulling at the object that had given him pause, unearthing a rusted horseshoe.

"Will you look at that." His voice remained casual even as he looked at me, studying me intensely like I was a specimen in his lab. "Seems you might be right."

I swallowed hard. Had what I saw really happened? Had it been replayed for me across the reaches of time through some kind of Wilder sorcery sewn within the stone?

"Told you I got kicked by a horse. If its ghost can pack that much of a punch, imagine what it must have been like in real life." My nonsense brought precisely the response I hoped for as he laughed and dropped a kiss on my forehead… the first time he had kissed me since graduation night.

I instantly froze. I liked Marcus, truly I did, but whenever he touched me in more than a friendly way, I felt like I was betraying Devyn.

Devyn who had pushed me away… to Marcus.

I needed to get over it, or I was going to have a rather awful marriage. A marriage to which it seemed I had become reconciled over the summer. It wasn't like my real match was an option anyway.

I smiled up at him, and in the hopes of covering my initial reaction I reached up and kissed him lightly on the lips. But I jumped back as the sound of falling stone interrupted the still warmth of the evening.

"Let's get you home, shall we?" Marcus's arm around my

shoulder urged me in the direction we had come. "Are you all right to walk?"

"I'm fine, really," I reassured him. I sincerely hoped I was. The last thing I needed was to add visions to my recent strange episodes.

I smiled tightly at Marcus and took the metal horseshoe from him, throwing it back on the ground. The sound echoed, and in it I heard horses screaming.

But there it was again, a cascade of rocks in the corner, pulling me back. I peered into the lengthening shadows, the sky still flame-orange above and the slight tang of burning in the air.

Nothing.

I couldn't dismiss the feeling of unease as we made our way out and home.

Chapter Thirteen

The next morning, I woke relieved in the knowledge that I wouldn't have to face Marcus watching me with concern – he had to get back to work. After the incident at the ruins, he had treated me like the fragile rose I knew I sometimes appeared to people. Petite but curvy, long silky hair, delicate fair skin, a cupid's-bow mouth, I was a veritable romantic dream, much to my own secret disgust. I didn't feel like the girl who looked back at me from the mirror very often these days. Vivacious and bubbly went with the old me, not this tired wraith who stared back at me. I dragged myself about the house until I noticed my father starting to give me the same watchful look Marcus had worn when he dropped me home at the villa the night before.

I felt drained; this last episode had left me on the floor. If it was just my imagination, I shouldn't feel like a stampede of horses had just mowed me down, surely? Could it have been real? Could what I saw actually be what had happened hundreds of years ago on that spot? For the thousandth time, I stood chewing my lip and contemplated calling Devyn. Would it really be so odd if I were to hail an old classmate? Why on earth would the authorities flag such an innocuous event? My fingers reached for the pendant I still wore around my neck, worrying it to and fro along the chain.

I had taken it off after I argued with Devyn but the distinctly Celtic pattern engraved on the back of the plain disk had left me nervous about leaving it lying around where someone might see it. Despite the permanent reminder of Devyn, I felt safer hiding the pattern by placing it against my skin.

Devyn would know what was happening to me. He had contacts among the Britons, like the people who had helped Oban and Marina. Maybe they would know what was wrong with me. It seemed to prove Devyn's theory that I wasn't city born – that, as a Shadower, there was Briton blood in my veins. Were these visions proof that there was even magic in my mixed blood? Or was it just the first symptoms of some strange new plague that we couldn't hide from, even out here in the luxurious country retreat of Richmond? But the episodes, the visions, didn't feel like an illness. Over the summer, as they had become more frequent and lasted longer, they had increasingly started to make me feel like I was more fully completely myself than I had ever been in my life. The sheer bliss of the moments spent chasing a light across the water or rustling in a bough left me nothing short of ecstatic in the moment. Afterwards, I reeled under the exhaustion with which even a few seconds of dancing in the air left me.

I just needed to curl up in the quiet somewhere while the fatigue passed.

More than anything, I felt drawn to the seclusion of the red and black brick walled garden at the top of Richmond Hill. The trudge up there almost finished me off but walking across the open heath I smiled into the sunshine in anticipation.

The air was warm velvet, the deer barely stirring to lift their heads as I drifted by. My feet tripped lightly across the bracken as I wove my way through the winding paths the deer had made in the tall ferns.

Finally there, I lifted the latch of the ornate gate and wandered through the cultivated paths of the garden inside. A haven of exotic plants and myriad flowers gathered from across the world was tended here in a protected enclave of the great park and it was my ultimate refuge.

As a child, I had begged my parents to bring me here to play among the fine-leafed, fiery coloured Japanese acer trees, whose names I had whispered to myself as I danced around them: crimson queen, garnet, red dragon. Now in full bloom, the rambunctious pink and white rhododendrons had hidden my secret den. I made my way past such children now, pleading with their parents to stay just a little longer as the sun started its mellow descent and picnics were packed away.

Deeper and deeper I went until I found the corner that was mine, past the exotic plants at the core of the garden, to a spot at the base of an ancient oak tree that overlooked the still pond.

Deep and darkly green, the pond was the epitome of reflective quiet and, after spending the summer running from my own thoughts, when I was too tired to run anymore this was where I curled up.

All the noise – my parents, my friends, my plans, Marcus, Devyn, the strange episodes I could no longer explain away, who I really was – all faded into the quiet of the pond. I felt as grounded as the oak, tethered to the earth, safe, when for so many weeks I had thought I might flutter straight out of my cage into a world that would batter me down.

It all faded away.

There was nothing but the still pond and the reflected sky, the trees, and the lengthening shadows. The silver moon brightened into gold as the sky darkened.

Finally, I slept.

And dreamed.

I dreamed of dancing, music swirling me down into the still pond where I lay stretched out, scarlet acer leaves reflecting, flower petals floating out of the sky, the twinkling laughter of a stream pulling me down its length and out of the walled garden, down the hill and up along the curve of the great river. The Tamesis was a comforting path that drew me along its curves and bends. Upstream. Through hills. By meadows. Further, away, further, along. Home.

I stopped. Not home. Not home.

A warning, a shout. Two travellers making their way along the river at night.

The teenage boy and the red-haired child from the Richmond palace ruins? I wondered. Another glimpse of the distant past? I wanted to know what had happened to her, that angry face looking back at me across time with fierce green eyes.

Somehow it didn't feel so thin or so far away. As the sentinels came into view, my guess was confirmed. What I was seeing was not now, not today, but days long past. This time, the uniforms were much more instantly identifiable, almost precisely the same black ones with their red insignia, led by praetorian guards, their collars glinting silver in the evening light.

The travellers had started to flee, their horses urged to make their way along the path, faster and faster. One of the horses stumbled and took its rider to the ground with it. The other paused and turned to go back. The rider on the ground stood and, reaching down, she grabbed a bundle from the fallen saddle bag, before continuing to run. She ran to the still mounted rider who paused on the path, caught indecisively between returning for his companion and fleeing the sentinels who were fast approaching.

My stomach swooped in terror for the woman who clearly knew she could not outrun her pursuers. She stopped and looked down at the bundle in her arms, then back to the rider. A small boy sat in front of the man, his arms reaching back to the runner on the ground, his expression one of horror and disbelief as he was held fast. Finally, the man averted his face before turning his horse and continuing to ride away.

The boy shouted but the woman was already whirling to face the sentinels, who were almost upon her.

She raised her hand, and the wind swirled.

"Cass."

My name.

"Cass."

No. I resisted. I wanted to know what happened, I wanted to see.

"Cassandra."

I looked back but the wind was up, mists starting to swirl over the river and across the still pond.

"Cassandra."

The voice was more urgent, insistent now. I couldn't see.

"Wake up."

It was an order, from a voice I knew.

I blinked and in the dark struggled to identify the shadow looming over me.

"Cass." A gentle hand trailed down the side of my face.

Devyn.

What was he doing here? When had it grown so dark? A moment ago it had been… somewhere far to the north of here. I tried to hold on to the last vestiges of the dream.

I whimpered. I wanted to know what had happened. Needed to know in a deep, soul-wrenching way. It was like something crawling on my skin, trapping me inside. Only finding out what happened would set me free. I needed to be free.

I pushed at Devyn. I needed to get him off because he had interrupted me. I had to get back there.

"Shhh, Cass, it's me." He caught my flailing arms and spun me around till he held me safe in his arms and my breathing slowed.

"Devyn." My voice sounded like I was about to burst into tears.

In fact, I could taste the salt of them with my tongue.

We lay there in the moonlight underneath my oak tree as I slowly came back to myself, Devyn holding me in his arms, occasionally lifting a hand to brush my hair.

I felt hollowed out, the only thing preventing me from splintering into a million pieces the strong arms wrapped around me.

My voice was smaller than I would have liked when I finally found the power of speech.

"What just happened?"

Even as I asked I wasn't sure I wanted to know.

"I'm not sure." So much for the great all-knowing Devyn.

My eyes narrowed. "What are you doing here?"

"Happened to be passing."

I didn't need to turn around to see his face to know it bore a smirk. I sighed.

Coincidences, I conceded, did happen. But Devyn, in the

middle of Richmond Park, in what appeared to be the middle of the night as I came out of the worst episode to date, was not one.

I didn't have the energy, didn't want to disturb the sense of safety I felt, the calm that had spread through my limbs in the comfort of his arms. I let myself relax into the lean length of him. For once I wasn't on my guard, I wasn't trying to be someone else – the good daughter, the dutiful debutante, the glittering girlfriend on the arm of the boy every girl wished she had. Just myself.

"Cass." His chest vibrated as he said my name. It was deep and rumbling in the dark.

"Mmm," I responded, too enervated to speak.

"What just happened?"

I huffed mutinously. "I don't want to talk about it." I wasn't entirely ready to admit out loud to the episodes I had been experiencing, much less give him the satisfaction that all signs suggested my veins definitely ran with Briton blood and without the pills suppressing it danced with magic.

I half turned towards him, snuggling into his shoulder, wrapping myself around his warmth. The summer evening had become chilly and I wasn't averse to taking advantage of that fact to get closer to him.

He wrapped his arm around me, tucking me closer, before bending his head to mine.

"Cass, please," he begged softly. "I need to know if I'm to help you."

"Help me with what?" I scowled into his chest. I really did not want to have this conversation.

"Really?" His sigh was exasperated in the extreme. "You've freaked out over handling a bit of tech and introducing chaos to the Code, fretted about the prison sentence involved in helping a sick girl escape the city, but discovering you have magic in your blood you feel you can just ignore? The moments you've been experiencing are only going to get worse."

I sat up.

"What? How do you know that?"

"How do I know you have magic in your blood?" He shrugged. "There was always a chance. That's why they're marrying you to Marcus, after all."

I frowned. "No. How do you know I've been having moments?"

"I just saw one."

"Right, *one*. You said 'moments', plural." I felt outraged and suddenly very sure. "You've been spying on me."

I could just about make out that eyebrow going up in the moonlight.

"I haven't been spying on you, Cass."

By now I was fully energised again, recovering quicker in his arms from my strongest episode to date than I had from the smallest of moments I had dealt with on my own.

"Liar." I straddled him as he continued to lie there leaning back against the tree but arguing with someone's profile in the dark wasn't very satisfactory. I stabbed my finger in his chest. "Li–ar."

Devyn sat forward until his face was mere inches from mine. Slowly, he reached up to take my accusing finger and wrapped his hand around it, lifting it away from his chest.

"I'm not lying, Cass," he said softly.

"I know you've been there." I recalled the sound in the ruins the night before. It was worth a shot. "In the old castle, you were there. Clumsy boy."

I tutted. His lips tugged upwards. It was him. I was right.

"Why didn't you say hello?"

"Cass..." he started, reaching to tuck a stray lock of hair that had blown across my face behind my ear.

"I missed you." I couldn't believe I'd put it out there but I couldn't contain it anymore. I did miss him. So badly. He was my first thought every morning and my last every night. Conversations became less interesting when I remembered I wouldn't be able to tell him about them. I suddenly realised I didn't care if he was using me to access Marcus; I didn't care what he wanted, as long as he was there. I know he didn't feel it as I did, that as far as he was concerned I was nobody.

He stood up and stepped back from me as he pulled in a long dragging breath.

"I'm not following you," he corrected. "I'm following Marcus, remember. Interestingly, his hospital is the only one to have had some success at curing the illness. I have my suspicions that he may be the reason they're doing so well at Barts. I was hoping to see some sign that he has... uh, opened up to his birthright."

"Magic?" I prompted, scrambling to my feet. Did Marcus have what I had? I hadn't seen any sign of him experiencing similar episodes.

"Yes, Cass, magic. His line is old, his blood is strong even this many generations on. It's not impossible," he explained. "But if he has magic, I haven't seen any sign of it. You on the other hand..."

His hands cupped my face in his excitement.

"You, Cass. You have magic in you, I'm sure of it," he declared.

This close, I could feel the beat of his heart, smell the warmth of his skin. I couldn't keep this secret from him.

"I think so."

His eyes were bright as he leaned in, as if he couldn't help himself, and touched his lips gently to mine. It was a soft kiss of sweet joy. In a heartbeat, the kiss deepened, and we were pressed desperately against each other, our hands roaming free to express the need we'd kept battened down until the touch of his lips released it.

I melted into him, breathing him in as the kiss deepened, dragging me down, down, deeper into the mindless haze. A haze where I saw the woman on the river cut down as she fled with the bundle still in her arms. There was blood everywhere and anguished blue eyes looking at me as the life in them dimmed and was gone. The horses' hooves danced perilously close and I screamed.

And screamed.

"Cass."

For the second time that night I came back to my senses to find myself in Devyn's arms as he struggled to secure me. Adrenaline raced through my veins. I felt terror and grief, a wild disbelieving sorrow.

"She's dead," I whispered brokenly.

"Dead?" Devyn repeated. "Who's dead?"

"The woman on the riverbank." My eyes danced wildly while the scene replayed itself again. "They never gave her a chance. They just ran her down."

I looked up at him.

"The sentinels ran her down. But the man, he just left her there," I muttered darkly. "He just turned tail and saved himself."

Devyn was looking at me strangely.

"Look, I know I'm not making any sense"—I was that aware of that at least—"but I know what I saw."

Devyn put his hand on the oak.

"Oaks are protective. They give strength and knowledge. It is a rare gift that comes to those in need of insight…" His face was pale in the half light. "…Or warning."

"Did you see anything else? Was anyone else there?" His voice was taut.

"No." I shook my head until I recalled the boy. "Oh wait, the man, he had a small boy on the horse with him."

The expressions that flitted across Devyn's usually controlled face were almost impossible to catch, they changed so fast: shock, hope, confusion, despair, resolve.

I looked at him, bewildered now. "What? Did I see something that really happened?"

There it was, the expression I was most familiar with: nothing. A stone wall would have more story to tell. My expression, I expected, was murderous. No way was he doing this to me again.

"Devyn, tell me what I just saw. I know you know something."

I was so tired of being locked out. Fury and frustration swirled inside me. I wanted to know. I *had* to know what he knew. I took one step and was back inside the circle of his arms. Reaching up, I put my hands to his face and forced him to look directly at me.

"Tell me," I demanded amidst the storm of emotions, my desperate need to know, and the echo of the woman's eyes as she held out the baby girl in her arms.

A girl I adored, would give my life to keep safe from the first time she wrapped her tiny fingers around one of mine and her blue eyes twinkled up at me. She was the happiest baby, stubborn when she didn't get her way and her mother laughed at me for being her pet griffin as we travelled across the wintry countryside.

It was my duty to keep her warm.

When I was big it would be my job to keep her safe, always. My father had told me so, but I knew this to be the single truth of my being without anyone having to tell me.

I heard the hooves before my father or my lady.

I told him, but he didn't listen. He told me no one was out this far from the cities this late in the season. But he was wrong, he was wrong. They were coming.

We started to gallop too late. My father's horse was bigger, faster, and we were leaving my lady behind. I screamed at my father, the terror rising as we looked behind to see my lady's horse had fallen.

The sentinels were closing the distance so fast. We needed to go back, we needed to go back. The urgency was pulsing through me. It was the only thought I could hold on to as my lady picked herself up and shielded her precious baby girl. My father needed to carry them to safety. My father wasn't moving. I didn't understand why he wasn't moving. I reached my hands out as if my will alone could transport that bundle from her mother's arms to mine.

Our horse took a step. My head turned as my father urged us away. Away from my lady. Away.

Nooooooo. The scream tore from my lips. I screamed her name, my soul hurling out all my despair.

The sentinels were riding her down.

My lady attempted to command the wind. I could feel it. I pulled away from my father to watch the scene we were leaving behind. The sentinels were afraid because they too could feel the wind being summoned.

They rode her down.

They rode her down.

The wave of grief as my lady fell swept in a wave across the land.

I reached desperately to feel the delicate connection that tied me to the precious bundle she had carried but I couldn't feel her.

I couldn't feel her, she wasn't there. The thread which carried that pulse of warmth I had savoured since her birth was gone. It was gone. Because I failed. The full impact of my lady's death hit me like a storm as the world went dark.

I had to find her.

I pushed away the hands that held me, that tried to stop me going to her.

I turned and stumbled away in the direction of the path.

"Wait."

I moved faster. The path should be right here. My oak tree was only four or five steps from it, my favourite perch above the still pond. I had been coming here since childhood. Why could I not find the way?

Where was she?

The frantic need and terror to find her pulsed in my blood and I crashed through the bush that blocked my exit.

"Wait, stop," a voice pleaded.

I needed to get away. I thrashed blindly at the branches in front of me. I had to get out of here. He was behind me… I turned to face him. My hand came up.

"Cass, no."

He needed to stay away from me. The trees rustled as the wind picked up.

"It's me, you know it's me. It's Devyn."

His words tumbled over each other as the trees started to sway. I couldn't listen. I would not let him get me. I raised my hand higher and smiled as the elements themselves surged in response. No one would hurt me this night.

The air in my lungs whooshed out as he tackled me to the ground, an oak branch crashing down where I had just been standing.

He was whispering gently to me as he kissed his way up my neck. His lips travelled across my jawline, my name a tender sigh on his tongue as his mouth caught mine.

His kiss was intoxicating and it was all that existed. I relaxed and the angry rustling of leaves died. He moved his head to kiss me more deeply. A hand swept through my hair to cup the back of my head and hold it safe.

Then he was laying tiny urgent kisses across my face, my name still tumbling from his lips. He returned to my mouth, softer, sweeter, gentler. I sighed, his tongue tangling in a tender dance with mine as I returned his kiss and whispered his name.

Devyn.

This was Devyn. I raised my hand to touch his irresistible black tangled hair.

"Devyn," I breathed.

He lifted his head away from mine.

"Shhh, it's all right." His hands again took up the reassuring stroking of my face and hair from earlier in the evening.

I trembled. What was happening to me? I felt exhausted.

"Devyn?"

"Cass." My name on his lips this time was a reassurance that all was well with the world. All was well with my world even though I was pretty sure my trembling limbs would not hold my weight.

"Your fault… you did this."

These visions, the dizzy spells, I had been so relieved to see him again, to touch him. This was all his fault. If I had never stopped taking my pills this wouldn't be happening and I would be in my old life. Safe.

I was safe because Devyn held me.

My eyelids were so heavy.

And I slept.

When I opened my eyes the next morning, I was in my own bed in the villa with the sun of another beautiful blue-skied Richmond day streaming in through the window. I felt strangely heavy as I pulled myself into the bathroom, and thirsty, so thirsty. I ran the tap to get some water.I cupped my hands in the cold running water to scoop it up to my parched lips and winced at a sudden sting. Refreshed, I stood gazing at my scratched hands.

Last night had really happened.

Chapter Fourteen

There was no sign of Devyn the next day, or the day after, or the day after that. In fact, the last days of summer passed entirely uneventfully and the episodes seemed to have stopped altogether. I thought maybe my own lack of energy was part of the reason, as though my heavy body was grounding me to stop me drifting away on a breeze.

Terrified that what had happened on Richmond Hill might happen again, I did everything I could to keep myself in this tired state. If exhaustion kept the episodes at bay… well, let's just say I was ending the summer much fitter than I had started it. As soon as my strength returned I pulled on my running shoes and tracked up and down the river. Always moving, always busy.

Night after night, I sat by the window staring up at the hillside, long after everyone else was asleep.

That night had left me blistered from emotion – and only Devyn could heal me. I had so many questions but he had disappeared, and left me with them.

I had trusted him. He knew what was happening to me, so

why wouldn't he tell me? The glimpse of the past that I had caught and the depth of terror, anguish, and grief that had ripped through the boy invaded my dreams so badly that I dreaded going to sleep.

Devyn had implied it was the oak that had allowed me to see the past, giving me access to knowledge. But as I watched the scene unfold the first time, the emotions had been my own, my own horror and fear for the woman attempting to flee the sentinels. I wondered who they were, this family that had been so brutally torn apart, that poor little boy. It nagged at me, night after night. In the first vision I hadn't even realised the bundle the woman carried was a baby. The second time around with Devyn had been so much deeper, so focused on the baby and the emotions she engendered in the boy. Had I invaded *his* memories? Was the baby the girl he had come in search of? I felt numb and shaky at the mere recollection of what I had experienced.

But it was Devyn that I tried and failed to push out of my mind. My cheeks burned at the memories which jumbled and tumbled over each other – Devyn's anger, the fear… hers, the boy's, I wasn't sure, but the lashing out had been my own. I could barely recall what had happened in those moments when past and present had blurred. I had barely known what I was doing, where I was. Who I was. It had felt like my mind had shied away from the feeling of violence, only to slam into the burning embarrassment of how he had managed to bring me back to myself.

He had literally seduced me back to sanity. In a world that had shrunk down to my emotions – fear, terror, the ferocious power that had promised to ensure my will was done – it was the tendrils of his kisses that had lured me back to him, back to reality. I had felt like a hurricane swirling fiercely across the oceans, devastating the land when it hit but ultimately blowing itself out on the ground to which it was drawn.

I cringed at the horror of those moments, though invariably it was at this point in the cycle of memories that my body was finally lulled to sleep, once more in the arms of the man who had brought me back from the brink. His arms around me, his whispered words comforting me, soothing me until my eyes grew heavy and I slept for a few hours.

Where had he gone? Why hadn't he come back?

When I returned to the city, the Treaty Renewal pre-season had already well and truly begun. There was a whirl of parties to attend and the city was hung with decorations and lights. It only happened every four years and the Province made the most of it from the moment of their entrance, revelling in the pageantry: the floaty Celtic Kernowans, the proud princes of Cymru, the martial leather of the armoured Anglian contingent led by the Steward of York. There were no Albans, of course; the Treaty only applied to those beneath Hadrian's wall because that was the furthest north the Roman territories had ever extended.

While the Britons were in the city, there was an undercurrent of wariness and danger that heightened the festivities, culminating in the masquerade ball at the Governor's Palace before they departed and everything went back to normal. Marcus, of course, unlike most of my friends, was already back at work, but thankfully he was able to make time to take me to a party on the first weekend after my return.

My mother watched me constantly. Apparently, she didn't deem the time I had spent with Marcus over the summer sufficient and she expressed her disappointment at the lack of attention my future husband was showing me in a hundred little ways. My appearance wasn't as polished as it had once been either, affording Camilla plenty to find fault with. My behaviour had changed and my new fitness regime and my constant air of distraction were both obvious targets. Without Devyn and the need to hide my meetings with him by keeping up appearances at home, I was left all too open to barbs but I just didn't care. My social butterfly days were behind me; I had become a moth drawn to a flame I knew would burn me. Now I was a forlorn, slightly singed moth drifting aimlessly in the absence of the light that had so dazzled it.

Attending a party on my return to the city with Marcus was somehow comforting because I was able to disguise myself once more in the glad rags and bright colours of the delicate protected butterfly I had once been.

At the sound of the door, I caught up my bag and, humming a tune, made my way to the entrance where Marcus was making small talk with my father. Their voices lowered as I approached. My father looked concerned but as Marcus turned my breath left me in a gasp.

"Marcus." I managed to catch myself and beamed warmly at him, my hand on his chest as I reached up to give him a peck on the cheek. But Marcus looked as I felt: a hollowed-out version of his former self. His lustrously thick, wavy hair hung limply, there were shadows under his eyes, and his high cheekbones sat gauntly in his face.

As we moved towards the door I placed my warm hand in his cold one – so often when I was with Marcus, I felt a little in awe of him. He was the golden boy of the city, stylish, charming, sure of himself, perhaps on occasion a little arrogant. I wondered if he felt as disappointed with our lack of chemistry as I did. Tonight though, that Marcus was markedly absent and my hand slipping into his was slow to be received before being gripped tightly, as if he needed the sliver of comfort it offered. Like dry soil absorbing a drop of water, the unexpectedness holding it on the surface for a second before the earth remembers its need and pulls down the much-needed moisture into its depths.

I winced a little as the grip became more than I could bear.

"Sorry," he mumbled, easing the pressure a little but not giving up my hand.

"Is everything well?" I asked as we waited for the lift. I was genuinely worried.

"I'm fine," he responded, "but I could probably do with a night out."

He looked like a party was the last place he needed to be.

"Are you sure?"

He turned, looking me up and down before lifting my hand to his lips in a light kiss.

"Very sure." He smiled. "You look beautiful."

I smoothed my skirt, nervous from his compliment. Given it was months since we had started seeing each other regularly, I knew our flirtation was much lighter than was the norm. Matched couples usually took full advantage of this period to properly get to know each other; I was just grateful that Marcus had shown as little interest in progressing things as I did… at least until now. Had putting my hand in his somehow indicated I was ready for more?

I caught a glimpse of us in the mirrors as we made our way through the foyer. We really were an incredibly attractive couple. I envied the girl in the mirror who was hand in hand with Marcus on her way to a party. If only the inside mirrored the outside.

"Cassandra, would you mind walking?" he asked as we approached the waiting car.

I gestured ruefully at my spiky heels.

"Of course," he said shaking his head. "I wasn't thinking."

Now I was really concerned. Marcus was a seasoned socialite when he wasn't doctoring. For him to have failed to consider that I was in full party regalia was highly unusual.

"Wait here." I pulled my hand from his and dashed back up to the apartment, popped my heels into a holdall to bring with me, and donned some more appropriate footwear. Then I made my way outside in my now less than coordinated outfit to where Marcus was leaning on the waiting car. "Now we can walk," I said with a smile.

"You can be a surprising little thing," Marcus said, swooping to place a kiss on the end of my nose.

My smile faltered a little at this further sign of affection and I saw him blink as he caught my momentary lapse. I smiled widely, tucking my arm through his to compensate. We walked companionably for a few blocks. Or at least, neither of us spoke.

"Cassandra," he finally said, "if you would rather not be with me, it would be best if you said so sooner rather than later."

"No, no," I got out breathily. "I'm sorry." How to explain why I pulled away when my future husband touched me… I cast about for a reason.

"I'm just a little new to all this." I grimaced inwardly.

"You're sure?" he asked. "It's not my bloodline that bothers you? I know not every citizen would relish the thought of marrying someone who is part Briton."

"No, really." I suddenly had a brainwave. "In fact, I'm adopted so I could be anything. Who am I to throw stones?

You are, what, fourth, fifth generation… as far as any of us know I could be a Shadower."

His eyes widened; perhaps it was time to dial it back. I needed to reassure him that it wasn't the old blood that ran in his veins that made me physically cool towards him, not give him a full confession of my own bloodline.

"I wasn't aware you were adopted," he said. "Do you know anything about your birth parents?"

I shook my head. "Very little. They were killed in an accident when I was a baby. I've never really given it much thought."

Until recently. Now I thought of little else. Over the last weeks I had wondered incessantly about the vision I had been given and the woman in it who had died trying to save her baby. What had happened to my own mother? Had she too been killed by the sentinels? Or was she still alive somewhere in the Shadowlands?

"You should get tested," Marcus said.

"For what?"

"For blood markers. We could tell you quite a bit about your genetic makeup. We've got a lot of DNA information on citizens from across the Empire. I'm afraid we have comparatively little information about Briton blood. Most of what we know is from diluted Shadower blood. We would at least be able to find out what you aren't and narrow it down a little."

"I don't know." I shifted uneasily. "What if I found out something I didn't want to know?"

"What?" he asked looking at me closely. "Like if you have mixed blood? It's incredibly unlikely, but it would be best to know."

"How so?" I asked, intrigued at what would be an unusual

statement for any citizen, but was even more so for Marcus given how self-conscious he was about his own mixed blood.

Marcus hesitated, apparently unsure as to whether he should say more.

"Cassandra, you cannot repeat what I'm about to tell you." He paused, I nodded, and he continued. "The latest outbreak... it's bad. More and more people are getting sick and we still can't figure out what's causing it. We're continuing to have some success at my hospital, more so than at any other, but we're struggling to pinpoint the reason for the recovery. One of the largest common denominators is that those with a high count of Briton genetic markers are more likely to get it."

What did that mean? Did a high percentage of Briton inheritance make them more likely to be latents? Was that who the illness attacked, those with magic in their veins? Were full citizens immune? Why were some recovering and others weren't? What was it that Devyn needed to find out, and could I get Marcus to give me something to tell him? I looked up at him to pursue it further and was again struck by how haggard he looked. What was I doing? I had refused to spy for Devyn for good reason. Marcus didn't deserve this.

"You've been working long hours at the hospital?" I prompted.

"Yes, I feel like I'm helping. I know I'm a lot more junior than some of the other doctors working at the hospital but I've had far more success at achieving recovery than any other doctor in the city."

I couldn't help myself as I smiled at his claim. He smiled back wryly.

"You think I'm exaggerating, tooting my own horn? I'm not, you know. If anything, I'm underplaying it. Very few patients recover. I'm the only one to have had any real success." He ran his hand through his hair. "If I only knew what I'm doing differently we could help more people. I could tell the other doctors so they could stop whispering every time I leave the room," he finished tiredly.

The sounds of music and the low hum of people announced our arrival at our destination. The oh-so-confident Marcus looked like a lost little boy in this moment, and I felt for him. I wanted to make him feel better.

"Let's pretend," I suggested, "that we are young, carefree, and in love. Let's laugh and dance, just for tonight."

He looked down at me, head tilting to the side as he considered my odd choice of words. Whatever he saw there seemed to satisfy him as a smile broke across his handsome face.

"Just for tonight," he replied, and he led the way into the party.

For a few hours, we were the perfect couple. We mingled, we laughed, we danced. His pale, gaunt look receded and the laughing charismatic Marcus resurfaced.

It was everything I would have wished for a year ago. We were the beautiful people in full dazzling flow.

Marcus pulled me close and whirled me onto the dance floor, his arm circling me, his hand on my lower back as he flashed his open smile my way. The fatigue and frustration that had engulfed him earlier seemed almost entirely to have dissipated. Anyone looking at him would believe he hadn't a care in the world. But I had spotted him looking at his comms device a few times during the evening, checking in on his patients, I guessed.

For now, though, he was the life and soul of the party. He twirled me around and I came back into his arms while my hand went to his very respectable chest; I laughed up at him and I felt a frisson of the awareness I had felt was so lacking previously. Marcus caught the change and his hand came up to caress my face as we stilled in the middle of the lively dance floor.

His bright eyes darkened and he leaned in just as we both felt the vibration of his comms device.

"Sorry," he apologised wryly, reaching for it. Whatever he read caused the glamour to drop away revealing the careworn doctor once more.

"I've got to go," he said apologetically. "One of my patients appears to have worsened. I asked a nurse to let me know. She says they've tried everything. I know it sounds arrogant, but I may be his last chance."

"Of course," I replied moving towards the door.

Outside, he placed my wrap around my shoulders as he nodded to the doorman to indicate he needed a hackney. "I can drop you at home on the way."

"No thanks," I returned sitting in the car already waiting for him.

He looked at me in consternation.

"I'm coming with you," I announced.

"Cassandra, you can't come to the hospital. There are a lot of sick people there. We don't know how this virus is spread. Your parents will go mad."

"How will they find out?"

He sighed. "That's not the point. You simply can't come."

"It's fine, I've already been exposed," I announced to reassure his fears.

"What? How?"

Uh-oh. I had failed to think this one through. I could hardly tell him I had nursed a young girl through her escape from the city.

"Uh… one of my classmates was ill with it," I concocted hastily.

"You never mentioned," he said.

"Yeah, well…" The number of people surviving the illness was not high and the chances he would recognise the name of a survivor were higher than if she had died, leaving me with little choice but to explain why I hadn't deemed the death of a classmate of the very virus he was battling worthy of mentioning before now.

"We weren't terribly close. In fact, we had… sort of had a fight a few weeks before graduation and I never had an opportunity to make it up with her so I don't really like talking about it."

"That's terrible." He wrapped his arm around me in sympathy.

"Yeah." I might as well make the most of it if I was going to go there. "Maybe seeing the victims will help me deal with the fact I wasn't there in the end for her."

There was silence while the wheels turned in his mind. He was a doctor; behind the image of the party boy lay the soul of someone who just wanted to help people.

"It would also be amazing to see where you work," I added, laying it on thick. "It would give me the opportunity to understand that side of you."

His arm tightened. That was the clincher, I knew it. At the back of it all, Marcus felt separate, whether because of his father or his blood or his profession I wasn't sure. He wanted closeness and here I was offering it up on a plate.

I was a horrible person.

"All right then," he said, confirming my prediction.

I was unprepared for the sights and sounds that threatened to overwhelm me as we arrived at the hospital where Marcus worked. I had always loved the romance of the ancient building, one of the oldest in the city. It was here, closest to the East End, where the poor of the city gathered with their sick. There were hundreds of people swarming around the entrance to the hospital. The feeds had indicated that the illness had got worse; I had even heard it described as an outbreak. But this, this was an epidemic of unprecedented proportions.

"Can't go no furver, Guv'nor." Our hackney drew to a halt at the edge of the human tide.

"That's fine." Marcus paid as I got out of the car, wrapping my silk throw closer around me, shamefacedly raising it to cover my nose and mouth as the smell of the ill and decidedly unwashed hit me.

"This way." Marcus led us towards a side entrance.

People lying on the ground plucked at my skirts as we made our way past them. I shuddered; I'd had no idea the situation was this bad.

The guard behind the barrier raised a hand in greeting to Marcus as he flashed his ID at him on our way past, giving me a nod to go through. While the seriously ill people who lay strewn across the street were clearly being denied entrance, as a member of the elite my access was unquestioned. Once inside, the cleanliness and quiet were a relief, if something of a shock. From inside the hospital, it was almost impossible to imagine the shivering, moaning mass of people on the other side of the wall. I looked to Marcus for an explanation.

"What… ?" I wasn't sure what question I wanted to ask, or how to ask it. How could he walk past all those people and not offer help? Why were so many ill outside while the hospital seemed serenely unaffected?

Marcus was already moving on, across the cold tiles of the lobby, and taking the stairs two at a time. I ran to keep up, following as he hurried through the quietly busy corridors. I caught glimpses of labs and white-coated doctors huddled together with an understated urgency to their movements. An occasional open door allowed me to glimpse a single or a handful of well-tended patients inside. The small private rooms and slightly larger wards all had their doors closed and a symbol I was unfamiliar with marked the entrance.

It was a sort of spiky inverted curve. I might not have seen it before but its meaning was distinctly sinister. Were all the patients behind the doors infected? If so, the scale of the epidemic was far greater than I had imagined, despite Marcus telling me that the number of incidents had increased dramatically over the summer.

Marcus remembered to look back at me a couple of times as he rushed along, but his pace remained a steady hurry until, at last, we came to a stop in front of another set of doors carrying the ominous spiky symbol.

"Cassandra, are you okay?

I nodded, though I was increasingly regretting the impulse that had led me to insist on joining him. I had no business being here and already felt hopelessly in the way. Casting a glance at the outfit that he had admired earlier in the evening, Marcus's lips pursed.

"Wait here." When he returned, he had donned a white coat and had a blue one that he handed to me.

"You're a little overdressed for this particular ward." He winked and pushed open the door.

The quiet, polite wards we had passed on our way in, which had been the cause of the building ball of rage in the pit of my stomach, were nowhere in evidence here. The long ward was heaving with people. Bodies lay on every surface capable of holding one.

I followed as Marcus wove his way to the far end of the room, averting my eyes from the pain-wracked bodies around me. These people were far sicker than Marina had been. I wondered if out there beyond the walls she had ended up like this? A nurse approached Marcus and whispered to him, shaking her head. He continued on, coming to a halt beside an older man who had somehow scored a bed in this mayhem.

He took the man's hand gently. "Otho," he called softly. The man in the bed stirred and groaned, his eyes lifting tiredly.

"Boy." He smiled weakly in greeting.

"Otho, what's going on, you old duffer? Nurse Miri tells me you've not been feeling too well this evening," Marcus said close to his ear so he could be heard above the din of background noise. The old man grimaced, his lined face wrinkling up in pain.

"Final stretch, lad," he answered.

Marcus looked momentarily alarmed before determination took over.

"No you don't, old man. We haven't made it this far for you to give in now."

As Marcus spoke, his free hand came up to rest on the brow of the sick man, who looked a little stronger. I edged closer. There was an odd aura around Marcus now. Watching him closely, I couldn't quite put my finger on what was different about him, but there was a distinct difference in the energy around him.

"Lad." Otho raised a hand and pulled Marcus's hand from his brow. "It's my time. You've done a miracle job keeping me going. I got to see my Marcella get married. Can't ask for more than that and she's well looked after with her Tony. But I'm tired now. I thankee boy, but I'm tired."

Marcus bit his lip as he stared at the older man before he straightened his shoulders and stepped away from the bed.

"All right, Otho," he said resignedly. Marcus looked shattered, his skin tinged grey as he took his hand out of Otho's to pat him lightly on the shoulder.

"You won't mind if I stick around though," he said, settling himself on the foot of the bed as if he no longer had the strength to stand. He raised a brow in my direction and, nodding, I took a seat on the other corner.

The old man, who had seemed so much stronger only moments earlier, sank back in the bed, not even noticing me as I took my place beside Marcus.

We sat in silence as I contemplated what I had just seen. Devyn was wrong. Marcus *did* have magic and he was using it, I was sure of it.

Marcus could cure the illness.

And it was killing him.

Chapter Fifteen

I pushed past the man obstructing my access to the side corridor into which I had seen Devyn slip. I hurried cautiously along the candlelit hall, unaccustomed to the flickering light and pools of darkness that the inconsistent light offered in these halls. At the centre of the city, the Governor's Palace was always ablaze with electrically generated light. It felt odd to be traversing its chambers in the half light, but now the Britons were in town, the Governor's Palace was suffering the same inconsistencies in power supply that their presence caused as everywhere else.

At last, I caught a glimpse of him up ahead.

"Devyn," I hissed.

He hurried on, oblivious. Damn it, Marcus was in trouble. He was using his own energy to help people, I was sure of it. Devyn might not want to talk to me right now but if I didn't get help for Marcus, he was going to die.

Besides which, Devyn would relish the sign that the old blood ran strong in Marcus. If only he would stop running away from me. This was the first and only sighting I'd had of him since returning to the city. I hadn't even been planning to come to this event as Marcus was working and my strange new abilities made me loathe to get any closer to the Wilders in our midst. I'd even skipped their entrance into the city, which was quite the spectacle, missing out on the unexpected arrival of the Mercian prince, which was all anyone was talking about. This was the first member of Mercian nobility to attend in years – the king had stopped attending decades earlier after he married the Lady of the Lake. The city was whirling in speculation about their handsome son. But I had concerns of my own. Whatever was going on with me, I needed to figure it out, to understand it. What if the Britons could tell I had magic? But my parents had insisted, so I had come.

A stuffy diplomatic social was the last place I had expected to see Devyn. On the plus side, my parents had been too busy sucking up to some senator to notice me slip away in pursuit. I came to a fork in the corridor. Left or right, I wasn't sure which way had he gone. Running through hallways and up staircases in full formal recital regalia was not recommended; I had dressed for light activity, not hot pursuit. I heard something from the left and started in that direction only to come to an abrupt halt at the sight of Devyn, half-naked, with some strange girl's hands all over him.

What in Hades?

His eyes were closed, a look of utter bliss soothing the strain I had glimpsed as he slipped out of the recital. The girl was dressed in garb every bit as elaborate – though far more exotic – than my own. One of the delegation. Who was this Celt Devyn was so clearly delighted to see and whose touch he welcomed? And in a manner in which he had never welcomed my own.

My breath left my body in a hiss.

Devyn opened his eyes, his head jerked back at the sight of me.

"Cass."

I raised a hand to stop him from speaking further. Bitter rage swirled within me as a wind snapped through the corridor, leaving us all in darkness.

A snicker sounded from the alcove before a ball of fire appeared in the hand of the half-lit Briton girl… and then all the candles came back on.

Oh gods. Was that *magic*? In the city?

Hers? Mine? Had I done that? Inside the walls? I couldn't breathe. Devyn's defensive illusion was one thing but an external event that people could have seen, with a Celtic delegate present? The consequences didn't bear thinking about.

"Looks like your delicate flower is miffed, Devyn," the girl trilled softly.

My jaw set. I literally had no words for how much I loathed Devyn Agrestis. He hadn't wasted much time.

"Cass," he attempted again, this time pushing the girl's hand away and tugging his top down. Better. The fury whipping through me calmed somewhat as he stepped away from the girl. I didn't want him. At all. That didn't mean he could start doing whatever he wanted with some Celtic stranger.

"This isn't what it looks like."

"How clichéd," I interrupted. "What you do and who you do it with are none of my concern."

The girl watching our exchange with an amused curl on her lips actually snorted at that. I glared at her in unison with Devyn.

"Shut up, Bronwyn," he snapped. "Cass, really I… we need to talk, but this isn't a good time. You need to leave."

"Why, so you can get on with your little groping session?" I waved behind him to the alcove.

"Ew," came from said alcove.

Devyn sighed, looking me directly in the eyes.

"Honestly, it really isn't what it looks like."

My stomach dipped. I really wanted to believe him. "Then tell me what it actually is."

The girl stepped out of the alcove, swaying up behind Devyn and patting his chest.

"I was looking after him. He needed a little fixing up after a tussle in a certain moonlit glade," she said archly.

I blushed, horrified.

"Seriously, shut it, Bron," he snapped, rounding on the girl.

I decided to ignore the fact that he had told this girl something about what had happened between us. In fact, I couldn't do this at all.

I whirled away, breathing deeply, but it was too late. I was spinning out of my body, drifting. The elements started to swirl overhead in answer to my call, a new wind killing the candle flames as it whipped through the corridor. Lightning from the storm outside crackled and split the darkness.

Devyn grabbed me, wrapping his arms around me, earthing me.

"Come back, come back, shhh," he soothed, removing the mask and brushing a hand through my hair as I stiffly resisted him. "Cass, shhh, it's okay, you're okay."

My body started to relax into his and I melted into his arms as the brewing storm calmed overhead. I pulled a deep breath into my lungs. That had been… I shivered. What just happened?

Devyn turned me in his arms so my head was tucked under his chin, continuing to stroke my hair and softly repeat my name until at last I felt fully restored to my body. Increasingly aware of the warmth of the arms around me, I pulled away and glared up at him.

"Don't touch me," I warned, my voice shaking, looking nervously around for cameras.

"Don't worry, we're safe here," Devyn said, realising my concern. "The Governor's Palace is one of the few buildings in the city entirely surveillance-free. The transparency of the Code isn't applied to those at the top, making it the safest place in the city to do things you wouldn't want to be seen doing."

"Well, that was dramatic." The girl had stepped out into the corridor, another flick of her fingers relighting the candles. Her voice was sardonic, but her eyes were sharp as she ran an assessing look over the tips of my daintily clad toes to the top of my elaborately done hair. "Certainly explains the broken ribs."

I was confused. "What broken ribs?" I asked.

"Shut up, Bronwyn," Devyn ground out, seemingly the only words he ever said to the girl.

I looked back between the two as they shared a complicit glance. A horrifying thought occurred to me and I scrabbled to open the shirt that was still hanging loose and exposed Devyn's chest. Bruises, purple, yellow, and green, were liberally mottling his lower ribs.

I looked up at him for an explanation but he was giving his stonewall face.

I looked to Bronwyn.

"Oh, it's fine, totally fixed," she gestured, wiggling her fingers in the air. "Hocus pocus." This came with an accompanying wink. "All better now. The colour will fade in a couple of days."

I struggled to process this information. The colouring was shocking and those bruises were old… from the night on Richmond Hill, when we had fallen? I was horrified. I'd done this to him. He'd carried me home like this?

Hang on. Hocus pocus? How much had he told this stranger?

I scowled, pushing aside my sinking suspicion and deliberately ignoring Devyn's friend, instead addressing him directly.

"Devyn, I need to talk to you." I sniffed. "Privately."

Devyn looked back impassively.

"Now is not a good time."

"Then when is? I haven't heard from you in nearly two weeks. You don't like me to contact you over the ether and Linus's home has other people living in it." I'd gone there looking for him, but the elderly woman who answered the door had been clear that no friend of mine could possibly ever have lived there before slamming the door in my face.

"I'll come to you." He paused. "Give me a couple of days. I just need to arrange something."

I wasn't sure Marcus had a couple of days. He looked really ill and judging by the number of people at the hospital, he was likely to make himself worse, very quickly.

"No." I planted my feet firmly on the ground. "Now."

Bronwyn shifted behind him.

"I don't think so. You can both catch up whenever you like. Devyn and I only have until somebody passes by, so if you don't mind, princess."

Devyn's mocking little nickname annoyed me at the best of

times, but out of the mouth of this person it was like a red rag to a bull.

"Who do you think you're talki –"

Devyn caught my arm as I started to round on the taller girl.

"Dammit, Cassandra, I really do need to talk to Bronwyn. I promise I'll find you after."

My mouth set mutinously. Okay, maybe I *was* coming across like some crazy stalker, but Devyn was too prone to disappearing for me to let him out of my sight now.

"No."

Devyn exhaled.

"Fine." He looked at the other girl. "Bronwyn, have you set everything up?"

The girl cast a sidelong glance at me, arching a brow. "I haven't spoken to her yet. Are you sure about this?"

"Yes," he answered without pause.

Bronwyn sighed. "Things are pretty tense this visit. You risk our lives for what is likely to be nothing."

Devyn looked at me as he answered.

"It's not nothing."

"So you say." Her head tilted to one side. "We've just had one miraculous resurrection, why not two?"

"What resurrection?" I asked quickly.

Bronwyn sent an unamused look at Devyn before responding.

"Well, up until those two little lost citizens arrived across our borders, we hadn't had word of Devyn here in years. We had to join this year's delegation to see for ourselves. We were pretty sure he'd got himself killed on his foolish quest."

"Quest?" I repeated. "What quest?"

I looked from one to the other. Devyn, at this point, looked murderous.

"Shut up, Bronwyn," he groaned again, which clearly tickled the other girl.

"I know why he's here… or rather, who he's here for," I threw back smugly.

"Ooh, really?" She arched a defined brow at Devyn. "You've told her why you've been chasing a ghost? All of it?"

"Enough."

Devyn clearly meant business this time and Bronwyn decided she wasn't going to share any further, much to my frustration.

Turning her attention to Devyn once more, she continued, "I've spoken to Llewelyn about it and he's sceptical. He believes you see what you want to see and that you've been citified for too long. Whatever the truth is, we cannot let even a hint of this reach the family. If there's even a chance she is who you think she is, they'll want her back at any cost. And the cost would be many, *many* lives. We need proof… more proof than your feverish suspicions."

Devyn swore.

"That's exactly why I need this favour. But Bron"—his eyes gleamed—"you've seen it now, with your own eyes."

Were they talking about me? Had Devyn changed his mind? Did he now think I might be the girl he sought?

Bronwyn shrugged. "Saw what exactly? The candles went out. Maybe the storm outside came in quickly. *Maybe*. Yes, she saw the past. She might have some power, but you've admitted you don't have any connection."

Devyn frowned at this, shaking his head. "I can't feel it, but sometimes there is something there. Something that's more than I would expect if I were nothing to her."

"But not a real connection?" Bronwyn pressed.

"No," he admitted.

This cryptic conversation was irritating me no end, but their hushed and hurried exchange suggested that explanations would not be forthcoming. I would have the truth out of Devyn as soon as I got him alone.

"Llewelyn says it's nothing more than a coincidence and that you should come home. Every so often a latent turns out to have some ability – that's all," Bronwyn continued.

"No." Devyn shook his head. "I know I'm right. I can't prove it, but the glimpses I've seen, the feeling I can't shake… I've suspected for years, and in the last couple of weeks I've grown surer of it."

"Devyn, please, you have responsibilities. You swore an oath. Enough of this. Wishing something is true isn't the same as it being true. You sent word yourself that you had given up on the search in Londinium," she reminded him. "The girl is matched to Marcus Courtenay, and that is of more use to us in current circumstances. That should be your focus."

Devyn shook his head again.

"Please don't be foolish. Do as they ask then come home." Her stern tone softened as she added, "The old Griffin is very ill. Don't you want to speak to him, just once, before he goes?"

Devyn's eyes went dead. I'd seen him shut down before but not like this. He wasn't just masking his emotions, it was almost as if he didn't have any. The light in his eyes was utterly extinguished.

"Bronwyn, if you won't help we have nothing more to say." He started to turn away, his demeanour cold.

"You're a fool, Devyn," she hissed.

My frustration finally bubbled over and I screeched.

"I am so entirely over all of this. If I have to listen to any more of this… this… cryptic, mysterious half-talk I'm going to explode." I turned stabbing a finger in Devyn's chest. "*You* won't tell me anything, *you* told me to stop taking the pills, and I did. Now I keep having these episodes which I need someone to explain to me. Everything I thought was the truth is a lie. Everyone I've loved would turn away from me if they knew. My parents, the people I should be able to trust above all, are the ones who have betrayed me the most. I finally believe that this is all true and the only person who can explain any of it to me disappears."

"Cassandra, you didn't want me to tell you anything more than the bare minimum," he reminded me placatingly. "You wanted nothing more to do with me."

I was so angry I could scream. How dare he throw that back at me. That was before, before… everything.

"Great," I responded scathingly. "Thanks so much for taking anything I've said into account as opposed to doing or telling me only what suits you at any given time. Thank you. Sincerely."

A snort from behind me had me twirling around.

"As for you, whoever you are"—I glared at the black-haired girl with her Celtic dress and her twisted torc—"I do know why he's here. I've heard all about the girl he's looking for as well as all about your interest in Marcus. But I'm not spying on him or anyone for you. I don't care about any of your nonsense. I had to find you because Marcus is sick."

"He has the illness?" Devyn asked, suddenly alert.

"No, it's not that," I said, putting my hand to my pendant. Despite Devyn's assurances that there was no chance anyone was eavesdropping inside the Governor's Palace, it couldn't hurt to be careful. "Marcus has been using magic. I've seen it."

Devyn's attention sharpened. "What? When?"

"You were right. He's the reason Barts hospital has been having some success treating the illness. I think he's been using it since before graduation." At this, Devyn exchanged glances with Bronwyn. "He's curing people, but he's using magic to do it. And it's killing him."

"You're sure?"

I nodded. "I've seen him do it. I know it was magic and you should see him… He's wasting away."

Devyn threw Bronwyn a triumphant look which was met with an acknowledging wry twist of her mouth.

"There is someone who could help," Devyn answered me, still grinning at Bronwyn.

Bronwyn groaned. "Fine, you win. I'll talk to her. Looks like we'll be getting two for one now."

I looked from one to the other of the Britons as they continued to speak to each other in cryptic, annoying half-sentences.

"Thank you," I gritted out before a thought struck me. "Why hadn't you noticed already? I thought your orders were to spy on Marcus."

"Ha." Bronwyn's eyes rolled. Hard. "Yeah, and Devyn is so obedient when it comes to his orders."

Devyn shot her a quelling look.

Bronwyn paid precisely the same heed to that as she had to his earlier verbal demands to shut up.

"Devyn isn't interested in Marcus Courtenay. He broke his oath and ran off to Londinium for one reason only, and that is the only reason he does anything," she said.

Finally, a cryptic statement I could actually follow.

"The girl, the one you came looking for…" I felt protective of him in the face of the other girl's mockery. For Devyn to have risked so much to come here, she must mean a great deal to him. Was I crazy to suspect he thought I might be her again? My brain went into overdrive, gears grinding as pieces fell into place. What else had happened besides the episodes, the visions? Maybe what I had seen was connected?

"The girl, the one you're looking for, was she the baby in my dream or whatever it was? Or does she have something to do with the red-haired man and child I saw in the ruins at Richmond?"

The mention of my visions made the Celt's eyes go round, her eyes flicking to Devyn for confirmation that she heard correctly.

"You didn't say she had seen Elizabeth Tewdwr as well," she said sharply.

"I didn't know. This is the first I've heard of it." Devyn smiled. "But I would say that was interesting, wouldn't you?"

Two sets of dark eyes turned on me.

"What? Don't you like it when I know something you don't? Too bad." My jaw set. Why did he always have to be the one with all the information?

"Cass," he demanded.

I let out an annoyed huff. "I would have told you if you hadn't disappeared on me. The night at the ruins, with Marcus, was actually the first time I saw something in the past. I saw the castle burn, and I saw her escape. I don't know why or how, or what it means. I don't know what any of it means. I don't know who that woman was on the riverbank in the other vision either, but I think the boy was you. I think the person you're looking for is the baby. But the baby and her mother died. You saw them die. You felt it."

"You saw her die?" Bronwyn interrupted, directing her question at Devyn. "You've always refused to confirm that...

So then why are you doing this? You threw away what little life you had left and have risked your head for nothing."

"Because I have to know for sure. Unlike everyone else, despite all the evidence, I never felt sure," Devyn replied before returning to the subject of my visions. "Cassandra saw my lady die. Why her?"

"Why Elizabeth?" Bronwyn returned just as quickly. "She sees things from the past. She's not connected to the first so why do you have to believe she is connected to the second?"

"Gods," I appealed to the ceiling.

Devyn turned back to me. "I'll explain everything, I promise. But I have to find out the truth first. Please, Bronwyn," he implored the willowy Celt.

Bronwyn looked from him to me and back again. She nodded.

"Let's see if we can find out the truth."

I gritted my teeth. "What bloody truth?"

They both looked at me, their dark eyes glittering in the candlelight, measuring me, before Devyn answered.

"Who you are."

Chapter Sixteen

I entered the tent cautiously. I wasn't sure I wanted to be here, but Devyn felt confident that the woman could provide some of the assurance he so desperately needed. He'd told me that one of the regular delegates was a wisewoman who Bronwyn had arranged to talk with us, to help Marcus, and to identify what type of blood flowed in my veins. I was less sure how enthusiastic I felt about the meeting beyond getting help for Marcus.

It was impossible to deny Devyn's belief that I had some element of magic in my blood in light of the episodes I had experienced over the summer in Richmond, especially that night on the hill.

I wasn't stupid. His conversation with Bronwyn, half-baked as it had been, was about me possibly being the girl he was seeking. I wasn't sure what that might mean for me. The glimpse of that incident by the river had tugged at me since the night on Richmond Hill. The strength of the emotions that had overwhelmed me on seeing it still occasionally swept through me, the echo enough to catch me unawares and steal my breath away. I wasn't entirely sure I was ready to learn more.

Passing through the carnival that had overtaken the main plazas of the forum, I had caught the occasional glimpse of some of the delegates with their long hair and outlandish clothes, patterned with swirls and images of leaves and rivers and animals. My fingers itched to reach out and trace them as I followed Devyn through the bustling crowd, citizens and Britons alike mixing in the week-long festivities held to celebrate the Treaty Renewal. It was a two-centuries-old tradition which kept relations with the indigenous peoples of the island on an even keel by inviting them into the city and throwing a party to show off our hospitality.

This year, though, there was a tension to the festivities, the city more aware than usual that these people were our enemies, an enemy that did not appear to be impacted by the illness sweeping through Londinium and the Shadowlands. It didn't help that this year the son of the Lady of the Lake, the single most feared Briton, was in attendance. A bonus for me was that, with the Britons being the main topic of gossip and conversation in the city, I didn't even need to look for information as it flooded my daily feeds.

Speculation about the Prince of Mercia was rife. Having the Lady of the Lake's son, a living reminder of the threat in the north, in our midst was making everyone nervous, the feeds full of the legends surrounding the generations of women who had stood with the Briton armies and the fearsome power they wielded. No Lady of the Lake had ever attended the Treaty Renewal; they only ever met the Empire on the battlefield. There were also bursts on the fashions of each tribe, from the martial Anglians to the whimsical Celtic styles of the western territories of Kernow and Cymru, and reports on the greater-than-usual impact of the Britons' presence on our tech, evidenced by the blackouts and power shortages. The discussion of what magical abilities they might have were half urban legend, half conjecture – nothing terribly helpful.

Weaving through the crowd in Devyn's wake was a frustrating experience as he avoided coming into close contact with the few Britons enjoying the street festivities.

Until we entered the tent.

There, sitting on a chair, was a small, older woman dressed in the Kernowan fashion, who looked up from the cards spread on the table in front of her as we entered. Devyn had brought me to a fortune-teller.

One of the few contacts any of my friends had ever had with the Britons had been to visit one of the fortune-tellers that were approved to ply their trade in the main square during the festival. The city council allowed the delegation to bring various such people with them for the amusement of the citizenry. Ginevra had booked a reading and dragged me along in support the last time they had been in town. I had waited outside during the session as my father had expressly forbidden me to speak to any Briton, but it had been fun to tag along in an attempt to peek at them. We had giggled over the experience together at school the next day, regaling our friends with the predictions of future love and wealth, despite not getting the thing I had most wanted: to see a Briton up close.

The woman waved us wearily to the seat at the little table opposite her, her steely gaze sweeping both of us. A small smile played around her mouth as she picked up the deck of cards marked with a Celtic symbol I didn't recognise and shuffled them deftly. The table and tent were covered in various Celtic designs and symbols, predominant amongst them the triquetra symbol from my pendant and from

Linus's house. I breathed a little more easily in the knowledge that any words exchanged in its presence would not be recorded.

"Citizens, welcome. I am the wisewoman Fidelma," she greeted us, her words welcoming but her tone wary. "What brings you here today?"

Devyn hesitated at her lack of acknowledgement of his true heritage.

"The lady Bronwyn sent us. We suspect my friend here may have magic in her blood but we aren't sure. Can you help?"

The silver-haired woman's eyes assessed him coolly.

"I know what you seek, foolish boy," she grumbled turning to me. "Give me your hands, child."

I looked at Devyn.

"Please," he coaxed me. "Fidelma may be able tell us more about your blood. Then we'll discuss your friend."

I laid my hands out, resting them palm up in her wizened careworn ones, a small ripple of unease going through me. I blinked. The wisewoman Fidelma smiled kindly at me before directing her gaze back to Devyn.

"The lady Bronwyn left a package for you. It's over there on the chair. She asks that you check the fit."

Devyn rose and crossed over to the bundle, unwrapping it to reveal some clothes in the Briton style. "What do I need these for?"

"My lady hopes you might use them soon."

Devyn's lips thinned. "I'll only need these if I have something to bring with me."

The older woman locked gazes with him until he shrugged, picking the clothes up to do as directed. I shifted as the woman's focus returned to me, her gaze locking with mine in a way that made me feel trapped, as if I couldn't breathe properly. Fidelma's brow came together in a frown, her head starting to shake.

"I'm sorry. I know what it is he hopes." She spoke softly, for my ears only. "I sense nothing at all."

I felt my heart sink slightly. Devyn had been wrong. I wasn't the lost child. At most I had mixed blood and Shadower heritage. I felt somewhat disappointed. My life could now go back to what it had always been, but my path was one Devyn wouldn't walk. Despite his orders to watch Marcus, with these clothes he could sneak out with the delegation and continue his search elsewhere. Stupidly, I felt my lower lip tremble as my eyes sought him out on the other side of the wide tent.

Unaware of the crushing news, he had started to lift his shirt over his head, the muscles of his back shifting under his smooth skin. As if sensing my gaze, he turned slightly, and his eyes warmed. I swallowed as mine pulled away from his and helplessly tracked down his torso.

"Argh," the woman gasped, clutching my hands harder. "What is this?" She turned an accusing glare at Devyn.

Devyn pulled on the Celtic tunic before responding.

"I'm not sure. She has magic, I've seen it. But it doesn't seem to be there all the time. Bronwyn saw her wield it but couldn't sense it at all within her. I need you to tell me… tell us if she is of the old blood."

The older lady cast a speculative look at me before indicating that Devyn should take his seat once more.

"I have never seen this before," she admitted, turning to address me directly. "I could sense nothing at all, not even a latency and certainly not special in the way that the Griffin's son hopes. There is a stillness in your blood that usually indicates a lack of magic. A person of the old blood has a different feel; our blood is alive, it swings and swirls, elegant and elaborate. Like the patterns that adorn our art, it is a mystery of interconnected patterns that sings through nature, with loops and tangles and unexpected directions that somehow achieve an unimagined symmetry and beauty. Your blood conveys none of this. It is less a stream or river than it is a shallow puddle. But the sight of our young friend"—her eyes gleamed with humour—"caused a ripple in that stillness, with a resonance that a shallow pool of water could not contain. This is a riddle to be solved."

At this the old lady pushed away from the table, going over to a drawer and pulling out some small bundles of twigs with leaves which she lit until they smoked.

Fidelma waved one in the air, the small leaves emitting a surprising amount of smoke that wrapped itself around the tent. She then went over and stood in front of Devyn, her sharp eyes gazing at him contemplatively.

"With the Griffin's son here as the key, perhaps…" she said thoughtfully. "Please clasp each other's hands in the traditional manner."

Devyn rolled up the elaborate cuffs of his tunic and laid his hands out face up and I did likewise. He then turned his palms, wrapping his fingers around my arm until our pulse points sat together. My entire being immediately focused on the feel of his heartbeat against my tender flesh, barely noticing as Fidelma moved behind my chair and laid her hands on my temples.

"The Griffin?" I murmured questioningly. Twice the wisewoman had referenced it and Bronwyn had also used the term, but to my complete and utter lack of surprise, Devyn shook his head dismissively. Unable to help myself, I rolled my eyes. His continual lack of sharing information, particularly about himself, was, without doubt, his most infuriating trait.

"Shhh," Fidelma admonished, "I need you to focus. Feel the heartbeat that lies beside your own. Concentrate on the pulse of life that flows from the heart to the heart."

The Celtic woman's voice was soft, mesmerising, and I felt every bone and muscle melt at her instruction, my entire being becoming nothing more than the swirl of blood in my veins, sweeping alongside Devyn's. My lids grew heavy even as my eyes lazily followed their favourite journey across the planes of Devyn's face, his high cheekbones, straight aquiline nose, lips that were neither too full nor too thin, and back up to the deep, deep darkness of his eyes.

I stood, pacing to the window, and found myself looking out across a beautiful storm-swept lake, lush green hills rolling beyond. The trees covering them were towering and ancient, so unlike the ones with which I was more familiar… from somewhere else.

I shook my head, trying to remember the trees I was used to, but the flash of a girl huddled on the floor in a dark room with tangled hair and grey eyes snapped up to meet mine.

Marina.

Heeled boots tracking quickly up the corridor made a racket on the stone floor, the rumble of masculine laughter tumbling into the room ahead of the dripping wet pair who entered.

"I'm fairly certain I was first, again," the darker of the two proclaimed.

"I'm fairly certain you cheated, again," the taller boy retorted, his easy smile taking the bite out of the accusation.

"It's not the game that's played but the battle that's won," he got in return as Devyn's brown eyes twinkled merrily in my direction.

I looked them up and down in disgust. "Dripping wet, the pair of you. You'd better hurry along before Mother sees you. You were supposed to be back an hour ago."

He clicked his heels and with a sharp laughing salute was gone.

I sighed. Mother's anger would be as rain before the sun. She could never manage to hold on to her annoyance at her laughing boy. I frowned. Mother was warm and beautiful, but a vision of cold eyes dripping with disdain flashed before me. It was but a fleeting thought as I was swept up in his arms.

"Stop, Dev." I laughed, catching his shoulders. "You'll ruin my dress."

"And no doubt your mother will be just as stern with you." He smiled down at me, following his words with a sweet kiss dropped on my lips.

I pulled away. "Stop, somebody will—"

A scream ripped through the castle. I tried to pull away, to run, but he held me fast. The light dimmed, blood seeping into the corridor from the direction the other boy had taken.

I reached up and touched the face of the man holding me. He was real, this was real, he was here with me.

Wasn't he?

He pulled away as the sound of approaching boots made its way into the room, which had previously felt so safe, so untouchable. I didn't want to be alone. Please.

I pulled his head back down to mine, pressing my lips determinedly, anxiously against his. A feverish fear overpowered me. He was leaving me. Why would he leave me?

No, I wouldn't let him.

My hands scrabbled to gain a hold of his shoulders and my kiss turned frantic. I could sense him trying to control the kiss, make it more substantial, reassuring me with the depth of it that he was here with me.

But he wasn't, he wasn't. He was trying to detach himself from me. Arms reached for me as he pulled away. Despair clawed at me.

"Enough," The command came sharply and abruptly, her nails sharp, her grip surprisingly strong.

I snapped back, almost falling out of my chair as I pulled myself off Devyn. A half sob escaped me, a symptom of the residual emotion ploughing through my body. Devyn reached for me, his arms about to go around me, but I pushed him away, anger rising to the surface.

"What in Hades was that?" I demanded of the two Britons. Devyn looked at Fidelma, his expression indecipherable.

"A projection. But whose… ?" the woman uttered softly and, from my point of view, unhelpfully. "How interesting."

"What do you mean?" I gritted again. The last time I had seen things it had been other people, people in the past. This time had felt like the present but not any present I knew. One where Devyn joked and twirled me in his arms when he entered a room.

"Sit," the woman urged me gently. "You've had a shock. Can I get you a tea?"

Tea? "No, no, thank you."

The wisewoman continued to indicate I sit back down, and I did so. Devyn, rebuffed from his attempt to hold me, had moved to the chair at the side of the tent, his head wearily in his hands, as if he too had felt the emotional punch of being wrenched back from the place I had just been.

"Has anything like this happened before?"

"Yes, I've seen things."

Fidelma tilted her head to one side as I recounted the

episodes I'd had in Richmond, seeing the Tewdwr girl in the stable, the travellers chased by the sentinels on the riverbank.

"Those were things that have been."

"The girl and her father survived?" I asked, unsure why I was so invested.

"Her father died in the attack, but the child lived," she answered abstractedly.

"And what I saw just now?"

"This is something else… a life that might have been." Her brows drew together as she turned to Devyn. "One that has been wished for."

She sat back in her seat, her head tilted, birdlike, examining me. "You have every appearance of a citizen – you feel like one to me. Your spirit is light, untroubled, ordinary. That is a lie. I don't know how, but there is another layer hidden beneath that one, a secret layer, hidden, trapped."

I leaned forward, urging her on. "What secret? Hidden by whom?"

The older lady reached a hand across the table and took mine.

"I'm not sure what was done to you, or perhaps you did it to yourself."

"I don't… what do you mean? What does this have to do with what just happened? With what I saw?"

"You saw a possible present that could have been but isn't," she continued in her riddle-laden way. Celts. Never a straight answer.

"I don't understand." My tone was brittle.

The wisewoman smiled sadly.

"The girl you saw was you and not you."

I exhaled my irritation. That made no sense. I looked over

at Devyn. He looked like a harsh word would shatter him. His eyes were haunted.

I frowned. "You saw it too?"

He nodded.

"Why were you there?" I asked, and, unable to stop myself, I whispered, "and why did you leave me to them?"

"It was a dream, Cass," he whispered.

He looked up at me, his eyes still glittering with pain.

"Just a dream."

His head bowed for another moment and then he stood, clearly shaking off the remnants of what we'd just experienced.

He addressed the wisewoman who sat watching us both closely. "Cassandra is the girl. She's alive. Right?"

Fidelma ignored him.

"Have you ever had any power to command the elements? Move things, create fire?"

I shook my head.

"Or any sense of the ley lines that run through the land?"

I shook my head again. I knew about the magical energy lines but I couldn't sense them.

Fidelma studied me intensely before spreading her hands widely.

"No. This dream means nothing. The girl you wished her to be is gone. The vision is a possible present that was yours, not hers."

Devyn's shoulders dropped. She exhaled tiredly before turning back to me.

"She has magic and her abilities are unusual – the ability to see is rare and more than could manifest in a Shadower with latent blood."

I had seen a possible present, not the past. A possible present in which I was with Devyn. I didn't know who his friend had been. Was that my life, or did it belong to his mystery girl?

Fidelma continued, "The depth I could sense means she is almost certainly a full-blood Briton with magic in her veins, but who knows of what lineage. If she were the one you seek, there would be signs of so much more. She has a gift to see but your destiny is strong. What she sees may be no more than a ripple of another version of your life, not hers. You must stop now. It is time to stop. It is time to come home."

Devyn shook his head and pulled away from her comforting hand.

"She's not dead. I have abilities that belong to the Griffin. If she were dead then my father would have been the last." His shoulders squared. "Magic has faded in my line, except in those of each generation who are chosen to protect her. Then we are given gifts we need: the ability to blend in, to manipulate perception. How is it possible I can do these things if she is not in this world?"

Fidelma smiled sadly. "It is a great gift indeed if you still have the skills of the Griffin. But is it not possible that these were triggered when you were a child and you knew her? You had a connection to her then, did you not?"

He nodded, his cheekbones sharp in his strained expression. The old woman was destroying his hope, reasoning away the source of his belief in his quest. It was painful to watch.

"Do you share a connection with this girl?" Her tired eyes flicked to indicate me as I sat trying to make myself as small as possible, not wanting to be part of this moment. Wanting to shield him – and myself – from the terrible pain in his eyes.

He didn't answer. He didn't need to. I had felt in my vision in Richmond the connection the little boy had to the baby that had died that day; they had shared a special bond. He'd been able to feel her mood, almost as if he could read her infant mind. I was drawn to Devyn more than any man I'd ever met, but there was nothing mystical about it. It was purely chemical. Just one of the components that usually made up a codified match. It was something I had expected to feel towards Marcus.

"But her vision…"

"She saw the fall of the Tewdwrs in the old castle and that was not related to you. She saw your past and it did not need to be related to her."

Fidelma paused as she contemplated her next words. "You have wanted a different reality for so long that perhaps you influenced what she saw. What you saw may have been less her vision than your dream."

She turned to me now.

"You have a great gift, child. When he leaves, you should go with him. You would be most welcome. I would be happy to teach you to master your gift."

Leave. Leave the city. Leave the safety and shelter of the only home I had ever known. I was sorry that Devyn hadn't got the news he wanted but I was also somewhat relieved. Wasn't I?

"Why would I leave the city?"

Devyn blinked slowly before standing and rolling his shoulders back.

"You heard Fidelma. You may not be the girl I sought but you are a full-blood Briton. You're not a citizen. You can't stay here."

I stared at him. I had been so wrapped up in what it meant for Devyn that I hadn't…

I was a Briton. With magic. How was this possible?

I shook my head. I didn't need this. I could start taking the pills again. All this could go away.

"No. I agreed to be here because you were supposed to be finding out how to help him. That's it. Maybe I was curious about who I really am but that's it. I'm not going anywhere."

I turned back to the wisewoman, who was looking alarmed at my raised voice. Her palms rose, indicating that I should lower my voice. I took a steadying breath.

"I don't know what I just saw, or how I keep seeing these things, but there are pills for that." I took a breath. "I'm sorry that that baby died. Truly I am. But I agreed to come here and meet you in exchange for something to help my friend. That's it. Can you help or not?"

Fidelma smiled softly. "Bronwyn tells me that your friend is using magic to help people with the illness. Yes?"

I nodded. "Can you help him?"

"Perhaps. I would very much like to meet him and to understand what he is doing. We have many of our own who are ill, and though we have our own ways, knowledge is always useful and I would be happy to help him, of course. We are only here for one more day. You will need to bring him to me."

"That won't be possible."

The wisewoman's brow lifted. "It is the only way. I'm told he is untrained and showing signs of fatigue? It's very dangerous to use this kind of magic untrained, all too easy to tap in to your own life-force as your emotions become entangled with your desire to help."

"I can't. He wouldn't be able to come here. Nobody is going to comment if I visit a fortune-teller in the year of my marriage but Marcus visiting a Briton privately would be noted."

The wisewoman's eyes sharpened.

"Marcus? Marcus Courtenay? This is of whom you speak? He is using magic, enough to cure people… and this is who you are to marry?"

Even though she was still technically directing her questions at me, she was looking to Devyn for confirmation.

"Yes." His voice was low as he uttered the single word.

"You're sure he's using magic?" There was a tremor in her hands as she brought them to her lips at my nod of confirmation. "You're right, of course; he cannot be seen with us. It would attract too much attention. But he puts himself at terrible risk if he continues to treat people in this way." The wisewoman nodded hurriedly. "I will help if I can."

She stood and began ushering us out of the room.

"You, boy, return later and we will discuss arrangements. The ball tomorrow night is our best chance." But she looked not entirely convinced as she said this.

"Now go."

As I made to leave, her delicately aged hand grabbed my arm in a surprisingly firm grip. "Tell no one of your abilities. Already too many know. Come to me and I will help you. So many lives depend on you making it home safely."

"I'm not sure…" The very thought of leaving the city—

No. If I started taking the pills again everything would be fine. "My path is here with Marcus."

"No, my dear," she said, not unkindly. "It is not."

My eyes flicked to Devyn.

"Ah." She started to smile then her eyes lost focus and her hand gripped my wrist tightly. "Your fates are entwined and you will be with him to the end, but he will not be with you."

"That makes no sense," I said. "What does—?"

"Better that way," she cut me off and ushered me out of the tent.

Chapter Seventeen

My mind was still trying to decipher the strange utterings the wisewoman Fidelma had made yesterday as I sat looking at myself in the mirror while the dresser fussed with the elaborate style my mother had inflicted on me.

Devastated by Fidelma's verdict that I was most definitely not the girl he sought, Devyn had been even less communicative than usual as we made our way discreetly back across the city from the forum. Predicting his insistence that we avoid public transport which could be tracked via our payment systems, I had worn a brand new pair of beautifully engineered running shoes that perfectly combined style and support.

Which was just as well as Devyn in full brooding mode had sped across the city, his long legs eating up the miles between the forum and my parents' home. It also meant he could avoid answering my questions as I trailed half a block behind him, unable to do more than seethe at his back.

On reaching the villa levels of Chelsea, he had peeled away

without a backward glance, by which point it was all I could do not to race after him and kick him until he spoke to me about what had happened at the fortune-teller's.

I couldn't stop thinking about the dream – or, if I understood correctly, the vision. A vision of a possible present that could have been but wasn't. Had I really caught a glimpse of Marina? Would she be imprisoned in this alternative version of the world? It worried me that I might be starting to understand after all.

In my vision, Devyn was the same age he was now, but his whole being had been lighter, his aura sparkling with a sense of mischief that I had never seen as he bantered with his friend. He was still recognisably Devyn: grounded by a fierce determination and purpose and a clear sense that he would be the right person to have around in times of trouble. The love and respect that had underlain his friendship with the other man told of the many shared scrapes that they had faced together.

Had I seen where Devyn was from in my vision? It had been beautiful and green with wide open spaces. And a sense of family. Such a deep feeling of home. I looked at my reflection in the mirror, at the sadness and hurt that lurked at the backs of the blue eyes that stared back at me. Was that what it felt like to belong?

The version of myself in the dream had felt complete and utter trust and faith in Devyn as he put his arms around me. I'd had no doubts that I was exactly where I belonged and that I was safe there, that Devyn would always be there for me. Had I been the girl he sought in that moment or had I been myself?

It had felt like me, particularly when the city had made its presence known. I had braced for what I knew was coming, what I felt to be utterly inevitable – the sound of approaching boots and Devyn's withdrawal. That other girl, the one who had been so secure, carefree, and at one with her world and the man in her arms, had frozen in wild shock. I knew he would abandon me as soon as they came to take me… her. She had turned to face them, alone. Always alone.

I wished I could be that girl. Even that taste of her happiness had left me dizzy. What would it be like to belong in Devyn's arms? Or, more than that, to feel wanted and accepted there? Would it be worth the devastation that had gutted me when I'd thought he was gone? It was an impossible question to answer, particularly as I was still reeling from the soul-deep feeling of grief that had hit me in waves after we left Fidelma's. I felt adrift in the wake of the meeting. Bereft. The vision, the news that I was not a citizen – not even a Shadower – and witnessing Devyn's hopes being crushed just all felt like too much.

When I had arrived home to my family's perfectly decorated apartment, I had sought refuge in my room. Curling into a ball, I had lain on my bed and sobbed. I had cried ceaselessly. I thought perhaps the door had opened at one point and maybe someone had sat with me as I lay there, wracked. Anna, our maid, the one who had mended my childhood hurts in place of my mother, sat with me now. I wasn't sure why I had cried so much. It wasn't really in my nature to take things so hard. When I had been a little girl, I'd had a toy doll that I took to bed with me every night. One day it had disappeared and my father often told the story with doting pride of his brave little girl who, when I found out that the doll I'd slept with every night since I was a baby had gone, had simply smiled and shrugged. But I hadn't slept well for months afterwards, lying awake, fearful of every sound in the night without my baba there to protect me. But I hadn't cried once.

Yet I had sobbed yesterday. I couldn't understand it. The shockwaves of that moment where I had realised he was going to step away as my dream turned to a nightmare had rippled through me like a physical thing. I didn't even know how to begin to describe it. But I had recognised it. It was not new to me; the tang of it sat in the back of my throat every time I saw Devyn and it had since the first moment I had seen through his mask. Was this the reason I had largely ignored him all those years? Was this the reason I was drawn to him like a magnet? Or, more accurately, like a moth to a flame? Some part of me had always recognised that Devyn was no good for me, that for every moment of joy I experienced with him, I was paid back double in pain and doubt.

My head was yanked back as the hairdresser tugged particularly hard on a lock of hair as she twisted it, snapping me out of the mire of my thoughts.

Joy? Despair? Pain? Were these really the emotions I experienced with Devyn? I examined my life before and after that day in school when the sentinels had come looking for him. The days that preceded it had been happy… no, content was a better description. I had been content. Endless days lived with no major ups or downs, no knowledge of hunger or pain, my time filled with petty interests and meaningless fashions. The colour that had blazed into my life since then was startling in comparison to that beige contentment.

Midnight eyes warmed as we nearly kissed that first time at my party. Purples and blues of sadness as my eyes opened to Marina's plight and so many others like her in the city. Oranges and reds of adrenaline and danger at the escape through the city and my fear that the sentinels would catch us.

I wasn't quite sure what colours I associated with Devyn, but in his arms I had experienced greens and golds of calm and safety, a deep, deep sensation that had made me feel more grounded than I had ever known in my flighty, shallow life. I felt like I was cocooned while the storms swirled darkly outside. I remembered us chatting over one of his beloved coffees, sitting quietly while we watched the warehouse activity before Marina's escape, the shared exhilaration after, our verbal dances as I tried to get more information than he was willing to give, and the moments when the chemistry between us ignited. Devyn's presence made that dark shadow throb and yet I never felt more alive than when we were together.

Was it because I was really a Briton? Because I didn't belong here? Because I belonged with him?

"Marcus will love your hair." My mother's voice was like being doused in cold water. I blinked, struggling to push my swirling thoughts away.

I met my mother's eyes in the mirror and smiled at her look of approval, pleased that she was pleased for once.

"I hope so," I murmured, putting a hand up to lightly touch it, the elaborate twists and twirls accentuating the lighter strands of hair which caught the light as I turned my head to admire it. Would Devyn notice the way they had done my eyes, accentuating their size and shape, the sparkly gold shadow highlighting their unusual turquoise colour?

Probably not. He was too focused on our mission of getting Marcus discreetly to Fidelma. But that was his problem; mine was convincing Marcus that he should meet a Celt in private.

After the emotional storm I had weathered yesterday, I hadn't been fit to go out in public, much less meet Marcus, and I couldn't speak to him of this over a comms device. He had been working at the hospital all day so I hadn't had any chance to try to explain anything. Not that I necessarily understood it myself.

Marcus had no idea he was accessing the magic that flowed through his blood… or did he? He had to wonder why he had some success at curing people while his colleagues had none. He was sensitive about his Briton heritage but it was a well-known fact – how had nobody pieced it together?

Unless they had. If Devyn was right and our match was engineered in order to try and strengthen the blood of any offspring Marcus might have, then they must have had some notion that the magic that ran through the veins of the Britons was stronger in some lines than in others.

Perhaps they realised that marrying the Courtenays to citizens was weakening their magic.

"…time."

I jumped.

"Pardon?" I looked across the room at my mother. "What was that?"

My mother sniffed her displeasure at having to repeat herself.

"I said, you'd better put on your dress, or you'll be late."

I took one last look at myself in the mirror, mentally bracing myself before jumping breezily up out of my chair and whirling across the room as excited at the anticipation of going to my first proper ball as the Cassandra of old would have been. Especially as tonight I would wear Oban's dress. Was wearing it a sign of my acceptance of the journey I had been on? Or a wish to be at my best when I saw Devyn again now that he no longer looked at me in the hope of seeing some missing girl but just for me? Did I need the glamour to hide or reveal myself?

I could sense immediately as I greeted Marcus with a peck on the cheek that he had reverted to his more customary façade of a confident, beautiful person. Presumably, the glimpse of careworn doctor he had shown me at the hospital was not here to stay. I used to be so in awe of his sophistication and the suave way he negotiated situations but I was coming to realise that, like Devyn, like me, this was a carefully maintained disguise that hid his secrets from the world.

One which would make my task tonight all the harder. This Marcus was much less approachable than the more vulnerable, weary doctor of the other night had been. I watched him covertly as we crossed town in the hackney with my parents. He still showed noticeable signs of exhaustion, but the slick man-about-town was not someone with whom I could easily discuss magic. Trying to convince him in this mood to meet a magic-wielding wisewoman who could show him how to deal with his own not-so-latent abilities seemed imprudent.

From our conversations over the summer, I knew three main things about Marcus: he loved science, he did not celebrate his connection to the indigenous people of these islands, and he loved and believed in our city and society.

Suddenly I felt coldly apprehensive of our plan. I could be putting Devyn and Fidelma in grave danger. Devyn would be revealed as a spy – if that was even what he was since he was less interested in what the council was doing than in what Marcus was doing.

There was also a strict edict about the use of magic within the city walls. Nobody had been caught using magic in generations – the savage punishments handed out in centuries gone by had seen to that. The arena hadn't been lit up with the fires deemed appropriate to end the life of magic wielders in generations. Anyone who knew their blood held any kind of ability had presumably fled across the borders a long time ago.

I had always assumed that there was sort of a reciprocal relationship between technology and magic. Just as advanced technology ceased to work well the further from the city you got, I had always thought that this was true of magic in the city, that behind the walls, where technology was at its strongest, magic didn't work. Judging by my own recent experiences, this did not appear to be the case.

Furthermore, technology became somewhat less reliable while the Britons were in town. Many of the delegates were important people in their society so did that also increase the likelihood that they wielded magic? There was speculation that the Prince of Mercia's attendance this year was the reason it was worse than usual. How much of his mother's power had he inherited? The city was uneasy at his presence – I couldn't even imagine the reaction if the Lady of the Lake herself ever attended. Her magic was feared. All magic was feared. There was a reason Britons weren't allowed behind the walls beyond this one week. Why traders from continents yet to stamp it out were forbidden from disembarking off their ships. Whenever magic appeared inside the Empire, it was stamped out. Swiftly and brutally.

I felt increasingly nervous about discussing any of this with Marcus. He was a loyal citizen of the Empire as well as someone who believed fiercely in the Code. Would his sense of self-preservation be enough to prevent him from betraying us, because surely reporting us would mean revealing his own abilities? Which would mean an end to his ambitions as a doctor and who knew what impact it would have on his citizenship, and on his place on the council.

For while his Briton heritage was a reasonably well-known

fact – and even part of his attraction, for some, as the last living descendant of the York princess whose marriage had ended centuries of open war – he was also the last scion of House Courtenay, which far outweighed any possibility of his Wilder blood being seen as a dilution of his right to citizenship. Marcus was a veritable prince of the city who lived a charmed life which was recorded by the social bursts so beloved of the city's housewives and teenage girls. It would be a great height from which to fall, and I doubted it was a future Marcus would willingly choose for himself.

But Devyn and the wisewoman were willing to risk all to help him, and I was convinced that to continue as he was would undoubtedly kill him. Squaring my shoulders, I slipped on my mask and took Marcus's hand as we stepped out of the car at the foot of the steps to the Governor's Palace, where the masquerade ball to mark the last night of the Treaty Renewal was being held.

The Governor's Palace had at one time stood alone, its glittering lights reflected in the river below, its height looming over the entire city from the Southbank. Now it anchored the urban heights that had grown up around it. It remained the building most faithful to the Empire, not just in its architecture but also as the home of the power it represented here in the most westerly reaches of the Empire. My breath caught as I was reminded of the might of the system I was planning to defy. The palace, like the amphitheatre and the forum, was privileged in never having had towers or layers of city built above it. I looked higher up into the night sky and took solace from the stars above.

I smiled at the slight lift of Marcus's brow, the first indication he'd given that he had noticed my odd mood.

The walk up the stairs was like being in the central ring at a circus. We were on display, the crowds there to catch a glimpse of the Britons in all their exotic finery, but a gratifying number of flashes greeted Marcus and me as we made our way up the stairs. I wondered if Oban would ever see the pictures of his magnificent gown – wherever he was.

The ball was far more formal than anything I had ever attended before and the sense of calm and grandeur in the marble-floored entrance was immediate after the chaos outside. Straight-backed attendants accepted guests' coats and wraps before indicating we should continue up either of the great curving stairs on each side.

As we followed the elegant couples towards the Great Ballroom, the perfume and colours of the flowers that lined the hall were incredibly distracting. My senses came alive, like a dancer who on hearing the music start unconsciously begins to tap their foot to the tune.

"Have you been well?" Marcus asked.

"Yes, quite."

Apparently we had moved from a comfortable if distracted silence to a stilted opener.

"And you? Did you meet with Otho's family?"

He nodded. "Have you been doing anything of interest this week?"

Right, so that was a topic not open for discussion… which was going to make it difficult to bring up my belief that he needed to see someone about his somewhat unorthodox healing technique.

"I met up with a friend earlier in the week," I said as I looked about to see how close the nearest guests were. "And we went to see a fortune-teller."

Which was greeted with a classic male upper-lip curl of disdain and no indication of any further interest.

"It was fascinating and we talked about all kinds of things," I pursued regardless. "I'd never spoken to a Briton before."

Still nothing.

"Wouldn't you like to know what she told me?" I asked, persisting.

At this, Marcus deigned to look at me. "I suppose so, though as our match has gone public, I'm hoping that she didn't fail to predict marriage to a gorgeous doctor."

Too easy.

"Maybe she did and maybe she didn't," I teased, now that I had his attention, before continuing with the bait hastily concocted when Devyn had sketched out the plan earlier this morning. "She did know something about the illness though, and she says that cases have been found beyond the borders."

"You shouldn't be discussing anything to do with the health or safety of imperial citizens with an outsider."

"But they've been having some success in treating it," I said, dangling the bait under his nose.

"What? How?"

I shook my head, indicating with a sideways look around us that I couldn't speak further in the presence of others. The procession had started to tighten up as we approached the entrance to what I assumed from the growing hum of the crowd was the Great Ballroom.

We shuffled forward slowly, Marcus's distraction swept aside by his frustration at not being able to discover if there was anything to the fortune-teller's claims, something new he hadn't thought of yet, something that might explain his own success where others had failed.

He couldn't hide his impatience at all the obsequious greeting, handshaking and air kissing that was required to make it past the senators lined up inside the door and over to the general crowd where we could speak more freely.

As we made our way through the sparkling guests, he pulled me across to a window where we could turn our backs to the room to peer through the tall panes of glass at the crowd below.

"Tell me."

"Tell you what?" What girl was ever going to be able to resist a little payback for having been pretty much ignored all the way to her first ball?

"Tell me what this woman told you."

"She told me I had met the great love of my life." Giving in too quickly would only make him suspicious.

"Cassandra."

"Oh, look." I pointed in the reflection of the window to a body across the room. "There's your father."

Despite the delicious edict that the ball be a masquerade, Matthias Dolon had lifted his mask as he greeted another rather portly man. Marcus stiffened but made no move to look around. Meanwhile, I scanned the window for any sign of Devyn or Fidelma. The masks didn't help matters but the wisewoman was likely to be in Celtic dress, and her distinctive long silver hair should narrow down the possibilities. Devyn was likely to be harder to locate. Despite his heritage, he was sure to be in the typical formal wear of a citizen – a long fitted jacket with an embellished shoulder scarf. Marcus's was a particularly notable example, interwoven as it was with the crest of his house and subtle golden Celtic swirls around white roses that nodded to his more exotic lineage. I rethought my strategy. I couldn't afford to pique his interest too early unless I could hurry him right in to meet Fidelma before he had too much time to think.

"I must dance," I announced.

"Now? No, not before you…"

I pouted, a proper full-lipped spoiled-princess huffy move. If Devyn could see me now…

"If you won't dance with me—" I threw at him before picking up my skirts and quite literally flouncing off. I was halfway across the room before I realised that with the masks I was unable to recognise anyone well enough to ask them to dance with me. Except for Marcus's father. I swallowed. At least Marcus was unlikely to ask for me back if I was in the arms of the only other man it was appropriate for me to be seen with.

"Sir," I began. His shoulder sash pompously included the Courtenay house he had married into as well as his own. The Dolons were a family of no particular note – unlike the one his son had been born into via his mother. "It's Cassandra Shelton. Would you care to dance?"

In the pause that followed, I could see his mask lift, no doubt from his violently raised eyebrows.

"It would be churlish to refuse my future daughter-in-law."

Wouldn't it though. Taking leave of his companions, he offered me his hand.

"Has my son been derelict in his duties?" he asked.

"No, not at all," I hastened to assure him so Marcus didn't earn another black mark, especially as it was so unwarranted. "I just thought it would be nice to get to know you a bit better."

"Did you indeed?"

"Yes, well, we had so little time to talk over the summer."

"That is true."

He twirled me away and then back into his arms, his lead rather heavy. "You and Marcus seem to be getting along well.

Or at least better since he has to see you at least twice a week."

"Has to see me?" I repeated his odd phrasing.

"If you are to marry next year, he cannot continue with this medicine nonsense to the detriment of his relationship with you, my dear."

Right, so not only was the reason I had started seeing more of Marcus because his father had insisted on it, it was also because his doting papa was threatening his career.

This man clearly cared little for his son and even less for me but Devyn's outlandish claims rang in my ears: that our match had been engineered in the hope that my probable Briton blood would increase the likelihood of magic in our children. Each of these little manoeuvrings on the part of our parents made my skin creep and chipped away at the belief that we were anything more than a genetic experiment to them. Suddenly I felt furious at the callous manipulations they were inflicting upon us. How dare they. A gust of wind suddenly swept through the hall. Heads turned.

"Do you mind if I cut in, sir?" Without waiting for an answer, the newcomer swept me away in an outrageous breach of etiquette.

"Do you mind?" I spluttered.

A soft chuckle came from behind the black and bronze mask.

"Would you rather I let you unleash your fury on the room?"

My new dance partner's voice was soft and low, his hair the tousled black curls I had imagined running my fingers through in many a moment of weakness. His movements were graceful, his muscles shifting under my fingertips as he spun me about the room.

I laughed, the sound a light trickle that drifted into the air and caused a couple of neighbouring Britons to turn and search for the source. I saw a tall, broad-shouldered man in a gold mask with long blond hair tied at the back of his neck standing at the edge of the dance floor and scanning the room intently before Devyn turned me, blocking my view. Rather too sharply.

"Do you know that man?" Even as I asked I knew the answer.

"Cass."

In an all too recognisable tone, Devyn shut my question down.

I exhaled my annoyance but that was forgotten in an instant as a hand wandered slightly lower than was appropriate and pulled me a number of fractions closer. *Excellent diversion technique, Devyn.* I was aware I was being managed even as my bones melted beneath his touch.

Speaking was no longer possible or desirable as Devyn twirled me about the room. Others parted in perfect timing as we swung by and it felt as if my feet barely touched the floor as he pushed me away and then pulled me back to him time and time again. My hand landed lightly on his chest each time, the beat of his heart underneath my fingertips a counterpoint to the one delivered by the music.

At that moment I felt as if I were the girl in my vision of the alternate present. The girl who knew true love, true happiness. Not one who was perilously close to irrevocably changing her future by revealing too much to the man she was supposed to marry.

A man who was currently watching me dance with another.

Chapter Eighteen

As the song ended, we moved back by the tall windows not far from where Marcus stood talking with a group of people. He never stood alone for long at any party. He was always surrounded by… I would say *friends,* but even his inner circle never felt like people he trusted completely, even as he enjoyed their company. Marcus was a prince of the city and they were his courtiers, beautiful, rich, witty, but not true friends. He didn't allow them to be.

"You need to get Marcus to a room where we can speak privately. We've found a place that should allow us to talk to him and hopefully help him if he lets us," Devyn said, leaning in as he led me off the dance floor.

"Where?"

"At 10.30 go through the door on the other side of the room, follow the hall to the end, and then turn right. Take the second door on the left by the painting of Senator Lewis. You can't miss it; he's the fat one holding the pug." Devyn smirked as he stepped behind me. "If anyone asks, you're meeting your father, who has sent for you."

"I haven't had a chance to say anything. Do you think he —" I stopped short as the blond man I'd spotted earlier stepped in front of us. Two other well-built men were positioned each side of him, apparently not there for the dancing so much as attending the man who was now blocking our route.

"Good evening." He paused as if waiting for an introduction. When nothing was forthcoming from behind me, I looked around to discover Devyn had melted away into the crowd.

Why on earth would he have left me to deal with this Briton on my own?

"Welcome to the city, my lord." I hoped that was the right form of address. In the feudal system outside the walls, most of the nobility were lords and this dignitary looked like he might be someone significant. His tunic was plain but well cut, the half sleeve revealing intricate swirling tattoos on his forearms, and his golden torc was one of the more elaborate I had seen.

The eyes that glittered behind the intricately embroidered mask turned back towards me, having also scanned the crowd for my erstwhile dance partner. They assessed me keenly.

"Am I?" he responded to my greeting.

I wasn't going to touch that political jibe with a bargepole. The last thing I needed was to further offend a prickly Mercian. While his long hair and clothes weren't too different from the Celtic lords from Cymru and Kernow, he was fairer and taller than would be expected. The swirling patterns on his mask and tattoos were distinctly aquatic compared to the martial ones the Anglians tended to prefer. I had been spending every spare minute studying the outsiders, comfortable that my new thirst for knowledge would go unremarked given the surge of interest caused by the festivities. The information in the feeds about their fashions at least seemed reliable, making me pretty confident this man was from Mercia.

"It's a lovely ball." I smiled brightly. "My first."

"Mine too."

Did that mean this was the first time he had been part of the delegation? He sounded young, but it was hard to tell without seeing his face. He held himself with authority. I extended my hand to introduce myself.

"I'm Cassandra Shelton," I offered, becoming awkward as my hand hung in the air between us. The man shook his head lightly.

"Not our custom, I'm afraid."

He was lying. I had seen other Britons this evening take the hands offered to them but that at least answered my previous question: if the other dignitaries were more accustomed to our greetings this one obviously wasn't. Or just didn't care how I perceived his rudeness.

"Your dance partner is returning?" he asked.

His guess was as good as mine.

"He had to go and say hello to someone, I'm afraid. Did you want to meet him?" Did this man know Devyn? If so it made Devyn's disappearance even more mysterious.

"Very much," he said.

I was taken aback.

"You know him?" I asked. Given the circumstances, I shouldn't be pursuing this line of inquiry, but I couldn't resist.

"I may have been mistaken," he answered softly. "It's been a while."

I smiled politely as I spotted Marcus coming our way. "I must go. My match is looking for me."

"Yet you were dancing with another."

Despite his refusal to shake hands, the stranger was well

enough acquainted with our customs to observe the breach of etiquette I had been committing. Unmarried girls of my social status might attend classes and parties with members of the opposite sex before marriage, but at a formal event it was frowned upon to dance with another man, especially here in the Governor's Palace. My only saving grace was that at masquerade balls the rules usually got bent ever so slightly; at the very least, transgressions were more difficult to spot when identities were concealed.

"Yes, I was." I moved to get past him before Marcus spotted me talking to the Briton in the golden mask but a small sidestep by the blond man prevented my escape. He gave a slight shake of his head. My departure was not permitted and I had a feeling that to force the issue would draw attention to us. Or rather, *more* attention; I had already noticed a number of heads turn our way.

"What?" I snapped, I needed to slip back into the crowd. He extended his arm in the Celtic manner and I hesitated. He had refused my handshake but now wanted to touch me in the more intimate Briton manner. People were looking and I needed to move on before I was identified but I reached out anyway and gripped his tattooed forearm. He tensed as our wrists touched and then relaxed as I pulled away.

"I had wondered if he had managed to do it after all," he said as if to himself, his blue eyes surveying me intensely. "But no. Hope is a cruel thing."

I kept my expression as innocent as I could. He did know Devyn. Was this the lord he had abandoned? That would explain his quick exit.

He stepped aside, allowing me to pass. "Tell your friend I am most keen to speak to him."

"Of course." I nodded even as I realised he hadn't given me his name but it was too late as he had already moved on. I went back to Marcus and played the dutiful fiancée all evening, making small talk with the hospital's board members, gossiping with Marcus's friends, the boys every bit as bad as the girls. Though I continued to scan the crowd for the black and bronze mask, there was no further sign of Devyn as the clock ticked down towards the allotted time.

"Marcus," I said, interrupting his conversation after having waited for it to end naturally for ten anxious minutes. "Could I talk to you for a moment?"

Marcus made his excuses and then followed as I made my way to the door Devyn had indicated earlier. Entering into the calm of the hallway was a relief; the noise was swallowed up as the door closed behind us.

"Cassandra, what's this all this about?"

I had already started to hurry along the corridor. We were late.

"I need to talk to you," I said as I walked faster.

A tug on my elbow pulled me to a halt.

"About what we were discussing earlier?" he asked. "I think we should wait until we are somewhere less… formal."

"No, it needs to be now. Here." I hesitated, unsure how much to say. "Please, Marcus. I need you to trust me. Please come with me. I need you to meet some people."

Marcus pushed his mask back from his face displaying his bewilderment.

"What people? The man you were dancing with earlier?" he said, casting me an icy sideways glance. I'd forgotten he'd seen me dancing with Devyn when I was supposed to be with his father.

"Yes, actually. I asked him if he would talk to you." I pulled my elbow free, already moving again, turning the corner. Which door had Devyn said? The first one, further along, I thought, and then I spotted the unorthodox cross little pug in one of the portraits. A smile tugged at my lips; it really was an odd thing to have in what was yet another staid dark portrait in a hallway full of them. I knocked on the door beside it, which opened before my knuckles had barely lifted away. Marcus followed me in.

"These are my friends, Devyn and Fidelma." I introduced him, fiddling nervously with my pendant before rushing on in a tumbling explanation. "They've offered to help you with your work on the illness. That is, *your* work, not the hospital's, because I figured it out, Marcus. I figured out what it is that you are doing differently."

Marcus frowned at me as I paused to take a fortifying breath before I put all our lives at risk.

"You're using magic."

Marcus looked at me like he didn't know me. Which I supposed he didn't – I barely recognised myself. I could practically hear his thoughts. I had everything a citizen could possibly want yet here I was introducing him to two Britons for purposes of which the State would not approve: offering him help with his magic.

"I don't have magic," Marcus denied once he had found his voice. He directed his words at me, and was yet to acknowledge the others in the room by so much as a flicker. "Even if I did, it doesn't work in the city."

"That's not exactly true," Fidelma corrected. "Magic lives within and it's subject to the power to contain it running in the blood. If the blood is strong, it will out."

"I don't have magic," Marcus repeated. I crossed to him

and laid my hand on his arm. He stiffened but didn't knock it off.

"Marcus, you have magic, and you are healing people with it. That's the difference between you and the other doctors."

Marcus's brow creased as he contemplated my words. He'd spent a lot of time searching for the answer to this question and there had to be a part of him that recognised the truth when he heard it. Hopefully, that same part was what would stay his hand in raising the alarm and summoning the authorities.

"No, I would know if I was using magic," he retorted.

"Healing magic is different to other magics. It flows from the spirit and the only outward sign it is being used is in the improved health of the patient," Fidelma explained. "If your patients are improving and there is no other cause then you have your proof, boy."

"Don't call me boy."

It was his first acknowledgement that he could hear Fidelma. It was a sign he was actually listening.

"It's true. I think it's why you're so exhausted all the time. I figured it out when you tried to heal Otho," I said.

"What? How?" Marcus interrupted, now taking a step away from me, causing my hand to fall from his arm. I looked at Devyn for guidance. Should I tell Marcus? Could I trust that he would not betray us? Perhaps if I gave him the knowledge that he was not alone he would feel like he could trust us too.

Devyn shook his head. He would risk his own life, but not mine.

I shrugged. "When he asked you to let him go he instantly became worse. And I saw you with your other patients. They looked so much better, even after you'd been with them for only a short few minutes. Each patient, Marcus, every single one. And with each one you looked worse. I think it's draining you, Marcus. You've got to get a handle on what you're doing so it doesn't kill you."

The crease on his brow deepened into a furrow. He looked from Fidelma to Devyn.

"I don't know you," he said taking in Devyn's formal wear, so similar to his own. "How do you know each other? Do you have magic too?"

Devyn's face betrayed no expression at all as he answered Marcus.

"I have some abilities."

He hadn't responded to the first the question.

Marcus stepped towards him. "Are you a citizen?"

"No."

There it was, the fact in the room that most scared me. That Marcus had magic in his blood was no fault of his own, and while it would make him an outcast, it was merely an unwanted part of his well-known heritage. The same could be argued for my own newfound gifts. Fidelma was part of the delegation and had the diplomatic protection that entailed. Her worst crime here was trying to help a beloved scion of the city. Devyn on the other hand…

Briton. Spy.

Accepting his help would be an act of betrayal against the city and Marcus believed in the city. Perhaps before his own self.

"What are you doing in Londinium?"

"I was looking for someone."

"Who?"

"I don't see how that's any of your business."

"To hurt us?"

"No."

"Then what?"

"The girl I was looking for was not a citizen."

"A Briton?" Marcus tone sharpened. "In the city?"

"Yes."

Marcus snorted his frustration. "Why would she be in the city? Has she committed a crime?"

"No crime. She did nothing to hurt your precious city. She was simply stolen."

"How does anyone steal a person?"

Devyn stepped forward, his face inches away from Marcus, barely contained anger seeping from him.

"When they are a defenceless baby. A baby whose mother has just been killed by your thrice-damned sentinels. A baby whom they… killed."

"You're looking for a baby who was killed? What?" Marcus was clearly confused, while my heart broke a little as Devyn finally faced the truth.

Marcus stopped and looked at me, clearly running the calculations in his head, his clever mind piecing together the tiny slivers of information he had been given.

"Cassandra," he breathed.

"No, it's not what you think. I'm not her."

"But this Briton thought you might be."

I couldn't deny it. I realised I didn't want to.

"Yes." He'd thought I was a missing Briton girl and it turned out I was. Just not the one he was looking for.

"Why did he think that?"

I opened my mouth to defend myself against his challenge. He knew I was adopted; I had reminded him of this *and* that my own heritage might be questionable not so long ago. I closed my mouth, raising my chin as I met his eyes. I would not deny the truth.

Marcus shook his head as he took in the realisation that our match was not what he had believed it to be. I was not who he had believed me to be. And that the very blood that ran in his own veins betrayed him. I knew all too well how that felt. I took a step towards him.

"Marcus."

He raised his hands to fend me off. "This is over. I don't know how you've managed to live here undetected all this time but we are not a match. It never felt right. You don't want… I am not marrying a Briton."

Devyn moved beside me, his body curving protectively in front of me. Marcus's eyes flicked to take in his position and his eyes narrowed. I pulled the promise ring from my hand and put it down on the table beside me.

Fidelma stepped in between us all.

"All righty then, why don't we try taking this down a notch before we attract an audience." She walked over to Marcus and laid a gentle hand on his cheek. "You, my boy, are in need of my help. Now. There's no time to waste. All of these other matters can wait."

Marcus brushed her hand away, though he had looked momentarily as if he'd wanted to lean into it. Despite the outward appearance of his charmed life, Marcus really hadn't experienced a great deal of affection.

"I've heard enough. I do not want or need your help. Thank you for your kind offer." He moved stiffly towards the door which audibly clicked as the lock was turned.

Marcus continued to stride to the door and attempted the handle but to no avail. Inhaling, he turned to face the room.

"Unlock this door."

"No. You do not seem to understand your situation here." Fidelma manhandled him in front of a mirror. "You are a doctor, I'm told, a healer. Like your distant granduncle, whom I served for many years before he died."

"I thought you were from Kernow," Devyn interrupted.

"I was married to an Anglian," she said tartly. "Why? Does it matter?"

"I don't know," Devyn said, eyes narrowed. "Does it?"

"I'm risking my life here by trying to help you," she said, dismissing him and turning back to Marcus. "Look at yourself, child. Look with a healer's eyes. You are draining yourself. Whatever you have been doing, we want to know, we need to know. We have a treatment that works but some of our people are dying too. And if I don't do something for you here and now, you will be dead before the end of the month."

I waited, watching, while Marcus shook off his anger and truly saw himself: the grey shadows under his eyes, the yellow tinge around his irises.

"A month?"

"Less," Fidelma corrected, not entirely without sympathy. "Whatever you're doing is tapping into a part of yourself you should not touch when healing others. It is your own reserve."

Marcus acknowledged that he had heard her while turning to look at me.

"Listen to her, Marcus," I pleaded. "You know something isn't right."

"You're exhausted, drained?" Fidelma asked. "But no fever, cough, shakiness?"

"I don't have the illness," Marcus answered.

"But it started at the same time?" she guessed. "Or have you felt this before?"

Marcus inclined his head, his lips a thin line. "I used to take something for it. With the outbreak I was busy and missed some. I thought nothing of it at first but maybe I did feel that I was better able to help people when I wasn't taking it."

Devyn's eyes met mine. Marcus *had* known on some level that he was using magic if he stayed off his medication. Just like I had.

"Sit," Fidelma ordered. "I need to look at you properly. You certainly have the height of the Plantagenets."

All the fight seemed to have gone out of Marcus and he folded in on himself as he followed her orders.

"You know members of the Plantagenet family?" he asked.

"Tsk, yes. I served the late King Richard XI of York, weren't you listening?" Fidelma reminded him.

"I've had a lot to take in," Marcus said, looking from me to Devyn, who had moved to the other side of the room in an attempt not to derail Fidelma's intervention.

"That you have, boy," she agreed, tilting his head back to look in his eyes before feeling around his lymph nodes. "That you have."

Her eyes, filled with concern, caught Devyn's across the room.

"Can you get him out of here if he loses consciousness?"

"What? What are you planning on doing?" This was not part of the plan. "I thought you were going to tell him a few tricks or something. What are you doing?"

Fidelma had her palms placed on each side of his head and Marcus was visibly sagging.

"Help me get him on the chaise longue behind that screen." Tiny Fidelma was trying to support him and I rushed to help her. Devyn's attempt to aid us was met with the last of Marcus's strength.

"Get away from me or I leave now," he said as he pulled

himself together to walk as much under his own steam as possible.

As Marcus lay back, I turned to Fidelma and Devyn.

"Wait, wait a minute." I held my hands up in front of them, palms facing outwards. "You can't knock him unconscious. How will we get out of here? We'll have to do this some other time."

"There is no other time, Cass. Fidelma will be gone with the rest of the delegation tomorrow," Devyn reminded me.

"Then we'll figure something else out. It's too risky. How will we explain why he's unconscious?" I argued.

"There's no time for something else," Fidelma said as she hustled me out of her way. "We do this now."

I looked to Marcus, who nodded weakly. Whatever Fidelma had already done to him to make him sluggish, clearly he could feel its benefit already… even though this was the last place in the world he wanted to be locked in with three Britons, one of whom was about to practise magic here in the very heart of Roman rule in Britannia. There was no way to make it worse.

"Fine." I moved away as Fidelma again put her palms to the sides of Marcus's head. Almost immediately, Marcus's eyelids fluttered closed and ten minutes later he was completely unconscious as Fidelma started to move her hands slowly down his body.

I stepped outside the delicate partition that stood in front of the chaise longue, crossing to where Devyn waited on the other side of the room.

"I'm sorry," he whispered.

"For what?" I asked tiredly.

"I was so focused on what I wanted that I never stopped to consider the impact all of this might have on you."

"You feel bad that I won't be Papa's little princess anymore?" I was aiming for humour but it fell pretty flat. Marcus knew now and he'd made pretty clear how he felt about our match.

"You'll always be a princess to me."

His aim, also for humour, felt similarly hollow.

"Sure. I'm not your mystery girl. And it looks like I'm not your way in to Marcus anymore either." I finally looked directly at him. "I don't know what I am."

He took a step towards me as if to embrace me. I waved him back. I had never wanted to be in anyone's arms more but I couldn't. I was on my own.

"It doesn't matter if you are a citizen, a Shadower, or a full-blood Briton. You are you. Damn everything else. You can be whoever you want to be. You're not tied to the future they made for you anymore."

I gave him a small smile.

"Neither are you."

His dark eyes widened as he contemplated his own future, the new one that had opened up in front of him. His life's mission had unravelled. He had finally accepted that this girl was dead.

"Right." He was completely stunned by the realisation.

A knock sounded on the door. We didn't answer, hoping that whoever it was would move on. Another jangle as the handle was tried again. Voices in the hall.

"Cassandra?" It was my mother's voice. How did she know I was here?

I looked at Devyn in alarm. "She must have seen us leave. She watches me all the time. What do we do now?" I whispered frantically.

More voices in the hall. Footsteps.

"They'll be going to get something to force the lock," Devyn guessed.

I hurried over to see how Fidelma was doing – her hands had barely moved below Marcus's shoulders. Fidelma shook her head. She needed longer.

"What do we do? They're going to discover us."

Devyn dragged me over to the couch in front of the door.

"Not if they never look any further than us," he announced moving behind me and starting to unlace my dress.

"What are you doing?" I pulled away.

"The one thing that guarantees your mother keeps this quiet," he said, continuing to attack the laces. My mother would go nuts if she came in here and discovered me half dressed—

Oh.

The laces gave and I turned and started to undo the buttons on his shirt, gnawing at my lips with my teeth in order to provide them with a fuller, reddened appearance.

"If we're going to have to serve the time, we might as well do the crime," Devyn grinned as he noticed what I was doing and claimed my lips for himself.

His lips moved over mine with purpose at first, firmly ensuring that there would be no mistaking the reason we were in the room alone together, rubbing his early stubble over my exposed shoulders before kissing his way back up to my lips.

My fingers brushed through his dark curls, tousling them as they had a thousand times in my dreams. I forgot about the people outside and got lost in the moment.

His kiss came again, claiming me in a way that had nothing to do with the people outside and everything to do with the revelations from earlier. Our tongues danced together, the rhythm at once questioning and reassuring, communicating without words in a way we did so much better than when we were actually speaking.

I should have been worrying about the impending doom clattering in the hallway, about Marcus unconscious on the couch, about Fidelma who was risking her life to help him, and what would happen to Devyn when we were discovered. Fidelma and Marcus had a chance of going undiscovered once my mother came through the door and I became the scandal of the city but Devyn would be completely exposed. Devyn, who of all of us needed not to be put in the spotlight. Fidelma, Marcus, and I all had protectors who would help us. Devyn had no one and he had so much more to hide.

The masks. I pulled out of his embrace and dashed across the room behind the screen. It wasn't there and I scanned the room in a panic, holding my dress up with one hand. Where was it? There, on the couch by Marcus's jacket and distinctive shoulder scarf. I grabbed his jacket and the mask. Comprehension dawned and Devyn quickly took off his own jacket.

He grinned as he shrugged into Marcus's jacket and sash.

I poured water from the jug on the sideboard into my hands and ran it through his hair, taming his tangled curls into a rough approximation of Marcus's hairstyle. I'm not sure how we would explain it looking like he had just stepped out of the baths but with his curls smoothed and suppopsedly darkened from the water, if no one looked too closely we had a chance.

"Come with me." His midnight eyes gleamed.

"What?" I didn't follow; go with him where? I could hear keys being tried in the door by my parents and whoever else was outside. I smoothed his hair one more time.

He grabbed me about the waist and pulled me to him.

"Come with me." He kissed me, the merest brush of the

lips. "There's nothing here for you now." He glanced at the door. "I'm not sure what I'll be taking you to. But come."

I smiled back. He was crazy, but I kind of liked it.

I kissed him once more then pulled back quickly. He donned the mask with only seconds to spare before the door finally opened.

My mother and father swept into the room with a senior council member.

"I told you," my mother pronounced, almost delightedly, her every expectation that I would disgrace the family satisfied in one fell swoop.

"Thank you, senator, we'll take it from here." My father blocked the entrance so the guards could not see beyond the door and ushered the elder statesman back out of the room. Having seen enough to have a tale to tell, the man was graceful enough in his departure.

I stood holding my dress up, my bee-stung lips and general dishevelment speaking for themselves.

"Papa—" I started.

"Cassandra, pull yourself together. It's time to go home." His voice was heavy with disappointment.

My cheeks glowed as I started to cry, my embarrassment and general frayed emotions giving me ample ammunition to let the tears flow freely – and helpfully covering any noise from the far end of the room as my fake Marcus retied the laces he had hastily undone only moments earlier. I donned my mask gratefully as I headed for the door, with Devyn in Marcus's costume a step behind.

"Have you nothing to say for yourself?" Camilla addressed what she thought was Marcus and he merely shook his head. Hopefully my sobbing also covered the sound of his teeth grinding together.

My mother didn't wait for any further response. She simply grabbed my hand and dragged her disgraced daughter down the hallway. Back in the ballroom, things were much the same as we'd left them – a little louder maybe as the party got into full swing. My eye caught the flash of long black hair as a girl in Celtic dress pushed through the dancers.

Almost at the exit, Camilla came to a stop as our path was blocked by the same tall Briton who had spoken to me earlier. His eyes blazed behind his golden mask as he quickly sized up the situation.

"Ah, Lord Courtenay, there you are. Might I have a word with you?" he said, his eyes glacial as he spoke to my masked partner in crime.

"Your Highness," my father said and inclined his head. My mother's grip on my arm tightened as the Briton I had spoken to earlier was identified as the Mercian prince. Ha. Was she afraid his mother would strike us from her lair in the north for talking to him?

Devyn shook his head.

My father looked at him aghast.

"I'm afraid I must insist." The Briton reached out and took Devyn's elbow, pulling him aside, and with an elegant bow he indicated to my mother that we should progress. "Donna."

My mother continued to drag me forward, my father bringing up the rear. Devyn was still attempting to free himself until a few curt words from the tall Celt stilled him. His rigid posture betrayed his agitation as I was dragged unceremoniously from my first ball.

Chapter Nineteen

In the days that followed I was kept under house arrest as I waited for the axe to fall. My mother barely spoke to me but it was my father's reaction that hurt most. He barely looked at me.

I had no doubt the scandal of my hustled departure from the ball was the talk of the city, if my parents' reaction was anything to go by. The scandal of a girl caught making out with her match before the handfast. If only they knew the scandal that awaited them.

I'd had no word from Devyn, of course, and even when I had access to comms it was no help as he didn't use them. Now that I was stuck up in my tower, there was no way for me to know what had happened. At least his Briton friend had had the sense to pull him away as we had made our way through the ballroom. What on earth had Devyn been thinking following me, each step bringing him closer to discovery? Unmasked – not just for not being Marcus, but potentially also as a Briton. As a spy. Who had knowingly entered the city and lived here for years illegally.

Sooner or later I was going to be exposed for what I really was. While nobody could say I had intentionally broken the Treaty, my life as I knew it would be over.

I had no word from Marcus either. The Briton delegation had left the city the morning after the ball. I hoped whatever Fidelma had been doing to him had worked. I was shocked at how genuinely ill he had been, at how close to death he had been.

But the one thought that I circled continuously was Devyn's invitation to leave with him. He was right, there was nothing for me here. I had been trapped in a cage that wasn't even mine. Now I was free.

Free to explore the world beyond the walls. The world to which Devyn belonged. He had friends there. Bronwyn. The blond Briton at the ball. At least, I presumed they were friends, though maybe not... What interaction I had seen between them, as brief as it had been, hadn't felt very friendly somehow. Devyn had known the prince though. And his swift intercession had been timely to say the least. Devyn had not wanted to obey the order to walk away from me, but whatever had been said had apparently been effective.

My house arrest came to an end a week after the ball with the arrival of Marcus and his father.

Matthias Dolon was his usual charming self, greeting my mother and father with just the right amount of superiority tinged with chagrin at his son's supposed part in my disgrace. Marcus held himself stiffly, his face impassive, but he looked a lot healthier. The atmosphere was squirmingly awkward while Anna served the tea before leaving the room.

"Now," Matthias announced as soon as we were alone, "what are we to do with our amorous couple?"

My parents both grimaced. What excuse could they make

on my behalf? It was somehow entirely my fault that we were in this situation, though I could hardly protest given that Marcus hadn't actually been a participant. Matthias's gaze was levelled at me, a sneer lurking at the corner of his mouth, disdain a shadow at the back of his eyes. It was a look I had seen before.

"What can we do?" my mother asked, a supplicant to the great senator.

"I think given the circumstances there is only one thing that can be done…" He held the pause for dramatic effect. Marcus had sworn he would not marry me and once the match was broken, even if he didn't reveal my true heritage, I would be ruined. It was a fate that lit a glimmer within me. There would be nothing left for me here in Londinium if the life I had been raised for was gone, leaving me with only one option, a new path and one that increasingly felt like the truer of the two laid before me: Devyn.

"…take place immediately."

I snapped back to realise I had lost the thread of the discussion. "Marcus has been reticent, but he has been made to see sense. It is the only way."

What? I looked to Marcus who sat in stony silence, refusing to look my way.

"Oh, but everyone will think that they actually…" My mother's cheeks reddened.

"Can we be sure they have not?" My father's voice was steady. That was why he couldn't look at me. He thought I… *we* had… in the Governor's Palace of all places.

"No, no, I promise we… nothing really happened," I stammered, helpless to stop myself defending my honour in my father's eyes.

"I think you've given up your right for us to have faith in

you, young lady. Thankfully Marcus has been chivalrously tight-lipped on the subject." The light in Matthias's eyes was calculating. "Unless you have something further to add, there's nothing else for it."

Why would I have anything further to add? What were we talking about? Of course, Marcus had refused to elaborate on what had actually happened. He'd been unconscious for most of it. But for the really important part, he had been totally lucid. Had Fidelma's healing wiped his memory somehow?

"Yes, you're right, of course," Camilla hurried to agree. "There's a great deal to be done in such a short space of time."

"Indeed," Marcus's father said, "I've taken the liberty of securing The Savoy. Given the time frame involved, I wanted to be sure we had a venue before I came here today."

I was thoroughly bewildered at this stage. What were they planning?

"Let me get my diary and we can start straight away," my mother proposed in an alarmingly giddy voice. Camilla walked over to her armoire at the other end of the room and the two men followed. Soon all three were in deep discussion as if they had forgotten Marcus and I were still in the room.

I edged along the couch, closer to where he sat on the armchair, still studiously ignoring me.

"Marcus," I whispered. He didn't acknowledge me with so much as a blink.

"Marcus."

I reached out to touch him and he pulled his arm away.

"Please, are you well?"

"Quite," came his abrupt answer.

I winced. I'd known he would be angry with me but it was a risk I had taken, backing him into a corner where he was already so complicit that he was forced to accept Fidelma's help and remain silent.

"I'm sorry I didn't warn you," I said softly. "I couldn't think of what else to do. You were so ill and you wouldn't have listened to me."

A muscle ticked in his jaw.

"Are you also sorry for the life in which you have trapped us now? You and your friend." He sneered out the reference to Devyn.

"You do remember."

"Everything."

Then why was this farce playing out?

"You didn't tell them?" My fingers were on my pendant.

His green eyes flicked to our parents.

"Tell them what?" He said, his tone hard. "About me? You? Him?"

So he hadn't said anything. But he had been so angry…

"Are you and he…?"

"No," I didn't want him to think I had cheated on him when we parted, and apart from a few stolen kisses I hadn't really, not yet. "That is… nothing ever happened between us, not really."

Marcus finally looked at me. "But you wanted it to."

All my protestations of wanting the life laid before me – marriage to Marcus and becoming the trophy wife of a future senator – had been exposed as a complete and utter travesty as soon as Marcus had said he didn't want me. And Devyn had said he did.

"Yes, I wanted it to," I admitted, wincing. Marcus had shared with me how unwanted his father made him feel and that I too had shown him that he was also not my first choice would hurt. I checked our parents to make certain they weren't listening, my fingers rubbing at the triquetra engraved on the inside of the pendant Devyn had given me. "You and I… we're not a match. We'll find a way out of this."

Marcus looked at me disbelievingly.

"We will, I promise,"

He exhaled. "It's too late now."

"What do you mean?"

"Cassandra, haven't you been listening?" His eyes gleamed with dull resentment. "We're stuck with each other."

"I don't understand," I said, reeling from the horrible emotion I could see in his face.

"We're to handfast imminently. Our wedding will kick off the winter season," he smiled mockingly. "Isn't it such good news, darling?

"What?"

"We're locked in now," Marcus confirmed grimly, our fate sealed by the ruse Devyn and I had staged. "What were you both thinking?"

"I don't know, I suppose our focus was on you not getting caught for unlawful use of magic and ruining your life," I hissed.

"Turns out it is anyway, but at least I'll have company."

I supposed I couldn't blame him for resenting the idea of being bound to me. It was one thing to realise that you didn't have the amazing connection everyone spoke of with their matched partner, but quite another to suspect that your partner would rather be with another.

Suddenly I recognised that the life I had been clinging on to, the one filled with a beautiful home and babies and a wonderful husband, had always been a cage barred by lies and false dreams. The thought of it suffocated me, and that was before I considered that my partner in that life was now looking at me with a resentment bordering on hatred; that our children would be regarded as genetic experiments was the absolute depth of all imagined levels of Hades. I had never really taken the time to think through the implications of Devyn's claim that this was the ultimate purpose of our match and it was something I would do well to consider now. With technology and magic in the city's arsenal…

I paused. I had been so busy refuting Devyn's assertion, that I had never taken the time to ask who was manoeuvring us this way. Marcus's father was powerful; there was no way that this could be happening without the full support of Senator Dolon. I no longer questioned Devyn's assertion that my own family were complicit. There was no getting away from the truth that my father's fortune had increased significantly after I joined the family – his payment for taking a cuckoo into his nest and raising the Wilder child. The idea caused my heart to rip a little. The father who, with infinite patience, had taught me to read, had played with me, treated me to little trinkets that came from far flung places on his ships. He was in on it. That my mother knew too I had no doubt. She had always been aloof and this explained why. Having to raise a Briton brat for breeding purposes would be beneath her dignity. My throat clogged up as my eyes burned.

Alone, used, betrayed, abandoned, I heard the words beating a self-pitying tattoo in my head, but I refused to let it break me. These were not my people. Outside the walls, that was where I would go. Devyn would help me; perhaps I even had family out there somewhere.

I would not stay for this. I would not allow them to do this to me. To us.

"I will not marry you, Marcus," I said, at last, looking up.

Somehow, I was still hurt by the flash of relief I saw in his face before his lips thinned. He looked over at his father.

"Much as I wish you were right, there's no way out. My father knows there was more to the night of the ball than the official story because I didn't return until the next morning. Your friend came back later and told me your cover story." I noted that he still couldn't bring himself to use Devyn's name. "I've spent a week being publicly accused of taking advantage of a well-brought-up young lady whom I've barely even kissed. One who is in love with a spy."

I was still holding tightly to my pendant.

"He's not a spy," I hissed, "you know he isn't. You need to keep your voice down or they will hear you. We can't speak here but I do need to explain,"

"Tell me now," he insisted. "I don't think we're likely to be left alone together again, do you?"

I glanced behind me again. Matthias caught me looking and his gaze was cold. Marcus was right, he suspected more but so far I had given him no reason to think anything more was at play. He could have no idea about Devyn or Fidelma, but what if it wasn't me he suspected? What if it was Marcus?

"Does your father know?"

Marcus raised a brow coolly, a not dissimilar look to the one I had just been on the receiving end of from his father.

"About your…?" I let the sentence hang, unwilling to say the word *magic* in this room, pendant or no pendant.

"No, no way." He shook his head. "If you recall, I didn't have any idea myself until last week."

"You mightn't have, but what if he does?"

Marcus sat back, giving the idea some thought. "Perhaps. He did ask a lot of questions about the night of the ball, like whether I had met any of the Briton delegates and he kept mentioning how much better I was looking. All anyone else has wanted to talk about is what you and I were doing."

I leaned forward. "Devyn believes that the reason for our match is that they want to strengthen the magic in your line. He thinks they're hoping that because I'm a… latent, that our children would be able to… well, I don't exactly know why they want to do it or what they would want from any children with magic. They've spent so long eradicating any trace of it from the Empire. But it would certainly adjust the balance of power if the city could wield magic too."

Marcus stared at me. I'd forgotten how outrageous it all sounded. I hadn't believed Devyn when he told me the first time either. It was all so far-fetched.

"I see."

"You see what? You believe me?"

Marcus shrugged. "These are strange times. I've been thinking a lot about it this week. Fidelma gave me some hints on how to continue to treat people without killing myself in the process and I suppose…"

But before he could complete his thought, our parents concluded their planning session and started to move towards us.

"I expect you two have a lot more to talk about, but I'm afraid it will have to wait until after the handfast." Senator Dolon smiled his false smile at us both.

I looked at my parents in consternation. "What?"

"Matthias feels it would be better if you both keep a low profile until the big day," my mother answered me when no one else spoke up. "It's for the best."

I shook my head. How were we going to get out of this mess if we couldn't speak to each other?

Marcus didn't protest. His father was undoubtedly holding

his career in medicine over him again – he had to toe the line or give up the only thing that meant anything to him. There was no way Marcus could call his bluff, especially now he knew he was the only thing that stood between the city and the epidemic.

I realised that marrying me had probably always been part of the bargain he'd made with his father and it was unlikely he would do anything to jeopardise that. If it wasn't me then it would be some other girl. It probably didn't matter to him.

It mattered to me though.

My first foray back into society elicited a flurry of interest, paps popping up as I met a friend for lunch or shopped with Ginevra on Governor's Road. Each day that passed without sight of Devyn made me increasingly anxious. Had he left with the delegation of Britons? Surely he wouldn't leave without me..

I took to meeting my friend Alianna in a coffee shop that I knew Devyn frequented. Alianna had twin boys, so we were both glad to meet up regularly – Alianna to get out of the house for a break and I in the hope of catching a glimpse of Devyn.

Each time I left the house I watched every person that passed, waiting for him to turn up. He wouldn't go without me. He wouldn't. Not now.

By the end of my first week of freedom, I'd started to notice that a couple of faces were becoming vaguely familiar to me. I wouldn't usually have noticed them but I had developed heightened powers of observation purely as a result of looking out for Devyn. I couldn't be sure if they were friends of Devyn or friends of whoever was pulling the strings in my life.

I started to look for them whenever I went out. There was a tall, lanky man and a smaller slighter one, both dark, both usually in smart-casual clothing which allowed them to blend in for the most part. The main reason I had spotted them was, in fact, their clothing, which had stood out when I went to the basilica library in the vague hope that Devyn might have used it to leave a note for me. I had told him one coffee-shop afternoon where I had hidden his tech and he had been amused; maybe he would think of it and try to communicate with me.

There hadn't been so much as a mote of dust disturbed on the anthropology shelf but an older guy had attracted my attention. His clothing was less overtly fashionable than the outfits of the latest set of citizenship students and a lot sharper than the academics. When I saw the same guy in the reflection of a mirror while trying on shoes a couple of days later, I paid much more attention.

I kept an eye out after that and realised there were in fact two of them. Initially, I was pretty alarmed at the thought of these two strangers watching me every time I left the apartment but if they were the reason I was allowed to leave at all, then it was something to be thankful for.

Trapped indoors as I had been that first week, there had been no chance of contacting Devyn. But if I could go out, I could find a way to contact him. All I needed was to slip my minders, who thankfully kept their distance. They had, I presumed, been instructed to avoid being seen – after all, how would anyone be able to explain to me why I was being watched? Especially since the parental policy had been reversed in the face of speculation in the gossip feeds and I was now under orders to be seen publicly on occasion with Marcus.

Occasions that wilted my soul.

Marcus had been right: we were never alone. There was no chance to talk privately as we were surrounded by people at every party we attended, every lunch. I was sure some of our friends must be under instructions to ensure we were never left alone together because it felt too deliberate to be accidental.

I cornered Ginevra about it when she insisted on going to the bathroom with me when we were out as a group for a pre-theatre dinner. I had chosen to leave the table shortly after Marcus – only because there was a break between courses. Despite my growing loneliness in a world where I couldn't be honest with anyone, I wasn't sure I wanted to speak to Marcus in private anyway; his behaviour was faultless but I could feel the antipathy radiate off him.

I was shocked when Ginevra laughed at my accusation. She confessed laughingly that they were all rallying to make sure the paps couldn't snap anything that could be used against Marcus and me. She was surprised that I wasn't aware of their plan – they had all assumed I was because the request had come from our parents and had been seconded by Marcus.

I had no idea why Marcus had become so active in hemming me in. Perhaps he was doing it for sheer spite because he must know I would be trying to contact Devyn, and he would have no reason to aid and abet what he considered traitorous behaviour. Not to mention the personal betrayal.

My frustration by the end of the second week must have been palpable as Alianna called me on it. Engaging and bubbly, she was also nobody's fool.

"What's with you, Cassandra?"

I could hardly tell her the truth. I didn't like to lie to her either, so I felt my way to somewhere in the middle.

"I feel a bit trapped," I admitted. "Everything has been so hectic with the handfast approaching and I feel like I never have a moment to myself."

Alianna laughed, indicating her two boys, currently entertaining themselves with tearing open the sachets of sugar. "I know how you feel. If I have ten uninterrupted minutes in the shower, I feel grateful. My husband is a darling but as soon as they go off script he's shouting through the door for instructions."

I laughed as Alianna had intended I would when I was struck with a thought. Highly sophisticated it wasn't, but they probably weren't expecting me to try to give them the slip. As far as my shadows were aware, I didn't even know they existed.

"Al, I don't suppose you'd like an hour or two of shoe shopping? My treat." I waved my credit tag in the air. Alianna and her husband were comfortably off but I knew her weakness and we both knew my tag could more than take the heat. I had complained bitterly to my friend that my parents had cancelled the year of freedom after college I had been promised now that my handfast date had been so sharply brought forward. I had been taking my anger out on my credit limit. If shopping was to be my only pastime, then my father could deal with the results. "You'd be doing me a favour. I'll take the boys for a walk and if we swap coats you can show the paps how a real society girl hits the shops."

"I couldn't…" Alianna's protest wasn't convincing.

"You could." I grinned.

And she did. I smiled as, moments after Alianna had swung out of the shop with her hair swept up under my broad-brimmed on-trend hat, wrapped in my electric-blue coat, my smaller shadow trailed by the window of the coffee shop.

I headed towards Ranelagh Gardens on the midlevel, pushing the boys and practically humming. It almost didn't matter if Devyn spotted his chance or not. I felt free. There was an aviary at the gardens and I thought the boys would like the birds.

I hadn't gone far before a casual arm slipped around my waist making us look for all the world like any other family out for an afternoon stroll.

"Clever girl."

A shiver thrilled up my spine at the sound of his familiar mocking tone.

I cast him a sidelong look, taking in his face like I hadn't seen him in years rather than weeks. I had missed him. I always missed him. But since the night of the ball, I had been beyond desperate to see him.

I smiled at the compliment. "I figured it out eventually."

We walked past an older couple who nodded admiringly at us and I laughed out loud at the joy of the moment. I had escaped my shadows and the bloody paparazzi, and I was away from people I no longer trusted – Marcus, my parents, most of my friends who had unwittingly made me feel even more trapped. I was walking on air. The image we were projecting was so far from reality but I didn't care. He was here.

"Are you well?" he asked, unknowingly echoing the words I had said to Marcus.

"I'm fine," I responded. "He didn't tell them anything. We're safe, for now. What happened after I left?

"Didn't Marcus tell you?"

"Not much." I sighed.

"Fidelma was able to heal Marcus, as you no doubt have been able to see for yourself," he said unhelpfully.

"He said she also showed him how to help people while protecting himself," I prompted.

"Yes, she still isn't sure how he's able to heal the sick though."

"They talked about magic? And he's accepted that part of himself?" I asked.

"Not very happily." His mocking tone was back but I felt for Marcus. Like me, he would be struggling to overcome his long-held prejudice which regarded Britons and their primitive magics with disdain. "He was curious to know more about his family in the North."

"But I thought… isn't he the last of the House of York?"

"Yes, Richard Plantagenet died years ago and he was the last of them. I suppose Marcus was curious about what they were like, especially as Fidelma knew old Richard. The Anglians certainly have a reciprocal interest because when Richard died Anglia became a stewardship, and they can't crown a new king while an heir still lives."

"Oh. You mean Marcus."

He nodded.

I vaguely recalled he'd said something about it before, but that was back when the lives and activities of the indigenous peoples of this island had seemed a lot further away than they did now.

"Do you think I might?" I asked, as the thought occurred to me.

"Might what?"

"Have living family out there beyond the walls?"

"Maybe." He smiled. "If we can figure out who you really are."

I grinned back at him as a new world of possibility opened up in front of me.

"The people of Cymru and Kernow are Celts and they tend to be dark, especially with the American and African influences on the coast. Mercians tend to be fairer because that region has had influxes of Northmen over the centuries. Anglia's a melting pot of Normans, Saxons, Anglians, Franks and so on because it was a refuge for all those fleeing the Empire. With that hair you're likely either Anglian or Mercian," he posited. "We'll start there."

I, unlike Marcus, was adopted. I had never looked at another human being and recognised a family trait that we shared. And I never would unless I had children. I checked on the boys, who were now happily sitting on the blanket we had laid out so they could admire the brightly coloured birds flapping about in the aviary. Their chubby little hands reached for the birds that were far too distant for them to grasp.

"Speaking of Mercia"—I was suddenly reminded of the end of the ball—"you know the Mercian Prince."

"I told you I served a house in Mercia." He was dismissive. "The royal house frequently hosts others in Carlisle during festivals."

"Did you ever meet the Lady of the Lake?" I persisted.

"Yes."

"Devyn," I cried. He had met the most famous woman in all Brittania and all I got was a one-word acknowledgement.

"She," he said, considering his words, "is a force to be reckoned with. But I've been gone ten years."

"I was afraid you'd left with them," I confessed.

He shook his head, chuckling softly as he reached across to untangle little Anthony's solid grip on his brother's hair.

"I thought we had an agreement," he said frankly. "I won't be leaving without you. You did agree, didn't you?"

I had kissed him. I guess he had taken that as a yes.

I smiled and nodded, feeling stupidly shy. He would be taking me with him. To his home. A home I had spent some considerable time wondering about during my long empty days of domestic captivity. I had gone over and over what little information I knew about him and pondered the life that waited for him beyond the borders.

"You were the boy, weren't you?" I asked him again. "The one I saw when we were on Richmond Hill, the boy with the man who ran away."

A terse nod was his only reply.

"The man was your father, the one you don't speak to."

Another nod.

Apparently, if I could put the pieces of the jigsaw together, he would let me know if I had put them together correctly. But old habits died hard because he didn't elaborate further.

"Who were they? Were they your mother and sister?" I asked tentatively, unsure if this was territory he would refuse to let me into.

He shook his head softly, sadly. "No, they were from a great house that mine have served for generations. You remember your vision of the burning of Richmond? Did you see anyone with her?"

I nodded, remembering the two horses, the big man falling, the teenage boy and the girl riding away. "The man that Fidelma said was her father and a teenage boy."

"The king's brother, Henry, and Rhys, he was the Griffin

then, her personal guard. The Griffin role has come through my house since the time of legend."

"Your father was the Griffin." This much I already knew. "And the lady he protected was also a descendent… of Elizabeth Tewdwr?"

I had tried to find out more about her in the quiet, dusty shelves of the forum since returning from Richmond, where nobody could track my activities, but it was impossible to find out what had happened on the Britons' side of the war because there weren't any records of that. I was glad to have learned Elizabeth had made it to safety.

"Yes, Elizabeth fled further north and found sanctuary for a time in Dudley. Eventually she married one of the sons of the house. The lady you saw would have been her great-great-something-granddaughter."

I connected the dots.

"And your father was supposed to protect her?" Which he had not, I recalled. He had ridden away leaving the woman and baby to die. "You mourned her?"

"We all did."

"We? Who's we?" Who else had mourned that mother and child? He ignored the question but offered me something else in exchange.

"My lady's death was a great loss to our people. The blood is strong in her line and without her we have suffered greatly; she tended the Belinus ley line in the north." He looked at me, his eyes dark. "I was surprised when my abilities, those gifted to the Griffin, appeared. I was built to be the perfect bodyguard. Her protector. I took it as a sign that her daughter was still alive. As soon as I was old enough, I came to the city to find her."

"Why did you think she was in Londinium?"

"My lady was killed near the borders and not many people live there. If there were someone in the populace fitting her description, I would have heard about it."

"What?" I laughed. "Are orphans so rare in the wilds?"

"No, Cass, unfortunately not. But those with abilities like yours are extremely rare. Which was why when you stopped taking the pills and showed some abilities I was so sure you had to be her." He smiled ruefully.

"Will I be welcomed by the Britons?"

"Far more welcome than me. I disobeyed them in coming here." He looked briefly less serious. "In fact, they were pretty sure that I had joined my lady and her daughter – until recently they'd no word from me since I left."

"They thought you were dead?" I interpreted.

He nodded, a mischievous look on his usually serious face.

"I'm not sure they were all so pleased to discover otherwise when I eventually turned up."

"Why not? Surely, you being alive is a good thing?"

He turned sombre. "I broke an oath in coming here. What my father did was unspeakable. I was given a chance to atone for his action, to be of service… and I left, on a wild goose chase. I'm not sure what I'll be returning to. What I'll have to offer you."

That explained Bronwyn's behaviour somewhat. She had demonstrated an odd combination of emotions, which I now recognised as relief, delight, and annoyance – all feelings which Devyn regularly inspired in me. I wondered who Bronwyn was to him. Did she have some claim on him perhaps?

Devyn glanced at the time. "How long do you have?"

"Damn." I had been so fascinated by his story that I hadn't

thought. I needed to get back to the café. Alianna would be frantic.

I started to gather up the boys and put them in their pushchair. Poor little mites, despite being thoroughly wrapped up their hands were cold in the autumn chill.

"I have to get back."

"So I gather." Devyn buckled in one of the boys and pulled a face, making the baby gurgle.

"I don't know when I'll be able to get away again," I told him hurriedly. "When I can, how will I find you?"

"Here." He handed me a sliver of paper – how incredibly quaint. He must have had it ready to slip to me in case our contact had been more fleeting. "It's my address. I can't spend all my days watching in case you give them the slip. I need to make preparations to get us out of the city. You can find me there most evenings."

I started to push the boys towards the park exit. Noting the address, my eyebrows shot up in surprise; it was only a few blocks away from my home.

Reading my expression accurately, he reminded me that he'd had to have an address in the area in order to attend the same school as me. He'd been nearby the whole time. I paused in dismay.

"There are so many questions I haven't asked you," I complained. "How soon do you think we can leave? Where will we go? Have you been able to find out any more about who I might be? Or where I'm from?"

What does me leaving with you mean for us? What did that kiss mean? Why did you try to follow me after that kiss?

These last questions of course I didn't ask out loud. The very thought of asking made me cringe. Maybe the kiss had meant nothing. Adrenaline had been high. Perhaps it had been nothing more than that.

I didn't believe that, not for a second, but I was still too chicken to ask him directly.

"I need a little more time." He pushed me towards the gate and when I resisted he smiled wryly before continuing. "I have the tech but I have to be careful. The Code feels sticky, like a web, and I have to make sure I don't set off any alarms. So it's taking more time than I'd like. We'd both need papers to go out the way Oban did and security at the gates seems to be heightened right now."

"Not too much more time," I said. "The handfast ceremony has been moved up and it's soon. The announcement will be this week."

"But I thought you had a year…"

Traditionally graduates had at least a year of freedom before marrying and that had certainly been my plan.

"Not anymore." I didn't need to explain why. "Why don't we go out the way we took Marina?"

He hesitated, his brows drawing together.

"We could, it's an option. But I would have to ask for help and that makes it complicated."

"More or less complicated than trying to mess with the Code?"

He sighed, running a hand through the messy curls that were starting to lengthen in his hair, which was way overdue for a haircut.

"I'll think about it. One way or another, I'll have a plan when we next meet," he said finally.

He pushed me more firmly towards the gate. "Go. You'll never get away again if you get accused of kidnap."

I reluctantly started back to my cage.

Chapter Twenty

"We wait until after the handfast."

I stood there stunned, unable to believe what I was hearing.

"What? Why?" Why would he let the ceremony take place? How could he bear the thought of me being publicly bound to another man? I would break in half if I were in his place and had to watch the bursts that had multiplied over the last couple of weeks since the ball. Marcus and I were the hottest couple in town; all aspects of our impending handfast were wildly speculated on.

With all the preparation for the ceremony it had been impossible to get away but after the bridal tea with my mother and her friends to celebrate my last fitting, I had finally been able to slip out under the pretext of buying a personal handfast gift for Marcus. The public gift had already been purchased and my mother had enjoyed being coy about what it might be with her friends.

All that had sustained me in the last weeks was the sure knowledge that if I made it to Devyn he would have a plan in place and we would be out of the city before I was even missed.

"I don't understand. You want me to be bound to Marcus?"

Devyn's mask was stubbornly in place. He'd activated a charm when I arrived, so we could not be overheard, but otherwise his home, which I had never been to before, was as perfectly civilised as any I had ever known.

It was a converted flat in Battersea and it had notes of the past woven amidst its chrome perfection, including a glass exterior wall which looked out onto one of the smallest but most delightful gardens I had ever seen. Even as I stood there immobilised, waiting for him to find the words to explain, I was mesmerised. It was an intimate verdant glen nestled inside the urbanity of his home and somehow seeped through the hard modernity, softening the edges.

"Those are my orders." He finally broke his silence but remained equally as still as me. He'd asked for help and this was the result.

I felt as though I was made of glass and one wrong move would shatter me from the soul out.

"I don't understand," I repeated.

Devyn took a stilted step towards me, entering my space but hovering as if he was aware of how fragile my composure was and afraid of what might happen next. I had never seen him so unsure of himself.

I moved away from him, needing distance to gather myself. To try and piece together what had happened. I moved around his flat, listlessly touching his possessions, abjectly curious about the place he had called home while he'd lingered on the periphery of my world.

I lifted the small objects that sat on the gleaming surfaces, innocuous and personality-free, as if a designer had created the perfect home and nobody had moved in yet. Nothing really spoke of Devyn. I walked up to the small mezzanine and backed away when I realised I was at the threshold of Devyn's bedroom. Here at least was some sign of life – clothes strewn on the floor, a couple of shelves robbed of their items, which seemed to have hit the far wall and lay broken on the floor. The tousled bed dominated the room as well as my focus. I wouldn't have put Devyn down as a restless sleeper; he was usually so self-contained. Maybe not so much at the moment though.

A cough beneath me reminded me that I wasn't alone and my cheeks heated as I realised I was staring at Devyn's bed while Devyn was watching.

I made my way downstairs, keeping my eyes carefully averted as he watched me prowl and poke around his home. I corrected myself, his *house*; this was not his home.

Drawn outside to the garden, I perched on the side of the fountain that bubbled out of the ferns that covered the wall and ran along the ground before disappearing through a drain on the far side. This at least spoke of more than the carefully constructed urbanite. I had never seen such a decadent, untamed garden.

"Cass…" His voice was tentative.

"I need you to explain."

He took a seat behind me on a couch tucked in an alcove out of any rain. "I made contact to ensure someone will be there to meet us once we exit the city. They *will* help, but I've been given orders to bring Marcus as well. We need him."

"Marcus. Of course," I repeated dully. "How?"

My mind turned over the possibilities. How would we persuade Marcus to leave the city? He already resented me, he loathed Devyn, and he bore no love for the Wilders.

The handfast. The pre-wedding ceremony to bind our pending union.

"You think… once the handfast has taken place, he'll follow me?"

The handfast ceremony was rumoured to produce some strange effects. Handfasted couples were known to be affectionate with each other even if they never had been before. It was traditional to be married within no more than a month or so of the handfast, but couples promised to each other from a young age, such as we had been, were also given the opportunity to break the handfast and call off the wedding entirely. It was an option that supposedly ensured no one ever had to marry against their wishes if they decided the match was not true. But this was unheard of. I'd witnessed couples that had been undeniably indifferent to each other before the handfast become utterly devoted to each other and desperate to tie the knot by the end of the period.

"That's our belief," he said.

There was no way that Devyn was unaware of the effects of the handfast. All he'd done for years was study the citizenry; he missed nothing. It also explained his strange mood. He was coiled tighter than I had ever seen him, every muscle wound tight, every emotion battened down, clearly preparing for a storm that would devastate us both.

But who would be the one to unleash that storm? Even as my own rage simmered to the surface, I sensed that underneath the rigid mask Devyn was not happy about his orders either.

"Marcus is barely speaking to me" I said, "ever since the night of the ball. He knows I feel nothing for him except as a friend. He wouldn't even call me that now. He blames me, I think, for the magic. He's convinced himself that somehow I'm responsible for it, for what happened with Fidelma, with you, everything. I think he's going along with the handfast, with the marriage"—I looked at Devyn for a reaction, but there was nothing—"in order to keep practising medicine. His father has been watching us closely. I'm sure he knows there's something we're hiding. I'm just a silly lowborn with mixed blood, but I think he knows there's more to Marcus's successes with the illness. The way he watches him is… like he's not *human*, like he's something he'd rather lock in a cage."

"You care for him?" Devyn asked emotionlessly, leaning further back into the shadows of the cascading plants.

Did I care for him? Marcus in public was still the perfect gentleman, but I found it increasingly difficult to be the girl on his arm as we attended events. I used to suppose him a vain party boy who played at being a doctor. I knew better now; he had allowed me to see behind the glamour, behind the public face that was Marcus Courtenay, and he had nearly killed himself trying to help others. He was struggling to accept the magic in his blood, and the tightening snare towards which we were being marched, and he blamed me for some of it.

It wasn't fair, but I was the one who had forced him to face the truth. I consoled myself by remembering that if I hadn't, he would most likely be dead by now. That didn't mean he'd thanked me though. Since the few minutes during which we had managed to talk while they'd planned our lives for us, he had treated me as an obligation, coolly aloof beneath a charming façade. It made my skin crawl… or at least want to very badly punch him in the face. Anything for an honest reaction.

"Yes," I stated. It was the truth. I *did* care. Not in the sense Devyn implied, but if I couldn't punch Marcus in the face then Devyn was an equally deserving target. Marcus might resent the fact that we were being hurried into handfasting, but for Devyn to stand by and do nothing when he had a viable alternative was unforgivable.

"What *is* the plan then? How will this work?"

"I'll use you." Devyn's smile was dark. "Handfasted couples can't be apart for long periods. It has something to do with the arm cuffs you wear in the pre-wedding period. I guess the powers that be really believe that artificially manipulated closeness makes the heart grow fonder."

"Won't they just take it off his arm if I leave the city without him?"

"I don't think they can. From what I've been able to discover it's triggered to release only on completion of the marriage ceremony. It doesn't seem to be in any way technologically controlled, despite what the Empire insists. I've researched it as far as I can. It was first used at the Treaty wedding because Princess Margaret and her Courtenay groom shared no love for each other after the generations of warfare. I'm assuming they've somehow managed to replicate the Celtic magic so somebody beyond the walls should be able to get it off you both."

"Should?" It all sounded incredibly iffy to me. "If that doesn't work, what then? After everything, Marcus and I would be stuck together anyway."

"We will figure it out," he promised.

I wasn't as convinced as Devyn that Marcus would be willing to flee the city, to abandon his medical career *and* his patients, all for me, magic cuff or no. But what choice did we have? It was too late now.

My blood was now riled by more than just worry about the logistics of our escape across the wall. The distance Devyn was keeping between us was noticeable. I thought things had changed between us the night of the ball, that I'd seen through the wall he'd built up, that he did want me. Yet I could feel him pulling away.

"And us?" I whispered.

Again, Devyn was slow to answer. "There is no us."

He couldn't be serious.

A rustle ran through the grove, disturbing the peace and alerting Devyn to the anger rippling through my veins.

"If there is no us, explain to me why I should leave my life here for some hovel beyond the wall with your barbarian friends," I hissed.

"Cass, you…"

He leaned forward and ran a calming hand along my arm. At least, I presumed he meant it to be calming. Instead, it was as though a lick of fire seared along my skin in the wake of his fingertips. It was all I could do to refocus on his words as he continued speaking.

My mind was reeling from the impact of the change of plan. We weren't leaving. I was handfasting with Marcus. But I was here now. We were alone. I had one last chance to remind him of what we were together, what he was now so casually risking to follow orders. He had promised me we were leaving together.

"I have nothing to offer you once we leave. Less than nothing, as I've just been reminded." His tone was flat, deadened. The words had the ring of a refrain that had been repeated over and over like a mantra.

I turned from the fountain to face him. He was much closer than I had expected and my eyes dropped towards his lips as I raised a fingertip to trace the outline of his face. He frowned.

"Are you listening to me? We can't… You need to handfast to Marcus."

But my eyes and fingertips were busy exploring every pore, every beautiful angle and plane of his face.

"Cass, dammit." He detached my hands from his face and pulled away. "I have my orders. I won't be my father. He brought ruin on our house, on our family, on our people that day. Because he loved me. Much good it did him. I haven't uttered a word to him since. I will not fail in my duty again."

I watched as the vein in his temple pulsed. He hadn't spoken to his father since that day on the river? But he'd only been a child himself.

"Nor will I be weak like him. I will do the right thing for our people. They come first, before me. Before you." He spoke like he was making a vow. He looked incandescent, like a righteous avenging angel. Steadfast in the face of temptation.

I realised I was that temptation. I smiled wickedly at him as I leaned in, but he leaned away until he fell back against the couch.

"Why does it have to be a choice? We can follow your orders and bring Marcus. Then we can see about everything else… It's not a weakness to want each other," I informed him gravely as I traced his face again with my fingertips. Nothing could be more certain. We wanted each other; everything else could be worked out later.

Wanting Devyn was all I had thought about for months and now it was the sole focus of my entire mind, body, and soul. Realising we were far too far apart, I moved forward, straddled his lap, and was rewarded by the sight of those dark eyes dilating. I squirmed closer and an intimate twitch told me he was not nearly as indifferent as he strove to appear.

"Cass, what the – what is wrong with you?" His voice was a husky growl.

Good question. I was furious with him… and apparently I

was pouring that rage and frustration into seduction. If tomorrow I was to handfast with Marcus, then I was making the most of tonight. Of what was real when Devyn and I were together.

After the final fitting, I had gone to tea with my mother and her sister and some of their friends, as was the tradition. But I had been served a different brew to everyone else, a traditional bridal tea that was taken during the handfast month. There had been a comment from one of the women that Marcus and I were hardly in need of it, which had earned her a glare from my mother. I had become so used to snide comments like this since the ball that I hadn't given it much thought at first.

There had been some knowing glances between the women as I sat there going through the motions, pretending to blush at their cringingly racy talk, wondering how I could get to Devyn this evening.

My mother's prompt to drink my tea had disturbed my ruminations on what it would be like once we were gone from here, out over the borders. Into the future. I had thought I'd be gone. Instead, I would have to continue living the charade my life had become. I'd lifted the tea to sip it and had caught another round of conspiratorially smirking glances between the women. Had they slipped something in my tea? It wasn't possible... or was it? There were rumours that more physical relations between a reluctant couple were actively encouraged during handfast. How actively encouraged?

I had taken a sip and felt the liquid warming me, confirming my suspicions. They wanted me to engage in illicit activities.

In that case, far be it from me to abstain. I traced Devyn's lips. Again, he grasped my hands in his own to pull them away but from my much more intimate position all I had to do was lean in to take his lips with my own.

Devyn groaned as my tongue replaced my fingers, tracing his lips, probing. His groan deepened as he gave in and finally kissed me back. Our tongues tangled and dived, enmeshed in each other. It felt like heaven and I smiled delightedly as I took a breath.

Devyn used the break to turn his face away and I mewled my frustration.

"Please, Devyn."

His hands were like a vice, moving to my upper arms and holding me away from him. I wriggled our lower bodies together to compensate.

"Cass, stop. What are you doing?"

"What does it feel like I'm doing?" I might have managed to pour out most of the drugged tea but the tiny sip I'd swallowed had heightened my senses and now I was inclined to indulge them.

Devyn groaned again. He stood, taking me with him, ensuring our bodies were no longer touching. The delicious warmth tingling through me cried out for more.

"Please," I begged. "Don't you care at all?"

"Of course I care, but I've told you we can't do this. We can't be together."

"Why, because you have nothing? When we leave I won't have anything either. It doesn't matter to you at all that tomorrow I'll be handfasted to another man?"

"Tomorrow?" he echoed. "Next week, you mean?"

"Tomorrow," I repeated. "Tomorrow is the big day when I get to be the luckiest girl in Londinium. Who wouldn't want the charming Marcus Courtenay, with his stunning green eyes, and that hair—"

"Cassandra," he cut me off, "not *tomorrow*; the ceremony is next week."

"It's tomorrow," I spat. "The other date was just to fool the paps. My dress is already sitting in my wardrobe."

He looked stunned.

"I'm supposed to be at home with my mother right now," I added, "fussing over last-minute preparations or sneaking off to meet my future husband – that's what other girls do the night before. She didn't seem bothered when I asked if I could go and buy Marcus a present; if anything she seemed relieved."

I stopped talking when I realised Devyn was no longer listening to me.

"Tomorrow…" he growled.

But then he leaned in to kiss me.

And it blew the previous one away. If the last had been a candle lighting the dark recesses of my soul, this was a trillion-watt bulb. His kiss was demanding, possessive, claiming. It told me over and over that I was his, only his, always his. I returned it like for like. For if he owned me, then I also owned him. Every part of him was mine. The flame licked higher, seeking ever more fuel. I felt his shirt tear as I tugged at the unwieldy buttons. Then his chest was bare, free for my hands to roam across and around behind his back, clawing at his shoulders.

He held me to him as I bowed backwards and his mouth pressed hard against mine, his lips moving across my throat like a man possessed.

"Yes," I sighed, hitching a leg over his hip. I wasn't sure whether it was my word or my action, but something snapped him back. He stilled, his breathing heavy as he tried to claw back his usual iron control.

"Cass," he rasped, "what is *wrong* with you?"

I giggled. Despite my frustration that he had put distance between us again, my eyes were still having a great time roving across all the bare skin on show now that his shirt was mostly off.

"Bridal tea." I smiled wickedly, though in truth it was merely an excuse to hide behind.

The lack of comprehension on Devyn's face tickled me enormously. Usually, I was the one trailing a step behind.

"Ah, clever Devyn, you don't know everything then," I teased. "Let me go and I'll tell you."

He might be a step behind on the bridal tea and my plan for what little freedom remained to me, but he more than saw my next move coming as he slowly released me and stood in suffering silence as I sidled up to him and started stroking his smooth silken skin. It was golden bronze, darker in the hollows. He stopped my hand and I looked up at him blankly.

I took a seat in the corner of his idyllic little nook in the wall and beckoned him closer, patting the seat beside me.

"The handfast isn't just about..." I paused until he complied and took a seat beside me. "Not just about the soon-to-be-happy couple spending time together. Though, clever boy"—I tangled my fingers in the glossy hair on his clever, clever head—"spending time together is certainly encouraged. You've got to know it often has certain... that is to say, what outraged everyone at the ball will be expected as soon as we are handfasted. My match is a lie foisted upon me so tonight I want to choose my truth. Tonight, I choose you."

It was outrageous, and the closer I got to being married the more I realised it was all a complete sham. There was no such thing as being matched; centuries ago, families arranged the marriages of their children – they still did. Now they used aphrodisiacs and other contraptions to ensure that the couple were happy to walk down the aisle together. At the end of the handfast, it could all still be called off, though I had never heard of that happening… and now I knew why. From the tiny sip I'd taken, I had no doubt that drinking the whole cup would have incited me to crawl across hot coals if it meant I could have Devyn right now, an urge that was supposed to be leading me in Marcus's direction were I not so distracted by another.

"If you don't tell me what's going on, I'm going to put a new shirt on," Devyn said very, very slowly.

"It appears the devious council pretty much guarantee that a handfasted couple will want to be together," I informed him. "I had tea with my mother today. It's tradition. Oops. I told you that already. But did I tell you it makes me want to do the most interesting things to you?"

"You mean you've been drugged." He went very still, flinching away from me.

"Mmm, that was certainly what they intended, although you are not its intended target. But don't worry, after I'm handfasted its effects will no longer be wasted on you." I moued sadly.

Every muscle underneath my roving hands tensed.

"You don't feel anything for him though," he said.

I kissed his lips softly, tenderly.

"No, but you don't want me," I sighed. "And he'll be there."

Devyn growled, capturing my hands and staring into my eyes.

"I want you."

"Then take me." I smiled. "Please. Let it be you."

His eyes turned sombre. "You're out of your mind. You don't know what you're saying."

"I know exactly what I'm saying." My hand came up and rested flat against his cheek. "I don't know what the future holds. Maybe I never make it across the wall. Maybe I marry Marcus and give the Empire what they want. Maybe I'm completely trapped in this life."

I willed him to hear me. I had put myself out there. I couldn't bear it if he turned me away.

I needed him. He was here. I had always wanted him. And I was here.

"But just for tonight. This one single night. Couldn't we be together? Then I will go and do as your friends ask."

Haunted eyes looked back at me. I could see the battle he fought inside. I had heard him earlier and I knew how important his cause was to him. How shamed he was by his father's weakness. That he prided himself on his strength of will. He was the most single-minded person I had ever known. I prayed to whatever gods existed that he would let that iron will bend. Just this once.

"You know," I said impishly, "on the night of her handfast I saw my oh-so-prim-and-proper older cousin push her groom up against a wall and then she put her hand down here…" My hand slipped just a whisper beneath the waistband of his trousers. "I wondered at the time what she was doing…"

I leaned into his unmoving figure and kissed him again, my teeth taking hold of his bottom lip and tugging.

"I only want to do that with you," I sighed into his ear.

He started to take hold of me to lift me away. "You don't know what you're doing. It's the drug."

"It's not the drug." Damn him, why couldn't he let me hide

behind the excuse of the tea. But I had been manipulated all my life. This, *this* was for me. I chose this. "I didn't drink it."

His dark eyes narrowed.

"I'm not saying it to…" I sighed. "I realised what it was and I only had a tiny amount. I'm in my right mind. And my right mind is telling me this might be our last chance. Our only chance."

Please.

He swayed. Actually swayed and then he pulled me to him once more in a kiss that was deeper and stronger than any drug.

"Thank you," I gasped as he moved to that corner where my neck met my shoulder and my eyelids closed as my head fell back.

He pulled back to look at me, but before I started to panic that he was going to say no again his hands started moving up under my top, cupping my breasts, teasing the tender tips.

"Thank you?" he laughed, repeating my words, his knee between my legs. "You will be the death of me."

"But what a way to go," I finished for him before all thought ceased as his hand moved up along my inner thigh.

There in the garden, we explored each other for the first time, both knowing it might be our last. We took it slowly, learning each other, feeling, sensing, tasting, hearing what we were together. How we moved together. Until he looked down at me and entered softly, gently.

We were one, and it was like a kaleidoscope of colour and sense as we moved together.

It felt like drawing a deep breath on a beautiful dawn morning, the world glowing with possibilities. It was an explosion of possibilities and beauty as I broke apart in his arms.

"I love you."

His voice or mine, I wasn't sure. We collapsed together, momentarily senseless, limbless.

I could feel the joy pulsing through him, the wonder mirroring mine. I felt so close to him, like we had opened up a connection. A bond.

I could *feel* what he could feel.

My breath left me in a long exhale, every particle of me relaxing into the moment.

Shock.

I was feeling his shock, no… his *horror*. He was horrified.

Pushing him off me, I scrambled away, my fist against my mouth, holding back the sobs threatening to overwhelm me as the shame and self-loathing rolled through him to me.

Devyn stared at me in the twilight. Bulbs set into the cascade of plants on the wall had flickered on as dusk fell. Then it was as if a door slammed shut and all those emotions were gone; his face was a blank mask and I was left alone with my own bewilderment.

I blinked. I had felt him. I had felt his emotions as if they were my own.

"Devyn."

He came towards me, then grabbed a blanket from the couch and placed it around my shoulders.

"We shouldn't have…"

"Please don't say it," I said. "I don't think I can bear to hear you say it."

He pulled on his trousers and ran his hand through his tangled hair.

I nodded, all of a sudden too tired even to pull my own clothes back on.

Only moments ago I had been a butterfly soaring in the

sunlight, glorious, beautiful, free… and now I lay broken on the ground, my wings crushed.

Being with Devyn had been so much more than I had hoped for. It had felt like the world clicking into place and everything that left me staring at the ceiling at night, all the worry and fear of the last months, had been as nothing against the sheer beauty of being with him.

The spectacular depth of emotion I had felt, the ecstasy, the love… not all of it had been my own. It had been *other*. Just like the following emotions that came crashing in, the shame and anger, had not been mine, they had been Devyn's. I had felt Devyn's emotions.

My brow creased as I looked at him standing beside the patio door, watching me with heavy-lidded eyes as I tried to process everything still curled up in the alcove where he had abandoned me.

"I felt…" I stumbled. "I *felt* you."

No reaction.

"Devyn. Don't do this. Tell me," I pleaded. "I felt you, didn't I?"

Glass splintered and smashed into a million twinkling pieces on the floor, catching the light as they scattered across the garden.

I gasped in shock at the violence that had exploded from him. I took in his bloodied fist, the shattered door. I started to get up to cross to him, anxious to examine the extent of the damage.

"Stop. Don't move."

My foot stilled inches from the ground. His dark head was bowed, his chest rising and falling as he inhaled deeply a couple of times.

"Crossing to me will only get you hurt," he said, his voice reflecting the irony he felt at his own choice of words.

"I don't care," I said.

He sighed. "You should."

He then began to cross the garden towards me, barefoot, still clad only in his trousers.

"Wait, what are you doing?" I cried, alarmed.

He shot me a weary smile.

"A childhood spent running barefoot around the mountains and valleys prepares one for walking across the destruction of a fool."

Reaching down, he swung me up into his arms, blanket and all, and carried me back to the relative safety of the inner apartment before returning to gather my clothes from the garden. I could do no more than sit watching him move about like a prowling cat, his movements lean and efficient. There was no sign of the heightened emotion that had caused him to punch through a sheet glass door. In silence, I pulled on the clothes he handed back to me before standing and lifting my head determinedly.

"Show me your hand."

"It's fine," he returned flatly.

"It's not fine, and I'm not leaving until you show it to me." There was nothing more I could threaten him with, but I knew that more than anything he wanted me out of there. He put his hand out in front of him, palm up, and reluctantly turned it over to show me the damage he had inflicted on himself. Blood covered his fingers and knuckles, welling and dripping onto the impeccably polished floor.

I crossed over to him and grasping him around the forearm resolutely dragged him across the room towards the small kitchen I had seen earlier when I explored his living space.

Running the cold water, I pulled his hand until he stood behind me while the water washed away the worst of the blood. I could feel the warmth of his breath on my neck, sense his body curve into mine as we stood there and watched the evidence of his moment of madness swirl down the drain. Closing my eyes to the blood in the sink, I breathed in his closeness, a small smile tilting my lips at the sheer comfort of it, the intimacy of standing here with him, our breaths synchronising, and again I felt a small tendril of shared emotion pulse between us.

I turned in wonder.

"How is that possible?" I asked.

His mouth was a thin line and the pulse went dead once more. I swallowed my disappointment and, still holding his hand, towed him over to the kitchen bar and sat him on a stool. Turning away from the sight of him still temptingly shirtless, I started pulling open drawers and shockingly bare cupboards.

"Top left."

I opened the cupboard above the fridge and found what I was looking for. Returning, I sat beside him and examined the contents of the first aid kit, pulling out antiseptic and bandages.

"Tweezers?" I clipped out.

"I'll get them."

He started to rise.

"You'll get blood everywhere." Laying my palm on his bare shoulder I pushed him back down onto the stool. "Where are they?"

"Bathroom, upstairs."

The bathroom was off his bedroom. I nodded and went back through the living room, trying not to take in the sight of the garden that had so enchanted me when I walked in an impossibly short time earlier. I studiously ignored the smashed door, glass-strewn patio, and the couch in the nook.

Climbing the stairs, I reflected that the need that had heated my blood on arrival was entirely gone. Truth be told, it had never been all that strong – as effective as a torch in daylight, its amplifying effect nothing to what already existed. It was merely an excuse to pretend it was brighter than the already blazing sun of my attraction to Devyn.

Collecting the tweezers from the spartan bathroom took a matter of moments when I needed hours before I would feel ready to face him again. He had rejected me. Again. After… after… I was an idiot. He had made it clear time and again that he did not want me. Or at least, he might want me, but he didn't want to want me. Time to get the message. I braced myself before entering the kitchen again.

Taking a seat, I began carefully to remove the first splinter of glass from his knuckle. Once it was out, I laid it on a piece of tissue and lightly swabbed the blood oozing from the wound before moving on to the next piece.

"Are you all right?" he asked quietly.

"Peachy," I threw out blithely.

His breath was warm on my bowed neck.

"Cass…" he began.

"No, really. All good," I said, cutting him off. "Message received."

"What message?"

"You know, it's been fun, but you aren't interested." I was incredibly proud of the casual tone I was managing to maintain. "This was a once off; let's put it down to the effect of my unexpectedly imminent handfast."

There was no response from above as I snagged another

splinter and set it on the tissue, where I now had quite the little collection going.

I felt that connection open and a questioning pulse tentatively beat across it. My head snapped up as I instinctively mirrored the action I had felt him do and slammed the walls down against it. My eyes blazed into his. At least he had the grace to look somewhat shamefaced.

"What is that?" I demanded.

"I…" He shook his head slightly, struggling for words.

"You can feel what I feel?"

"Yes," he admitted curtly.

"When I saw the sentinels attack you on the riverbank, I sensed a connection between you and the baby," I said aloud as I recalled the memory I had seen.

"Yes."

"Is this what it felt like?"

"Yes." He ran a hand through his hair again. "That was an awareness, usually triggered by danger. She was a baby; I don't know what this is… it's more."

I felt as if I… Actually, I didn't know how I felt. As if I was the baby and the woman I had seen was my mother. The little boy screaming for me was… How could I have been so slow to realise what he had figured out almost instantly? Fidelma had been wrong. I wasn't some random girl who happened to have magic. My dream hadn't been *her* alternate present; it was the life that should have been mine. The girl he was searching for and I were one and the same.

"Does this mean…?"

His eyes were glowing as he nodded. "It must be."

"I'm her."

"Yes."

Even without the connection between us I could see he was

bursting with emotion. The connection… as soon as he'd felt it he'd known. And his reaction had been to punch a door. And I knew that being with me had made him feel ashamed. My lower lip trembled and, unable to process it, I resumed my task.

"Cass." His soft use of my name was concerned, questioning. His good hand rose and lifted my chin until I faced him."What is it?"

"Why is it so bad?" I asked, sucked in by the intimacy of our closeness to betraying the cause of my dismay. "Being with me?"

His eyes darkened. "I broke a vow. I gave up everything to find you. And I have." His voice was velvet gravel. "You're alive. That's all I could have hoped for. All I ever wanted. This – you and me – cannot be. This was a mistake. If I had known… I would never have…" He steadied himself. "Cassandra, I've found you. I can finally take you home."

Cassandra? I blinked.

"You're saying that me being this girl means we can't be together?"

"Yes. We must forget this ever happened. I had no right to tonight." At this, he kissed me softly. It was as clear a goodbye as I could imagine.

I stood up, pushing away from him. "No. You promised. I'm leaving the city for you, for us. You can't just change your mind."

"I have a duty, and that duty comes first. Always. Do you understand? I will not break my vow; I will not put anything before it. Certainly not myself. Not anything."

I could barely breathe as he spoke. It wasn't that he didn't want me. What he was saying was that no matter what was between us his duty came first, and he would never betray it for me. Though he had tried to push me away before he found out who I was, it seemed that his rejection was even more emphatic now that history and magical vows and whatever were involved. Fine.

I needed a minute. I resumed my seat and dropped my lids to cover my eyes. I picked up his bloody hand and returned to my work, only to find I couldn't see through the blur caused by my tears. To my horror, one escaped and splashed on the surface of the counter as I tried to blink them away.

His hand came again, this time to cup my shoulder, and I shrugged him off. Eyes cleared, I checked his knuckle for any further evidence of glass and, finding none, started to wrap the bandage around his calloused hand. I marvelled again at how nobody noticed the slight oddities that marked him out as not being one of us, not a citizen, and certainly not an elite.

"Catrio..." he breathed. Was that the name I'd had as a baby? Even my name wasn't my own anymore. But he stopped himself and just said, "Cassandra."

"No." I stepped back, my legs wobbly, my hand raised to keep him away. My thoughts were bouncing from one to another, careening wildly with no control. *I was the girl he had come to find.* That baby had been connected to the little boy, the little boy whose grief had been mindless when the connection was broken. It was a connection that had been made whole once more. And his first act was to push me away. I was alone. I'd been alone for so long. He had what he wanted, they all had what they wanted. What about what *I* wanted?

I tied off the bandage, and once I was sure I had myself under control, I found my best careless tone.

"You still expect me to leave the city with you."

His head jerked back up to look at me, thrown at the suggestion that for me this might no longer be a given.

"Now more than ever. You must—" He stopped the rush of words and took a breath. "Cass, you must see you can't stay here now. It's too dangerous. If you are discovered, if they realise who you really are…"

"And who am I?"

His eyes shuttered.

"Right," I exhaled on a laugh that teetered on the edge of not entirely stable. "Of course, you're not going to tell me."

I had no idea who I was or where I'd come from but the only thing that was clear, even from here in the dark, was that I couldn't stay. I felt trapped, and that trap was growing ever tighter. I was no longer leaving to go towards a future I had imagined with Devyn, the only thing that had been real to me about this future beyond the city walls. But I couldn't stay here either.

"When do we leave then?"

For a moment it looked as though he wanted to continue the conversation I had just drawn a line under before he conceded that I was telling him exactly what he wanted to hear.

"You're all right?" He wasn't convinced by my hastily erected façade. But he had pretended to be other than his true self every day for years and now I needed to do a better job to get me through this one conversation.

I wondered briefly what would happen if I closed my fist and punched him. I picked a spot on his face. In my mind, a punch would hit one of those high cheekbones and I probably wouldn't come off the better of that exchange. Square on the nose, while less elegant, was my better option. At least I wouldn't break my hand. I settled for some hefty side eye. Appearing to be over it was clearly going to be more of a process.

"Right," he echoed my previous response.

He stepped away, entering the living space and coming to a stop as he inspected the same scene that had given me pause before him. I needed to leave. Suddenly I couldn't stand being in this space. The gleaming fake apartment where every shining surface, every piece of furniture in its groomed perfection, was a lie stood in stark contrast to the verdant garden strewn with shattered glass and its rumpled nook. The lie and the truth; it was hard to tell which one in that moment was more difficult to look at.

There was movement as Devyn finally dragged a shirt over his broad chest and it drew my attention back to him.

"Tomorrow then." He moved on to the life I was somehow supposed to return to now. I had come here thinking it was the beginning of my life with Devyn and instead it had been the end. And to top it off, now, after being with Devyn, I had to stand in front of everyone and commit myself to Marcus.

I stared at the nook. Would I go back and change what had happened, if I could? It was my own fault I had thrown myself at him, tea be damned, I'd known exactly what I was doing. I had made my own bed and my cheeks heated at the memory.

"Is it usual…" He hesitated, each word sounding like it was dragged from him. "Is it… customary… for the couple… your cousin…?"

I had no idea what he was trying to ask me until he glanced at the now shadowed nook. If it was possible, I blushed even harder. Good to know that despite reeling from life-changing information we were both still freaking out about what had happened out in the garden.

"No"—I shook my head vigorously—"no. My cousin – or rather, my mother's niece – she was in love with her match…

that is, they were already into each other… ah, that is… I don't think it works that quickly on most couples."

Had anyone ever in the history of the world wished harder for the ground to open up and swallow them? It seemed unlikely as I all but told the man who had walked on broken glass to get away from me that I loved him. Admittedly, technically, the broken glass had come later. But it had been a consequence of being with me. Now my thoughts were as garbled as my tongue.

I tried again. "It's supposed to be a gradual thing, you know"—an imp stole my tongue—"climaxing on the big day."

He looked startled. But catching the mischief in my eyes at my innuendo, he flashed a smile in spite of himself.

"Good to know."

I grimaced. "Anyway, Marcus can barely look at me right now. I hardly think he's going to want to jump me any time soon."

"The handfast has that effect on the groom as well?" Devyn looked distinctly sour at this news.

"Of course. No point if only half the couple wants it," I returned sharply. He blinked in acknowledgement of the hit.

"The date of the wedding, is that false too?"

"No, my mother felt we would only get away with the false date once," I clarified. My mother had been the one to insist the handfast be as private as possible; she too remembered her niece's behaviour and, given what had supposedly happened between Marcus and me at the ball, Camilla was terrified we would embarrass her in front of the city a second time.

"We can stick to the current plan then," he stated.

I waited for him to elaborate. Unsurprisingly, he added nothing further.

"Well?" I prodded.

An eyebrow rose.

"What is the plan?" Even to my own ears, I sounded snarky.

"Don't worry about it. I have it figured out. I have a lead on some new tech. The firewalls have been amped up, but we should still be able to get out through the barrier on the river; it's the least guarded option. There will be people waiting for us on the other side. With Marina it was relatively easy to slip away unnoticed. To get the city's most celebrated sweethearts out, we'll need to do something a little more diverting."

For Devyn, that was practically laying out the step-by-step of the plan; he must be feeling bad. Good.

"How long do I have to pretend to be the excited soon-to-be-bride of the city's darling son?" I asked, twisting the knife a little in the process. I wasn't entirely without bitterness. That interesting little tic in his jaw flexed again.

"I'll let you know in due course." My dig wasn't to go without riposte then. Or rather, my intended strike was deflected, batted away by superior strength. He held all the cards, and I would do well to remember it the next time I wanted information.

"Fine." I'd had enough. Time to go back to my gilded cage. I grabbed my coat and headed for the door.

"I'll be in touch," Devyn said to my retreating back.

I wish, I thought as I closed the door behind me.

I wanted to turn around so badly. He wanted me to turn around.

I didn't.

Chapter Twenty-One

My knees threatened to give way as I bared my teeth in the expected smile and took Marcus's hand on arrival at the Savoy. I had felt curiously light-headed all morning as I had been primped and preened into a concoction I barely recognised as myself.

The girl on the arm of the boy that was reflected back at me from the glass in the door as we walked into the lobby was a complete stranger. The intricate hairstyle, perfectly applied makeup, the layers of silk from the distant Orient adorning me elicited gasps from the guests who gave a smattering of applause as they commented to each other how beautiful I looked, how handsome the boy was by my side. His clear green eyes looked down at mine, searching for something. I looked up at him blankly. What did he want? I didn't care.

"Cassandra," Marcus said softly. "Are you all right?"

My hand reached for the comfort of the triquetra charm necklace only to be met by the string of pearls temporarily replacing the plain necklace at my mother's insistence.

I blinked. The numbness that cocooned me was warm,

comforting. His hand squeezed mine. I looked around – so many people, friends from school, important people I recognised as senators. Were they the ones who had arranged all this, manipulating Marcus and me for their own purposes? The hand holding mine tightened.

"Cassandra," his voice came, more urgent now. I smiled blankly up at him.

"Yes?"

"Are you all right?" he repeated his eyes searching mine. "Are you ready for this?"

Ready? The handfast. He meant the handfast. I cocked my head to one side. The handfast. I was here to be handfasted. To Marcus.

I drew in a breath. My head spun. I couldn't breathe. There wasn't enough oxygen in the air. I looked up at the tall man in front of me. I sucked in air again.

"Hold on," he reassured me, his eyes assessing me quickly, using his doctor voice. "I've got you. We'll just go in here."

His hand nudged the small of my back, pushing me towards a small hallway. People moved to let us pass, smiling uncertainly at me. I smiled back, the automatic smile I had been using all morning, the one I had been training to use for weeks, months… ever since Devyn had come into my life and there had become two versions of me: the unchanged, public Cassandra and Devyn's Cassandra.

I couldn't do this. Going through with this ceremony was a travesty. I couldn't do it. I was leaning against the wall, concentrating on breathing. The green eyes looking into mine were grave. Concerned.

"Just breathe, easy, in… and out," he said gently. It was an anchor to hold on to. Marcus checked the door marked "private" beside us and, finding it opened freely, gently ushered me into the small office.

"That's it," he comforted, as my breathing became more regular.

As my grip on my body became steadier, so too did my grip on reality. I shook my head. How had I got here? I remembered leaving Devyn's apartment the night before, walking back to my parents' house.

I had felt so alive. Pissed off. Resolute. But alive.

So unlike how I felt now. I shook my head to clear the wooziness.

"Cassandra, are you back with me?" Marcus asked.

"I don't feel right."

"I think you were having a small panic attack," he informed me grimly. "Good to be clear on how you feel about today."

My mother had been waiting when I got home. Her lips tight, her expression stony when I walked through the front door. She had pulled me into Father's study.

"Where were you?" she hissed.

I had never got around to buying Marcus's gift. My cover was nonexistent. How could I have been so foolish? The events of the evening had scrambled my brain and I had left myself seriously exposed. I gave my mother my most innocent expression.

"Shopping."

Camilla looked pointedly at my distinct lack of packages.

"Not very successfully, it would seem. How unlike you."

To be fair, this was the first time in weeks I hadn't come through the front door laden with things I didn't need in my feeble attempt to punish my father for using me. If I was the reason for his mercantile empire, then I was going to reap the rewards.

"I couldn't find anything," I excused myself

"Is that so?"

"Yes, I was thinking about Marcus and I just really wanted to see him. I couldn't concentrate. I'm so excited about tomorrow and being with him," I elaborated wildly, trying to stick to the cardinal rule of lying under interrogation: keep it simple. Camilla had been so accepting of my plan to go out on my own on a Marcus-related expedition earlier that she had lapped it up. Why not use that to my advantage?

"I wanted to see Marcus, straight away." I bit my lip at the confession. "I'm sorry. I went over to the hospital. Just to say hi really quickly."

"Did you?" Again with the short question. How unlike my mother. She would usually have thrown a snide comment in there. I'd just handed her the perfect opportunity to have a dig at my duplicitous nature; after all, she'd caught me in a direct lie. She wasn't to know I was actually trying to cover it with yet another.

Camilla looked towards the side door. "Darling, you have such a big day tomorrow. It's important you get your sleep."

She sat, waving for me to do likewise, and rang the little bell on the side table beside her armchair. Mother was just going to let it go?

I shrugged mentally, taking a seat as indicated. The family was going to be in the full glare of a watching audience at the handfast; maybe she really was willing to shrug it off for once.

Anna entered carrying a drink on a little tray and set it down on the low table in front of me without looking at me once. I looked up at my mother. Why was there only one drink?

"Just a little something to help you sleep, dear."

Now I was nervous. This was the second time today that my mother had offered me something to drink that she was not going to partake of herself. Fool me once shame on you, fool me twice shame on me. She was also using an uncomfortable amount of endearments. I gnawed my lip.

"I'm exhausted actually. I think I'll just go straight to bed." I started to rise.

"Sit," Camilla said sharply. I sat down abruptly.

"I would like it if you drank your hot tea, sweetheart." *Sweetheart?* Who was she kidding?

"Unless you want to talk about where you were all evening?" Camilla leaned in and whispered the question softly.

I swallowed uncomfortably. I lifted the cup and took a sip, smiling brightly at her over the rim. Her eyes narrowed as she watched me.

"I was with Marcus."

"All of it." Camilla nodded at the cup.

I tipped it up, and drained it. I could already feel my lids growing heavy. My mother really was very keen that I should sleep. My hand felt heavy as I lowered the now empty cup and missed the table as my vision blurred.

"Mama…" I mumbled. I felt odd.

Camilla leaned down and elegantly picked up the fallen cup from the carpet. Catching my hand, she rubbed the finger missing the promise ring which had been absent since the night of the masquerade.

"Marcus called here looking for you, Cassandra."

My lids closed and I rubbed my eyes, trying to shake off the lingering mugginess, careless of the immaculately applied makeup I had so carefully retouched on my way home.

Now I looked up and took in my surroundings – the plush couch on which I was sitting, Marcus sitting opposite looking at me strangely. I started laughing. Not a regular laugh, a slightly hysterical laugh.

"What's going on with you?" Marcus asked sharply.

I smiled up at him, the fake one at which I had become so expert.

"It appears my mother put a little something in my drink last night," I explained.

"That's crazy, why would she do that?"

"Well, apparently she thought I might make a run for it. Seems Camilla's not as convinced as the rest of the city that I'm blissfully running into your arms," I sneered. Unfairly. After all, it was hardly Marcus's fault we were here. In fact, the only person who wanted to be here less than me was Marcus.

"What does she know?" he asked.

"I don't know. Nothing really." At least, not as far as I was aware. "Only that I wasn't where I said I was last night."

He frowned.

"Where did you say you were?" he asked.

"With you."

"Oh." He quickly put two and two together. "Where were you really?"

The somewhat annoyed look in his eyes showed me that he had arrived at four all by himself. I lowered my eyelids and looked away.

"Right." His tone was grim as he stood up and moved away from me. "With him."

He exhaled deeply.

"Sorry for blowing your cover." He didn't sound too sorry. "I don't exactly want to be here myself, you know."

"I know," I answered in a small voice.

A knock came at the door. He moved to answer it and spoke briefly to whoever was in the hall.

"We need to go back out there."

I shook my head jerkily. My breath started to come too quickly again.

"I can't do this."

Marcus crossed the room in two strides, his hands gripping me as he lifted me to my feet.

"You are doing this," he gritted.

I felt physically sick. The final vestiges of whatever I had been slipped by my oh-so-loving mother finally burned out of my system. I was not going to do this. They couldn't make me.

"They bloody can make you," Marcus glared at me.

I must have spoken out loud. I frowned, my jaw setting mulishly.

"You think you're the only one playing games here, you stupid little girl. While you and your boyfriend were running around saving one urchin from the stews, I've been doing everything I can to save the city. They know everything. That device didn't work; they let you get her out."

Marcus's cheeks were flushed; he was practically spitting in his anger.

"For one girl." He shook his head. "I have hundreds of patients, hundreds of people who are dying. I marry you, and I get to continue to treat them. For every one of the elite I treat, I can treat twenty more of the poor, as long as I don't burn myself out."

I was struggling to follow what he was saying. How did he know about Marina? I had never told him, I'd never had a chance. I had suspected his father held his career over him but this… they were bargaining with people's lives. My head spun.

He had made a deal. He had betrayed us. He saw the realisation dawning in my eyes.

"You really didn't know they were on to you? You ridiculous little fool. Everything you did fed right into their plans."

"I don't understand."

"They arrested him months ago for some subversive behaviour. Hacking or something. Praetor Calchas persuaded the Governor to let him go after he was taken from the sands of the arena to see if they could catch more fish."

My blood ran cold. Devyn had been the hacker on the sands at my first Mete. The red flecks splaying out across the sand… But he had no injury afterwards, no memory… What was I thinking? Our advanced medicine would easily have resolved such things.

They'd been watching the whole time. If they weren't worried about me knowing now, their game was played out. They had what they wanted. They would be coming for Devyn.

I opened up the connection between us. I couldn't sense him so I threw myself at the wall where he had done the same. *Let me in, Devyn*. I battered at it frantically.

"By the time the handfast is in place, they'll have thrown him into a deep, dark hole. You'll never see him again," Marcus informed me, not entirely without compassion.

RUN.

I battered at the wall again. There had to be a way through. I concentrated harder, blocking everything else out. He was okay, I could feel he was okay. Bitter and dark though his mood felt, at least he wasn't as indifferent to my impending nuptials as it had appeared last night.

He was sitting in his room nursing his bandaged hand. I was outside the window, banging on the glass. *See me. See me.*

His head raises, he sees me.

RUN. RUN.

His eyes widen. The connection opens. He senses me. My alarm. My despair. My fear.

RUUUUUUUNNNNN.

He's up. Away.

Gone.

I smiled at Marcus. The genuineness of the smile clearly startled him. Standing, I offered him my hand. "Shall we?"

I pulled myself together. I couldn't let him see what I was thinking, what I was feeling. If the authorities had been a step ahead of us all this time, I wasn't going to give away the slight advantage we held now.

"Who did you make your deal with?" I asked idly. Knowing exactly who it was that was manipulating us was a question that had started to niggle at me. We were fighting someone who knew everything about us, while Devyn and I were fighting blind.

"My father."

No surprise there.

"But he's not in charge," Marcus added reluctantly, as if the words had been dragged from him. But he clearly needed to speak about it… and who else was there to talk to? "I don't know who's pulling his strings but when I asked for a greater number of patients he had to go back to someone. They refused, and their answer was final, so whoever it is clearly holds all the cards."

I nodded absently, most of my focus on the connection with Devyn. He had left it open and I could feel the adrenaline charging through him.

"Nobody ever holds all the cards."

"Well, it sure seems like they do. We're both here, aren't we, doing their bidding?"

I grimaced. If only he knew it wasn't entirely the mystery puppeteers' bidding that had brought us here. I was here at the command of a boy who held my heart but gave me to another.

As we exited the room, I found that I needed to know if *everything* had been a lie. I had thought for a while there that Marcus and I were becoming friends.

"You knew all along?" I asked. "All this time you were playing me, this summer, the hospital..."

Had Otho's death been nothing but a gambit to draw me out? Bait that I had totally fallen for? After all, they couldn't ask the Briton delegation for help with their golden boy, so I had helpfully provided it, not to mention handing them further evidence condemning myself and Devyn.

"No."

"No?" I asked as he stilled.

He looked down at me.

"Cassandra, I may not agree with whatever it was you and your boyfriend were doing... I believe in the Code and the Empire; the council want the best for our city and the Britons would only tear it down and drag us all back to the dark age." He paused. "But I didn't know then. How could I? I didn't even know what I was doing myself until the night of the ball."

I was confused. Marcus hadn't known until after the ball?

Guests had noticed our re-entry into the reception and I could feel eyes on us. I laughed up at Marcus.

"You didn't tell them about...?" I didn't give Fidelma's name, conscious that without my pendant we were having this conversation in the open.

He shook his head.

"Who do they think helped you?" I messed with his cravat, straightening a nonexistent crease.

"Devyn."

"You told them Devyn has magic?" I asked through my teeth.

Marcus looked uneasy. "I had to give them someone."

I hated him suddenly. The pampered city boy, always looking out for himself. Devyn hadn't needed to help him. If I hadn't persuaded him to help Marcus then perhaps we would already be a long way from here.

"Not me?" I fluttered my lashes up at him for the benefit of our audience. Underneath those lashes, Marcus could see the murderous expression in my eyes.

"How could I give them you?"

How indeed. As far as Marcus knew I didn't have any abilities. Marcus had been keeping our conversations strictly public since the ball, presumably so he wouldn't give himself away. Little did he know it had also prevented me from telling him too much, believing I could trust him after the ball.

Relief and a certain jubilant smugness speared through the connection. Devyn must be safe.

I smiled a blazing smile up at my intended.

"Let's do this."

The handfast ceremony was mercifully short. I had attended a few over the years, mostly children of the extended family of my parents – such as the cousin whose antics had so inspired my behaviour with Devyn last night. At least we had that.

They knew about Devyn. It was going to be nigh on impossible to get out of the city now. I could only assume that as Devyn had acted on my alert, he knew we were betrayed. And Marcus was the prime suspect.

I had to tie myself to him for now. Surely Devyn would figure a way through this. I breathed deeply again, attempting to steady my nerves.

I didn't care about this ceremony anymore. It meant nothing. Marcus had sold us out. I wondered just how much information he had given the authorities.

He took my arm as we began our walk to the circle under the beautiful Art Deco dome that I had admired on previous visits. In the summer it was radiant, the sun lighting up the roses that twined through the design. Real roses now decked the folly in the centre of the room where the civil celebrant waited to perform the binding. My step faltered. I wanted to run. Find Devyn and run. How could he have sent me to do this?

A pulse came through the connection, warmth and support. Faith that I could survive this. That I could survive anything.

I lifted my chin.

Looked my parents in the eye as I took my place beside them.

Looked Senator Dolon in the eye as Marcus stood in front of him facing me.

I could do this.

I repeated the vows as they were dictated. Reaching for Devyn, I directed my words to him. I lifted my hand and placed it in Marcus's when told to do so. The positioning of our hands, wrist to wrist, was the increasingly familiar Briton style. Fidelma had also done that when she'd wanted to connect magically.

I felt a shimmer through my body as the metal cuff was attached to my upper arm.

Something felt wrong.

Why could I sense Devyn?

I watched as they placed a similar but slightly larger band around Marcus's bicep. He was shaped more like a soldier than a doctor. I was so proud that he was a medical professional. He put his patients before everything else and I admired that about him.

I could feel confusion seeping from my connection to Devyn. How inconvenient that it was Devyn and not Marcus I was connected to. Not that it mattered really.

As the ceremony drew to a close, Marcus was invited to kiss me. He smiled into my eyes and leaned in.

A warm sensation shivered through me.

A dark emotion nudged my bliss… How bothersome.

Then it was gone.

Part Three

SO SILENCE BUILDS HER WALL

Could there have been a wind
That haled them by the hair,
And blinding
Blue-forked
Flowers of the lightning
In their leaves?

Tap… Tap…
Slow-ticking centuries…
Soft as bare feet upon the snow…
Faint… lulling as heard rain
upon heaped leaves…
So silence builds her wall
about a dream impaled.

– *After Storm*, Lola Ridge

Chapter Twenty-Two

I loved my life. It felt amazing to let all the madness of the last few months slide away. Being properly back in reality was like slipping on a luxuriously comfy robe, much like the one I had spotted while lunching in Knightsbridge last week. I hadn't even been looking but how was a girl to ignore an iridescent aqua silk robe? It was the perfect match for my eyes.

I was trying to be better about my spending though. I had burned quite a hole through my credit tab in the run-up to the handfast which I felt bad about now, so I was laying off the shopping for a while, which my father was greatly relieved about. He had an impending dowry tightening his purse strings, I supposed. It was only fair I acted a little bit more responsibly. I did love that robe though; maybe I could drop a gentle hint my mother's way. After all, even if a girl wasn't expected to have an entirely new wardrobe when she entered married life, she couldn't begin such an auspicious phase of life still dressed as a student.

Especially if the groom was the city's most talented physician. Marcus's star was definitely on the rise. Word had somehow leaked to the press about his singular success, which I mustn't feel too happy about, especially as I might be ever so slightly responsible. Who could blame me for telling a few close friends about how brilliant he was? Isn't the point of being handfasted to get to a better understanding of how amazing your partner is before the big day?

Marcus had grumbled a bit when I confessed my little indiscretion, but not too much – after all, I was utterly adorable. He couldn't possibly stay mad at me. He didn't like when I mentioned Devyn either… not that I did really, but sometimes I wondered why I'd been willing to turn my life upside down for such a nobody. Marcus got this sweet little frown line between his meltingly gorgeous eyes, which was half the reason I did it.

I was starting to get excited about the wedding too now. It was so close, only a week to go. It was such a shame I hadn't shown more interest earlier as a lot of the big decisions had already been made, though I had no one but myself to blame for not being more involved from the outset. Thankfully, I liked what my mother had organised well enough, but if I had paid more attention instead of moping after Devyn, it would probably have felt a bit more like me.

My mother had suggested pre-wedding revels, which meant my actual friends would have the chance to put together a party that felt more *Cassandra*. My mother was being an absolute angel; she really had thought of everything. Over the last weeks, we had grown so much closer. We had finally developed the bond that had always been missing and there was a part of me that was sorry we wouldn't have more time together. A very tiny part. After all, staying at home would mean that Marcus and I weren't living together. Shudder.

As it was, I just felt underfoot at home with all the wedding stuff, which fortunately meant I could escape to the hospital. Yet another one of the benefits of being handfasted was that couples were permitted to spend time in each other's company, to get to know each other more fully. I didn't have a job, which meant I could spend all the time I wanted at Marcus's.

The hospital was crazy these days so they were actually grateful for the extra set of hands. Marcus was doing such important work and it was such a privilege to help him. It was hard to believe he had had to bargain to be allowed to treat people. What had they been thinking? The hospital would be lost without him.

As would I. Spending our days and evenings together had shown me just how right we were for each other. I could practically predict what he would need before he asked for it; truth be told, I put his nurses in the shade. One of the few dark spots of this time was the paps continued to show far more interest in us than was entirely decent. The hospital had to tighten security around us while we were working, which was a terrible waste of resources. There had been an incident a week earlier and the hospital board had seriously debated whether I would be allowed to continue working there, which was unheard of. No one kept handfasted partners from each other. It was the thought of not being able to work that had made me most nervous. The fatigue I had felt in the summer had returned but it made me feel useful and I was easier in my skin when I kept busy.

I tidied a locker here, wiped a brow there, updated the numbers on a chart, my route always taking me closer to where Marcus was dealing with a patient. Tucking in a sheet in an adjacent bed, I watched as he treated his patient. The nurse was making notes, but while she was busy Marcus had taken hold of the patient's hand while using his other to pull the man's blanket up to his chest. It was a manoeuvre that he employed to hide the positioning required to most effectively use his magic. I skirted the bed and, coming up behind Marcus, laid my hand on his shoulder. I really didn't approve of him using means other than the medical ones the city provided – it was against the Code after all. But if he absolutely had to then it didn't hurt to support him in this way, letting him syphon off a little of my energy. I didn't need it, after all.

"Cassandra, would you mind taking this bouquet up to the fourth floor? It landed here by mistake, and with changeover, it'll be ages before anyone here is able to run up. Would you mind terribly?" a harried-looking Miri asked me as she tucked stray locks behind her ear. Matron did not love messy hair, and Miri's hair was terribly flighty, though she was terrific with the patients.

I smiled, taking the vase from her. "Shame to have such a beautiful bouquet not find its rightful owner."

The bouquet was charming – unusual though in that it was the opposite of the sublime cultivated blooms I had been looking at for the wedding. This was made up of autumn berries, rowan, spindle, wild rose and hawthorn, set in ferns and autumn leaves, including fiery acer and golden oak. I never went to the fourth floor, so it took me a couple of turns around the corridors to find the room on the note. Entering the room and pulling the curtain back to deliver the flowers, I expected an aged grand dame but I was somewhat wide of the mark.

Very wide of the mark.

"What are you doing here?"

I hadn't seen Devyn since the regrettable night before the handfast. I did my best to put it as far out of my mind as I could, but occasionally a sliver of an image would flash before me. Midnight eyes smiling… the slide of skin on skin. Even the damned sound of running water would bring to mind that stupid fountain in his garden.

Devyn frowned.

"You're a hard lady to get time with." He smiled crookedly.

"I've been busy," I answered tersely. "I'm getting married."

"What?" He tilted his head as though trying to comprehend what I'd just said.

He hardly needed an interpreter.

"I'm getting married," I repeated slowly.

He took a step back, his face going blank. It was usually his default setting, which was the moment I registered how pleased he had looked when I came into the room.

"Devyn, I'm so sorry if you thought I would be waiting for you to whisk me away. In fact, I'm truly sorry if you feel I led you on in any way, but I'm marrying Marcus," I explained as nicely as I could. It wasn't like I'd had time to finesse a speech – I'd assumed he had fled the city. He should have.

"Led me on…?" he echoed.

I smiled stiffly.

"Maybe I chose my words poorly. I totally accept that I was a participant in what happened between us," I said.

"A participant…" He repeated my choice of words.

He should be worrying less about my inability to find the perfect wording and more about what would happen when the sentinels got their hands on him.

"Devyn." I tried to get him to focus. "I'm not sure if you're aware, but the authorities are looking for you. I really don't want to be involved any further, but you should know that security here is very tight."

"Not involved?" He gritted his teeth.

This was getting ridiculous, and I had things to do.

"Look, it was really nice seeing you, and I'm glad we got a chance to clear up any unfinished business, but I really must be getting back to the ward." I started to back away, which seemed to wake Devyn up from his strange dazed state.

"Cass, what… ? It's taken me weeks to get to you. And now I'm getting the nice-to-have-known-you treatment?" He did not look happy.

"Like I said, I'm really sorry. Experimentation happens. What we did… was a mistake. I would have thought you'd be happy I'm with Marcus now." There was a chance this wasn't just about what had happened between us. Maybe his concern was that he was still trying to get Marcus and me across the wall. "Our lives will be here in the city."

"You can't be serious." Devyn looked like he'd just heard that cats had landed on the moon and started making cheese there. As though the words he was being presented with all went fine together but utterly and completely lacked any sense.

"Marcus and I are happy together," I explained, as simply as I could.

"Happy?" Devyn spat the word back at me. "Happy to be manipulated into marrying someone you're not attracted to, to bear children they will take off you?"

I laughed at his dramatics.

"Don't be ridiculous. I am marrying Marcus Courtenay. No one will take our children from us. The city wouldn't stand for it. They love him." I lifted my chin as he came closer. "And so do I."

"Really?" He was like a cat prowling closer to its prey. "You love him. Have you been with him?"

I frowned. How uncouth.

"Of course not." It wasn't unheard of for couples to slip up before the big day, but Marcus and I didn't have that kind of relationship. His kisses were nice, but… My eyes snagged on Devyn's lips. I shook my head.

"Goodbye, Devyn." I whirled away, heading for the door, but hadn't even made it a step when he grabbed my arm. Pushing me up against the door, he reached behind me to turn the lock. It felt like a fog was lifting in my head.

"I don't think so, darling." He smiled down at me, his body surrounding mine. "We aren't ready to bid farewells yet."

"Devyn." I blinked up at him.

His eyes dropped to my lips, his hand coming around my head and trapping me, ensuring I couldn't evade his kiss. Why would I want to?

His kiss felt like heaven, his lips moving warmly against mine, his tongue flickering, waiting to be invited in. He was always welcome here. I wound my fingers through his familiar tousled curls. I breathed him in. I had missed this.

"Cass?"

I smiled brilliantly up at him. "Hi. Where've you been?"

Chapter Twenty-Three

Devyn exhaled in relief, his forehead leaning against mine. "Cass."

I leaned up for another kiss and my beautiful boy obliged.

I opened the connection between us. I'd never experienced what he felt when we were kissing. The pulse between us felt muggy, cloudy, but I could sense his relief, some residual anger, and a lot of quickening passion.

I understood the latter, but his anger, and relief were… that I wasn't running away from him. Why would I be running away from him? He was the one who did all the running. What in Hades was going on?

I pulled away to take a breath. *Think.* Why was I in the hospital?

"Devyn?"

"Mmm." He sounded like a grumbling teenager resisting his wake-up call, but in a minute he was going to remember that he—

Pushed me away.

And there it was.

He stepped back and took a breath before he turned and paced away to the windows, putting some distance between us. I felt the fog in my mind gather once more. My eyes widened in distress and I whirled round, desperately attempting to open the lock. He quickly crossed the room until he stood behind me, his hand touching my waist.

"Cass, what is it?"

My hand stilled on the lock and I turned back to him, evaluating the last few moments. "Don't go anywhere. I think you being near me is the difference."

"The difference?" he asked.

"Will you stop that?" I sniped, my memories of the last time we met returning. "When did you lose the ability to choose your own words? You've been acting like a damned parrot from the minute I walked into this room."

"Well, you've been a little off yourself," he said. "What's going on?"

"I don't know," I said, trying to work through the time since I had walked out of his apartment. "It's like I'm there but I'm not."

His concerned dark eyes watched me, urging me to explain. Now I was the one struggling to find the words.

"Since the handfast, I've been happy… with things. That is, it's like I'm the old me. I remember everything that happened but I don't care. That stuff, you, it's not important." I couldn't find any other way to put it. "All that's important is Marcus."

I shrugged.

"Looks like I'm finally on board with everyone's wishes."

He ignored the hit.

"And you don't feel that way now? Whatever they did has worn off?" he asked.

"I don't think so. I think you being close just makes everything clear again. I'm truly me again."

We stared at each other. There was so much that had been left unsaid when we were last together but there was no time for that now. Our first priority was getting out of the city; everything else would just have to wait.

Things were complicated enough but whatever had been done to me during the handfast ceremony made any attempt to escape almost impossible. The most wanted person in the city would have to get close enough to practically touch me, and I was now the most secured person in the city. Well, maybe second only to Marcus. Even Governor Actaeon and Praetor Calchas didn't have the kind of security we did. I realised now that the increased and obvious security around me was less about the paps and all about Devyn.

"They know everything," I told him, recalling Marcus's revelations before the ceremony.

"How do you know?"

I grimaced. "It was Marcus."

"It was Marcus who told you, or Marcus who betrayed us?" he questioned closely. "Think carefully."

I wracked my brain as Devyn took my hand and entwined our fingers, leading me over to the chairs on the other side of the empty bed. I looked down at our hands. Apparently maintaining our link trumped his duty, his obligations... or whatever it was that had made him push me away.

I shook it off. One problem at a time. Marcus had told me that the authorities knew everything but that only meant they knew what he knew. What else had he told me in that little room in the Savoy? I'd been so out of it and then the lights had gone out entirely. Sort of.

"Everything is so confusing. At the hotel, before the

handfast, I felt out of it. When I got home Camilla knew, she knew I hadn't been with Marcus. I think giving me my freedom that evening was a test, and I failed." I looked up at him, a slight warmth on my cheeks. "Spectacularly."

Devyn looked away. I felt his emotions; they were still faint but I could make out his shame clearly enough. He was still angry at himself for what had happened and some of that anger was not unfairly aimed at me. He resented that I had made him betray his principles. I had known how much he wanted to honour his stupid promise. But I hadn't made any bloody promises. A squeeze of my fingers brought me back.

"They gave me something to get me to sleep that night – maybe they were worried that I was planning to make a run for it before the handfast. I guess they knew what we didn't – that once handfasted I was pretty much locked in." I shook my head at our naivety; we didn't have a clue what we were up against.

Devyn ran a hand through his dark curls. "I didn't know. I'll look into it. We'll figure it out. What does it feel like?"

I thought about the last couple of weeks. I had been so blithely happy, like the girl I had been before. The pampered princess, back up in my ivory tower. I was aware of everything that had happened, everything I had learned, everything I had felt over the last months – the trap for which I had been raised, the illness that was sweeping the land, the mother who had died protecting me, the music that sang in my bones, the way I felt when Devyn was with me. I looked down at our joined hands.

"I don't care," I shrugged. "I don't care about any of it, magic, the illness. You."

I looked up to see if my words had any impact on him but the stoic mask was firmly in place.

"It's like all that happened a long time ago, to someone else, and this version of me is… sort of indifferent to all that stuff. My parents are lovely, my fiancé is handsome. That's enough." I tasted salt as a tear hit my mouth. All my hopes for life beyond the city were crushed. They'd never been the strongest anyway, based as they were on a boy who told me he would have to betray everything he believed in for us to be together. A boy who had allowed me to be handfasted to Marcus rather than leave with me. Here, there, I was still pushed at Marcus by people whose endgame I didn't understand. "And maybe a part of me was happy to go back to that."

His rejection had been devastating. But he had also been hurt, and I was the one who had thrown myself at him. I needed to say something now, while I was still myself. Once he let go of my hand, I didn't have the same belief as he did that we hadn't been completely outmanoeuvred.

"I'm sorry. I'm sorry for what I did. I'm sorry that you're unhappy about it."

"Don't be." His fingers tightened around mine. "I've been thinking about it. If we hadn't been together like that then the connection might never have re-established. That said, if the sentinels don't kill me here, they will definitely kill me there if they find out at home how it got triggered." He shook his head, refocusing. "Since your warning I've been trying to reach you but I can't sense you at all. You can still feel it?"

"No, I mean yes. That is, I can feel it now. During the ceremony I could feel you but as soon as they put the cuff on it went. Or I turned it off. I'm not sure. Now I can feel something, not clearly, but I can feel you a little again," I explained.

"The cuff. Show me."

I lifted my sleeve to show him the intricate band of silver wrapped around my upper arm.

"I can't see a catch. Can you take it off?" He traced his finger around the band to see if his touch could discern something his eyes were missing.

I shook my head. "No, you know it only comes off during the marriage ceremony."

He huffed and sat back in his chair.

"That's going to be a little late for us."

"What do you care? Marcus is just as likely to come with me if I leave once we're married."

His dark eyes locked with mine. I could feel traces of his emotion – anger, a swirl of jealousy, and denial.

What did it matter if I married Marcus? After all, Devyn had made it clear it was impossible for us to be together. Why not let me marry Marcus… except for the fact that I felt nothing for Marcus. Not the way I felt about Devyn, even despite the fact that he wouldn't tell me what I needed to know, that he kept me following along on half-truths and bits of information he fed me at just the right time, that he had rejected me.

I didn't care. None of it really mattered in the end. I would cross the earth to be with him.

"If you're not married and you don't want Marcus, maybe there's still a chance for you and me," he said quietly, staring intently at his fingers rubbing mine.

My heart jumped one way as my stomach dipped the other. I was stunned.

"You mean it?" He would fight for us? Who was the fight against? Himself or the people who gave him orders?

He nodded. "I'll try."

I beamed, radiant. There was a chance. Whatever other

forces stood in our way, if Devyn wanted something then I believed in him. He had found me after all.

"First things first. We still need to get you both out of the city." His words brought me back down to earth.

I frowned. "It still needs to be both of us?"

"My orders remain unchanged. I haven't told anyone I found you; it's too risky to try. We should stick to the original plan and try to bring Marcus."

"Even though he betrayed us and told them everything? Okay, so he didn't tell them about Fidelma, but he still wants to stay in the city and he has no interest in living with the barbarians in the woods," I said angrily.

"Not like you, my love." He laughed, pecking my cheek. And stopping my heart in my chest.

I focused. I couldn't let him see how much that one little affectionate peck had affected me. Passion, anger, desire, despair, all of these I had seen, all too frequently. But affection was new. Affection to me was off the charts. I smiled. I would scale the wall with my bare hands for that peck on the cheek.

"Marcus didn't tell them about Fidelma?" Devyn picked up the subject at hand.

"No, he told me he didn't tell them about her. He gave you up instead. They know you have magic, but he didn't know about me. We never told him."

"That's something, at least," Devyn said, his expression thoughtful as his mind searched through our options. "What else did he say?"

I tried to recall the conversation with Marcus. It felt like so long ago and there had been so much going on at the time. I had been so angry... he had been my friend. How could he have given me up like that?

"He did it so he would be allowed to continue to treat the

sick, all of the sick and not just the elite." I found myself defending him again, a fact that did not pass Devyn by.

"If he came with us, we could treat many, many more," he stated.

"How?" I asked. "He's been given permission to treat at least twenty for every elite he treats, as long as he doesn't get too drained again."

"Who did he make the deal with?" Devyn probed, ignoring my question.

"His father," I answered. "It wasn't his father's call though. Marcus said he had to take it away to get confirmation. Someone more senior must be in charge – Praetor Calchas, maybe the Governor."

There was something else, something important I was forgetting. I wracked my brain. My chest was also starting to get tight. I was going to have to leave this room soon; I was aware that I had already been gone far longer than I should. Hopefully in the chaos of the public ward I wouldn't be missed straight away. I didn't want to go back. I looked at our linked hands. I loved Devyn with everything in my being. But a slight niggle tapped at me: did I trust him? I had trusted him before and he had let me down. He always kept something back, always hid secrets from me.

He'd waited for years, watching from the shadows before making a move. He'd left his home, his family, his people, put everything on the line in order to find me. I had to believe he loved me too and that once we got across the wall, no matter what his people said, he wouldn't let them force me into staying with Marcus.

I knew why the puppeteer who pulled the strings here in the city wanted me to be with Marcus. Why would anyone care who I was with beyond the walls? Magic was everywhere there. It was what stopped the Empire taking over the whole island. That they wanted Marcus to help with the illness I understood. I was their only way to get Marcus out, a leash that could drag him with me. Would I even be wanted though? Devyn had implied that there were others who would have looked if they knew I was still alive. There were still so many unanswered questions.

"The illness," I said, shaking off my wandering thoughts as I made a connection, "Marina. They've known about us since then. Since before then. That day they took you from class, Marcus says you were on the sands, that Calchas persuaded the Governor to release you so they could find out who else you were in league with."

His brow drew together. "What?"

"You were on trial at the Mete, the same night as Oban. That's why you didn't remember. They must have healed you then set you free. That's how they knew about us. Whatever you plan to do, you can't use the way we got Marina out. They let it happen; they let us get her out. We're trapped here."

I could see his quick mind absorbing the new information, filling the hole he must have been aware of on some level.

I stood up, panic building in me. We were never going to be able to get out of the city. The authorities had been a step ahead of us the whole time. There was no way out.

"Cass." His arms came around me. "We will get out. I will get you out."

His dark eyes were unwavering as they looked deep into mine, steadying me.

"I'll figure it out. Our biggest difficulty is that once I let you go, you aren't going to care about any of this. I'm going to need to get near enough to counteract the handfast in order to have a conversation with my Cass," he said.

His Cass.

"What about the connection? Can't we talk through that?" I asked urgently.

"That's not how it works."

"But you heard me when I screamed at you to run after Marcus told me they were coming for you," I reminded him.

"I didn't hear the words, just sensed your fear, your urgency. It was warning enough. I left the house immediately. I was coming to find you, to figure out what was wrong. I went out through the garden into a side gallery and moments later the sentinels arrived at the front door," he explained. "I've been battering against that connection ever since and you've felt nothing."

I shook my head, confirming that I hadn't felt anything. There had to be a way or Devyn was never going to get near me again. That he had managed it this once was a minor miracle but with less than a week to go to the wedding I wasn't willing to risk it.

"There's no way this is going to work. You need to make a plan, without talking to me, and find a way to get close enough to touch me before I'll even consider doing anything off script. A plan, may I add, which involves getting both Marcus and me alone and ready to run." I felt ill. "It just isn't possible."

"Anything is possible."

"Now you decide to become an optimist?" I teased. Where was my stoic Devyn who, despite his magic, dealt in facts and careful planning?

"Let's try this. Let's separate and see how quickly your will disappears," he proposed. I considered his phrasing. Was it my will that went away, the will that wanted to break free, or was it that their will was imposed onto mine until I couldn't tell the difference anymore?

I stepped back and our hands dropped away from each other. Initially it was fine but as he continued backing up I felt Devyn begin to drift away. The anxiety that I would never be able to escape, the fear that he would be caught, the joy that pulsed through me in his presence just dissipated. Marcus, Marcus would be wondering where I was. The sentinels would surely have noticed that I had disappeared and I would be reprimanded. Perhaps they would tell my parents. How would I explain why I had spent so much time with Devyn? Why was I still here? I needed to get back so I turned to go.

Devyn caught my arm to hold me.

"Oh."

We had no chance. I had been gone. My real self, the real Cassandra, had vanished as if I had never been mere moments after Devyn had let go of my hand.

Devyn stared at me, his eyes dark and intense.

"I can't take it." He closed his eyes. "I can't bear to look in your eyes and see myself disappear. Once I let you go I'm no one. I'm no one to you."

"But you have to let me go." I would be missed soon.

We stared at each other in despair. I stepped into his arms and held on to him as if my life depended on it, tucking myself into his chest. The clinical room faded away and all that existed for me was Devyn's solid chest and his heartbeat. He put a finger under my chin and lifted my face up, giving him access to my lips. His kiss was tender and soul deep conveying his desperation, his need. We pulled away breathing heavily; time was not on our side. Our hands remained tangled together as we stepped apart.

"No, I don't."

He looked back at me, his expression becoming resolute.

"We go. Now," he pronounced.

I gasped. "What about Marcus?"

"Damn Marcus. Damn them all." He assessed our options. "You're right. Without you at least as a willing participant in your escape we have no chance. I came here for you and I have you now. I will not lose you again. If the handfast has done this to you, once you're actually married I may never get you back. I'm not willing to take that risk. To the bottom of the Tamesis with them. If they want Marcus they can come here and get him themselves."

"Are you serious?" I couldn't believe what I was hearing. "But you said you had orders. Won't you get into trouble?" I raised a brow. We were the only chance of getting Marcus across the borderlands. "Are you sure?" He had been so adamant about his orders.

He shrugged. "No, but I'm hoping that bringing you home will take the sting out of it."

"Your home?" I asked. To be honest, beyond crossing the wall I had no idea where we were bound. North Cymru had taken on a mythical aspect in my mind, all mountains and mists, valleys and castles, and I wondered what it would be like for Devyn to return home after all this time. I had heard the note of longing in his voice when he spoke of it, how desperate he must be to get back there, having been trapped inside the city all these years.

"No, *your* home," he corrected me sombrely.

"*My* home?" I asked, my heart bouncing in my chest. I had a home. Out there in the wilds there was someone who waited for me.

"Yes. I promise I'll tell you everything but first we have to get out of here," he said hurriedly. He pulled back the curtain and looked out on the street below, a frown appearing on his face. "If we're going, we have to go now."

He looked me up and down.

"Where's your pendant?"

My hand lifted up to where the pendant usually sat. My teeth pulled on my lower lip.

"I'm not sure. I couldn't wear it with my handfast dress. It didn't go so I had to take it off."

He pulled an annoyed face at me as he drew me over to the door and unlocked it.

"What?" I asked. "It's not like the other me has any need for it. No sneaking, you know."

He gave an irritated humph and, taking my hand and laying it on his shoulder so we maintained contact, started to pull off his wristband.

"The charm doesn't just keep your words hidden from the microphones. When it's activated it should obscure you to the cameras. As soon as you disappear, every camera in the city will be scanning for you." He winked. "Obviously I have my own way of disappearing in a crowd. You need it more."

He put it on me which was a good thing as I was now starting to shake so badly I wasn't sure I could have managed the clasp. Were we really doing this? This moment was the last I would ever spend in the life I had always known. From now on I would be considered a traitor, a fugitive to be hunted down.

I reached up and pulled Devyn to me, kissing him, deeply, hungrily. I could do this. There was no way I was living my life without him.

The door opened and Miri's head appeared around it. Devyn ended up on the other side of the door so the flustered nurse failed to see him.

"Oh my gods," she exclaimed. "There you are. What are you still doing up here? Everyone's going mental looking for you. They've called in sentinels, for crying out loud. What took you so long?"

"I... I..." I stammered. They'd called even more sentinels in. There was no way we were going to make it out of here. "Sorry, I got totally lost and then I sort of got chatting."

I waved distractedly at the curtain behind me and realised that Devyn had let go of my hand when the door opened. I wasn't touching him and I was still myself, though I wasn't sure how long I had left. I caught his eyes as he stood unmoving behind the door. He'd already realised our mistake and was watching me carefully, waiting to see if I would turn him in to the authorities. I looked down at the wristband – that was what was making the difference, I was sure of it. I looked back up and Devyn took my meaning, a slow smile appearing on his face in the shadows.

"Come on then." Miri ushered me to follow her.

"Ah, I just need to say goodbye." I attempted to delay our departure. I just needed a minute to talk to Devyn. We needed a new plan. Obviously, walking casually out of the hospital wasn't going to work now that it was crawling with sentinels.

"Are you crazy? Have you not been listening? They're tearing the place up looking for you," Miri said urgently, reaching out to grab me to pull me along with her.

I looked at Devyn in desperation. What should I do?

"I'll talk to you again, donna," I called over to the curtain where my supposed new friend lay admiring her unusual bouquet. Unusual, I belatedly realised, because it was made up of berries and leaves that grew in the walled garden on Richmond Hill.

"I'll go and fetch more of those gorgeous bright autumn colours for you soon. I know just where to find them," I improvised hastily. If I could make it out to Richmond, surely Devyn could meet me there?

I couldn't see whether or not he understood my message as Miri had already pulled me out into the hall and was marching me back towards our ward and Marcus.

Chapter Twenty-Four

He knew. We made our way back through the chaos of the ward and the stern-faced sentinels standing back to let me pass through to where Marcus stood with the more senior officers. He watched my approach, coldly furious. He knew. I didn't know how but this wasn't just about the fact I had disappeared for thirty minutes or more. Marcus knew I had been with Devyn.

"Where is he?" His tone was clipped, restrained.

"Who? I'm sorry, I don't know what happened. The time just went. I'm so sorry everyone went to all this fuss." I was playing for time; every second they spent talking to me was one more that Devyn had to get away.

The grim-faced officers exchanged glances as I widened my baby blues for all I was worth. My mind was racing. If they knew I was fully conscious again then I had no chance of making it out to Richmond and I would be under lock and key until the vows were exchanged. By now I was firmly convinced that whatever it was about handfasting that made me so compliant would be impossible to shake off once we were actually married.

Marcus stepped up to me, taking a grip on each of my upper arms and pulled me into him. His green eyes were flinty.

"I know he's here," he said. "I could feel it. My body was on fire. Is that how he makes you feel?"

I gasped. Did the handfast cuffs imitate the connection I had with Devyn? Could Marcus feel my emotions? If so, how much had he been able to pick up from our exchange? But no, we had been wearing these bands for weeks and I'd never sensed anything from Marcus.

"Feel?" I echoed.

"I felt your desire," he bit out angrily. "I know it's because he was here. You've never felt that way with me."

Fire. Desire. The cuffs transmitted passion. Of course they did; they were a courtship device. That's all they knew for sure, that I had been with someone… who was not Marcus. My brain just wasn't working fast enough. There was no way Marcus would accept I had felt that way for some random person I had bumped into on the fourth floor. Had Devyn had enough time to get away? I hoped so because I was out of options.

I shook my head as if trying to shake off a foggy confusion. I allowed my eyes to open as if in shocked horror.

"Oh no. Oh, oh. Marcus. Guards," I exclaimed as if only now coming to myself. "Quickly, Devyn Agrestis is here. He's in the hospital."

I pointed in the direction from which I had come. The officers moved quickly, dispatching the men who had come to a standstill when I arrived back into the ward.

"I don't understand." I lifted a shaky hand to my brow, a

tad afraid I was overplaying it. "He was here. I… I… how is it possible? What was he doing here?"

Marcus watched me narrow-eyed.

"We were about to ask you the same thing."

"I don't know. I don't understand what's going on. I went upstairs with a bouquet…" I lifted a hand to my lips. "Oh Marcus, I'm so sorry. He kissed me. I remember now, he kissed me. I should have stopped him. Why didn't I stop him?"

I looked up at him in apparent confusion and fear at my recollections. I really was laying it on thick. How much did they know about the weaknesses of the handfast? How much should I tell them?

I stepped into Marcus's arms and tucked myself into his chest, just as I had done only moments earlier with Devyn, and let a sob shake me. We had been so close to escaping.

"It's okay. We'll find him, it won't happen again." Marcus's attempts to comfort me actually fed my worst fears. I closed my eyes, wishing with everything in my being that I could go back. If only we'd realised earlier that the protection charm in the wristband somehow interrupted the compulsion of the handfast cuffs. Because I was under no illusion now that it was a compulsion and that my will was being suppressed in favour of whatever had been coded into the armband. At least I was still myself, and while I was in control there was still a chance.

We were moved into a quieter room that lay just off the entrance of the large ward, usually used for nurses' meetings as well as being a place to sit and observe the ward at night. Or rather, it had been in quieter times.

The seconds ticked by while I made occasional noises of distress about having gone off script and how it wasn't my fault and I couldn't understand it etcetera, etcetera. With every minute that passed, my emotions rollercoastered. There hadn't been any word yet so he must have gotten away. Nobody was coming for me so they must have caught him. Around and around I went. I reached for the connection between us but while the charmed wristband appeared to counteract the handfast cuff's ability to subdue my will, it didn't allow me to access the link I had with Devyn. It seemed only physical proximity or contact made that possible now.

I eyed Marcus warily. Could he detect the façade I was presenting to him? I didn't think so. Maybe it was only desire that pulsed through the handfast bond – it made sense since the handfast period was all about the couple bonding with each other. It was revolting. It was all so conniving and manipulative. I wondered how many happily married couples in the city were living a lie and didn't even know it. Did they love each other or were they just conditioned to think they did? I checked the door for the millionth time. Where was Devyn?

The door opened and a grave-looking officer stepped through, one of the ones that had been standing with Marcus earlier perhaps, but I wasn't sure.

"Dr Courtenay, Donna Shelton, forgive me for delaying you here," he started warmly, but it was a warmth that didn't make it all the way to his sharp eyes. The laurel emblem on his chest was silver, not the standard dark red.

"Praetorian Alvar, I really must get back to my patients." Trust Marcus to get straight to it, utterly dismissing one of the praetorian guard, the security force that personally served the council, as though all this was just a most inconvenient interruption in his important day.

"I can only apologise, doctor." Those sharp eyes flicked to Marcus before coming straight back to me. "We have concluded our search."

I couldn't breathe. *Don't react. Don't react.*

"And?" Marcus's tone was impatient. "Did you catch him?"

"I'm afraid he has eluded my men."

And breathe. *Don't react.*

"He was here in the hospital and you let him get away?" Marcus was furious. I moved closer to him and took his hand; I figured it would look good. I swayed at the contact. Something had changed – my feelings about Devyn seemed remoter. Not as remote as they had before but less raw, less overwhelming. I looked down at where my hand was held in Marcus's. Should I to step away to preserve my freedom? Was physical contact with Marcus going to be my undoing? I searched my consciousness... no, I was still me. My feelings towards Marcus were warmer and my feelings about Devyn a little more distant but I was still myself.

"It's all right," I reassured Marcus. "They'll get him next time, darling."

"Indeed, Donna Shelton," Alvar intoned. "We'll get him, but there won't be a next time."

I glanced up at him before looking back at Marcus, our physical contact urging me to reassure him, to make him feel better. He had to feel bad about what would seem like my betrayal of him, cheating with Devyn, and he *had* felt it. I checked myself. Was I just using the motivations being dealt me by the handfast in order to cover or were they taking over? I unlinked our hands gently.

"I would greatly appreciate that, sir." I shuddered. "I'm not sure what happened but I'm to be married in a week and I need you to keep that Codebreaker away from me."

He bowed his head sharply. "Indeed, Donna Shelton, let's get you home."

I frowned, it was early in my shift.

"I'm not due to finish until six," I informed him.

"Unfortunately, given today's disturbance my orders are to see you home immediately." Again with that smile that failed to meet his eyes.

"But I've barely seen Marcus at all today." I gripped his arm as I spoke which enabled me to gaze adoringly up at him, though my reason for doing it was less out of the all-consuming need to spend every moment of every day with my groom than it was to stay in the hospital. Perhaps Devyn was still here.

"I have orders."

Marcus patted my hand. "Don't worry, darling, as soon as I've finished my shift I'll come over to your house for dinner."

I couldn't argue with that so I reluctantly followed as Alvar led the way out of the hospital.

When we arrived at my parents' apartment no one was home, so I let us in and was politely asked to remain in my room. For my own safety. Because if Devyn found a way past the guards stationed at every entrance to our tower, and through the ones outside the apartment and in the hallway, he was so much more likely to get at me in the sitting room than in my bedroom. But I smiled sweetly, thanked them for keeping me safe, and retired to my room.

I couldn't settle. I hated being caged up in my room. I watched the walkway below but the only signs of life were the sentinels and the occasional paparazzo getting moved on. I scanned the bursts about the commotion at the hospital today. We appeared to have made both the gossip columns and the main news. There was some speculation gathering that I had been the subject of an attack by a patient. Pictures showed the sentinels arriving at the hospital and me being led to the awaiting car by a praetorian guard. Eventually, a photo of Devyn appeared as my attacker. Way to make the news work for you. Now the entire city would be looking for him.

I turned my room upside down looking for the pendant I knew I had carefully put aside the morning of the handfast. I had only intended to be without it for a few hours. I frantically pulled out drawers and jewellery cases before taking a moment to calm myself. Devyn had got away, I was sure of it now. They wouldn't catch him; he knew every back alley and secret tunnel in this city. Besides which, the sentinels weren't well loved in the stews and the hospital was on the edge of the tangle of the financial district. As long as he had made it there he'd be able to hide.

My mirror. I'd hung the pendant on my mirror after we'd applied the last touches to my outfit. And there it was, the chain hanging off the corner and the pendant tucked behind the back of the mirror, to hide the looping Celtic symbol on it. I pulled it out and felt the familiar weight of the rose-gold disk in my hand. Putting it on I immediately felt calmer.

I took some ribbons and other bracelets and wrapped them around Devyn's wristband. I felt better with the added security of a second Celtic charm but, while it had gone unnoticed so far, it didn't suit my usual feminine style so it was better hidden away from prying eyes.

When I was finally summoned from my room, I was in control and feeling surer of my version of the afternoon's events. I knew the line I had to walk.

Anna led the way down the corridor which still held two guards. I entered our front reception room to find myself facing Marcus and his father as well as my own parents and the praetorian, Alvar, of course.

"Cassandra." My father held his arms out to me and, given

the censorious reception I was receiving from everyone else in the room, I was glad to go to him. Pulling away, I crossed over to Marcus. The charmed accessories Devyn had given me hadn't entirely cancelled out the effects of the handfast and I was still genuinely drawn to Marcus. I had also evaluated my options while in my room and I felt my best chance of convincing everyone of my story was by appearing to be what they expected: a girl half in love with my groom. And I felt more like that girl while in contact with Marcus – not so much that I was completely under the influence of the handfast and likely to give up everything, but enough to make my performance convincing. I hoped.

I tucked myself in beside Marcus as we sat down, making sure to take his hand and hold it tightly. He kissed me reassuringly on top of my head.

My parents sat down to the side, my mother with a sniff having barely looked at me since I entered the room. Matthias took the seat opposite while Alvar stationed himself behind him. These two were the ones I really needed to convince.

Matthias smiled at me – or at least his mouth widened. If he thought stretching his lips across his teeth was going to make me feel more at ease, who was I to point out his mistake.

"Now, let's discuss this afternoon's adventures," he began. Right to it then.

I nodded demurely. "Of course, Senator."

"In your own words, my dear," Matthias prompted me.

I smiled nervously, inhaling deeply before I began.

"I was asked to take a bouquet up to a patient on the fourth floor," I started.

"Is this usual?" he interrupted.

I shook my head.

"No, not really, but we were busy. I'm not a trained professional so it made sense to send me," I replied.

"Who sent you?"

I hesitated. Would Miri get in trouble? Would they think she was an accomplice? I had to trust that her innocence would protect her.

"Sister Miri. She was the one who found me later and brought me back to Marcus." I watched as the praetorian made a note of her name, a sick feeling in my stomach.

"Continue."

"I carried the bouquet up to the room. At first, I went the wrong way as I'm not too familiar with the other floors of the hospital. I got hopelessly lost." I figured that the more time I accounted for before I met Devyn, the less time I would have to account for once I was in the room. "When I finally found the right room, there was no patient. *He* was waiting for me. Devyn Agrestis. I tried to tell him that whatever had been between us was over, that I'm marrying Marcus."

I smiled tremulously up at my groom.

"What was his reaction?" Matthias probed.

"He was angry. No," I corrected myself, sticking as close to the truth as far as possible for the less incriminating parts of my story. "He seemed confused, like he couldn't understand what I was telling him. Like he expected me to be glad to see him."

Matthias nodded. So far, so good.

"I told him the sentinels were looking for him, that he should hand himself in. I told him it wasn't his fault he has magic," I fabricated, while still feeding them a truth they already knew.

"What else happened?" Alvar asked, unable to restrain himself. Matthias threw him an annoyed look.

This was where I had to be careful. They knew this wasn't the end of the story. They knew because of the event that had alerted them to the fact I was with Devyn in the first place.

I bit my lip, looking anxiously up at Marcus, before looking down at the ground.

"I… well, he started saying something in a language I didn't understand and I tried to leave the room but he grabbed me and he was, I don't know, I guess it was magic or something," I glanced up to see how my audience were receiving my little tale. My parents were horrified but Marcus was braced against the bit he knew was coming; my main interrogators were revealing nothing though. "Then he kissed me."

"And?" Matthias prompted.

"Well, I don't understand it but I kissed him back." I took my hand back from Marcus and sat wringing my hands together in my lap, the very image of the penitent Codebreaker. "I don't know what came over me."

Matthias's cold gaze remained indecipherable.

"Was this the first time you had kissed?"

What to do here? Did I make a full confession and hope that the scandal of my past behaviour became the focus of this fun family evening, or lie and say it was the first time? How much did they know? Did they know the handfast compulsion could be broken? I decided to stick as close to the truth as possible without telling them anything that further incriminated me.

"No, sir," I said in a small voice. I felt Marcus stiffen beside me.

"You had kissed this man before?"

"Yes, sir," I repeated my confession, bowing my head as if unable to look them in the eye.

"The night of the masquerade ball," he said knowingly. I'd forgotten that they must know now that it had been Devyn I had been with at the ball.

I nodded, unable to trust my voice not to betray my relief at being caught in the truth.

"No need to rake over past transgressions," my father said, defending me.

Matthias cast him a cutting look before returning to pin me once more.

"What else was discussed after the kiss?" If the kiss had been the moment Marcus alerted security that I needed to be found then I still had quite a bit of time to account for.

After the handfast ceremony I had admitted to helping Devyn get Marina out of the city, which they had already known. I hadn't offered much more, not about my magic and not about my feelings for Devyn, and nothing about what he had told me about the truth of my origins. Perhaps I had failed to offer up the entire truth out of fear that Marcus would reject me or think less of me and reject me. Whatever the reason, I was grateful for it now.

"He told me that I was being manipulated," I informed Matthias earnestly. "That the city wanted Marcus and me to marry and have children with magic in order to strengthen the council. But it doesn't make any sense. Why would the council want magic in the city?"

"What an outlandish tale." Matthias smiled at everyone in the room. I could see Marcus watching him closely.

"He really believes it to be true," I assured him. "He even told me that I'm a Briton. But that can't be true because Britons aren't allowed in the city."

I looked to my parents for reassurance and caught a flash of disgust on my mother's face. Even though I had long since been convinced of the truth of this, it hurt to see the proof that I had never been more than a cuckoo in this particular nest. I allowed the tears that came at her visible rejection to well in my eyes.

"You will catch him?" I asked the praetorian. "He's crazy. I thought he was a friend, a citizen. I don't know who I thought he was but he's obviously not entirely sane."

I watched to see if they'd bought my story.

"Of course. We're doing everything in our power to detain him," Alvar assured me.

"He didn't say anything else?" Matthias checked.

I shook my head. "No. Miri came and saved me and I went with her back to Marcus."

I threaded my fingers through Marcus's resisting ones. One person here wasn't entirely convinced.

"But you didn't alert her to the fact that a wanted man was in the room you had just left," Matthias observed.

"I felt really disoriented, foggy, and light-headed. I'm not sure what I said. Perhaps it was the after-effects of whatever spell he cast on me?" I offered.

"Indeed."

Matthias seemed satisfied enough with my answer – at least, he chose to let it go.

The praetorian left when we sat down to dinner. Matthias stayed and made it clear that he felt it would be better if I remained in the apartment until the wedding. Marcus concurred, which pretty much sealed my fate. There was no way I was going anywhere, at least not without permission. I felt even less confident when I was assured that I would be guarded around the clock, which meant the sentinels were staying.

The days passed slowly in the apartment. I was going stir crazy, the only relief coming from Marcus's daily visits. I tried to speak to him about what had happened at the hospital but he was firmly under the influence of the handfast. He would talk about his patients and my day and any topic under the sun but when I tried to broach anything to do with Devyn or magic or the fact that we were being manipulated he shut it down. The easy physicality we had fallen into since our handfast had also disappeared. Before Devyn's visit we had become more comfortable with each other, lots of hand holding, hugging, occasional doting kisses, but any time Marcus attempted to touch me now I pulled away. The only thing from that day that appeared to affect him at all was what he had felt when I was with Devyn.

I had asked some questions about what had tipped him off that I might be in trouble. He'd been suspicious at first, or rather he believed my questions were innocent enough until he started to recall the feelings he'd received second-hand. Then he was less sure that my interest was purely about my own security and my hope that he would always come to my rescue. As he attempted to recollect what he'd felt, I saw a flash of something, perhaps jealousy or hurt; he knew the desire I'd felt while kissing Devyn and that it was something we'd never experienced together.

He baulked at describing it to me but I was fairly confident that desire was the only emotion transferred by the handfast. I had also been paying more attention to my moods, trying to assess exactly what influence the handfast had. I was beginning to suspect that there was something to do with absence because I missed Marcus dreadfully during the day and my anxiety levels skyrocketed by the time he called to see me in the evening. I was fairly certain he felt the same because his relief as he walked into my room was palpable.

I changed tactic and started to raise certain topics with Marcus under the guise of working through the outrageous things *that* boy had suggested. Marcus, despite himself, was intrigued by the claims Devyn had made. He also asked me more about the time I had spent with Devyn before we were caught.

He had no one else he could ask about the magic that he now knew he was using to help victims of the illness. I couldn't tell him much more than he already knew from Fidelma – I knew no more than he did as my magic had manifested too late to allow me any time to grill Devyn about it. It was quite a dance we led each other during the conversations in my room. I was unwilling to reveal more than Marcus already knew while trying to convince him I was still under the influence of the handfast, while Marcus was trying not to show his increasing suspicion that I was hiding something even as I was sowing the seeds of doubt in his mind that there was something more behind our match. Despite the handfast and its coding making him want to comply, I could see the clever scientific mind sucking in the pieces of information and chewing them over night after night.

I whiled away my days scouring the newsfeeds for any mention of Devyn, my interest in my alleged psychotic attacker being apprehended only natural, surely. The gossips had noticed that I no longer went to the hospital each day and there was speculation in some areas that Marcus and I were on the rocks. Most defended me though – Marcus and I were a romance for the ages and it would take more than one crazy man to take us down. If only they knew. I was locked in my room, contemplating cutting off my own arm in order to get to that crazy man. Not seriously of course, but it had crossed my mind. My biggest hurdle was getting out of this room; the handfast armband was a concern but not a major one. I had already reasoned that they couldn't track me with it or they would have found me sooner that day in the hospital.

But I was starting to panic. My ivory tower had become a prison and I had no way out and no allies.

Or so I believed.

Chapter Twenty-Five

Anna helped me with my dress after my final fitting. I was running out of time – the wedding was just days away. My chest tightened and my heart pounded like it was going to burst every time I allowed myself to think on it. The feeling of being trapped was insidious, ever present, and I felt like an animal in a snare trying to remain compliant lest the trap tighten, but the need to thrash against my bonds was overwhelming as I almost tore the dress off, clawing at the pressure in my chest.

Anna's cool hands calmed mine and she helped me take it off, wrapping my robe around me before sitting me down.

"Donna Cassandra, would you like me to fetch your mother?" Her concerned voice came to me as if from a great distance

I shook my head frantically as I struggled to draw breath.

I was going to have to marry Marcus. There was no way out.

I whimpered.

I would never see Devyn again. Never know what he

meant when he said he would take me home. It was one of the many things I had spent my days fretting about. Home, he had told me. I had a home with him, out there in the wilds.

I looked into Anna's eyes, my own filled with the despair I could no longer hide. Anna's hand came up to hold my trembling one as I tied the clasp on my robe.

"I'll help you," she whispered.

"What?" I asked, certain I must have misheard my carefully proper servant.

"I've watched you since you was a little girl," Anna told me. "It ain't right. My dad, he was a Shadower, you know. My mum loved him despite his blood. If you want to be with this boy… I'll help you."

"You will?"

"Yes, donna. I watched you in that dress. I see your heart's breaking. If I can help you, I will."

I beamed at her.

"Thank you, thank you," I gabbled. Anna would be risking a lot to help me. But beggars can't be choosers and this was it, my one slim chance at escape. I was going to take it.

"If we're going to do it, now's our chance. I can get you out. Do you know where to find him?"

I hesitated. Was this the same trap Devyn had fallen into after the sentinels let him go? He'd thought he was in the clear but they'd followed him and he'd led them to me. I gripped Anna's hand in the Briton manner, pulse to pulse.

"Can I trust you?" I asked.

Anna looked back at me, this woman who had always lived in the shadows of my life. I remembered her picking me up and dusting me off as a toddler, or sitting on my bed stroking my hair as I cried. I had wanted so badly to be loved and I had missed it where it had been freely given, all this time.

"Yes," I said, "I'll be able to find him."

"All right then. If you need anything, best you be gathering it now," she directed me.

I looked around the room that had been the centre of my universe. It held all my treasures, luxuries, fancies, and mementoes. The pictures on the wall documented the things I had cared for as a girl. I was that girl no longer and none of it meant anything to me.

I'd thought about what I needed to do if I got my chance – after all, I'd had little else to do. I accessed my online account and selected the image I had identified a couple of days earlier. It was a picture of a red dragon acer, the scarlet leaves reflected in a lake – not the one that grew on Richmond Hill but close enough. I indicated I was a fan of the pic and shut down my comms. If Devyn was watching, I hoped it was enough of a flag to tell him I was on my way. I ran to my wardrobe and changed into some of my more practical clothing, which wasn't saying much. My outfit was still more aesthetically pleasing than sturdy and who knew how long it would have to suffice.

I shrugged on a jacket and squared my shoulders. "Ready."

Anna took a quick look into the hall before beckoning me to follow her. We quickly took the corridor to the door at the end and down the backstairs to the kitchen.

"I can get you as far as the lower level exit," she told me, wrapping a long servant's cloak about my shoulders. "The cleaners will all be leaving in about twenty minutes. Go out with them; nobody will take any notice of one more. I've been watching and them sentinels don't take no notice of the servants, leastways not on the way out. As long as nobody comes looking for you in your room, you should have time to get away."

"They'll know you helped me," I said, gesturing to the cloak.

"I'll cry and say you nicked it, donna." She smiled at me, a genuine smile that I hadn't been on the receiving end of since I was a child. Was it my fault Anna had grown distant or had I been the one to put the distance between us as I got older?

"I… thank you, Anna," I said, hoping the older woman understood the depth of my gratitude.

We made our way down the stairs with Anna in front in case anyone met us on the stairs. When we reached the lower level, she opened a storeroom door and gestured for me to go inside.

"Wait till the others are passing, then you join them," she instructed me softly. "Good luck, my girl."

I slipped out into the night with the servants and, as predicted, nobody so much as looked my way. I walked a little behind the main group headed south when they splintered between those headed east and south, the two areas where the cheaper housing in the city existed. When we got to the river, I peeled off and headed west into the lowering sun.

I needed to be out of the western gate before the sun set and traffic was halted for the day. My plan was to simply walk out. Devyn had mentioned that the charm would conceal the wearer from the cameras when active – maybe not conceal so much as cause a person to be overlooked. I was wearing two now; hopefully that meant double the strength. All that remained was to keep my hood up and my head down and hope the guard didn't look too closely.

I picked up my pace as I made my way along the embankment. Even if it wasn't double the strength, the western gate tended to be on the lax side as there was another level of security on the other side of Richmond. My plan wasn't an elaborate one but I was hoping that therein lay its strength.

I took a deep breath as I approached the gate. Ducking my head into the recesses of the hooded cloak, I queued up with the last few stragglers hurrying through the gate before it closed. The guards informed us that only those already in the line would make it through. We inched forward. Was the queue slower than usual? Were they being more conscientious or was I imagining it? I didn't usually queue in the foot-traffic line on my way to Richmond; we normally took a boat and the guards would check our passes on the river.

A moment later, an argument broke out at the back of the queue as a man protested why he had been denied entry. Or rather, exit. His loud excuses for his lateness received short shrift from the guards but as I approached the front of the line his protestations started to sound increasingly aggressive and the guard checking the passes barely glanced at me as he waved me through.

On the other side, I breathed deeply and headed into the red sunset. I had decided to stay off the main roads, instead using the river path as it wound its way from the city to Richmond. It would take me longer, but with night falling there would be fewer people on the path and if I was pursued it would surely be the last route they checked.

I passed joggers and strollers taking in the last rays of the day, the oranges and golds of the trees along the bank mirroring the reds and pinks of the sky in the water. I rarely came out to Richmond once the summer was over, which was a shame really as it was truly spectacular at this time of year.

I was passing through the gardens of Kew by the time darkness fell and what would have been beautiful and rustic became sinister and gloomy as the shadows took over. I walked as fast as I could without calling attention to myself. I was starting to feel even more tired than usual and the cuff on my upper arm felt uncomfortable. It was an odd sensation – I almost forgot it was there most of the time but this evening it felt noticeable. I rubbed my arm as I walked on.

Finally reaching Richmond, I started to fret about where in particular I should go to meet Devyn. If I continued on the path I would pass by the old ruins – my parents' villa was only a little further on from there – but if I took a small detour and then came back onto the path and headed west until I got to Petersham Meadows, I could then hike up the hill to the walled garden. He would be in one of those places. He would.

The ruins felt even lonelier than usual as I picked my way through them. No Devyn. It had been a long shot but I felt it had been worth checking. He knew I had witnessed the start of one escape from the site. I padded quietly up the familiar road to our summer villa. Strange to think I would never walk this path again. Once I left the city I could never come back. My old life would be gone forever. I would never run along here on my way back from tennis, planning my outfit for that night's party.

I nearly jumped out of my skin when a figure emerged from the trees.

"Cass."

I sagged in relief, tears springing to my eyes. He was here. I turned back and practically fell into his arms.

"You're here." We stood in the dark, careful not to embrace and attract attention but just the sight of him was enough to ease me.

"Of course. Didn't we have a date?" he teased. He took my hand and we headed back the way I had just come, towards the river. "How did you get away?"

I told him as we walked, increasingly conscious of the cuff which was starting to feel warm in the cool autumn air. I rubbed at it; it felt prickly, like I'd developed an allergy.

"The guards at the gate didn't challenge you, the lovely Cassandra Shelton in servant's garb?" he asked, indicating my plain cloak.

"No, not everyone reads the gossips, you know," I retorted, "though to be fair there was a bit of a commotion so they were a little distracted.

"Ah, good. You came through the western gate then?"

"What… how did you know? That man was a friend of yours?" I guessed and received a cocky look in confirmation.

"You think of everything," I cooed, only half mockingly. Even after the fact, it made me feel better to know that he had been there helping me.

"Ow," It felt like the cuff had stung me. And it was growing still warmer. I rubbed at it again.

"What is it?" he asked.

"It's nothing."

"It's not nothing." He stopped walking and pulled my sleeve up so he could examine the armband.

"What the—" he exclaimed, finding the skin red and inflamed around the band. "What's going on?"

"I don't know. Just now it felt like it emitted some kind of sting or something." A prickle of unease ran down my spine. "You think it got triggered when I left the city?"

Devyn shook his head. "I'm not sure. I don't think so. You've seen handfasted couples out here in the summer," he reminded me. "It doesn't seem to harm them."

"Let's just go. The sooner we get out of here the sooner we can find someone who can get this off me." I tugged on his arm and he joined me in heading purposefully up river.

We hurried along the path which was almost completely deserted now. After Petersham, we ducked into the woods where Devyn had two of the most beautiful horses tethered to a tree.

"The boundary on the other side of the park is patrolled but if we're moving fast enough we should be able to get through," he explained as I admired our new equine friends.

"Uh… I've never…" I started, eyeing the tall beasts.

"Just sit in the saddle and hold on."

Right. This was it. He cupped his hands for me to step into and I swung myself up. He untied the horses and climbed onto his chestnut, then we swung their heads back towards the river. It was the best path west – at least until dawn when we would be able to head cross country in the light.

"Is your arm feeling better?" Devyn checked.

"Yes, it stopped hurting a few minutes ago." Devyn frowned at my admission that it had actually been causing me pain.

We emerged back onto the bank and turned left to continue to freedom when I spotted the lights. Many lights approaching fast. My breath stopped in my constricted chest.

"Devyn," I whispered. He turned and looked at me, then his eyes moved to take in the lights behind me. He looked back at me.

"Back," he instructed. Turning back into the woods, we picked our way as fast as we could through the trees on horseback. The lights were gaining on us and had started to follow us through the trees, the sounds of men and dogs in pursuit.

We raced across the open field. Devyn was holding back so he didn't get too far ahead of me. I looked behind at the mounted men in pursuit. We weren't going to make it.

As we arrived at the treeline, I made a decision. My punishment for trying to escape would be severe but Devyn's would be fatal. I couldn't let him be caught.

"Devyn," I called, my throat so tight I could barely manage his name.

He turned, holding back his horse until I came alongside.

"Go. It's me they're after."

His eyes widened as he took in my meaning.

"No," his tone was resolute. "We stay together."

I shook my head. "No, we stay alive. If they catch us they'll kill you. I need you to go. I'll be fine. Just go."

His jaw was set, his eyes looking behind me, judging the approaching sentinels. He reached across and tore my reins from my fingers.

"If you won't come with me, I will lead."

He started forward again holding my reins, setting a pace that was reckless in the uncertain dark terrain.

I held onto my horse's mane and kept my head low as we charged along. I could hear the hooves pounding behind us; our pursuers were gaining on us. There was no way we could make it. We exited the woods into an open space and Devyn picked up the pace, heading towards the hill opposite when lights suddenly appeared over the crest. Torches and men and dogs.

We veered left, heading back for the cover of the trees. Devyn slowed some as we approached the woods and I threw myself off the horse and tumbled onto the ground.

Feeling the change, Devyn turned and saw me on the grass behind him.

He roared, a sound filled with anguish, echoes of the child's pain mingled with the man's.

"Cass." He came back towards me. "Get on the horse."

I shook my head, backing away from him.

"You've got to leave," he pleaded. "I'll buy you some time to get away."

This had to be his worst nightmare – the past repeating itself. A repitition that every fibre of his being would protest against, the idea of riding away from me in the face of oncoming sentinels.

This was not the same. I was not alone. This was my choice.

"No." I looked back over my shoulder. They were nearly here. I ran over to the chestnut and held his hand so he could feel my strength, understand my decision. "Please. Please, ride. I'm begging you."

He stared down at me. I could barely see his face in shadow with the moon bright behind him. How I wanted to see his face. I could feel the turmoil within him, the pain, the fear… not for himself, for me.

"Please. You've got to go now." I willed him to heed me. If he was caught they would kill him.

"I'll come back for you."

"I know."

He would always come back for me.

He leaned down. He was going to do it. He was going to leave. I smiled into the kiss as our lips touched. He straightened up and I let my hand fall. With a thundering of hooves he was gone.

I turned to face the oncoming sentinels. He needed more time. I could give it to him.

I let my pain and fear swell and swirl within me. I called out into the night and felt nature herself answer.

The leaves started to rustle and the trees started to sway as the winds built. The moon disappeared as the clouds scudded across the night sky and thunder rolled. I gave myself up to it, lifting my head to the night sky as rain started to fall.

Devyn rode further away, north to home, to safety. The creeping lights slowed; they knew they had me now. The rain poured down great sheets of water, the wind whipping through the trees behind me.

The lights flickered and extinguished.

But the dark shadows edged ever closer.

They hesitated as the world became mine. Energy crackled through me.

Lightning flashed and forked into the open field in front of me, giving the oncoming sentinels pause. Again and again the world lit up in a stark white flash.

I laughed as power rushed through my veins.

Let them try to ride me down.

A flash cracked through a great oak in front of me. My protector, it gave itself for me, the flames licking up into the night sky.

A single figure appeared through the storm, a shadow in the night.

"Cassandra."

The fiery tree revealed his identity. Marcus. What was Marcus doing here? The storm lessened as he approached. He stopped when he was only a couple of feet from me. The rain plastered his hair and clothes to his body.

"Cassandra, you have to stop," he ordered.

"Make me." I grinned.

He looked back at the sentinels, his hand taking mine tentatively. The touch brought me back and I felt my energy waning. "Cassandra, he's gone. You have to stop now."

The wind that whipped across the field gentled and the sheets of rain eased off. I swayed on my feet, suddenly exhausted. Marcus leaped forward and caught me as my knees threatened to give way from underneath me.

"He's gone?" I asked Marcus, my lip wobbling, from exhaustion or a sense of abandonment I wasn't sure. The latter was hardly fair as I wanted Devyn to be far from here, where he couldn't be caught. Where the sentinels lined up before me couldn't lay their hands on him. He must be a long way away by now.

"Yes," Marcus said, his voice reassuring. "Long gone."

I nodded. I'd wanted him to leave me here. I'd asked him to go. Finally, the rain ceased and the wind died completely. I felt better for having Marcus here.

"I'm sorry."

I wasn't sure why but I felt bad for Marcus. Nobody was going to enjoy the fact that their match was willing to bring a storm down on the world in order to get away from him. Of course, it wasn't that I was trying to run from him so much as I was trying to run *to* someone else.

"I want you to have this." I scrabbled at Devyn's wristband. I didn't need two charms and maybe if he could see through the fog of the handfast he might help. It couldn't hurt to try. It was a gamble but what if Marcus was able to think clearly again and wasn't just marrying me because of the handfast bond? Before the handfast, Marcus hadn't been entirely their puppet. He'd manoeuvred things in order to be able to get his own way at the hospital. He hadn't told them about Fidelma and I had to believe that he wouldn't marry me knowing what he knew now were he free of the fog blanketing everything.

Marcus looked at me slightly bewildered as I placed the charm on his wrist.

"Please, help me."

"What?" He blinked.

"Why are you here, Marcus?"

He looked down at the wristband again before answering.

"I'm afraid I was the one who alerted them to your escape," he confessed ruefully. "Again."

I leaned wearily against him, his broad chest supporting me. I was so tired. "You did?"

"The handfast cuff… I didn't know it caused pain when your partner got too distant," he explained. "I complained to one of the senior doctors and the next thing I knew the world had erupted. Sentinels were pouring out of every nook and cranny."

"Ha," I laughed weakly. I really did feel most appallingly weak and sentimental. I wondered where Devyn was and whether he would be worrying about me.

"How on earth did you manage to get out?" he asked.

"I just walked," I told him simply.

"Well, you'd think they were mobilising for war the way they reacted when they discovered you were gone. And that was before you actually rained Hades down upon us." He raised a brow. "I'm presuming that was you."

"I think so," I admitted, biting my lip. I looked across the field. It looked like they had finally gathered up their courage and were coming across the field.

Even though I wore my pendant, I felt better for holding Marcus's hand as I watched the uniforms march towards us.

"Donna Shelton." I recognised praetorian Alvar as he stepped forward. "That was quite the display."

I met his gaze rebelliously. I would not cower before them.

"It appears you are a girl of hidden talents," he commented. "What an interesting turn of events."

Wasn't it though? If they were surprised, I was shocked. My hand reached for the comfort of my pendant. I looked around at the destruction I had wrought. The field was flooded, the trees split and aflame. I had no idea how I'd managed it.

"Bring her," he ordered, indicating that two of his sentinels should take me from Marcus. Marcus attempted to hold on to me but a quelling glare from Alvar put an end to his protestations. Alvar looked back at me and stalled as something caught his eye. He beckoned for me to be brought forward.

"What is this?" he queried, taking my pendant between his fingers, turning it over and finding the Celtic knot on the back. "A triquetra, what an unusual design choice. In the city."

"No," I cried as he pulled it from my neck with a snap. "Wait."

"Is there a problem, Donna Shelton?"

A problem? Why would there be a problem? He could have the pendant. I had far prettier ones at home.

"No, of course not, sir." I smiled demurely at him, looking in confusion at the guards who held my arms. What on earth did they think I was going to do? "Can you take me home please?

Alvar's head tilted to one side as if he were considering a conundrum before his eyes lit up and he looked down at the pendant before looking back at me.

He smiled.

"Of course, Donna Shelton. It would be my pleasure."

Chapter Twenty-Six

With only days to go until the wedding, the apartment was a flurry of activity. Praetorian Alvar had left after we had another long chat about the pendant and what had happened in Richmond. He really was incredibly curious, and while I was happy to talk to him, I did find walking him through the events of the other night incredibly tedious. If I knew where Devyn was, I would tell him. Asking me the same questions over and over again wasn't going to catch me out in a lie. I'd told him everything but you had to admire his thoroughness, I supposed.

"Marcus, you're here at last," I cried as his head poked around my door. "Come in, come in."

He stepped over the clothes and general detritus strewn across the floor.

"I know, the room is an absolute mess. I don't know where Anna is," I complained.

Marcus looked at me strangely.

"Anna's been arrested, Cassandra." He looked vaguely disapproving as he said it.

"Oh yes, I keep forgetting. She shouldn't have got caught up with Devyn Agrestis." I dismissed the whole affair and his judgey expression. The old servant had made her bed and now she'd have to lie in it. Shame, I'd liked the way she tucked the sheets in on my bed. I didn't like them too tight.

"Anna didn't get caught up with Devyn Agrestis. You did. And she didn't do anything to help him, she did it to help *you*," Marcus said slowly as if speaking to a small child. One he was running out of patience with.

I arched my brow at his tone. "Yes, well, it's not my fault." Yet part of me was squirming. Just a little. "Do you plan to spend the evening lecturing me?"

"No," he said. "I've been wondering, your magic abilities… did you know all the time?"

"What? Here we go again. Yawn. Everyone is very interested in my magic."

He came over and sat on my bed facing mine. "Cassandra, you created a storm from nothing to protect your friend. Did you know you could do that?"

"I've already told Alvar that I didn't so I don't know why you're asking me again," I protested. I didn't like talking about it. Magic was against the Code and there was still a chance they were collecting the wood to burn me at the stake. As soon as the wood dried out, I smiled to myself. Funny. I reached out for Marcus to take his hands in mine. "I don't know what happened or why I did it. I just want to focus on the wedding and put all that behind us."

"Cassandra, you're in love with another man. You were willing to set the world alight to keep him safe. You do not want to marry me." Marcus's jaw was set, his eyes conveying his hurt.

"No, no, that was all a mistake. I don't know why any of

that happened. I don't care about him. I want you and our life here together. I want you," I told him frantically, my hands reaching up to cup his face, forcing him to look at me.

Marcus smiled wryly at me. "Why, so we can go and have those children that the state wants us to have? Who will undeniably be strong in magic. You warned me, and I didn't believe you. I didn't want to believe you."

Why was he talking about this stuff? I didn't care about any of it. It wasn't relevant. It would be fine. He was Marcus Courtenay. There is no way they would take his children from him and if the city needed our children to help them by using magic for some reason, then who were we to argue?

"Fidelma showed me how to target my magic. How much better would it be if I had been trained," he mused aloud. "The Wilders have some kind of medicine that treats the illness. Did Devyn tell you what it is?"

"Marcus," I reprimanded, looking towards the door Why would he even mention that person? "Shh, we don't need to get in even more trouble. Let's just focus on the wedding."

Marcus got up from the bed and paced up and down the floor. What on earth was going through his mind? I'd never seen him like this.

"Okay, I'm sorry for talking about things you find upsetting," he said, coming to sit back down beside me. It wasn't that I found talking about Devyn and magic upsetting so much as that I didn't care; it just wasn't relevant to my life. "I was hoping to discuss our last night before the wedding actually, our one last night of revels."

A much better topic. I clapped my hands. A party. My face dropped mid-celebration. I was not going to be allowed out.

"I'm not allowed to leave the apartment."

"We'll see about that," Marcus said, giving me his most charming smile.

"I don't know how you did it." I laughed as we stepped out into the night two days later.

But I did know how he'd managed it. He'd thrown a massive fit and said the city would expect to see us having our pre-wedding revels and that we must show the city that everything was normal. Nobody knew anything about my attempted escape, just that a freak storm had hit. There might have been some whisperings of magic but what reason would the Britons have to hurt the city that way? It had been generations since anything like that had occurred. Marcus mounted a convincing argument that what the city needed was something new to gossip about, and what better than Marcus Courtenay and his bride ripping it up before their big day?

It was amazing not just to be out of that horrid stifling apartment, but to be partying at the outer walls. Was this what married life would be like? No father frowning on your behaviour with boys, no mother saying where you could and couldn't be seen. I gripped Marcus's arm and laughed up at him as we were ushered to the front of the queue.

All our friends were in the club and it had the makings of the best night of my life. To Hades with the wedding, *this* was the party I'd wanted. Everyone dressed to the nines, dancing and drinking at the outer wall. I couldn't believe I was here, couldn't believe that Marcus had managed to convince my parents to let me come to this side of town. The club was dark and decadent, full of loud music and writhing bodies. I was having the time of my life. I swirled from one partner to the next.

My new partner twirled me into the thickest part of the dance floor, his hands on me, and my entire body stilled. I leaned in and inhaled. Him. It was him.

"Devyn."

"Cass," his voice whispered in my ear as he continued to sway to the music, our hips moving together. I looked around; no one was paying us any attention. My hands roamed over him, reassuring myself that he was really there with me. His broad chest, his muscular arms. He had come back. He had come back for me.

"What do we do?" I whispered frantically. "Tell me you have a way out."

"I have a way out."

We moved towards the side of the dance floor and wound our way through the crowd until we came to a staff door. Devyn pushed it open and that easily we were through.

In the darkness of the corridor I threw myself at him, wrapping myself around him. If I could have I would have buried myself inside him. I was desperate for his touch, need surging through me. I didn't want to be the Cassandra I became when he left, I wanted this. I wanted Devyn.

"Thank you, thank you," I murmured as I pressed tiny kisses to his jaw, his throat, wherever I could reach.

"For what?" He pulled away so he could look down at me.

"For coming back," I said, my eyes glistening.

His head went back in shock that I had ever doubted him.

He took my head in his hands. "I will always come for you."

He hugged me to him fiercely. I was in his arms. I was safe.

The horror of the last few days was over. The endless questioning, Anna's arrest.

"Anna, they took Anna," I told him. If anyone could find a way to get her out, Devyn could. He had untangled us but was keeping our hands threaded together to maintain our physical connection as he started dragging me along the corridor. "They took her. She helped me and they arrested her."

"I know," he said softly. "I'm sorry, Cass."

"You won't help her? We have to help her," I told him.

"It's too late."

"Too late? Too late for what? We can find her, we can bring her with us."

Devyn paused before opening the fire exit that would lead us to freedom.

"She's dead," came a grim voice from the darkness behind us. My heart stopped. We had been caught.

We both turned to face the shadow behind us. It was Marcus.

"Dead," I echoed. What did he mean, dead? My mind couldn't process what he was saying. We had been caught. It was all over. Dead. Anna was dead. What? How?

"They executed her for helping you get away," Marcus informed me stonily.

I gasped, a sob welling inside me.

"What? They barely even reprimanded me. Why would they do that?" My grip on Devyn's hand must be cutting off his circulation. He was the only thing grounding me right now. I felt like somebody had taken a giant cleaver and split me in two. Kind, gentle Anna, who had never stepped out of line, never done anything against the Code except help me. They had killed Anna for helping me.

"They need you. You can give them something they want.

Anna crossed them. They eradicate all chaos in the Code. You know that," Marcus elaborated coldly, his handsome face outlined by the neon red of the fire exit light.

I leaned heavily against Devyn, his body warmth the only comfort in a world that was so much colder, so much darker than I had ever imagined. Anna had been a good person and they had killed her. Now they would take Devyn.

"They're going to have to kill me too then," I said throwing my shoulders back and lifting my chin I held Devyn's hand and stood tall. "Because I'm never going to give them what they want."

"Really?" Marcus asked. "What happens when he lets go of your hand?"

I felt the pulse of fear and dread through the connection.

"What?" I stalled for time. Though really, at this point I was starting to wonder why the hall wasn't packed with sentinels. Why was it just Marcus?

"I figured it out." He nodded at our hands. "It's his touch, isn't it? That's how you manage to break the compulsion, why you stop being compliant and just wanting what the city has told you to want. Me. Marriage. Babies that they can use."

I didn't answer. I didn't know what to say. He had figured a lot of it out – at least the part about Devyn's touch – but he didn't seem to recognise his own thought process was less clouded than it had been before I gave him the wristband, but I wasn't going to educate him further when there was a risk that information could be used against us.

"What do you want?" Devyn asked. Like me, he also had to be wondering where the sentinels were.

"I want to help you," Marcus replied, shocking both of us.

"Why?" Devyn asked quickly.

Marcus looked at me before looking back at Devyn. "It's

not right what they're doing, what they did to Anna."

"Really?" I asked softly, not sure what to believe.

"Really," he replied. "I don't like being used. I've been pushed around all my life. I've spent my whole life trying to please, doing what I was told, working within the boundaries of what my father permitted. I thought it would be enough. But it's not. It's not enough. You've fought, really fought. Why shouldn't you get to be free?"

I nodded but I could feel Devyn's reservation. He was less willing to believe Marcus had merely had a change of heart.

"You won't say anything?" Was this how he was going to help, by not raising the alarm?

"Not say anything?" he echoed. "I'm coming with you."

This was the last thing I had expected. Devyn's reaction was also surprising: he wasn't as pleased as I'd thought he would be. His suspicion was almost tangible, even without the connection. He was right to be, but I also knew Marcus better than he did. Marcus was more than a party boy; he felt responsible for people. What happened to Anna would not sit well with him. Perhaps he even felt a little to blame since he was the one who had raised the alarm. I'd given him the wristband for a reason, for *this* reason. Now that he was seeing clearly, now that he was helping us, I had to trust him.

"You want to leave the city? Devyn questioned. "I don't believe you."

"You don't have any choice."

"I think you'll find we do," Devyn responded, moving towards the door and taking me with him.

"Not if you open that door," Marcus warned him. "Every exit is covered by sentinels. They're not stupid. They know there's a chance you'll try to get to her tonight. It's your last opportunity."

I looked from Devyn to Marcus. We were trapped.

"Why should we believe you?" I pushed, hoping he had a good answer.

"That there are sentinels outside that door? You'd be idiots not to." Marcus rolled his eyes. "Look, if I'd wanted to out you both I could have done so the minute you touched her in the club. He does make your heart go pit-a-pat, Cassandra, and when your pulse races… well, by now I know what it means."

Of course. I'd forgotten in my delirious joy at seeing Devyn how we'd been caught before. I turned to Devyn who was looking to me for an explanation.

"Marcus and I… the handfast bond has some interesting elements we weren't aware of." I picked my words carefully; given the intimacy of my connection with Devyn and how seriously he took that, I didn't want him to think for even a nanosecond that the handfast bond connected me to Marcus in a similar way. "When I'm with you and we uh, kiss and stuff…"

One furious eyebrow rose practically to Devyn's hairline.

"He can sense our emotions?" he demanded.

"No, no," I rushed. "That is, not exactly."

"Oh, for the love of the gods," Marcus snapped. "When you guys get it on, I start feeling the heat. Though the effect was barely noticeable tonight," he mused. "I thought I was mistaken until I saw you both slip through the door."

I could feel my cheeks lighting up. Anyone looking from as far away as the moon would be able to see the blush on my face.

"That's how you knew I was in the hospital?" Devyn asked, the tic in his jaw moving.

"Yep."

"That doesn't explain how you caught us so fast in

Richmond," Devyn observed.

"Ah, I'm glad you brought that up," Marcus said. "Reason number two why you need to take me with you. It appears that the cuffs start to react when the handfasted couple are too far apart. They don't just make us feel like we need to be in each other's company all the time. They start to cause physical pain when we are too distant."

I recalled the discomfort I had felt as I made my way to Richmond.

"It's not that bad," I dismissed.

"Maybe not for you sweetheart," Marcus grimaced, lifting his arm to show me Devyn's wristband. So, he'd figured it out. "I'm presuming these little accessories may have suppressed the worst of it. Our homes are in the same neighbourhood so the furthest apart we ever are is when I'm at work which is where I was on the night you decided to head west, in the opposite direction to the hospital. Once you passed through the gate at the outer wall, my arm started causing me a lot of pain. It took us a while to figure out which direction you'd gone in, and far too long to get me on a boat so we could follow. By the time we started after you, I couldn't stand. I spent most of the pursuit on the floor of that boat writhing in agony."

I stared at him in horror. He wasn't exaggerating. His breathing had shallowed, his skin greying as he spoke of the remembered pain.

"I had no idea," I gasped.

"Yes, well." He leaned against the dark corridor wall. "I think it came as rather a shock to the authorities as well. I'm not sure anyone has ever separated that far before. Most couples would pull back long before it got that far. Their first instinct is to seek comfort from each other, thereby ending their pain. I presume that pendant Alvar took from you protected you somehow."

"I didn't know," I repeated horrified. Devyn had posited before that the handfast connection would somehow manage to bring Marcus with us. It had never occurred to me to wonder how exactly.

"I didn't think you did," he assured me. "They wanted to know how you did it. Luckily you gave me your backup before they took your necklace. It gave me a chance to think about things."

Clever Marcus had figured out the wristband and then everything else.

"And you decided to join us," Devyn finished for him.

Marcus smiled his broad smile. "Well, if I can't beat you…"

Devyn stilled, looking down at me thoughtfully. He'd been told to get Marcus out, and now he could get me out too and obey his orders. Win-win.

"…he should join us," I finished and Devyn nodded his agreement. It wasn't like we had other options, anyway.

Marcus hurried us back along the corridor. "For the guests of honour, we've been gone a little too long. We need to get back." He cast a sideways look at me taking in my messed-up hair and distinct lack of lipstick. "Anyone looking at you, at least, will assume we snuck away to do what handfasted couples do."

I could feel Devyn tense protectively. He didn't like Marcus talking about me that way. Marcus stopped and looked back at us as we approached the door leading back into the club.

"I had a plan to get us out of the city"—he looked at Devyn—"not one that included having the city's most wanted man along with us. Unlike the sentinels, I didn't plan on you being stupid enough to come back for her."

It was Devyn's turn to smile at Marcus – a cocky grin that said he was more than happy with the title and didn't really care if that was causing Marcus any extra difficulty.

"How much do you remember when you aren't touching him?" he asked me.

I frowned.

"You know I remember everything," I said. "You've heard me telling Alvar what happened."

Marcus looked at me assessingly. He'd been there for the first round of questioning. He'd been there after the hospital incident too.

"You don't tell everything," he said. "You missed out certain things. You didn't tell them you'd given me the wristband."

He was right. I did manage to hold things back. Relevant things that the authorities would want to know but where they hadn't asked the question I hadn't offered up additional information. Was that enough though? I wasn't willing to bet all our lives on it.

"I'll tell them this," I assured him. "Trying to get us out of the city is the epitome of noncompliance. It goes against everything the handfast is programming us to do which is for us to be together and do what the city wants."

Marcus rubbed the back of his neck. "You can't maintain contact with Devyn. They'll be watching us as we leave. I don't suppose you have another one of these handy charms with you?"

"I didn't know they had taken Cass's from her." Devyn shook his head. "We don't have to be touching, exactly. It seems as long as we're no more than a few feet from each other the interference with the handfast bond holds."

"We'll have to work with that. I can't give you the

wristband, as I'm likely to give you both up." Marcus stepped closer and looked deep into my eyes. I could practically feel Devyn bristle through our connection. "I think you'll go along with it if I ask you to."

He was going to risk all our lives on the hope that I would stay quiet about Devyn if he were with me. Was he mad?

"It's the only way," he said as I opened my mouth to shoot down his crazy idea. He turned to Devyn. "I'll get us out. You'll have to find another way."

"No." I wasn't going to be separated from Devyn. Not again. I couldn't bear it. I also didn't believe that Marcus would be able to keep me from spilling the beans if Devyn wasn't around. "He stays with me."

"Caesar wept," Marcus exclaimed exasperated. "Fine. We'll need to disguise him or something."

His eyes lit up as inspiration struck. "Maybe tonight won't be a completely fun-free night after all. Stay here."

He pushed out into the club, leaving Devyn and me alone together, the noise and heat momentarily invading the dark where we stood,. I tucked myself into Devyn's chest and his arms went around me. I needed a minute to steady myself, I needed this moment of comfort with him.

"Can we trust him?" Devyn asked quietly in the dark.

"I don't know," I confessed. "But it doesn't feel like we have any choice."

He grumbled into my hair.

I smiled up at him and took the chance to kiss him. I loved kissing him. I loved his lips, so firm, so soft against mine. I missed this when he wasn't there. His kisses made me feel warm. Alive.

"Can you two bloody stop that?"

The door opened and the noises of the club invaded our

space again. Devyn and I pulled back guiltily from each other. It was somewhat discomfiting to know that a third party was affected when you kissed.

"Here you go, lover boy." Marcus threw a white cloth at Devyn.

Devyn caught it in the air and shook it loose. It was just a white cloth and he looked up at Marcus in confusion.

"What's this?"

"It's your outfit for the party." Marcus looked inordinately pleased with himself. "I've just hired some traditional entertainment for the next part of the night. You're one of them."

Devyn looked at me for an explanation. I didn't have one; I was just as bewildered as he was. What on earth did Marcus mean, entertainment? The white cloth was his costume?

"What tradi—" I started to ask when enlightenment dawned. "Oh."

I swallowed. Was Marcus really proposing what I thought he was? He was going to hide Devyn in plain sight, right there out in the open, the centrepiece of our decadent prenuptial revels. The one night where innocent girls like me could play in front of everyone, and nobody batted an eyelid because it was all in fun.

"It's not much of a disguise," I pointed out, at which Marcus pulled a chestnut-haired wig from his pocket and threw it at the still none-the-wiser man at my side.

Devyn's annoyance at not understanding was loud and clear; no need for a connection for that one.

"I'll be back in our area. Hurry up." Marcus threw over his shoulder as he left us.

I explained quickly to Devyn as he changed and five minutes later we followed, my lover boy trailing along behind as I tugged him towards the VIP area where our party was congregated.

Catcalls and whistles followed us as the crowd parted to let us through. As we made our way up the steps, I noted several other entertainers strewn about the party. It was camouflage for Devyn, and good thinking on Marcus's part. Having boys and girls of this type at a revel was going to raise eyebrows. It was licentiousness on a huge scale, especially if we were going to exit the club with them in our company. I couldn't help but shudder at Camilla's reaction when she saw this all over the gossips in the morning. At least I wouldn't have to face her. If this worked I'd be long gone.

I pulled Devyn up the stairs after me until we reached Marcus. I then trailed my fingers down his bare torso while I laughed up at Marcus.

"Why thank you, darling, he's perfect." I pecked Marcus on the lips in full close-up view of everyone.

Marcus met Devyn's eyes in devilish delight at the sight of my Briton attired in an old-fashioned waist toga and wig. If I was to have a lover boy on a string at the party, he had to look like my soon-to-be husband – it was all part of the fun. The fun was a little taken out of it for me as my friends and acquaintances cooed and ran their hands all over Devyn's well-shaped broad chest, not recognising the handsome, sharp-featured, toned version of the unremarkable Devyn Agrestis they had known.

"Oh, my." Ginevra cast me a sideways look as she ran her hands along his six pack. "He's delicious. I'll have to hire him when my day comes."

I wanted to tear her fingers off. One. By. One. I couldn't do it now, so I pushed Devyn away onto a seat between us, sending him my deepest apologies along our connection. He was furious, repelled by the pawing at his body, and loathing every minute of this. When was Marcus going to make his move?

Ginevra turned Devyn's face up to her. The fingers she was soon to lose traced his features, turning his head from side to side.

"Does he remind you of anyone?" she asked. *Yes, the last man you will ever touch before you die slowly.*

"Uh… no. No one comes to mind." I smiled mischievously as I ran my hand down his chest, lower and lower, distracting Ginevra with his muscles as I made my way down, tantalising her with the potential of where I would stop. Or fail to stop. It was working; Ginevra was mesmerised as she followed my fingers.

"That's enough," Marcus said as he snapped my hand away, and I turned dilated eyes in his direction. He shook his head. "Time to get out of here, my love. Why don't we bring the entertainment with us?"

I took a deep breath to steady myself.

Marcus jumped up on a table and announced to the delighted group that it was party boat time. The crowd roared, and we surged towards the door. The entertainers came with us as our decadent trophies. I wondered if anyone ever did more than look and touch. I supposed they might – there was a reason my father didn't like me to come to this part of town. There was also a reason that this tradition had mostly died out, belonging to a much freer, more debauched past. The old Romans would roll in their graves if they could see us using this as the disguise that got us out of the city.

As we exited the club, Marcus took my hand firmly in his grip, nodding at Devyn to back off as the sentinels approached us. I felt a pang as I unhooked my arm from his and he stepped back as far as he could into the crowd behind us.

"Do as I tell you." Marcus glared down at me. "I'll speak to the sentinels and you will do as I want."

Why would I go against what Marcus wanted? I was put out at his tone; it was very unfair of him to speak to me that way.

"Dr Courtenay." A praetorian I recognised blocked our path. Kasen was Alvar's right-hand man, the one invariably left in charge of the sentinels when Alvar was away. They no longer trusted the sentinels alone to keep an eye on me without supervision.

"Praetorian." Marcus inclined his head, his pronunciation less than crisp, to imply he had drunk more than was good for him. His hand gripped mine. "We're off to the next venue. Are you coming?"

"You only have clearance for the club." Kasen frowned, indicating we should go back inside as our friends jostled by him.

"Don't be such a bore," Marcus mocked, moving on and dragging me with him. Where was he going? If we only had clearance for the club, we really should return there.

"Sir, I really must insist." Two more guards arrived, blocking our way. They were immediately surrounded by scantily clad women in loose togas who started to fawn all over them. Attempts to shake them off were thwarted by the growing attention we were attracting from partygoers and the paps who had stationed themselves outside the club once word had got out of our location.

"You're more than welcome to join us," Marcus invited the praetorian as he stumbled, wrapping his arm around my neck and leading me onwards towards a boat. Kasen watched us depart, hesitating, clearly torn between forcibly preventing us from leaving and not wanting to create a scene in front of the paps.

He hesitated long enough that Marcus had already started to usher me up the gangway onto the boat. I began to protest. This wasn't right. We shouldn't be leaving the club. Marcus wanted to board the boat because he was trying to leave the city. And Devyn was here.

"Wait," I called towards the sentinels, waving my arm to attract their attention. They were starting to follow the party, but they were too far away. "Praetor—" I started to call, Devyn Agrestis was here and Marcus was trying to leave the city, and now he was… preventing me from shouting by kissing me. I was caught between kissing him back and trying to push him off so I could run to the guards. I needed help, I needed to stop him.

The crowd started to cheer us as they pushed past us onto the boat, lapping up the display that Marcus was putting on. Then an arm went around my waist and I went still, the fog lifting.

Devyn's barely subdued jealousy poured through me and in reaction I bit down on Marcus's lip. He pulled back and his eyes gleamed as he met Devyn's glare over my shoulder. The crowd roared at the sight of the half-naked fake Marcus pulling me away from the real Marcus in what they thought was a pretend jealous tantrum. If only they knew. Devyn could burst into flames at any moment, he was so angry.

I turned, laughing for the crowd and dramatically pretending to beg the forgiveness of my fake lover for kissing my actual handfasted match. The crowd lapped up my antics while my eyes pleaded with Devyn to get control of himself.

He pulled me up into the prow of the boat while the

sentinels boarded after everyone was on and we headed east along the Tamesis.

"Long time since we last made this journey," Devyn whispered to me. I thought back to that first trip along the river with Marina, my fear that we would be caught, when he had told me something real about himself, and later that night when we had kissed back in Linus's flat.

He ran his fingers up and down my arm, the movement hidden by the large cloak he now wore. The entertainers had all been supplied with them for the duration of the trip down the river. It was a cold night in October and the captain had insisted that the paid help be appropriately cared for. In fact, he had not been at all impressed by the sight of the hired entertainment and our displays of wealth and overindulgence.

I was all too aware, as my lover boy wrapped me in his cloak, with me sitting in his lap, that he was still only clad in a tiny piece of cloth. Every sense trained on the warmth emanating from the exposed sculpted body behind me. His fingers ran along my arms and then slipped to trace my waist, then upwards and in until they were at the underside of my breasts. My entire being was focused on the movements of those hands.

"Enough." Marcus was suddenly looming in front of us. The charm he wore might dampen the leakage but it didn't block it entirely, so this was unfair.

Devyn slanted a smirk up at him. It was clearly payback for the earlier kiss. I threw an elbow into Devyn's ribs.

"Seriously, our lives are all in danger and you two decide it's a good time to play games with… argh," I let out a cry of annoyance. "Idiots."

I felt like a rag doll being pulled in different directions by schoolboys more interested in the competition than the prize.

My life was being turned upside down. I was dragged this way and that, first by the compulsion of the handfast to do whatever made Marcus happy, then by what I felt for Devyn whenever he drew near. It was the only thing strong enough to break through the handfast, not to mention my lifelong conditioning to live by the Code.

"Cass," Devyn's concerned whisper came to me as he felt the emotional turbulence that buffeted me. Not even my feelings were my own anymore. Could I even trust myself?

"Cass." Devyn's voice was insistent. "Are you all right?"

I half turned to him and gave a little nod. I certainly hoped so.

Marcus was watching us, his eyes dark, our exchange excluding him.

"We'll need to move fast once we get to the warehouse." He looked back at the sentinels at the rear of the boat. He reached out and caught the locks whipping across my face from the cold estuary wind. For the sake of anyone watching, I hoped, and not just to annoy Devyn. Which it did. "I'm not sure how long we'll have; Kasen has been in contact with Alvar. It's only a matter of time before they call a halt to our little party now that we've gone off plan. I just hope they wait until we get there."

"You have a way out?" Devyn asked quietly from his position nuzzling my neck, keeping in character as my plaything. Marcus looked down at him thin-lipped.

"I hope so," he said and walked back into the middle of the party.

I sat quietly beside Devyn watching the revels as we made our way downriver. We were occasionally engaged by our friends as they stumbled out into the fresh air for a breather. I gritted my teeth as pretty much every female on the boat found an excuse to talk to me so they could play with my new accessory – mostly running their hands over his torso and arms but one had asked my permission for a kiss. I stood there and watched Devyn perform the tricks of what everyone assumed to be his unofficial trade. While party escorting was legal, I supposed that most of the entertainers who earned their living that way would do a lot more if the price was right. A question Lucia Lonis was clearly asking by putting her hands where they had no business being, at which point I accidentally spilt my red wine all over the other girl's flamboyant costume.

I was still attempting to mop it up, accidentally-on-purpose making it even worse, when we started to pull in to the north bank.

Kasen approached me and Lucia flounced off.

"Donna Shelton," he addressed me courteously while simultaneously managing to convey his disapproval by ignoring Devyn who lounged against the boat railing a foot or so away, which was the most inconspicuous way we had found to maintain proximity. It did look a little odd for the hired entertainment to be continually hovering by my side.

"I would prefer it if you remained on the boat until praetorian Alvar gets here," he intoned formally.

Alvar was on the way then. We needed to be out of here. Kasen was an impeccable guard but Alvar was better. Devyn's disguise wasn't that clever if you looked too closely at his face.

"But sir, I must go where my lord directs me," I trilled flirtatiously at Kasen as I pointed to Marcus who beckoned me from the dock. I linked my arm with Devyn's.

I danced off the boat, throwing Devyn's borrowed cloak back to the captain.

"I may need that," he grumbled as we made our way down the gangway.

"Now, now," I patted his face affectedly, "everyone else was returning them. We'll get you another."

"Or not." Ginevra laughed, appearing behind us and putting her hands on Devyn's chest. *Again*. I really was going to have to kill her.

Marcus came over and grabbed my hand. "This way."

He waved us all on, directing us through the docks to a large warehouse by the outer wall. The locals watched us go by, stopping what they were doing at the sight of the elites frolicking by – and what a sight we made in our fancy party outfits, with the scantily clad entertainers and the sentinels trailing in our wake.

Music emanated from the brightly lit warehouse that Marcus led us into, the entire party *oohing* and *aahing* at the elaborate interior. It was the most enchanting, frivolous thing I had ever seen in my life. It must have cost Marcus a small fortune to set this up. The entire building was festooned in weird and wonderful decorations, lights, and hangings, with exotic and elaborate themes in each room. And most of all, it was dark and concealing. Everywhere we turned, people were disappearing into the fantastical maze Marcus had created. It was an illusion which would allow us to disappear.

"This way."

He pulled us through a winter wonderland, cold white light and snowflakes falling from the ceiling. How had he managed to prepare this in such a short space of time? It seemed Courtenay wealth and influence were able to work their own particular kind of magic.

Marcus peered through the window out on to the street below where additional vehicles were pulling up outside the warehouse. Sentinels. No, praetorian guards were teeming out, including Alvar, who looked up at the building. We pulled sharply back from the window.

"Come on."

Ginevra had caught up with us and had her hand on Devyn's arm while he looked determinedly down at the floor, resentment blistering through him.

"Don't touch him." I slapped Ginevra's hand back and she turned a shocked face to me.

"Oops," I called entirely insincerely as we moved away, picking up our pace and diving down some backstairs. This room was a chaotic buccaneers' bar, with wenches and billowing sails, some more entertainers who were better dressed than the ones we'd hired at the bar, costumed as pirates and engaging in a swordfight as we ran around the room to the delight of our guests.

"Here." Marcus pulled us behind the bar, and the barman grinned, lifting a trapdoor and holding it open so we could climb through. But he frowned in confusion as Devyn preceded us in.

There was a small exchange as Marcus handed him a credit. "Not a word." He winked at the man. The barman shrugged his shoulders as he started to close the door.

"Wouldn't know what to say, sir." He shot me a roguish leer.

"He'll hold them off for a while, but we've got to move fast," Marcus explained as he perched on the bed in the room under the bar, pulling off his shoes.

"He won't tell them we're in here?" I asked.

"Not for as long as he thinks we're doing what I told him we'd be doing." He grinned, throwing a bag at me. "Change."

What did he think we were doing in here? I looked at

Marcus on the bed… Of course. What *else* would a handfasted couple be doing in a secret bedroom at a prenuptial party? No wonder he'd looked askance at Devyn joining us.

I emptied the bag onto the bed. Out tumbled sensible travelling clothes and I hurriedly started to change.

"Do we have time for this?" I asked.

"I can't be sure they haven't put trackers on us. I think it's best to change now. The rooms outside should conceal the fact that we're missing for a while," Marcus replied. He smirked over at Devyn who was less than prepared for a long journey in his waist-wrap toga and sandals. Devyn glowered back at him.

I stopped to also glower at Marcus who begrudgingly pulled a spare pair of trousers and a shirt from the pack on the floor. Devyn put them on with ill grace. They were plain, nothing like the Celtic outfit Bronwyn had tried to get him to travel home in.

As I tied on the cloak that had been in the pack, Marcus pulled aside a barrel strategically placed over another trapdoor.

"It will drop back into place when we close it," Marcus explained. "They won't give up this exit too quickly."

"A smuggler's passage," Devyn identified, sounding grudgingly impressed. I was too. Marcus had unexpected talents.

We stepped down into the passage and Devyn picked up the light that lay waiting. We heard the thud as the barrel snapped back into place as Marcus lowered the trapdoor on us.

The passageway was dark so Devyn led the way with the light. We moved quickly together, staying in the pool of light, which shone brightly against the total black of the tunnel. I was coming to hate the passageways that lay underneath the city. I'd always thought that crime in the city was low, given the severity of the punishments handed out at the Mete. However, it appeared that evasion of taxes was a thriving industry in the city. I wondered if other crime too was much more prevalent than the public displays of justice suggested.

I would do well to wonder less about crime in the city and more about what awaited us on the other side of the walls. Devyn should be pleased that Marcus had decided to come with us, instead of which I could feel waves of distrust and suspicion rolling off him. He was wary, and I could understand why. Marcus had betrayed us before, but he'd had no real choice; he'd been caught and in order to keep treating the sick he'd had to comply. The wristband had allowed him to think clearly, to understand the trap closing around us. I too had once been happy to go along with the life that had been laid out for me since birth. Or rather, as it turned out, since I was ripped from my dead mother's arms. With all the facts laid out before me and the rise of magic within me, it seemed downright suicidal to remain inside the city walls. We no longer had lives here. We were just prisoners, puppets on strings being pulled this way and that by our parents and whoever was behind all this. I wasn't sure I ever needed to find that out.

The roughly paved path beneath our feet turned to shallow steps which went upwards for a few minutes until the passageway came to an end at a doorway. Marcus stepped forward and tapped on it.

"The door only opens from the outside," he explained.

I took Devyn's hand as we watched the door slowly open. I couldn't bear to be so close to escaping only to be once again pulled back as we had in our last attempt. I dreaded the sensation of my own consciousness ebbing away again. We had to make it this time.

Marcus reached out to take the torch from Devyn.

"Wait here," he instructed. "They're only expecting two of us."

Again I felt that pulse of distrust from Devyn. I tightened my grip on his hand in reassurance before pulling away. I followed Marcus through the door to find myself surrounded by trees. In fact, looking back, it sort of appeared as if we had stepped out of one. How clever.

The boy in Shadower clothing who had opened the door had stepped away and was now leading two horses towards us. The horses were saddled and carrying packs. Marcus had prepared well. How had he done this? I guessed that he had recently come into contact with a much wider spread of the population than one would expect of a member of such an exalted family, many of whom might have felt obliged to help him if he had reached out to them.

Marcus went to the boy and explained we had another person with us, asking if the boy had another horse. With a shake of his head and a shrug, the boy indicated he hadn't. His hand went out for the money promised, apparently keen to be on his way. Marcus put a small pouch in the boy's hand and he scampered off into the night.

"Looks like we're going to be a horse short," he sighed.

"We'll be all right."

I stepped back to the door which had remained ajar, thus maintaining a close proximity between myself and Devyn. I beckoned him out, and he stepped out into the opening before closing the door behind him. He immediately scanned the area before turning to look up at the wall looming behind us.

"Time to get out of here," he suggested, introducing himself to the larger of the two horses and rubbing its velvet neck. "You won't mind carrying two, will you, girl?"

Marcus watched as Devyn bent over, interlocking his fingers to help me mount before hoisting himself up behind me. His arms came around me, instantly making me feel more secure. I wondered if Marcus was annoyed at Devyn's automatic assumption that we would ride together. If he thought anything, he didn't show it as he climbed onto his own horse before looking to Devyn to indicate which way we should go.

"Stay close," Devyn advised as he turned the horse's head north. And we took our first steps to freedom…

And immediately halted as out of the darkness an entire squadron of sentinels stepped into view. They had the Shadower boy in their custody.

No, no, no.

We had been caught and this time they had all three of us. My instant panic whirled into the air, the trees stirring in response.

"Donna Shelton." There was a shout and a black uniformed figure stepped forward from the shadows. Praetorian Alvar.

His weapon was raised and pointed directly at us. Luckily, Devyn was behind me and I didn't think he would risk hurting Marcus or me.

I exchanged glances with Marcus. We were mounted; if we rode straight at them, maybe we had a chance of breaking through. Devyn's arms were bound tight around me.

They would kill him if they took us. Decision made, I looked back at Marcus and willed him to understand me. I took a deep breath, tensing my muscles in readiness.

Suddenly, a shot rang out.

My hands jolted to my chest as a burst of adrenaline went through me.

"No, no…" But I was all right; it wasn't me. Devyn's arms had tightened around me and I looked over at Marcus who was still seated on his horse, and then he was off, racing across the glade.

It was then I saw the fallen Shadower boy on the ground.

I looked back at Alvar in shock. He had killed the boy, an innocent boy. The storm whipped overhead.

"He's not dead," Alvar shouted over the rising wind. "But if you aren't off that horse in five seconds the next shot will be through his head."

Marcus was crouched over the boy, his body taking a protective position. Alvar must be telling the truth. Another sentinel emerged from the trees behind where the boy lay. From there Marcus would be able to do nothing if they took another shot. There *had* to be some way out. More sentinels emerged behind us and Devyn was now exposed while Marcus was off his horse.

"Get down."

It was over.

We dismounted. Alvar walked over to us and I gripped Devyn's hand tightly, my breath fast and shallow. Marcus was busy trying to help the fallen Shadower.

Alvar smirked and nodded to someone over my shoulder. Devyn's hand went limp and I turned to see what had happened. There was a sharp pinch in my neck, my limbs went limp, and I blinked to clear my vision as everything faded to black.

I came to slowly. My head felt woozy, like everything was slightly distant. I tried to raise my hands to my brow and realised they were tied tightly in front of me. I couldn't see. I couldn't hear. Nothing. I was in a total sensory void.

What was going on?

We had been taken. The sentinels had us.

Despair started to fill me.

I tried to use what senses I had left. I could smell something sharp and pungent.

"Hello? Devyn? Marcus?" I called, my voice thrumming strangely in my throat as I realised I couldn't actually hear myself make a sound. The sensation of calling out and failing to hear the corresponding cry was unnerving. Even if Devyn and Marcus could, I wouldn't be able to hear their responses. I stuffed down my rising panic.

Hands went under my arms and I was pulled to a standing position. My own hands were untied and someone grasped my upper arm and dragged me along. I stumbled as I blindly moved forward.

A strange vibration began to pulse through the building, growing to a steady thud. It was heavy and regular and felt oddly familiar. The stone beneath my feet surrendered to sand, and my footing grew less steady as the ground gave way and my knees weakened.

Realisation dawned as I came to a halt. The noise hit me in a wave the second my hearing was restored. The roar of the crowd beat down on me like a physical force.

The jeers and yells of the mob died as I heard the familiar tones of Praetor Calchas.

"You are accused of crimes against the Code. How do you plead?"

Acknowledgments

Thank you so much to all at One More Chapter, having been an editor in the past I've gotten such a kick out of being on the other side – thank you so much Bethan and Sophie for the pixie dust of tips and nudges that pushed me on to better versions.

I set out to capture a daydream, doodled for years and never expected to be here – thank you Kim for lighting the stepping stones to this castle in the sky and Charlotte for your encouragement and most improbably that magic nod that got us here.

My thanks multiply to all those who helped in the creation – Andrew, who added the shimmer I needed at just the right time. Lydia, for those words and especially for waving your wand to better ones. Tony, for that final polish. Laura, for whispering life into a world of my imagination. Melanie and Claire, and all the folks who breathe into the palms of their hands and float the dandelion seeds out into the winds to let the world know this book exists, thank you.

Special thanks to Jennifer for braving an early read and

lending your thoughts to help me knock down some of the neverending decisions. To Ashley for allowing me to pepper an otherwise idyllic Joshua Tree trail with musings about how to unravel some major worldbuilding knots and Ida for inspiring a work ethic when sun and palm trees called.

Last but not least – Úna, my port in the storm, and Eilish, my calm in all storms – it's been quite a year. Thank you for being there.

And to all of you who find this world… I do hope you enjoy your time here.

Cx

Author Q & A

How did you go about world-building an alternate history?

'What ifs' are something I'm endlessly fascinated by; battles in ages past that decided the fate of countries were often fought by surprisingly few. There are so many 'what ifs' as we look back on history.

If the king of Leinster, Dermot McMorrough, hadn't liked the look of another man's wife, he wouldn't have invited Henry II to Ireland, and this book may not have been in English. The Normans conquered England with 10,000 men, the attendance of a lower tier football game. Washington marched on Yorktown and won the American War of Independence with 9,000; a Friday night high school football game would easily accommodate them, plus the French navy assist.

In this version of history, Western Europe and Northern Africa would have been a single political entity for two millennia, which meant I had to consider what impact that might have had within and without. If the Romans had maintained their presence across Europe, one of the earlier pillars of this world was the easy conjecture that technical advances would have happened earlier, another was that some of the societal structures would have been inherited from ancient Rome.

Without the Imperial colonisation driven by Spain, France and England, what might these cultures and development of other cultures have been like? A world where the nations of native north and south Americans had continued uninterrupted, the Aztecs, the Incas, the Apache, the Comanche all thriving into the modern day. The African nations benefiting from the wealth of the land they lived on, making them less Conrad's *Heart of Darkness* and more Marvel's *Wakanda*, or so I had fun imagining. Rich magics and more traditional societies made... well, more of that in book two.

What challenges did you face in crafting this world?

Choosing a turning point so far in the past left me with a lot of explaining to do. *And* everybody has different interests or periods they believe are key and want to know how they went in this alternate universe.

I did do a parallel timeline; unfortunately, I couldn't put it all in, as my characters are themselves only interested in certain points in the past. Some key turning points remain but are twisted, or never happened at all: the Danes came and ultimately merged kingdoms with Mercia (putting Mercia further north than it was in reality), the war of the roses became a Union, Oliver Cromwell simply never rose to prominence; in that era my Britons were in a raging war with the Romans; or maybe he did... and, if so, he lived in Anglia.

What inspired you to write this series?

How we interact with the world around us, how it shapes us and how our cultures and beliefs shape it just fascinates me. Hundreds of generations in the past, present and future will see the same rivers and mountains; landmarks change or remain the same. The architecture of our cities tells tales of the past – the wealth or poverty of different eras, the changing tastes and capabilities of the people who live in them.

I've always particularly adored older buildings and the histories contained within those spaces – spaces we now occupy. As a child, I passed a Round Tower on my way to school, a building for early Christians to flee to when Vikings or less Christian folk raided. *Vikings*.

The fields around abounded with the remains of bronze age ringforts or *raths*, protected in Ireland for centuries by the belief that the little folk would have their revenge if their home was damaged, leaving the landscape dotted with the homes of those who lived millennia ago. Across the road was an estate where once lived the disgraceful rake known as the Fighting Fitzgerald, a famed Georgian duellist who kept a pet bear. My local town had seen pitched battles between the landed French and the English stationed at the barracks there. These days I walk through a movie studio lot in Los Angeles to my office, in the footsteps of Laurel and Hardy, Judy Garland, Jennifer Aniston… it absolutely blows my mind.

Growing up with so many eras and histories around and thinking about those who trod the same paths before us has inspired many a daydream. No matter where I've travelled in the world I've easily been transported to times and places past, from hidden Templar temples in southern Italy in the time of the crusades to Moorish castles in Portugal to Aztec empires in

Mexico to the sophisticated urban spaces and societal structures of ancient civilisations in Greece, China, Mexico, Peru. The list is endless.

When I started to capture this story, I was inspired by the city around me; London tumbles with stories and locations evoking different times, I just tripped over these ones.

Exploring the World of The Once and Future Queen

LONDINIUM

The Roman Walls

The roman walls are still visible in multiple places around the city of London from the Tower of London up to Liverpool Street Station, along to the Barbican Centre and down to the river by St Paul's Cathedral.

Spare a thought for the enslaved Britons ripped from their once peaceful homes to build it by the red-cloaked invaders. I added a second outer wall to account for an expanded city in later more populous centuries.

The Amphitheatre

When I started to explore Roman London in a bit more detail, I had no idea that London once held a site where gladiators fought to entertain the elite of the outpost. Much less that I would be able to visit… and you can too. Discovered in 1987, part of the excavation is open to the public visiting the Guildhall Art Gallery.

The Forum

Again, there was a basilica and forum in London, nowhere near the size of the one in Rome with its multiple basilica, but the basilica in London stood as tall as present-day St Paul's. Leadenhall market now sits in its place, still somewhere for people to shop, eat and generally gather.

The Governor's Palace

There are three suspected locations of the original Governor's Palace in London.

A large structure under Canon Street Station that is now largely believed to have been administration buildings.

There is also a likely site under Suffolk lane.

The last is the one I went with, the site of the medieval Winchester Palace, for no better reason than I have always enjoyed stopping and wondering at the lives lived there on my way to Borough Market for my cheese fix. But also because, given the growth of cities, I figured during a period of dominance the Romans would have pushed south of the river, and leaders in power do like room to spread out.

Richmond Palace

My first proper job in London was in Richmond and the path to our Friday pub lunch took us through the remains of Richmond Palace where Henry VIII once lived. My mind explodes at the idea of strolling across the grounds where such intrigue and power plays existed before he moved further west after putting poor old Wolsey out of his Hampton home.

Isabella Plantation

There is a gated Victorian woodland garden in Richmond Park in which I have spread out a blanket and spent many a happy summer afternoon reading. It's full to the brim with native and exotic flowers and trees, overflowing with colour, including wonderful crimson acers and bright rhododendron circling tranquil ponds…